BLUE DAWN

BLAINE L. PARDOE

DEFIANCE PRESS
& PUBLISHING

ISBN-13: 978-1-948035-79-8 (Paperback)
ISBN-13: 978-1-948035-77-4 (eBook)

Published by Defiance Press and Publishing, LLC

Bulk orders of this book may be obtained by contacting Defiance Press and Publishing, LLC at: www.defiancepress.com.

Public Relations Dept. – Defiance Press & Publishing, LLC
281-581-9300
pr@defiancepress.com

Defiance Press & Publishing, LLC
281-581-9300
info@defiancepress.com

DEDICATION

To my uncles, Jim Pardoe and Don Miller. To wife Cyndi, who has always been an inspiration. Enjoy!

ACKNOWLEDGEMENTS

My thanks to the year 2020 which demonstrated so clearly that millions of Americans were prepared to surrender their freedoms out of fear. It is a lesson that our leaders are not likely to forget. That kind of thinking makes books of fiction like this possible and utterly believable.

INTRODUCTION

It began with a virus. It ended in a coup.

In the spring of 2020, the American nation had been filled with bitter divisiveness and anger, with pent-up and undirected rage—the nation struggled with who it really was both morally and fundamentally. The media intentionally fueled these tensions to push a progressively liberal political agenda for mere ratings and to flex their political clout. The country had endured political division before and prevailed, but in the past, it had never been so connected digitally. Politics toyed with people's health and welfare simply to sway opinion polls. Uncertainty about the economy and the handling of the pandemic were kindling for a fire that was already starting to roar in the hearts of many citizens. Fear was used to convince people to give up their rights. The nation had become a hot stew of frustration on the verge of boiling over.

Anarchist cells sowed further division. Their desire was that the entire political system be violently taken down. Many politicians looked the other way and even funded their efforts, hoping it would damage their political opponents in the upcoming elections. Little did they realize at the time that they were empowering people that were willing to take them down as well as their opposition.

The Presidential election became a quagmire of fraud—both perceived and real. The lawsuits drew bitterness and only added to the insecurity of daily life. The drawn-out legal process led to protests which morphed into rioting across the country. Brute force was applied to restore law and order, but it only generated more resistance and hate. Law and order began to dissolve. Indecision as to who had really won the election tore at the American people. Months of being suppressed by restrictions tied to the virus made their anger transition to undirected violence.

A cascade of chaos began in the late autumn, early winter. The self-proclaimed President-Elect suffered a cerebral aneurism and died before being able to take office. It was a tragic event that only fueled frustrations and spawned conspiracy theories. The Vice President-Elect was then assassinated by a right-wing extremist, further piling onto racial and political tensions. What had begun as a Constitutional crisis boiled over into full-fledged mayhem. What sounded like a madman's crazy conspiracy theory became a reality for many people.

The enemies of the United States abroad capitalized on the chaos, using social media to fan the flames of division even more. Some nations took a more hands-on approach, funding the violence and arming the anarchists. They knew that the only way to take down the United States was to have its citizens do it from within.

By the early winter the enemies of America organized the factions that sought to bring it down. The time had come, at long last, to make the U.S. suffer. Matters were set in motion that could not be controlled or predicted. What followed was bloodshed and carnage…

PROLOGUE

"Tyranny is what you make it."

Washington DC

Secret Service Assistant Chief Jack Desmond sat in the hot seat in the Service's Emergency Response Center (ERC) two stories under the White House and glared at the screens. The protestors had been getting bolder in the last few weeks—a few clamoring over the fence in Lafayette Park and then attempting to scale the perimeter fence around the White House. Each night the numbers grew, each night new tactics were employed. The majority of the perpetrators had been apprehended, but there was method behind their madness. The increased use of fireworks was part of a strategy. Desmond saw a pattern, which was part of his job, to go beyond the raw data. *They are testing our response, watching how we react.* It spoke to him of a level of sophistication that the FBI and DOJ were not assigning to the leaders of the protests. When two groups hit the perimeter fence at different times, he finally convinced his superiors that they were planning something bigger, something far worse. "They are coordinated, organized and upping their game." That had been last night, and while the crowd eventually had broken up, Jack had a feeling in the pit of his stomach that it was going to get worse.

As he looked at the monitors, he had never felt so bad about being so right.

The crowds were at least three times larger than what the Department of Homeland Security had predicted, which only confirmed what he thought about their intelligence apparatus. He had long suspected that a lot of old schoolers in DHS and FBI didn't like the President and skewed their intel to make him look bad. It was well known by folks at his rank, but little seemed to be done to fix the underlying problem—disloyalty. The agents he worked with were competent, but some did not hide their disdain for the policies of the President. Normally he wouldn't care, but if something went down, would that hate cloud their decisions? Jack Desmond really didn't want the answer to that.

There were cameras everywhere around the White House—on microdrones, some planted on the fence—some camouflaged as nothing more than bolts, satellite surveillance, not to mention the agents that mingled with the protesters, decked out in ANTIFA black. The protesters had taken out some cameras with paintball guns—low tech but effective. Some carried strobes designed to overload night vision gear, and others used signs, large banners, and makeshift shields to conceal their nefarious activities. The resulting blind spots had been tolerable on the other long nights of riots; Jack and the other Service staff could compensate for the gaps. To Jack, it was as if someone had tipped off the protesters as to Secret Service monitoring. That was a thought that ate at him as well as he tried to wade through the barrage of visual data that hit him and the ERC team.

Jack knew that the best thing was to be responsible to his oaths. He served the office—if not the man. He had voted for the man, but like all men, he knew the President was flawed. So were his predecessors in some way or another. As long as his colleagues did their jobs and ignored their political slants, things generally worked out. His job was to protect the President and the White House—in that order. With the crowd like this surrounding the White House, he had a nagging feeling that if push came to shove, a number of DHS agents might just stand down. He had privately sworn that if he saw anyone neglecting their duty, he would take care of it—one way, or another.

His wife Barbara had tried to call him twice, but he had ignored his cell phone. Duty first—that's how it had always been with Jack. From his eight years in the Army to his fifteen with the Secret Service—he had always put his job first. Barbara and the girls knew the drill. He was sure she was just trying to reach him to tell him to be careful.

Begrudgingly DHS had set up teams on top of the Old Executive

Office building and the Treasury. He had counter-sniper teams deployed at the Department of Veteran's Affairs, the Freedman's Bank Building, and the White House Conference Center, giving him overlapping fields of fire if things got out of hand. The rules of engagement for a massed assault were known, but he knew people would hesitate. Thoughts of mowing down American protesters on the front lawn of the White House was the kind of thing that got you hauled up to Capitol Hill. He had reviewed the rules carefully with the teams at the start of his shift. As he watched the screens, he saw that the crowd was monitoring his people on the rooftops and on their assorted perches.

The problem was that the crowd was willing to risk it. Fueled by hate and organized by ANTIFA and other radical groups, they had gotten more sophisticated. The arrest of several cells in Portland and New York had resulted in bombings and two assassination attempts on Department heads, leaving one Director in the hospital. This was beyond protests; this was now war—though the press played down the entire thing as 'minor incidents of violence in otherwise peaceful protests.'

"Sir," the Captain seated in front of him spoke up, pointing to the far-left monitor. "Look. I think those are collapsible ladders." Jack saw them too; in the crowd they were hard to make out, even with night vision. They had used them before to toss up makeshift barricades, but tonight, tonight felt different.

Leaning in, he toggled the microphone on and tore off the black mask he had been forced to wear since the pandemic began. He couldn't afford to have his voice muffled, not now. "This is Rabbit to all stations. Southeast corner, ladders spotted. Prepare for breaching attempts."

One of the emergency phones flashed on and the communications officer picked it up. Jack saw the color drain from the young man's face as he lowered the phone. "Who was it?"

"Capitol Police. The rioters have penetrated the Capitol. The Speaker has been taken hostage. They are calling for help."

"Shit," he cursed under his breath. *That's it, they are coming for us next.* Hitting the mike again, he spoke as crisply and professionally as he could. "All stations, this is the Castle. We are at red—say again, we are at Condition Red."

As he spoke, it was as if the crowd outside heard him. They surged forward to the fence like a wave lapping up on the shore. Ladders went up and like an army of ants, they began to scamper up them. This time dozens were being set up, laden with rioters, all seeming to head right at him. The lawn sensors triggered all around the White House. "We have perimeter breeches. All units, engage." He could not hear the gunfire in the ERC, but he heard it over the speakers. Rubber bullets at first sprayed a swath of the rioters, but they did not recoil like they had before, though a dozen or more dropped from the kinetic impacts. Most got right back up and continued the climb. *Body armor. Fucking Amazon and eBay!* They would run out of rubber bullets soon; then things would get ugly and bloody.

His eyes saw they were hitting everywhere at once. The gunners switched to live ammo, but the sound of explosions tore up the front lawn and rocked the house above. "Mortars!" Jack said. Strobes flashed from the crowd, overloading the night-vision. "Comms, get the Pentagon on the line. The Castle is under siege. Tell them to send in everything they have, Case Jade. Get the FBI HRT at Quantico. We need cover and possible extraction. If we can, open a line to the Marine barracks."

For a long moment he stared at the rioters and felt the weight of the world on him. *This might not be reversible.* He hit a switch next to the microphone, then barked out, "Rabbit to Slingshot. We have Shattered Spear, repeat, Shattered Spear. Get Excalibur to Camelot, now!" One of the screens flickered off, shot out by the attackers. Jack checked to make sure his sidearm was still in its holster at his side. *If anyone can pull this off, it's Charli. Don't let me down Slingshot!*

Secret Service Lieutenant Charli Kazinski heard Jack Desmond's words in her earbud and the sounds of semi-automatic gunfire outside filled in all of the blanks she needed. Something was going down, something bad. Years of training and instinct kicked in. This was a scenario they had anticipated, one they had planned for. There was no time to think, only to act. She entered the Oval Office and saw the President rising, looking out the windows.

"Sir, we need to get you to the EOC now!" she commanded. He turned to her, with a mixed look of disorientation and concern.

"What is happening?"

She didn't have to respond. Several shots hit the bulletproof glass of the Oval Office, snap-cracking on the armored glass. The President rose as another explosion went off outside, this one throwing tiny bits of grass and dirt on the window. He moved to her side as two additional agents rushed in, flanking him. "My family... my wife and son..."

"We will get them," she promised, tilting his head down as they made for the door. "We need to get you secured and fast," she snapped back. They moved into the hall and another rumble shook the White House, this one above them. *Mortars... they are using fucking artillery!* The lights flickered for a millisecond as the backup power kicked on. Plaster dust drifted downward as they sprinted to the elevator. She pushed him, harder than she would have liked, but it was clear time was not on her side.

As the doors hissed shut and the elevator started down, she hit the mike pinned to her collar. "Rabbit, this Slingshot—Excalibur is on the move." As they pushed the President forward, she caught a whiff of his cologne. It was such an odd thing, that tiny detail, yet it stuck in her mind.

"Roger that Slingshot," Jack Desmond's clearly strained voice came back. "Be advised, we have perimeter breaches, north, east and west. They aren't using fireworks this time—they have mortars." As if to confirm that, she heard a rumble in the White House above her.

The elevator stopped and the door opened. She and the other two agents hurried him down the hallway to the Emergency Operation Center, the EOC. "We are in Camelot," she said as the heavy blast door closed behind them. The President was breathing hard, his face red, his eyes wide as he gave her a quick glance.

"Inform the President that they have overrun the Capitol. Cap police say that the Speaker has been taken hostage." Charli looked over at the President who nodded that he too had heard the words. *Taken hostage? I call bullshit. Chances are she was behind this.* The Speaker and the President had been at odds for years, and she had made a point to say that she supported the protests from the beginning. Charli suppressed those thoughts. There would be plenty of time for conspiracy theories—right now she had a duty to perform.

"Engage access shut-down procedure," Charli said and one of the agents hit a button on the control panel. It would kill the power to the elevator, meaning anyone trying to come in would have to climb down four stories. Certain parts of the shaft would be electrified enough to kill anyone trying to access. There was also a gas system that could pump a knock-out agent into the shaft if it were breeched. Anyone trying to come in would have a hell of a time doing it. For a short second, she felt secure. She ran her hands back through her short blonde hair and drew a long, deep breath as she gathered her composure.

Turning to the President, she locked a gaze on him with her pale blue eyes. *I have trained for this and I need to do my job.* "Sir, the communications system is lit." In the center of the room was an oblong, polished table. A panel rose at the far end where the President sat, and the monitors flickered to life. "Green light gets you the Pentagon, yellow the FBI."

He nodded. Presidents get training for this moment, but none had ever had to endure it. The protests had started months ago, and they had steadily gotten more daring, more violent. *But this? Attacking the Capitol and White House? This has got to be organized.*

The President activated the channel to the Pentagon. The face of the Secretary of Defense came on, wet with sweat, each wrinkle on his face shimmering. "Mister President—thank God you are okay."

"Dave, I need you to scramble the troops. They are shelling the White House and have overrun the Capitol."

The Secretary looked as if he were going to have a heart attack. "They have us under fire here too, sir. Joint Base Bolling was just hit by two car bombs and is being shelled; so is Andrews."

"You've got to get someone over here," he ordered. "This situation needs to get under control and quick."

The Army Chief of Staff stepped into view on the screen. "Mr. President, I am going to scramble the Old Guard out of Myer-Henderson, and we have the Marine barracks mobilizing in the District. The streets are clogged with protesters though, sir, and we are not equipped for riot duty. These protesters are well-organized sir, more so than before."

"Your President and the White House are under siege," the President said angrily. "Tell your people to get their asses in gear!"

"Sir," the General hesitated, Charli could see it from where she stood. "The Joint Chiefs have *reservations* about using our forces on American soil against a clearly domestic threat."

"What are you saying, General?"

"Sir, this situation should be handled by DHS and the FBI. They are equipped to handle it and, frankly, there are statutory concerns about using our forces in the manner you have prescribed."

"I am the Commander and Chief," the President barked. "I am ordering you to send in the troops and restore order."

"Respectfully sir, I am not sure I can comply with that order."

"Then you're fired! Put someone on that will do their job," the President snapped. The General stepped off screen and another officer stood facing the camera.

"This is Brigadier Cooper, Mister President."

"General, send in the troops to secure the White House," he ordered.

General Cooper's face went red. "At present, we are unable to comply, sir. We have talked with the FBI, and their Hostage Rescue Team is at Quantico now boarding helicopters. They are still about thirty minutes out, best case scenario. Can you hold until they arrive?"

The President looked over at Charli who nervously nodded. "You heard my orders. You *will* send in the troops, General."

"I will do what I can sir," he said. The screen went off. Charli's stomach felt as if she had been punched. *My God, the military is hanging us out to dry.* Looking down at the President, she saw that he was as stunned as she was.

He regained his composure first. "Where is the Vice President?" he asked.

Sergeant Donaldson of the Secret Service pulled out his mobile device and checked. "He's at a fundraiser in Arizona, sir. We got him in his limo and on the way to his plane the minute this started."

The President nodded nervously. "Good. What about the DC Police?"

Donaldson shook his head and Charli dipped hers. "They are overwhelmed, sir. We didn't expect this big crowd tonight. DHS has teams at Treasury and they report engaging with the hostiles." Charli had her own thoughts. The DC mayor hated the President; he had shut down her bid to make DC a state. *She will order her people to stand down and let us burn if she can.* The President knew it too, but he had to ask. "Tell the mayor to get this under control—now. I want the DC National Guard to move out." Charli didn't hold out hope. The mayor would contradict that order; she had on previous nights. The Guard would be paralyzed with conflicting orders.

It is almost like they had this planned. Charli hit her own mike on her collar. "Slingshot to Rabbit, sit rep," she said.

"Perimeter defense just went off line, Slingshot," his ragged voice replied. "We have formed a defensive ring around the ERC and are coordinating here. Hostiles are in the house, numbering over a hundred. They are heavily armed."

"Can you hold?" she asked.

"We will," he said, trying to assure her. There was something in his voice though, something she had never heard from Jack before. It was a hint of fear. *This is worse than I thought.*

There were ways out of the Emergency Operation Center, last ditch tunnels that led to different parts of the city. A distant rumble of another mortar round going off made her start mentally crunching the math, determining if it was time to move.

No... not yet. We might still retake the building. The thought of the President out on the streets filled with violent radicals made her more nervous. *For now, we hold here and wait for the cavalry to arrive.* A line she had been taught years ago came to her and filled her with resolve. *Hope is not a strategy.*

Five blocks from the White House...

Abel Brummer stepped out the back door of the building and was shocked by the number of people on the street. It was late, and at this hour, usually the streets near federal buildings were empty, but tonight that was not the case. At the front of the massive government structure where he worked, hundreds of people in a raging mob were throwing objects at the building. Eight men wearing black hoodies and black masks were carrying a large pole-like object—a battering ram. They were climbing the steps a block from where he stood.

Abel clutched the package tight to his chest. The protests had been getting worse. Anarchists, angry young men and women, had been commonplace. Tonight, had seemed different. That was why he stayed late, along with a small cabal of men and women. The package had to be saved, and the time had come to take the extreme actions needed to preserve them.

And Abel had drawn the straw… literally.

As he moved onto the sidewalk, he collided with a young black man wearing a mask. Able clutched the package tight to his chest and the young man eyed it instantly. "Where you going man?" In the distance, Abel could hear the sounds of helicopter rotors, a sign that the protests were growing, larger than on previous nights.

"Home," he said, lying. In the distance he heard a rumble, not thunder, something else. Explosions. There were pops, rapid, uneven, echoing in the streets and off of the buildings. Gunfire. *God, it is happening.* He hated being right, but he was. He told his supervisor he thought something was wrong—too many people out at mid-day, the size of the protests swelling far beyond what they had seen before. "If we don't act now," he had told the small group in the office, "tomorrow may be too late. They will destroy it because of the threat it represents." Now his words were taking flight as the city began to burn.

"What's in the big bag, little man?" the youth asked, poking at it. For a moment he feared me might try and rip it from his hands.

"Work. With these riots, I thought I better work at home. The streets are not as safe as they used to be."

"Protests," the man corrected. "These are peaceful protests. Rioters are breaking laws. We are making the law." Another rumble in the distance and the sounds of gunfire, a lot of it, seemed to invalidate that comment.

"Of course, *protests*," Abel corrected with another lie. The gunfire did not faze the young man in front of him; in fact, he seemed to be savoring it.

The eyes of the man were almost all he could see of his face. He eyed Abel up and down, focusing on the package. Then he nodded. "Look old man, get off the fucking streets. It's going down. The people are taking back everything that is ours!"

"Thank you," Abel said. And with that he moved into the shadows. No Metro tonight… he would have to work the backstreets to get to his house. If he got there, he could plan the next phase of his trip.

He clutched the heavy package even tighter as he fast-walked into the darkness. Behind him the staccato of battle grew, roaring like a thunderstorm over the District of Columbia.

CHAPTER 1

"Only the downtrodden are truly free."

NEARLY FIVE YEARS LATER...
Wheaton, Illinois

Andy Forrest sat beside his father's hospital bed and clutched his withered hand. His father was asleep thanks to the drugs. At least when he was asleep, he wasn't in pain. Andy looked at his dad's face and struggled to recognize him; he had become so gaunt. *Fucking cancer.* His father, Arthur, had faced numerous obstacles in life and had overcome them—but this was an enemy that seemed to be winning, consuming his father a bit more each day.

National Hospital 114 was supposedly one of the better ones, but he didn't see it. The Ruling Council had implemented nationalized healthcare as soon as they came to power. The new national hospital system was supposed to be better, more efficient—at least that was what the media said. Andy's experience was the opposite. He'd had to go and slug it out with the Local Medical Tribunal to get his father treatment. Arthur was classified as non-essential, non-contributing; so there was a debate about whether his recovery would be worth the cost. Andy had yelled, lied, and pleaded to get the treatment. Even with the steady trickle of chemicals, Andy was watching his dad die a little with each passing day. *And I had to fight for this.*

He hated hospitals. The Nationals were physically fine facilities, but the staff were FedGov workers and acted the part. No one ever seemed to know what was going on. His dad's doctor wasn't one person but a steady stream of unfriendly faces and they never had the answers. Then there was the smell, the mix of disinfectants, cleaners, and his father's own faint body odor. Andy wished he could afford private health care, but at the same time was glad he couldn't. *If I made that kind of money, it just would have put a target on my back.* In Newmerica, making money was a curse.

The door opened and he saw his sister enter the room, making his stomach knot. The woman wore her black shirt with red piping on her collar showing her rank in Social Enforcement. Where the National Security Force (NSF) was a potent arm of the FedGov, Social Enforcement was less-controlled, and thus more dangerous. Born out of the ANTIFA and BLM mobs during the Liberation, they acted as informal police, dispensing social justice as they saw fit. She was proud of her membership in an organization bent on intimidation, one that had ruined her father. That told Andy all he needed to remember about his sister, Karen.

It bothered him instantly that she would show up wearing that garb for their father, especially after all they had done to him. He hadn't seen Karen in two years; nor had he missed her. She looked as if she had put on some weight which gave him a little satisfaction. His sister had changed her last name to Forrester early on after the Liberation, claiming she had been forced to do so because of their father's political affiliations. Andy knew better. There had not been any forcing of the matter, his sister had shed the family deliberately for personal gain. She only gave him a passing glance, instead turning her focus on the father who lay between them. Karen Forrester eyed him as if he were an inanimate object, not the man that had raised her.

The fact that she had gone to the effort to get a permit to fly from the regional office, that she ran in the Midwest, to Chicago for the visit seemed odd to Andy. She and their father did not speak, and with damned good reason. Karen wasn't one to give in to sympathy, not unless there was something in it for her. *It has always been about her.*

"Karen," he said softly from the side of his father's bed, giving her minimal acknowledgement.

"Andy," she said, leaning over her father as if to study his face, never making eye contact with him. "I thought you would be at work." That was Karen's way of saying she had hoped to avoid seeing him altogether.

"I took off early."

"How is he doing today?"

"They keep him sedated most of the time. He's still taking food, still in the game."

"He always was a fighter," she acknowledged.

"When the cause was right," Andy added wryly. "He always fought the good fight."

She finally looked over to him. "That was supposed to be a shot, wasn't it?" Arrogance rang in her voice.

"You can take it any way you want."

Her eyes flared slightly. "You are like a dog with a bone, aren't you? I haven't seen you in two years or more and you go right back to the argument we last had." There it was, Karen's trademarked anger. Andy knew he was pushing her buttons but didn't care. *Our last argument never got resolved.* She *stormed off.* He didn't believe it would be today either.

"Karen," he said, mustering what composure he could and keeping his voice low so his father wouldn't be stirred from his sleep. "You and your social justice goons got him fired from his job. Because of the SEs, he lost his house, our mom, almost everything he had, and his reputation because of the investigation."

"Me?" she snapped. "I had nothing to do with it. All he had to do was cooperate and recant. If he had given up a few associates' names, everything would have gone fine. God knows I told him to. He brought this on himself. Don't try and lay this at my doorstep."

"Why should he have to turn on his beliefs? Because it didn't fit your social commentary at the time?"

"You know very well why," she spat back, running her hand through her short cropped black hair. "He supported a domestic terror group. He didn't change his class curriculum to the standard. The man was a professor at Sojourner Truth U and refused to adhere to the rules."

Sojourner Truth—you mean Mary Washington University. With the national purge of offensive names and symbols, the school dropped any association to the Washington family since they had been slave owners. Mary Washington had been just another victim of the Great Reformation. To Andy, the new name had no meaning; it had been imposed rather than honored. His father had been a respected historian, but the NSF had ruined him. Surely Sojourner Truth would have been opposed to that? They had sent Social Enforcement Teams to follow him everywhere, harassing him to the point where he couldn't even get to his classroom. They broke windows at the house, set fire to his car, and relentlessly followed him screaming and shoving, to the point where businesses wouldn't allow him in. Everything he typed was monitored, screened, and often edited. Big Tech monitored every keystroke he made, or so he claimed.

And Andy's sister was part of The Social Enforcers, or SE, a part of what the FedGov called, "The Great Reformation." The overthrow of the government was called the Liberation by almost everyone out loud; in whispers, however, it was called the Fall. Karen had consumed the Kool Aid of the riots, the violence, and the takedown of the government. It was a fact that steeled his disdain for her.

Yes, their father had dug his heels in against teaching the state mandated changes to his teachings. But rather than due process, they had resorted to physical and virtual thugs to cow and bully him. The school fired him, out of fear for their reputation and because of a handful of vocal students who claimed his presence 'oppressed' them. It was an easy choice for the university, one that garnered favor with the FedGov. *They didn't even care that he had done nothing wrong.*

Then came the NSF interrogators. Separate from the SE, they were just as bad, if not worse because they had a fragment of legitimacy that the Social Enforcers lacked. The NSF claimed he knew 'radicals' and that he had 'incriminating materials' in his possession—materials that were never produced, only alleged. They allowed him to be hauled before two People's Tribunals, the kangaroo-courts of the SEs, with no evidence, and he lost two years of his life, exiled to a Social Quarantine Camp—denied his freedoms. He had come back from social quarantine a hollow-shell of a human being. In the end, Karen had done nothing for her father, other than attempt to persuade him to provide names of his associates. She had been in Social Enforcement and could have vouched for him, perhaps called off their dogs. Instead, she let their father die emotionally. Now the cancer was going to do the rest.

"That terrorist group you alluded to was the Republican Party for Christ's sake," he said. "The only thing that made them terrorists was you and your goon squads calling them that."

She glared at Andy and her eyes narrowed. "It was more than that. He had ties to the Sons of Liberty."

"So you claim. When did it become illegal to support a cause?"

"You may want to watch what you are saying big brother," she replied coolly.

"Or what? You'll send me off to a concentration camp like you did with Dad?" There it was—the line that had started the argument two years ago. Andy said it with no regret whatsoever.

"It wasn't a concentration camp. It was a social quarantine facility." Her implied threat was real, but Andy was in no mood for addressing it. Karen loved threats. *They are her pacifier, what makes her comfortable.*

"Same thing."

"No, it's not. There were no cells, no one was tortured. There are worse facilities, believe me. Dad got off light, probably because of me." *Pride*, there it was, ringing in the last word she said.

"He couldn't leave," Andy countered. "That made it a prison."

"It was for his own good. You know what my people are capable of. Some SE squads don't play nice and he was no spring chicken. And if he had only cooperated a little bit, he could have left a lot earlier."

How much would you have to give up to satisfy them? What was the price of his freedom? "It wasn't a choice he got to make, Karen. The fact that you can't see that as wrong is a big part of the problem."

"He *did* make a choice," she said, moving to the foot of the bed. "He could have given us what we wanted. He chose not to. *I* didn't send him to the facility; that was the Tribunal's call. It was for his own good. He was going to get hurt at some point by the Social Enforcement Teams, maybe killed."

Andy shook his head in disbelief. "You just don't get it, do you?"

"What?"

"Your Enforcement teams are a bunch of thugs. The fact that the NSF lets them go out and administer 'social justice' is little more that state-sponsored intimidation. You know what they are, what their tactics are, what they do to innocent people."

"We don't go after innocent people," she replied flatly. "Innocent people have nothing to fear."

"That lie works for a lot of people Karen; not for me. Who makes the call as to who is innocent? We used to believe you were innocent until proven guilty. Now we start with guilt and force people to prove their innocence. History is filled with groups that take justice into their own hands. Most of them are sponsored by the governments that spawned them."

For a long moment, Karen said nothing but glared at him. "Andy— you might want to think about the words you are choosing. As the son of a known violator, your files are already flagged. That kind of talk is sedition."

The irony of her using that word made him angrier. *Sedition—you people overthrew the government!* Andy knew a threat when he heard one though and kept his anger in check. Karen never would say it out loud—that was part of her passive aggressiveness that he remembered from their youth. *We used to be close… family. Now, she's just one of the thugs.* Worse yet, he knew that she would carry through on the threat. *She never lifted a finger to help Dad when he needed her.* "You know what, maybe I should go. You probably haven't seen him in a long time," he rose from his seat.

"What does that mean?" she snapped, refusing to step down from the brink of the argument.

"Nothing," Andy lied. "I just know from what he said that you stopped coming by, that's all."

She moved one step to the same side of the bed he was on. "I couldn't Andy; did that ever occur to you? I have my own life to think about. Our dad was a criminal, a traitor. You just don't want to admit it. He associated with criminals and he performed criminal acts by not teaching what he was supposed to. I tried to get him to turn over something that could help him get out, but he refused to cooperate. His stubbornness is what landed him here. It's the same thing that drove Mom away."

Her words struck home. Yes, Arthur Forrest could be seen as stubborn. He preferred to think of it as staying true to his principles. Where Karen saw him as flawed, Andy saw him as a man who honored his friends. The mention of their mother hit hard. When their father had lost his job and was tormented non-stop by the Social Enforcers, she had left him. His mother lived under a cloud of fear that she would be attacked while stepping out to get groceries. That was part and parcel with the tactics of the Social Enforcement Teams. Harassment was a weapon in their hands.

She moved in with a friend but was unable to get work; her name was on a list because of their father. She took her life six months later, never even speaking to Andy's father. He had not been released for her funeral. Karen laid the blame at their father's feet. Andy saw it for what it was, the FedGov had killed his mother and had stolen his father from them.

He drew a long, deep breath. "What drove Mom away wasn't Dad, Karen. It was the people you work for." As he finished, he saw crimson rise on his sister's cheeks. Her mouth opened slightly, but no words came out. He decided to beat her to the punch. "I need some fresh air," he said walking past her. "Take your time. I'll be with him tonight anyway." Andy walked past Karen, not looking back once.

He left the hospital and walked aimlessly for two hours. Karen wouldn't stay that long, but he did not want to risk seeing her when he returned. She was not the kind of person that was supportive. Guilt was what brought her there. There was nothing that could be left to family other than a few personal possessions. The new laws prevented people from having inheritances. He suspected her of a deeper motive. It was a well-founded distrust on his part. Even as a child, Karen never did anything that was not to her benefit. Sacrifice, even for family, was not in her DNA. She was masterful at weaving the words so she sounded like she was supportive, but Andy knew the façade far too well.

He stopped his stroll in front of a long-abandoned Starbucks, its windows now gone and the exterior spray-painted with protest slogans. A government poster was plastered up under the spray paint, barely visible. "Trust! It begins with you!" Andy wanted to chuckle. The revolutionaries had preached to not trust the government, now they wanted that trust back. As he looked into the shell of the building, he found himself wondering. Why *had* Karen come to visit her father? He had endured cancer treatment for a year, and she had not come. What had brought her from The District to Chicago now?

There had to be a reason.

The District

Caylee Leatrom entered the conference room and surveyed it quickly. Her instincts had served her well; she determined who represented the greatest threat and what she might be able to use in the conference room to kill the others. The pitcher of water offered some possibilities. Jagged glass was perfect for the throats of victims. She slid into her seat and glanced out the third story window of what had been the Hoover Building before the Liberation. If she had to, she could punch through the glass and make the jump, but landing was going to be a bitch.

She could remember when The District had been called Washington DC, although the memories were fading a little bit with time. The purge hadn't done as much damage as its critics had said, at least in her mind. *What was one of the mottos of the FedGov? "Change is for the better."* She didn't subscribe to all of that rah-rah bullshit. Caylee was also smart enough not to say anything about her opinion, not out loud.

The Secretary of the National Support Force came into the room, a perky woman probably the same age as Caylee, in her mid-to-late thirties. The Secretary had a quasi-Hispanic look to her, dark skin, pristine long straight hair and almost perfect makeup. She wore the single gold pip on the collar of her jacket that signaled her rank. Other than that, she wore a small black flag pin, adorned with the white-outlined fist and the arrow lightning bolts stabbing downward. The old flag had long been banned, deemed far too racist and prejudiced to ever be shown in public. Caylee wondered for a moment how a piece of cloth could possess such qualities, but knew enough to keep her mouth shut.

Her only other decoration was a shiny brass-ish pin with the emblem of the party. She wore it over her heart. Caylee had inquired about the pin before, not to the Secretary personally, but with her manager, Burke Dorne. It was special—only members of the Ruling Council had them. When she found out what it was made from, she understood.

There was an arrogance as the Secretary sat down, a rigidity in her spine. Her light brown eyes cast a penetrating gaze. It was designed to intimidate, but Caylee was unimpressed. Instead, she contemplated how easy it would be to use her tablet to give the Secretary a concussion, if it came down to a fight. A part of her wished it would. Smugness was one of the many things she had a disdain for.

The Secretary preferred to be called 'Madam Secretary,' despite the obvious sexist overtone of the title. Caylee had heard that she insisted on it because it made people uncomfortable, wondering if it could be used against them at some point. She used the male version of her name as well, Alex, rather than Alexandra. From what Caylee saw, that too was to assert her dominance. Word games didn't play well with Caylee Leatrom, but she also knew just how far she could go in rocking the proverbial boat.

The fact that the Secretary was still in power said something about her, something frightening. In the last few years, a number of the original 'Liberators' had turned out to be traitors to the cause. Many were in jail. Many were ashes. *The fact that she is still here means she has enough shit on other people to make it risky to try and remove her.*

"Operative Leatrom," the Secretary said coldly. "Have you been briefed as to why you were brought here?"

She leaned back in her seat, crossing her legs. "No. I presume it's because somebody fucked something up and you need me to unfuck it."

"Watch your language, Caylee," her direct supervisor, Burke Dorne said from his seat next to her. Dorne was the oldest man in the room and had been FBI back in the day. When they formed the National Support Force, the FBI, DHS, state and local law enforcement had all been combined. The word 'police' had been dropped because it had been deemed offensive and potentially racist. Dorne was old school. Back in his day, he had done some pretty dark work for the Bureau, which was one of the reasons she nodded and sat upright when he spoke. *He knows where the bodies are buried because he put them there himself.*

"Apologies, Madam Secretary," she said, not really meaning it.

"Not needed," the Secretary said. "Besides she's not that far off," she said to Dorne before turning back to Caylee. "Let me tell you what you need to *unfuck*.

"Remember back during the Liberation—a group named the Sons of Liberty, the SOL?"

She nodded. "I worked several ops against them back in the day. We bagged and tagged their leadership. I wasn't part of the last roundup, but as I recall, we got even the small fish. That refrigerator was empty the last I heard."

"So we thought. But there have been some recent acts, bombings, cyber-swipes, and an assassination or two. We had our friends in Silicon Valley crunch it and they say there's a pattern."

"You think the SOL are back?" Her use of the acronym was important. The use of the full name gave terrorist groups identity. Using an acronym dehumanized them. They weren't people; they were just a thing and needed to be dealt with. It was the language of the FedGov which made it the language of Newmerica.

The Secretary nodded. "We do. That or someone has taken their MO and is running with it. We've seen tags in several cities that are clearly SOL."

"It could be posers—wannabes."

"Perhaps. Regardless, we think they are legit and are treating them as such."

"So, you want me to take them down again? No problem."

"It's a little more complicated than that," Dorne said at her side. All eyes shifted to the Secretary.

"We have had several suspected members under surveillance for a while. We had some drone runs that spotted a unique Class One target at a gas station in Gettysburg, Pennsylvania a few weeks ago, standing next to the vehicle of a former member of the SOL. At the time it was a routine sweep, we were in the process of apprehending some cartel smugglers and caught him in the background of the images during a routine scan. His face showed up again last week outside of Nashville."

Intelligence ops should be left to those of us in the profession. "Who's my target?" Caylee said, trying to cut to the chase.

The Secretary stabbed her long, painted, pink nailed fingers at the tablet, pulling up the image, and sliding it in front of Caylee. It was crap for an image, which told her it was a rover—a fast-moving drone that had snapped the shot. Still, the face was familiar, damned familiar. *That can't be him.*

"You're telling me that—"

"What follows," the Secretary said, cutting her off, "is classified, I mean classified at the highest levels of the administration. Our facial recognition experts say there is a 53% chance that it is him."

"Fifty-three percent is not very high," she countered. "We usually don't move unless we get in the sixties or higher." That was her CIA training creeping out.

"It's high enough for us to take action, which is why you are here," Dorne said.

"Forgive me," she said, ignoring how fake the words were. "I'm confused. He was arrested and put in prison. I saw the pre-trial motions. He died of a heart attack in his cell—everyone saw the body. It was all over the net."

Dorne diverted his eyes to the conference room table and the Secretary drew a long breath before continuing. "What you saw was what the country needed—closure. Our friends in Hollywood helped us craft something that would help everyone heal."

"He survived?"

"We were unsure. We haven't seen any trace of him or his detail since the Liberation. We believed that there was almost a zero-percent chance of him being alive. The city was on fire and citizens were roving the streets. The Traitor-President wasn't a quiet man; if he had been alive, he would have popped up. We did some good CGI with our Hollywood associates and gave the people what they wanted, justice. The consensus was that he was dead after all. If we didn't do it, conspiracy theorists would have had a field-day with rumors of him out there. A heart attack seemed plausible… we couldn't have him Epstein himself. He was dead, which is what we all wanted."

Caylee glared at the image on the tablet, picking it up. "Until this."

The Secretary said nothing for a few seconds. "You understand the sensitivity of all of this. I mean if it *is* him, and the public finds out, it will erode their trust in the administration."

"And the SOL is protecting him?"

"That's the thinking. For all we know, he's leading them. It makes sense," Dorne said from his seat beside her. "The SOL was thought to be eradicated until a few months ago. There were some rumors floating that they were planning something big, something that would really offset some of the advances the administration has made. Initially, we thought they would try and take out some high-value target, an assassination attempt. We started trying to monitor known associates of the former Son's leaders and we spotted this," he nodded at the tablet Caylee held.

Several things hit her as she zoomed in on the blurred image on the tablet in her hands. The administration had lied. It wasn't some small exaggeration or twisting of the truth either. They had manufactured a complete fiction in the death of the former President. They had told and sold the world on the President having a heart attack. What bothered her more was that she had been tricked by the massive deception as well. *I must be losing my edge—I can usually see through the lies.*

Setting it down, she looked over at the Secretary. "So, what is my mission?"

"You are one of our top people," the Secretary replied, templing her fingers in front of her. "You aren't messy like some in your profession. This needs to be handled without drawing a lot of attention. We can't afford for anyone to pick up on this."

"I'm an operative. Technically, I don't exist."

"More so than usual on this one. Thanks to the Truth Reconciliation Committee, we can control the message with the mainstream media, but things like this have a way of being made public. We want you to locate this target and eliminate him. No traces. Bring back the body, leave no witnesses."

Caylee leaned back in her chair. "You want me to assassinate the President of the United States."

"He is *not* President, not anymore." The Secretary had rage in her voice. It was understandable, she and the President had been sworn enemies years before the Liberation. *On top of that, they have already declared him dead.* "The United States is what we have made it, not what he was in charge of. That country is no-more. He is a war criminal. The man is a monster, an abomination. What I want, operative, is for you to do your job. The world thinks him dead, so we need to maintain that. Can you do that?"

A death you faked. Caylee knew this was the right time to keep her mouth shut. The information that they had provided her was dangerous to know. That fact made her exercise caution she rarely relied on. Another part of her brain was already formulating what it was going to take to pull this off and do it right. No witnesses meant just that. It added to the complexity. "I can. It is going to be expensive. I will need a team too, one I pick."

"Money is no object," Dorne said. "No team though. This information is too sensitive as it is. We need to keep a tight lid on this."

"The SE might get wind of this." Social Enforcement had a way of interfering with NSF investigations. The lines between the two groups were blurry at best.

"You have a reputation for being, shall I say, 'harsh,' with SEs. We both presume that you will handle them with your usual tact."

In other words, I can break a few bones. "Understood. I need everything you have on the Sons of Liberty," she said.

"It will be on the NSFcloud for your access only," the Secretary said. "Leave no traces Operative, nothing for anyone to latch onto. Only the top members of the Ruling Council know about this intel. If you don't do this right, you could turn a dead man into a martyr. We can't afford that."

Caylee put the tablet down and rose to her feet. "Secretary, I am the model of discretion."

The Secretary waited until the door closed, then turned her full attention to Burke Dorne. "She will raise hell with any SE teams she crosses paths with," he warned.

She allowed a slight smile to her face. "I assumed as much. I remember the phone calls I received from the Director of Social Enforcement regarding her actions in Florida a few months ago." *I wanted her for that very reason.* She had not risen to this position by not being able to read and manipulate people. *Six years ago, I was an outspoken junior Congresswoman, a radical in my own party. Now I control the most powerful agency in the FedGov.*

The National Security Force had combined all law enforcement in the nation. The impetus had been that racism and prejudices tainted every agency. The solution she had proffered, through her Restore Civil Liberties Act, was to roll all of the agencies together and root out those that were responsible for such acts. She knew that many of the officers that lost their positions during her infamous purge of the newly formed NSF were innocent of the charges leveled at them, but their guilt was never the issue. It was about making the public believe that she was attacking the problem. Even with the losses of so many officers, she still managed the largest internal armed force in North America when it was all over with. *The loss of a few thousand careers and reputations was a small price to pay to restore public confidence. Now the Newmerican people can feel a sense of confidence in their law enforcement.*

She had hoped that the Restore Freedom Act would have spelled the start of a gradual decline in Social Enforcement. On this front, she had failed, though she was never going to admit that out loud. The SE units all over the country had gotten a taste of power. Their riots, looting, acts of physical and psychological intimidation; these were things that were difficult to surrender. Some SE teams controlled entire cities, where others dominated neighborhoods. *That kind of power has to be absorbed, not destroyed.*

"You *want* tensions between us and the SEs?" Dorne asked.

"The tensions have been there all along Burke," she said. "We are law enforcement. They are self-appointed social justice enforcement. We have the law behind us; they have their self-involved sense of righteousness and brute force. We constantly are stomping on each other's feet. The problem is that the rest of the Ruling Council doesn't see this as a problem."

"How can increasing tensions help the situation?"

"People either react or overreact in such situations. I'm counting on Social Enforcement to overreact. When they do, justification will emerge for us to *reconcile." They will either be put in a position where merger is the best option, or I will take steps to make it happen. The time has come for this interagency rivalry to end. And I intend to be on top of the heap when that happens… no matter what it takes.*

CHAPTER 2

"Everyone is a minority."

Alvarado, Texas

Raul Lopez wasn't entirely sure if he wanted to join the Youth Corps. At 18 years old he wasn't sure what he was going to be doing in a week, let alone the rest of his life. While the press said the economy was strong, he couldn't find a job. Most of his fellow high school graduates stood in line for reparation points and stimulus relief rather than to land jobs. The TV news said that Newmerica was prospering, but he never saw it. Many businesses had been damaged by the riots and closed up forever, and others had simply left—their buildings gutted for copper wire and plumbing. Wherever the supposed prosperity was, it wasn't in Alvarado. It was easier to do nothing and get paid for it, but that was not how Raul had been raised.

His school counselor had suggested he go to the Youth Corps building and talk to someone there. His mother had thought it was a good idea and it was impossible to argue with her. The building was new, even the air smelled like fresh paint. The air conditioner had chilled the air to the point where he felt cold, despite the heat outside. The building seemed to be a recreation center as opposed to a work assignment facility. There was a networked video arcade, some pool tables, and several classrooms. Raul wondered what he really knew about the Youth Corps when he saw the recreational activities. *How is this place going to help me with a job?*

The recruiter's office was nice, very clean, every stack of paper in the right place. Her last name was stitched onto her jumpsuit, "Thomas," and she had a small triangle insignia on her right collar—probably a rank of some sort. He leaned back in the seat and eyed the recruiter with a gaze more suited for a school dance than for an office, and with good reason. She was young with deep, dark green eyes and a stunning figure. Her gray jumpsuit, the field uniform of the Youth Corp, was tight around the waist, accentuating her hips and breasts. A part of him knew that they had put her in her job because she was good looking, and he wasn't complaining at all. Ms. Thomas looked at her DigiPad, scrolling through the material he had sent her on his background.

"Let me ask you, Mr. Lopez, what other options are you entertaining after high school?" Her voice was so crisp, so professional, it helped Raul focus.

That question always made him uncomfortable. He was going to graduate high school in a few months and everyone seemed to want a decision about his future. His mother especially had been drilling him with the question. Raul was the first person in the family to graduate high school, and she wanted him to go to college.

Raul had tried to explain to his mother that his grades had been low, that jumping straight into college was not really an option. The problem was that when college had been made free, everyone wanted to go. The colleges couldn't handle the massive influx. Students got in based on race, sexual preference, poverty level. Even with that ranking, there were too many people wanting to go to school. Grades became a measure at that point. With the lowering of standards and his bonus points for being Hispanic, he still simply didn't have the smarts for college and he knew that. Raul had never had the patience for classes. His cousin had suggested going back to Mexico and getting a job in one of the factories just across the border, but for him that felt like a step backward. Mexico had been his family's past, Newmerica was the future.

His mother had crossed into the old United States in the middle of the Liberation when things had been in chaos. The Americans had fought so much about sealing the border that it just didn't get done. Millions of people had fled Mexico as its economy collapsed, hoping for new lives in the U.S. The first few years had been rough. Everyone had talked about a civil war, but it never materialized as they thought it might. It had not been fought state against state, but rather neighbor against neighbor, mostly in the cities. Protests had turned against those that refused to accept the new government. Politicians that had supported the Traitor-President had been rounded up. Raul had tried to drop out of school, but his mother had hung tough.

Now he was graduating and another person was asking him about what he wanted to do with his life. He hated the question because it made him feel stupid. *How do I know? I want money, a good life. I want to make sure my mother is taken care of.* "I'm not really sure. I would like to go to college, but my grades were not good enough."

The recruiter smiled. "I understand completely. My grades were not very good either. Consider this. Two years of service in the Youth Corps guarantees you admission to any Federal college."

"What about my grades?"

"Grades are not nearly as important as they were when our parents and grandparents went to school," she replied. "Federal service in the Youth Corps gives you a place to live, pay, and automatic admission to college after your two years with us. Our camps offer classes in the evenings to help you prepare for school and those class grades can actually boost your high school grades. No matter what, you will get into the college of your choosing and be ready for it—if that is what you want to do."

Do I really want to go to college? He wanted a good job and the money that came with it. That was more important. "What if I don't like the Youth Corps? Can I leave whenever I want?"

She slid a brochure in front of him, covered with brilliant photos and a lot of words he couldn't begin to scan in the millisecond he glanced at it. "You are able to leave after your first six months of service. Most people don't do that though. That's one of the keys to our success."

"What if I don't go on to college?"

The recruiter flashed him a thin grin. "Raul, a lot of men and women wonder the same thing. The Youth Corps is all about building Newmerica. The Ruling Council created this organization to help rebuild the country and you can be proud to be a part of it. If you don't want to go to college, we don't pressure you at all. You will get job experience ranging from construction trades to small manufacturing. I know of many people who went on to be plumbers, electricians… all sorts of craftsmen. The first camp I went to build a new school in San Diego and I learned how to do basic carpentry and painting."

"Does it pay?"

"We pay off of the Freedom Scale. It isn't a lot, but we are providing you room, board, and training. You would be ranked by reparation points. You are Hispanic, so that would give you some points, but being male will hold you back for points based on sex. By any chance are you gay, transgender, or part of an oppressed religion?"

"No," Raul said, slightly confused by the questions.

"Well, you'd still make more than, let's say, a privileged white man."

"Even if we did the same work?"

"Of course," the recruiter said with a smile. "The scale ranks people by their oppressed status. The more oppressed you are, the more you are compensated. It's based on the reparations scale used for monthly checks. It is all designed to make things fair."

To him, it seemed somewhat strange that people doing the same work would not be paid the same. Still, he knew about reparations. His mother got a larger check each month than Mr. Pasquez across the hall because she was a woman. *What prevents someone from simply lying about being gay just to get more pay?* He decided not to ask that question aloud.

The recruiter pushed on. "The Youth Corps is one of our nation's greatest success stories—Newmericans helping Newmericans. And you can be a part of that. No matter what, the Corps gives you the first leg-up on the rest of your life."

Raul had heard those stories before. The media seemed to have a story every week about the Youth Corps building a new bridge or a school somewhere. The footage always seemed to be the same to him, so he never gave it much thought. It was always young people wearing the gray jumpsuits, doing some sort of building or work. All of them were smiling—they seemed happy. To him it seemed corny when he watched the news, but now it made sense. These people were all getting something out of the Corps; they were getting good jobs.

The recruiter was quiet for a few moments as Raul looked at the brochure in thought. "Getting a job is hard without some training, be it experience or some trade school. I'm sure your family would be proud if you decided to join us. You will have plenty of time to figure out what you want to do and get the skills to do it. Working in the Corps introduces you to new friends and gives you the capability to succeed."

Family, to Raul, meant his mother. He didn't really care what his siblings thought; they were all younger than him anyway. None of them had to face the choices he was being forced to make. No, he had to worry about his mother and what she thought. She wanted him to be successful, that much he knew. To her that meant college. Now he had found a way to satisfy her desires and his own. "I have to tell you Ms. Thomas, I am very interested."

She smiled an almost pristine grin, her stark-white teeth almost shimmered in the white light of the office. "Good. I don't want to pressure you. This is a big decision and you're smart enough to talk it over with your family and friends. Take the brochure and some of the data I'm shooting over to your DigiPad." She held up her unit and whipped her thumb side-to-side, sending the data to the unit in his pocket. "Look it all over, and when you're ready, I'll be here."

Raul rose to his feet and extended his hand. She grasped it firmly. "Thank you."

"I hope we'll end up working together." Raul picked up the brochure and walked out. He passed two other youth, a little older than him, wearing the same gray jumpsuits. Both nodded to him and one said, "Hello." Everyone seemed so friendly. Maybe this was a good idea.

Lexington, Kentucky

The man known as Mike Raymond sat alone in a booth in the back of Mahone's roadside bar, playing with the sweat that ran down the sides of the glass of beer. Word was there were two good old boys, brothers of the Watson family, that wanted to meet. It had been an odd request, one that he intended to fulfill.

Mike Raymond was a truck driver these days, doing pick-up gigs for a number of customers. The money was decent, but he was not a young man anymore, and moving cargo and jostling along the road made his joints ache. He kept in shape, but there was no escaping time, and time was taking a toll on him.

Mike's background was solid, impenetrable—he had seen to that. He had to. The person he had been before the Liberation was still a wanted man. Staying mobile, driving around the country as his job, made him more difficult to put under a magnifying glass. To the rest of Newmerica, he was Mike Raymond, high school dropout, whose parents had divorced and were both dead. Never married, no known kids, he had served a fictional stint in prison for a bar fight that had left a man dead. He had been granted his rights back under the Parole Freedom Act and had a good upright citizen ever since. His truck was his home, his livelihood, everything.

Of course, it was all a lie.

It had been easier than anyone thought to manipulate the records in the post-Liberation days. The Service had given him some burner documents that he could use—a parting gift for a man that had failed. No one blamed him, it was clear that what went down had been masterfully orchestrated. That didn't make him feel any better about it. Mike Raymond and the man he had been both hated to lose.

He saw his intended targets enter the bar, a pair of red-headed good-old-boys, right down to their bib overalls. Mike's eyes looked at those overalls carefully, noticing their lack of wear and tear. The pair spoke with Sampson at the bar and he gestured toward Raymond's booth. "You the driver, Mike?" the larger of the two asked.

Raymond nodded and the boys slid in. The larger of the two struggled because the table was bolted to the floor and his gut spilled out like a loaf of French bread onto the top of the filthy table. Mike nodded to Sampson who came over with two fresh beers for his table. The Watson boys wasted no time in taking long drinks.

"I got word you wanted to meet, and I have to admit, I'm a little surprised. No one knew I was passing through these parts this month," he said.

"Cliff here," the chubby one said nudging his brother, "He did some asking around. They said there was a chance and the bartender said he had a way of getting you a message. I'm Dale. We sure are glad we could meet you face to face." He extended his hand but Mike simply nodded to him. After a moment, Dale Watson pulled it back under the table.

"I'm just a truck driver. You need a load hauled?"

Cliff Watson grinned, leaning over the table slightly. "We heard rumor that you might be able to connect us with the Sons of Liberty," he said in a low whisper.

Mike feigned surprise. "Boys, what in the hell would I be doing with a domestic terror organization? Besides, the SOL is DOA last I heard."

Cliff looked a little confused, but in fairness, that didn't look like it took very much. He ran his hand back through his reddish hair as Dale grinned. "Oh, I get it," he said in a low tone. "You can't talk about it."

Mike took a sip of his beer and the brothers did the same. He shot a quick glance over to Sampson at the bar who responded with a long deep nod. If they were wearing listening devices, they were now picking up static. "Look fellas, I don't know you and I don't know a thing about the Sons of Liberty. I'm just a driver doing my job. Whoever fed your corncob asses that information is a damned liar."

The pair looked at each other with sideways glances, then back at Mike. Dale maintained the negotiation position for the pair. "Look Mike. Word is you are recruiting and we are ready to join up." There was determination in his voice that Mike largely ignored.

"Gentlemen," he said sarcastically. "I sure as hell would be interested in knowing who it was that told you that I was a front-man for the SOL. Who was that again?"

"We didn't say," Cliff replied.

"Let's just say it was a mutual friend," Dale prodded.

Mike paused. "Well, whoever it was gave you boys some bad information. I'm just a truck driver. I'll spring for your beers since someone sent you on a wild goose chase, but I'm not the guy you're looking for." He nodded at their beers and Cliff took another gulp.

"We ain't leaving," Dale said, until you hook us up."

Mike nodded slightly. "Let me play along, just for the fun of it. Let's assume that I *am* some sort of terrorist operative masquerading as a truck driver. Why in the hell would I ever want to recruit the two of you?" His eyes darted to Sampson who tapped his watch from behind the bar. Then he locked gaze with Dale Watson.

"We've got skills," Dale said. "We're good shooters. Cliff here has some explosives background from a job he had in construction. We know how to live off the land and stay off the grid. We ain't afraid of the FedGov. We've been hunting in these parts most of our lives. You need guys like us."

Mike raised a thin grin to his face. He took another small sip of his beer and the brothers did the same with theirs. He opened with a slight chuckle; it was hard to suppress. "I think you're going about this all wrong," he said putting his glass down on the cardboard coaster. "If I were with the SOL, the pitch you'd have to make is not about what skills you have or don't have. What I would want to know is what you could do for us from an intelligence perspective. What kinds of contacts you have, how you could help the Sons take the fight to the NSF or the Social Enforcers. I'd like to know what kind of computer skills you have, sources for data, things like that. That is, *if* I were a member of the SOL." He loved being coy with them, but saw they were not amused.

Mike glanced over at Sampson again out of the corner of his eye and got another long nod. *Showtime.* Dale was frustrated. "You know, I get the feeling Mike, that you're not taking us seriously. That you think this is some sort of game. Well, it's not." He reached down and pulled out a .357 long-barreled revolver, putting it on the table in front of him, pointed at Mike.

"Whoa, whoa," Mike said waving his hands in front of him. "There's some sort of mistake here."

"Damned right there is," Cliff said, with a noticeable dragging out of the 's' at the end of the last word. "You have fucked with the wrong guys. We're the Black Hats," he said, slurring the last 's.'"

"Yeah," Dale said with his hand resting on the handle of the gun. "We know who you are Mike. We tried to do this nice, but now you're going to go with us. We're going to walk out of here nice and slow. We're going out to the parking lot where we have a car waiting."

"And if I don't?"

Dale picked up the gun. Mike eyed it, but only smiled more.

"What's so funny?"

Mike relished the moment. "Take a look around you." Dale and Cliff swept the patrons of the bar and they all had weapons trained on the brothers. From behind the bar Sampson held a double-barreled shotgun. The bar maid Sarah, held an old AR-15 perfectly aimed at Cliff's head.

Dale took a moment to grin. "So, you're all in on it. Well, there's something you should all know. Outside we have an entire squad of Social Enforcers. The Black Hats SE have this place surrounded. None of you are getting out of here alive." There was a cockiness in his tone that bordered on arrogance.

Sampson spoke up. "You mean the ten pussies that were waiting around the parking lot? Yeah, we got them tied and bagged already. Now I suggest that you put that gun down on the table nice and slow and slide it in front of my friend there."

The cockiness slid down their faces and into oblivion as they realized their plight. "I'd listen to my man Sampson there. He's a Navy SEAL and not likely to miss."

Dale's face went red and he slowly pushed the gun over to Mike who took it as his own. "You boys get up if you can," Mike said, waving the gun.

They rose, but staggered, especially Cliff. "What the fuck?" Dale said, fighting to keep his balance.

"We laced your beers with horse tranquilizer. Nasty shit if it doesn't kill you. I have to admit, I struggled a little bit with the dosage—this wasn't made for humans after all. It makes you easy to control, and surprisingly talkative when properly enticed. You'll be sleeping for a long while, long enough for us to get you to where the interrogations are taking place."

"We won't talk," Cliff said, staggering a bit, finally grabbing the bar for support. "We are loyal to the Social Reformation."

"Too bad," Mike said walking behind them on the way to the door. "Because if you don't talk, there's no reason for us to keep you alive… other than the fun it will provide us."

"I ain't afraid of dying. We took down your shitty government. We know how to deal with fucks like you," Dale said, staggering a half-step before somehow regaining his balance. "Jess remember, we know who you are. Your days are numbered, all of you." His words slurred and sloshed as they marched him out across the dark parking lot.

Mike shook his head. "I love amateurs like you when they try and play this game," he said smirking. "You thought this op was to infiltrate *us*. We set you up from the start. You got played. Our mission was to take out your cell, each and every last one of you. You planned on coming for us, capturing me, but you walked right into the trap.

Dale Watson looked at him, his mouth half-open, at a loss for words for a few seconds as he was patted down for other weapons. Finally, he forced out the words. "We beat you once. We can do it again."

Mike Raymond shook his head. "Doubtful. Last time you had the element of surprise. You're in the hot seat now, dancing to our tune. Your black-shirted friends will talk if you don't. Don't worry though, they won't find your bodies right away when we're done. That will give us time to track down your families and kill them." There was coldness to his words as he spoke them. No remorse, no guilt. His own wife had been killed. When that happened, the person within him that possessed the capability to feel guilt died as well.

Dale Watson reeled about, his face filled with rage. "You wouldn't dare!"

"We took the page from you. This is the same bullshit you pulled on the police during your revolution. You see, when you make the rules of the game, you are bound by them. Your wives and kids, they are going to die. It's going to be messy too. And just like you did to us, it will send a message to the other cells what's going to happen to them."

Dale teetered for a moment, long enough to spit on him. He wiped it from his chin, still smiling. "That's going to cost you a finger or toe during our interrogation Mister Watson." He pushed him through the door and out into the parking lot. Lined up in front of his truck were the rest of the cell, zip-tied with bags pulled over their heads.

Sampson came up beside him. "You got this?"

"Yup," he replied. "We will pinch these guys, get some names for some promises—then do the deed. I'll be taking them to the graveyard per the plan. I'll lay them out all nice and pretty, something to scare the living shit out of the black shirts. You all set?"

The former SEAL, if there was such a thing, nodded. "It will be like we were never here. Bleach and fire cover up a lot of potential problems."

Mike nodded. "Good. Follow the plan. Somehow these guys have figured out how to find me, and that makes me a liability. I'm going to have to take on a new persona."

"You got the paperwork, or do I need to get you some?"

"I have a handful of burner IDs still. Stuff that was never on the grid," former Secret Service Assistant Director Jack Desmond said. "Mike Raymond will disappear in forty-eight hours. That alone will make them worried."

"Anything I can do for you brother?" Sampson asked.

"Yeah," Mike said, tucking the .357 into his belt. "Look, we out-thought these dumb-fucks this time. They are not used to dealing with our skills and expertise. They will get better. The big-guy has some new high priority targets for us, some stuff that will make them sweat at night worrying.

"In the meantime, I need some help, someone whose moral compass is a little skewed."

"You have someone in mind?"

He nodded. It wasn't going to be easy to find her, not after all that had gone done—but he had to try. Besides, she was the only one that knew what happened to the President the night of the Fall.

CHAPTER 3

"The past is lies—trust the future!"

Wheaton, Illinois

Andy Forrest felt his dad stir and watched as his eyes opened slowly. Andy got a cup of water and moved the straw to his father's mouth. "Dad, you thirsty?" Arthur Forrest nodded and Andy fumbled for a moment with the glass, finally getting the paper straw in his mouth. His father took several long sips before pushing the straw away.

"Do you want something?"

"Sit me up," Arthur said. Andy found the bed controls and raised him to a sitting position. His father moaned slightly but Andy did not react to the sound. The last time he had moaned, his father had told Andy it was nothing.

The last two weeks had been a struggle. Andy's job had laid him off when his leave had run out. He had told them why he wasn't able to come to work, but they said his father had coverage at the hospital, that there was no reason for him to be there. "Your father is a Class 4 Patient—Terminal." He would be able to appeal it to a People's Tribunal, but their dockets were full. In the meantime, his father was wasting away.

The loss of his job bothered him, but only slightly. His job was as a change manager, helping companies move 'undesirable' jobs overseas. When Andy was brought in to a company, it was because a lot of Newmericans were going to lose their jobs to China, Mexico, even Jordan. He loathed his work, but did it because the Labor Tribunal in his company had assigned him to it. Being good at the nasty task didn't help. Each time he stood up in a factory or office and told the people they were going to need to retrain for their new jobs, he felt like a bit of him died inside. In some respects, losing his job was a good thing—it relieved the nagging pressure of his work that he often described as, 'filthy.'

Karen had been to visit their father four times before simply disappearing. When she came, Andy left, with neither of them exchanging a word. To him, she was more a stranger than family. He had more interactions with the nurses and doctors than with his sister. One nurse said that during her last visit, their father had been visibly upset. Andy was prepared to grill Karen about what she had said, but she never came back. As with all things in life, Karen had dodged any responsibility.

"Andy," his father said. "What day is it?"

He had to think about it himself for a second. "Saturday."

His father gave a nod to the response. "I always liked Saturdays."

Andy smiled at memories of the family weekends together, the trips his father used to organize to museums or battlefields. Things were much simpler then. Now many of the museums were gone. The battlefields had been sold off because they commemorated people that were on the Red List of banned individuals or entities.

"Are we alone?" his father asked.

Are we ever alone these days? It struck him as a strange question. "Yes Dad, just you and me."

"Power down your phone," Arthur said. Andy complied. "Done, Dad."

"Good," Arthur said. "I had them change my bed the other day. I figured Karen would have planted a bug in my old one."

Andy had never spoken to his father much about Karen. *Would she attempt to bug him?* Given a millisecond of thought, he realized there was no doubt that she would. The real question was, 'Why would she?"

"I'm dying boy," his father sighed as Andy leaned into his field of vision.

"Dad, you're going to be okay," he said unconvincingly.

Arthur shook his head slightly on the pillow. "History is coming for me," he said with a gravelly voice. "I'm ready. This cancer… it's the last straw. I'm only sorry I won't be around to see it."

"See what?"

A gleam came to Arthur's gray eyes. "When they turn on each other."

"Who?"

"Them... Newmerica. Goddamned ANTIFA and their Social Enforcement squads, and the others."

"What do you mean?"

Arthur drew in a long breath and spoke with a firmness that Andy had not heard in weeks. "Revolutions rarely go the way you want, long-term. Look at the Chinese and their Cultural Revolution. Look at the French. When the crazies overthrow the government, they get what they want... for a time. Then they become a thousand times worse than the people they overthrew. Give them enough time, and they turn on each other. The revolutionaries become the victims of their own madness. Look to Robespierre," he said with a faint smirk. "The media always supports them at first, but eventually the media needs a good enemy and turns on them. The organizations that were taken down, they find a way to fight back. The revolutionaries... they start hanging each other. History is on my side with this one son."

It was a strangely warming thought to Andy. "You may still see it, Dad."

"No. What they didn't take from me, the cancer will. But that doesn't mean I'm out of the fight. I have a chance at hitting them even after I'm dead."

"What does that mean, Dad?"

Arthur reached one hand up and Andy took it. His father squeezed his grip tight. "They thought they got them all, but they didn't. A friend of mine, Abel Brummer, got a package out the night it all went down in DC, the night of the Fall. He worked pretty high-up in the federal government, and somehow he got it out through the riots and the mobs. We met afterwards and he left it with me. A friend of mine kept it hidden all of this time, right under their noses. That was one of the reasons they ruined me; they suspected I had it but couldn't find it. Even your sister was asking about it when you weren't here. It bothers them that it may have survived. And if it does, it's a threat to them. Symbols are important, they bring us together."

Andy shook his head, still not fully understanding what his father was talking about. "What is in this package?"

Arthur creaked out a grin. "Hope… pride. The things they can't take away from people. They've tried like hell, but it is still out there, waiting to show itself. It's a threat to the FedGov. You can crush institutions, kill people, but an idea? Ideas always live on."

His mind raced at the concept of what might be in the mysterious package. It was only tempered by the thought that the possession of it might bring the same wrath that had come down on his father. "You need to know where it is," his father said. "Take it, and when the time is right, use it. Take it public, something so big they can't ignore it. When people see it, it will reignite the dream… you'll see. Revolutions can't squash who people are in their hearts. It will remind them of that." Before Andy could respond, his father motioned for him to come closer. Andy put his ear in front of his father's lips and he whispered where it was kept. The information overpowered his father's bad breath. It took the better part of a minute, leaving Andy with his mouth hanging open. He almost slumped back to his chair beside the bed, but instead remained in his father's field of vision.

"Dad—you're kidding," he said as he drifted to his seat. *He has to be kidding.*

"It's right where I told you. I took it there to make sure it was protected. It is the last place those dumb-shits would look."

"They don't allow people in there."

"I know," Arthur said with a hint of pride in his voice. "As a historian, I know the value of irony. I was there just weeks after they were destroyed, before they banned people there. Idiots—they couldn't even get that right… did a half-assed job."

"Dad—"

"I had help. There was a construction worker, name of Dick Farmer. If he's still alive, he should be able to help you when you go. He was there when I took care of it, did the heavy lifting."

"I don't know what to say…"

"Don't say anything," Arthur said, mustering his last bit of strength. "I was in the fight, but you saw what they did to me. The final indignation was my daughter becoming one of them. Karen talks brave, but she's weak. They attract the weak, the uneducated. The radicals always convince people they are victims and deserve justice or revenge. That's why professors like me were a threat. I didn't follow their little rules. Totalitarians can't have free thinkers.

"I hate doing this, but you're the only one I can entrust it to. Your sister, she was asking about it too, so she suspects something. She will have her eyes on you now. Anyone you tell about this is as good as dead. She may even bring you in for social quarantine to try and squeeze it out of you." Those words chilled Andy for a moment. He remembered how drained and emaciated his father looked when he was released from the camp.

"Don't give into fear. For them, it's their go-to drug. It keeps the masses complacent. You remember the pandemic—people gave up all of their freedoms for a bug with a 98% survival rate. But fear has a downside. Fear makes its users paranoid, and eventually afraid of each other. You'll see. They fear things they can't control. Dictatorships are all about control. It's not enough to win, you have to hold on to what you seized.

"Do this right and you light the fuse for the counterrevolution, boy. They haven't squashed America just yet. There are people out there who still feel the way I do. If anyone can do it, you can."

"Dad, I'm no freedom fighter," he protested. "Is there someone else I can tell about this? Maybe they can handle it?"

Arthur feebly shook his head on the pillow. "They squashed or killed everyone I ever trusted. They tortured me too, physically, psychologically. They figured they had broken me or that when they let me out, I would lead them there. Karen and her buddies, they will follow you now. Be careful with your trust, Andy."

"I—I don't even know what this package is. Why is it so important? If you could have gotten your life back, why not give it to them?"

Arthur smiled, looking deep into his son's eyes. "It is our past and our future. I could have folded, surrendered it, gotten them off my back. They would have likely just killed me the minute they had it. The administration is not big on loose ends. Historians love a good tragedy, and I'm happy to play a part in theirs.

"Not telling them was like being a soldier, fighting them my own way, being stubborn. I had something they couldn't have, no matter what they threw at me. They ruined my career, scared away my friends, took my daughter—but they couldn't make me sing the song they wanted to hear. I *beat* them. Now you can do it too. It will be hard, but you will love it, trust me." His eyelids closed, suddenly leaving Andy very much alone with his thoughts and the grim realization that his life had just become more complicated.

San Jose, California

Angel Frisosky sat at her desk and her eyes fell on the same thing every morning, the digital display that covered the far wall of the Third Precinct of the San Jose National Security Force, the illustrious NSF, as she liked to call it. Today the slogan displayed was a rerun from months ago. "Feelings = Facts." Most days she ignored the slogan. Today though it frustrated her. *What a load of bullshit.* To her, the slogan was just another reminder of things that had been lost over the last few years.

God, I hate Wednesdays. That was her day to patrol a desk. At least on the street, she felt less-monitored, a tad freer. Being in the Precinct was sometimes annoying duty, with people walking in off the streets, demanding counseling or support, or simply turning in their neighbors for some minor, often perceived, infraction. *When you pay people to snitch on their neighbors, you get more people snitching on their neighbors.*

The National Security Force was a quasi-controlled clusterfuck in her mind. It had federalized all police forces into one unified, and most importantly controlled, entity. Sheriffs, police department, the FBI, DHS, state police... all were combined. The population was told that it was for their own good, it allowed them to root out systemic racism and injustice in the old order. Angel saw it for what it was, a blatant power grab. Combining all policing gave the FedGov an army at its disposal. It was only really hindered by the massive bureaucracy that came with its formation. The NSF, which was supposed to help provide security for the people, was more of an instrument of fear. To Angel, it was just as it had been planned. *This was what they always wanted, total control.* If the NSF didn't act, the local Social Enforcement Teams would, and they didn't have any rules.

There had always been a lot of tension between the two entities. The NSF was sanctioned, it was official. The SE, they were just roving bands of black-shirted thugs. They didn't play by rules. Where the NSF arrested suspects, the SEs dealt out justice as they saw fit. More than once she had come across dead bodies spray-painted with tags from a local Social Enforcement Team, labeled as 'racist' or 'homophobic.' The NSF had politics and structure. Early on the progressive politicians had some nominal control of the SE Teams and used them as their personal army… or so they thought. Angel knew the truth; no one controlled the angry undirected mob. They could be aimed at a target by some congressman, but that was where the influence ended. The two groups hated each other, both seeing the other as part of a larger problem.

During the Fall—which was a word you weren't allowed to use to describe the Liberation, the SE targeted not just police officers but their families. In one week, lovingly called the Freedom Week, well over three thousand family members of local law enforcement were executed by Social Enforcement teams. It crippled the police at every level of the government. It allowed the ANTIFA-led mobs to do what they wanted, intimidate in order to seize power. There was a lot of sympathy for police officers after that, but that did not bring back the dead. Most officers stepped down, opening up the ranks to new officers, more willing to tow the party line.

Angel remembered those days all too well. *We should have struck back. We should have killed every one of those teams. Fuck the law, they made this a war.* None of that happened though. The problem was the old police organizations played by rules, where the SE didn't. Police officers had been painted as the bad guys, and the mass-firings during Freedom Week was seen as divine retribution for crimes that may or may not have happened. The civilians let it play out, not wanting to become victims of either side.

"Angel," her partner, Bobby Dale, said. "Remember we have cultural de-escalation training this afternoon."

She rolled her eyes. "Oh, I remember," was all she could say. Speaking what you thought was a quick path to getting unwanted attention.

"Eyes are everywhere," was another FedGov slogan that got tossed about, and there was truth in that. The NSF spied on everyone, including itself. The population helped… they were encouraged to report individuals that refused to support the FedGov policies. Free speech was permitted, as long as it wasn't offensive, and the NSF determined what was offensive. As it turned out, anything could be labeled offensive, so more often than not, the complainer got what they wanted. Angel kept her mouth shut just like her peers. Though for her, there were other reasons. It was best to just blend into the background, not draw attention.

She went to the three-hour session on how it was important to try and convince people of different cultures to stop yelling or fighting and allow themselves to be taken in. She girded herself so that she would not doze off, paying just enough attention to pass the test at the end to prove that she had been there and had been trained. The instructor was some college puke who had never had to face down a six-foot-eight naked man with mental issues, covered in his own vomit, high on meth, swinging a tow chain at officers. No amount of kind words appropriate to his culture were going to persuade him to stand down. That required force, brute, unadulterated physical contact with intent. A part of her wanted to pose that scenario to the instructor, just to expose how stupid the concept was, but that too would draw attention she did not desire.

As her shift ended, she prepared to leave, and she was surprised when a group of officers rushed past her and surrounded patrolman Ron Juarez. They immediately slapped him in cuffs and patted him down. Bobby moved in beside her, watching the brief pointless struggle as they took Juarez away. "What's this about?"

"An Hispanic perp filed a complaint against Ron, or so the story goes," Bobby said. "They claimed he made a racial slur during an arrest."

"That's bullshit on a stick. What about his bodycam and the drone footage?"

"Drones were elsewhere, as usual," Bobby said. "His bodycam wasn't working right, so it only caught part of the arrest. The local SEs are calling for a People's Tribunal. You know the drill."

That was all it took and the perpetrators knew it. It was their word against the NSF, and in those fights the perps almost always won. Ron was a racist now; his FedGov ID would have him tagged as such. He wouldn't be able to get work, all because of a likely false accusation. The Tribunals acted as courts and she could not remember them ever siding with law enforcement. "Too bad. He was good," was all she said.

"Yeah," Bobby said, following him being marched out the door by his fellow officers. "Good doesn't always count. You know that."

Angel flashed a smile but didn't say anything other than, "See you tomorrow," and she grabbed her lunch bag and purse and went back to her one-room apartment on the south side of the city. Saying what she was feeling was going to lead to trouble, and she had endured enough of that for a lifetime. Juarez was a good man—he didn't deserve the bullshit he was going through. *How could he be racist? He's Hispanic too. He's actually experienced racism.*

She flopped down in her only easy chair for what seemed like a few minutes, but when she looked up, twilight was setting in. That happened a lot lately, the loss of time. Her thoughts had been twisted and dark, memories of days and friends five years ago, before the world was turned upside down… memories of officer Ron Juarez. *Poor bastard. They will ruin his life just on the word of a criminal.*

As she sat there, she heard a siren off in the distance. It was getting harder to remember how things were before the Fall. *I miss the old holidays the most.* The Fourth of July, labeled as a 'nationalist travesty' by the Ruling Council, had been renamed Liberation Day. In her youth, she had enjoyed playing with sparklers and watching the fireworks over Washington DC from her parent's Arlington townhouse.

President's Day died a quick death, replaced with a National Day of Remorse for the Indigenous People. Christmas was gone, replaced with Workers Respect Week. Being a Christian or Jewish in Newmerica was not a good thing, it was seen as a mark of scorn. They were labeled as 'religions of privilege.' You didn't dare put up a Christmas tree or a menorah where it could be seen from the street without someone complaining and getting the SEs involved. Her parents had learned it was a quick way to get a brick thrown through the window.

There were other perversions of traditions, all tied to the FedGov's great Reformation. Veteran's Day had become Equality Recognition Day. A half-dozen other insipid holidays had sprung up, so many in fact it was hard for her to keep track.

Angel stared out the window to see the building across the street… it was a shitty view for a shitty mood. There was only one thing that could make her feel better. She went to her bedroom and put on her black night-ops jumpsuit and mask. Her rifle was in the black kit bag, in parts. Guns had been long outlawed, but then again, so had she. For Angel, there was only one way to make things right for Juarez. A life for a life.

49

She had learned during her time in the District during the Fall, that you had to respond to the bastards. *The Social Enforcers are going to ruin his life; time to ruin some of theirs.*

The FedGov loved putting up cameras and monitors everywhere, but they sucked at maintaining them. There were blind spots everywhere. And with a little discreet work from someone else's workstation, larger ones could be created by simply repositioning them or shutting them down. She had created several over the last few months. Every time somebody she knew got fucked over by the system, she took the fight to the Social Enforcement Teams that roamed the street.

Tonight, it was going to be the Chantillerys, the local SE team. They controlled their little slice of San Jose with intimidation and violence. Twice, when she made an arrest, they had interfered, the last time nearly breaking her arm. As she made her way down the carefully selected streets that were blind to her passing, she made her way to an abandoned Wendy's that had been torched during the riots. The roof was perfect, right on a street corner overlooking Santa Theresa Boulevard. Angel had been there a dozen nights before, scouting, planning.

She assembled the rifle and scope carefully and used a handheld sweep device to make sure she was not being monitored. Getting a gun illegally was easy, impossible through normal channels. Hers had been taken during a raid on a cartel drug den.

As she finished checking the weapon and loading it, she settled in for the waiting game. The hot roof gravel made her legs feel like they were sizzling, even in the darkness, but she ignored it. After an hour or more, she got her chance. The Chantillerys arrived at the Taco Bell II parking lot a half-block away. They were loud, boisterous—making their presence known. That was the way of the SEs; it was a form of intimidation. ANTIFA had taken kids who played video games and lived in their parent's basement and convinced them they were warriors fighting for a cause. She wanted to laugh, but they had been successful; they had helped take down the U.S. from within. Tonight, she would demonstrate that this was not a video game.

Angel slowly raised the rifle and adjusted the scope for the range based on the laser. Under the dull light of the parking lot lights, she zoomed in on the loudest of them. He was gesturing wildly, waving his arms, going off about something. Sitting on the hood of someone's car, he was the perfect target.

Angel slowly squeezed the trigger. The suppressor muffled some of the crack of the gun firing, enough to confuse any possible witnesses. Silencers didn't work the way they did in movies, but thankfully the sound didn't carry far. Her target flew back, off of the hood of the car he had been sitting on. The Chantillerys were stunned for a moment, and in that moment, she lined up a second target and fired. This one hit in the lower body, sending that chubby girl into a ball of agony on the hot parking lot asphalt. The others drew weapons and scattered, hunkering for cover behind cars, leaving their comrades to die gurgling on the pavement. She could see the legs of her first victim quaking as he tried to grasp the wound at the base of his throat. The girl wailed in agony. *Play adult games… win adult prizes.*

It felt good to Angel, better than she had felt in weeks, since her last outing. It wouldn't help Officer Ron Juarez in the least, but for a moment, it felt good to be able to strike back without fear of recrimination. Every time she went out and killed one of the SEs, it made her feel as if she were still in the fight, if only in a little way.

Disassembling her rifle, she faded into the night, part of the shadows. Two less SE members terrorizing the community. It was not a big victory, but a good start. She slid into her apartment and locked the door behind her. Then she heard it, a breath, not fast but deep. Ducking and rolling, she drew her sidearm and aimed it at the figure sitting in her easy chair. The man there did not react, a wise move on his part.

The face was one she knew but had not seen since the Fall. Time hadn't been kind to him. His hairline was an inch further back and peppered with gray. His eyes had bags under them. He made no movement, no threat, only looked at her and smiled.

"You," she said rising to her feet and lowering her pistol.

"Hello Charli," Jack Desmond said. "It's been a long time."

It's been a hell of a long time since I've heard my name. "Where in the hell have you been?" she cursed.

Jack gave her a coy smile. "I stay on the move. Harder to hit a moving target."

She took off her mask and tossed it to the tiny island that separated her appliances from the rest of her apartment. "I figured you'd be dead by now. I checked the list of those presumed killed at the White House. Your name was there."

"A lot have tried, but like you, I beat the odds," Jack replied. "How in the hell *are* you?"

Former Secret Service Lieutenant Charli Kazinski shrugged. "Doing what I have to do. Hiding right in plain sight. Word is that I'm still pretty high on some FedGov wanted lists. I figured the best ID to use was one that got me into the NSF. Hiding right on their doorstep."

"You always were resourceful," Jack replied.

"I did what I had to do," she said. She paused for a moment. "I read about what happened to Barbara and the girls."

"Please, don't go there," Jack said flatly. The narrowing of his eyes told her it was a prudent move to heed his words.

"Sorry," was all she could muster in response.

"Both of us have paid a high price, higher than most."

It was a statement she could appreciate. "Agreed. Some of us carry a curse… the curse of knowledge."

Jack leaned forward. "You want to tell me what happened?"

"No," she replied flatly.

"The whole bit they put out, the President in jail, his heart attack, the photos of his dead body, I know it was all fake," Jack said.

"How do you know?" she said with no conviction.

"If they had captured the President, you would have been killed or caught as well. You were always the best at your job."

She allowed a thin smile to come to her lips. "Yeah, they faked the whole thing. For the first time ever, the conspiracy theorists got it right."

"Charli," Jack said. "I need to know if he's alive."

She eyed him carefully. Jack Desmond was a solid performer, dedicated to a nation that no longer existed. That meant something to her. "I'll tell you if you tell me how they got into the EOC."

"Drake Barker," Jack said, leaning back in the chair. She pulled a bottle of water out of her tiny refrigerator and drew a long gulp. "He flipped on us. Fucking mole. Practically opened the door for them. He handed them our protocols, code words, everything that he knew of. Fucker gave the ANTIFA boys our personnel files."

Charli snarled and took another sip. "I always knew he was a back-stabbing asshole. It doesn't surprise me that he turned on us."

Jack nodded. "Word is he's in charge of security for the Ruling Council. They rewarded the prick who handed the mob the White House with the job of protecting them. I doubt they even see the irony."

"You should kill him," she said with a complete lack of emotion. "Or I will." *Hell, I might enjoy it.*

"That time will come. After he doxed us, I managed to get out. I couldn't get down to you, but I had to buy you time. I presume you got out by one of the emergency egresses?"

"Something like that," she replied.

"Your turn Charli. Is he alive?"

She shook her head slowly several times. "We got out. He died a few days later." Pausing for a moment, she studied her old superior's face. "Why? Why do you need to know?"

"We got a legitimate successor," Jack said.

"Impossible," she replied. "It can't be the Speaker, she sold us out as fast as those dickheads over at the Pentagon. She was shot at the Capitol. I saw the footage of the Secretary of State's murder scene, so it couldn't be him either." Memories of that night, the desperate orders for help, the denials, it all rushed back to the forefront of her mind. She had long pushed those memories down, but Jack had taken those glowing embers and blown air on them. Now they were a roaring flame.

"Their winning was supposed to be impossible too. So is your still being alive. Me too. No shit. We got him, a true-blue successor."

"What good does it do you?" she countered. "Even if he is sworn in, the United States is gone. They won't recognize him. In fact, they will bomb him into oblivion the moment they know he is alive."

Jack smiled and somehow that made his words more palatable. "Newmerica may not recognize him, but the people will. They have had over four years of chaos, four years of having their rights and beliefs stomped on. Four years of being treated like shit for things they never did. He represents a chance to reset all of that."

She chuckled, for the first time in a long while. "So what? You think they're going to just rise up?"

Jack rose to his full height, standing in front of her. "I do. Some will.

Most need something to believe in, and he embodies that. They have been waiting for the right chance. Last time, they caught us off guard. We didn't see it coming, not on the scale it came at us. It's time to switch roles, let them get caught with their dicks in their hands. You know me. For what it's worth Charli, I have a plan." There was something in the way he said it, a confidence, that caught her attention.

"A plan?"

"Yup," Jack replied. "And I need your help. *We* need your help."

"Who is *we*?"

"The Sons of Liberty."

She shook her head quickly. "Jack, the SOL was taken down. No one has heard a peep from them in years."

"The NSF took out the people that made up the SOL, but you can't capture or kill an idea. They taught us that much with ANTIFA. The group reformed just as it has since the nation was born. We learned our lessons from those that overthrew the government; we operated in the shadows. We are a rumor on the wind, spread word of mouth. We are growing, building strength. When the times comes, we'll take back what was our country." There was a passion he could not suppress as he spoke; she heard it. For a second, it surprised her.

"Your opposition is entrenched, Jack. They are in every nook and cranny of society. They have created a culture where citizens report on each other. They have made the government integral to every aspect of a person's life here. Breaking that apart, tearing it down, is going to be hard."

"I wouldn't be a part of it if it was easy. You know me, Charli. We both got dealt a nasty hand of cards during the Fall. Both of us are survivors. We did our duty to the best of our ability. That doesn't mean that our duty is over. In fact, I would say, our responsibility to our nation is just starting." She heard pride in what he said and remembered how much she admired the old Jack Desmond. A part of Charli wanted to feel that kind of enthusiasm too, but realities and guilt stood in her way.

"I've been under the radar for a long time," she countered, half-heartedly. "And I failed in my most important mission. I didn't keep him alive."

"You got him out," Jack said firmly. "And I'm willing to bet you've had it up to your ass in regards to all of this Newmerica bullshit. I need you, Charli. You are the best tactician the Secret Service ever produced. You think on your feet and are unstoppable when you put your mind to something. The Sons need someone like you."

Charli felt something stir in her brain... excitement. Not the kind of fear that had dominated her life since she had 'died' during the Fall. "Jack, you always knew how to punch my buttons. You also never do anything without a plan. So what's the plan?" she asked.

Jack stepped towards her; she could see the fire in his eyes. "First we put their nuts in a vice—then we tighten it until they scream." He held up an image that appeared to be the President, aged years from the last time she had seen him.

"It's fake. I know that. He's dead."

"*They* don't know that. And that fear of him being out there will send them on a lot of wild goose chases. We have a great prosthetics guy working for us. We let them get these images, just to get in their heads. I had to know for sure though; that was why I came to you. Now that I know he's gone, we can move to the next phase."

"Which is?"

"Getting them to turn on each other. Then we start to hamstring the NSF, hinder their ability to do their jobs. We need to blind them to what we are doing."

Revenge—payback. Those words seemed hollow to her, but they were all she had left. She was a wanted woman, the same as Jack was wanted. Loose ends that needed eliminating. Her fate would be worse. They would want to know if the President was really dead, who had helped her, and details that would cost others their lives.

Charli drew a long deep breath. Setting her bottle of water on the island, she stuck out her hand. Jack grabbed it hard and shook it firmly with both of his. "Good. I'm in, but with a condition."

"And that is?"

"I want to meet this successor."

Jack's face reacted with a ripple of tension on his brow.

"We keep him on the move. It's not easy."

"I don't care if it's easy or not. If I'm going to get back in the game, I want to make sure I'm backing the right horse."

Her former supervisor said nothing for a long moment. "Deal. But only after you first do some things for us. I need you and your special set of talents."

"Agreed."

In that moment, the person that was Angel Frisosky disappeared. By morning the fire in her apartment would make tracing her real identity difficult, and there was no reason for anyone to try. She was just another dead or missing cop. Nobody would even care.

The District

Burke Dorne, the Director of Special Operations within the NSF, took his seat opposite the Secretary. Many people looked at her with a glint of fear in their eyes, but Dorne was not one of them. He had been an Army Ranger, three tours of duty, a top law-enforcement officer in the U.S. Marshals. Unlike so many sycophants she met, Dorne didn't feel that he had to curry favors. He refused to play politics. He just did his job and did it well.

She had chosen evening for their meeting. Outside a thunderstorm rolled over the District. Strained roars of thunder occasionally shook the old FBI building where her office was located. Looking out through the half-closed venetian blinds, she could hear the splatter of the rain being blown against the window. *A dark night for dark thoughts...*

"What can I do for you, Madam Secretary?" he said as he settled into the seat opposite her desk.

"Your handling of the Spec Ops team has been exemplary," she began.

"Thank you."

"I will be relying on your talents in the near future."

"Spec Ops has never failed you."

"No, it hasn't. But I fear that these upcoming missions are going to be a little more challenging than ones I've tasked you with in the past."

Dorne leaned forward. "How so?"

"I have long suspected that the Chief of Social Enforcement's loyalties to our cause have been somewhat questionable. It may be necessary to effect some changes in their structure and leadership." She paused, letting her words sink in.

"I think I understand. And you see my people as helping *implement* these changes?"

She nodded. "We have had a trying few years since the Liberation. I would hate to think that the Chief and his top people are disloyal, but the evidence seems rather conclusive. We are unsure of how deep the corruption may go, but as the Secretary of NSF, it is my responsibility to maintain law and order."

"Understood. When are we looking to move forward with this?"

"Not fully determined at this time. It could be any time, however; a week from now, a month, or less."

"Okay. Should I presume these will be targeted arrests?"

She hesitated, deliberately. "The problem is that arrests and People's Tribunals would damage much of what we have sought to build. These people are not likely to go quietly. Public displays of justice might further fan the flames of dissent. We will need to be more *complete* in our solution."

The Secretary paused, and Dorne leaned back in his seat. "So you would like Spec Ops to make these problems disappear?"

"It is the conclusion we have arrived at," she said. The use of the word 'we' was deliberate. Dorne was no fool, he could catch that. It implied that others on the Ruling Council had endorsed the action. If he testified ever, he would say he inferred that. There was that thin veil of plausible deniability that she and he wrapped themselves in.

"We have taken crimson level actions before," he said, using the code word for assassinations. "But never against members of the administration or the party."

"I know," she said, leaning back in her chair. "And it's not something I take lightly. We both have known for some time that there are tensions between the good work we do and the SEs. As such, I anticipate that they will be folded into our team here. It will be the best way to ensure that if there is any further dissent, we can deal with it internally, before it festers and becomes a problem."

"I will need to use our best people," Dorne replied thoughtfully. "I know you have personally tasked Operative Leatrom on this Sons of Liberty assignment. She has a reputation for stirring the pot when it comes with the SE teams she interacts with. It might be best to bring her back in, put her on this. She is one of my best people."

"Normally, I would agree," the Secretary said. "But her assignment is just as important. In fact, her head-bumping with the SEs has helped us ferret out some of the more rebellious elements. She will, for the time being, need to remain on her assignment."

"Madam Secretary," Dorne said. "I don't have to tell you, this has the makings of a public relations nightmare when it goes down, even with the best planning. Caylee has a tendency to stomp on toes out there in pursuit of her objective. It would be best, in my opinion, to have her here, where we can govern her actions a bit... just until things settle down."

She rested her elbows on the desk and templed her fingers in thought. *In fact, her clashing with SEs will help give me impetus to take action.* "While her actions have been useful, I'm not sure I can afford for this to look as if we deliberately provoked the Chief of Social Enforcement or his people into action. Her unique form of inquiry has already raised some eyebrows."

"So, what are you saying?" Dorne pushed.

"I never played chess, but as I understand it, one of the strategies that is often employed is to sacrifice a pawn in order to achieve a winning position."

"So, Operative Leatrom..."

"She is serving us well on her current assignment. Let her continue. You know her target. I cannot afford her being hauled up to Capitol Hill to discuss her actions in dealing with the Traitor-President and having SE people claim she was roughing them up. We told the people of Newmerica that the President was dead years ago. The fact that she is even on this mission generates risk for us. I'm sure you'd agree."

"I do," Barker said, a frown tugging at his usually flat expression. "She's a loose cannon, but one we have always been able to aim. I think it would be a shame to lose her."

"As would I," she said, placing her hands palm-down on the desktop. "But when you consider the implications of the two operations—hers and the one we just discussed—I think it best that we remove her from scrutiny."

"No loose ends," Dorne said flatly.

"Exactly. Once she has achieved her mission, Operative Leatrom needs to vanish."

CHAPTER 4

"The greatest heroes are victims."

Detroit, Michigan

Raul Lopez surveyed the blocks of burned-out buildings, noting how even the empty shells were now overgrown with vines and weeds. Woodward Avenue had been on the rebound until the Liberation. The riots that started on the west coast spread and Detroit had a historic reputation for rioting. It was a puzzling thing for Raul. The fires had destroyed the neighborhoods of the people that were allegedly behind them. *Why set fire to places in your own block?* The looting and rioting spread over a series of months until the suburbs felt the same wrath.

And the Youth Corps was there to clean it up.

They had been giving an orientation to the city. How it had been built off of the sweat and toil of workers, many minorities and other oppressed groups. The Youth Corps officer that gave the lecture had talked about how the companies had taken billions in profits and had made the workers get by with paltry bonuses. Some of the factories he saw were massive and impressive and it struck Raul as wrong that the businesses had taken advantage of their people in such a way. When he saw all of the neighborhoods on their tour-drive, he found himself wondering just how bad off the employees were. *We never had homes like this in Mexico. For oppressed people, they seemed to have good places to live.* Still, if the Corps told him it was one way, then that was the way it must be. *Why would the government lie to us?*

Raul adjusted his uniform work-shirt after he set down the wheelbarrow at the job site. The shirt was a distinctive gray, with the eagle patch of the Youth Corps on the right sleeve. He was proud of being in the Corps… even prouder now that he had been given his first assignment. When he was younger in Mexico, he had never thought he'd own such a uniform, let alone be part of such a prestigious organization.

Paco came up alongside of him and surveyed the bricks in his wheelbarrow. "Are you trying to make us look bad, carrying that many?" he cracked, half sarcastically.

Raul grinned. "I'm just doing my share."

Paco looked around at the old factory building that the Corps was demolishing. "They say that Detroit was once a boom town. Now, not so much, eh? My father's truck, it comes from China and the parts were from our home country."

"American engineers designed it though," Raul countered.

Paco shrugged. "Maybe. But things are not built by engineers."

Raul took a sip from his water pack. "It will take us most of the summer to tear down this plant and the rest of the block."

His friend nodded as he surveyed the old factory. "Still, it's better that we do it by hand. Running the heavy equipment, that only pollutes that air. Yes, it is faster, but look at all of the material we are saving for reuse."

There were so many Clean Air Acts out of The District in the last few years that it was hard to keep track of them. Everyone said they were worried about pollution. *No one makes the Chinese or Russians comply though. They are the biggest polluters.* The Chairman of the Ruling Council summed it up best: "It's not important what *they* do; what is important is what *we* can do." That meant the Raul and his Youth Corps troop were dismantling the factory one brick at a time. There were over 250 Corps members, 25 squads, working on the project. He had heard there were at least a half-dozen such projects going on.

It made him proud to be a part of something so big and important. "It will take time, but we have months to get it done."

Raul grabbed the handles of the wheelbarrow and moved it along the well-worn path to the sorting area. Dumping it there, another squad worked to separate the usable from the unusable bricks, stacking the good ones in bins. Pivoting, he turned around and headed back to the dark confines of the old factory. The air stung of grease and rotting wood and wet paper. The facility had been abandoned for decades. According to the troop leader, it had been used by homeless people as a shelter. That area had been the worst to demolish—the stench of stale urine and garbage mingled with body odor. Those days were gone. The homeless didn't exist, not according to the administration. There were Economically Displaced, In-Transition, and Shelter-Dependent People, but the word homeless was never used; it was simply a banned word. Though Raul had to admit, he didn't understand the distinctions so well. The ones that had been in the abandoned factory had looked homeless enough to him.

Once out of the sun he began to load up the bricks that had been knocked off of the old wall by members of his troop. As he carefully loaded the wheelbarrow, making sure that it stayed balanced, he noticed the old graffiti on the wall. 'Freedom Lost,' in fading orange paint. Looking at it he wondered as to its meaning. *What freedoms had been lost?* He felt free to do what he wanted, as long as he followed the rules.

"What are you doing Cadet Lopez?" his Troop Leader Avalon Winston barked out to him.

"I was just looking at the wall."

"That's subversive content," the Troop Leader replied, looking at the wall as if it were a piece of pornography. "You shouldn't even read it."

"It doesn't say much, only two words."

The Troop Leader walked over to him. "You probably were just a kid at the time—you don't remember the right-wing radical standoffs with the NSF, the bombings, and violent protests. The people who wrote that were clinging to long outdated ideals that went back to the founding of the country. They wasted the rights that they had and corrupted the rights they believed were theirs. Look at guns. Gun crimes are down because we rounded them up. Those people fought against safety that we offered. They said we were anarchists, but in reality, they were."

Raul nodded slowly. He wasn't so sure that gun crimes were down. Shootings happened all of the time. Even in Texas he had heard the pop-retort of gunfire almost every night. You didn't see them as much on the net as you heard about them. Since they had been in Detroit for two weeks, he had heard the occasional crack of gunfire in the distance. *I'm not about to raise that point with the Troop Leader though. He'll pull me out of work to do some forced reading if I do.*

Still, the words bothered him. *How could the loss of freedom be bad?* "*Si.* My mother told me about those times. They told me that they rounded up the opposition party and sent them away to prison."

"Not prison," the Troop Leader corrected. "We sent them for rehabilitation and education. They needed to learn to be more tolerant of others. They advocated violence. They resisted change, a change that was for the better. Prison indicates laws. We sent them into social quarantine—for their own safety and protection." The words he spoke were so passionate that Raul was sure they were rehearsed by the leader. *He has been told what to say and believes it.* So did Raul. There was no reason to doubt what the Ruling Council said. At the same time, this was just words painted on a wall. *How could that be a threat to anyone?*

"Perhaps it would be best to take that wall down next," Raul finally uttered as he looked at the word 'Freedom' again.

"Not yet," Winston replied. "Before we go to the bivouac tonight, I'll bring the troop here. This wall is a symbol of the violence of the old days. It will make a good lesson." Suddenly he cocked his head off where one of the walls had already been removed.

Standing in the sunlight just outside of the building were five young men. They had dark complexions and they seemed to be angry; Raul could see it in their faces and the way they stood—arms crossed, their mouths drawn to tight frowns. An air of defiance emanated from them.

"What can I help you with?" the Troop Leader called out to them.

"Your people—they didn't stop when the prayer siren went off," the tallest of the men said bitterly. "They continued to work through the prayers now for several days. You must stop when you hear the siren. It is *Fajr*. It is sacred." His voice was thick with a Farsi accent. Raul thought back. They had heard the short sirens several time a day since arriving in Detroit, but had ignored them. Suddenly, they made sense.

Avalon Winston stepped toward the men as the rest of his troop stopped what they were doing and watched. There was a hint of tension in the tone that the young man had used, almost as if he were making some sort of accusation. "I heard the siren but don't understand what you are talking about."

"It was a call to prayer," another man snapped. "You are defying the will of Allah and insulting us when you continue to work while we pray." *Ah... they must be Muslim, that makes sense.* He had been told when they arrived in Detroit that there was a large Muslim population in the area.

Troop Leader Winston tried to diffuse the situation. "I'm sorry, we meant no offense. We don't practice your faith. Most of my troop are Catholics, some follow no religion at all."

The lanky man stepped closer, only a few feet from Winston. "You will stop your work at the times of our prayer." His tone was filled with a rage. Several members of the troop began to move forward, closing on their leader. Raul was shocked, but he too found himself stepping towards them in response.

"I respect your right to worship, but we are here doing the work of the administration."

The man stabbed his slender finger right into Avalon's chest as he spoke. "I do not care about your administration. You are violating our law. We are not going to tolerate it."

"What law?" Julian, another of Raul's friends, called out. "There's no law that says we have to stop." Raul noticed at that moment that Julian was carrying a pick in his hand. Suddenly it looked like a weapon to him. *This is getting out of hand.*

"It is Sharia law," another one of the men spat back. "It is the law we live by. If you are here, you need to adhere to it."

"That's religious law," Avalon said. "That doesn't apply here."

The man poked at his chest again, this time harder. "It *is* our law." As he did so, he noticed that the troop stepped forward. Even Raul stopped for a moment and grabbed a brick from the old factory floor. The weight of it gave him confidence.

While his flared instincts called for action, his Troop Leader retrained some degree of calm and control. "Look, we don't want trouble. At the same time, we are not Muslim. You go about your business and pray as you want. We will go about our work here. There's no need for violence." He held his arm at his side and his hand horizontal, as if beckoning his troop to stop advancing on him.

"You are making a big mistake," snapped the tall man. "You're disrespecting our faith. We don't take that from anyone, especially a bunch of *Meksikanen* brought into our city. It is bad enough that your Youth Corps takes jobs that our people need. We will not tolerate your ignoring our religion. You had better do as you are told or there will be blood." He spoke boldly and loudly, so all of the troop could hear him. It almost looked as if he were speaking to them, rather than the man in front of him.

"We don't want any violence," Winston said with a calm in his voice that Raul doubted he could muster in the same circumstance. "If we offended you in any way, it wasn't intentional."

"Your being here offends me," the man snapped back, as his posse took a step closer toward him. "This building is in our neighborhood. We are responsible for the social justice here. It belongs to us. You can't just come in here without the permission of our elders." His men all nodded and muttered something in agreement.

"This property was confiscated by the Federal Government," retorted Shin, one of the troops who was holding his shovel as if it were a weapon of war.

The thin, dark-skinned man was unmoved. He forced a chuckle, then retorted. "You're not listening. Your government has no rules here. This is our property because we claim it. Your courts and the NSF have no say here. We are the Social Enforcement here. We govern ourselves according to our traditions and beliefs."

"You can't just do that," Winston replied. "This is Newmerica."

"It is—and here, it is *our* nation. You cannot interfere with our religion. When you continue to work during prayers, you degrade us, mock us. You are restricting our rights to pray as we see fit. We will not stand for it."

It was too much for Raul, who finally spoke up. "We're not interfering with you at all. You can still pray."

The lanky leader glared at him. "Who are you to say what is interference? I will tell you what is interfering, and your working here does that." Despite the numerical odds against him, he seemed unwavering in his defiant tone.

"We don't want trouble," Winston tried again to diffuse the tension. "We will try and work quieter. Will that help?"

The skinny leader surveyed the members of Raul's troop, locking an icy silent stare at each of them, one at a time, working his way around to all of them. *He's sizing up the odds… coming to the reality that we outnumber him.* Almost a half-minute went by before he turned back to the Troop Leader and spoke. "You infidels don't even realize how much you insult us. That will cost you. Not today," he nodded to his compatriots who seemed to relax their stances. "You should leave before someone gets hurt." Before Avalon could launch a response, the men turned and slowly walked way, each giving quick glances back at Raul and his companions.

The Troop Leader turned and looked at them a moment later. Raul could see the relief wash across his face. "Alright then, let's take a break so as to not provoke them more." Slowly the men turned and found whatever they could to sit on. Raul turned as the Troop Leader moved in beside him. "Sir, what do we do when their sirens sound the start of their prayers?" he asked.

"We will work quietly," he replied almost under his breath. "I don't think we want trouble with these men."

Raul nodded in response. That much was true. They were tough looking and angry. *Their religion fuels their anger… and that is a dangerous combination.* He moved over next to his wheelbarrow and began to pile up bricks that other troop members had tossed there.

Where do you draw the line with such men… between what offends them and getting our job done?

Raul didn't have the answers, but he knew the questions alone were complicated. That Sunday, he and several of the other troop members went to the church. Once it had been a splendid building, but time and the community had not been kind. Nasty spray-painted words plastered the magnificent stonework. Avalon had limited their time for church but never said why. Raul had promised his mother he would go and he enjoyed the singing and praying… it reminded him of home.

The congregation was small, huddled in the first five rows of the immense church. There had been more Catholics here at one time; that was evident. Many were older people, though a few Latino families were there as well. Some pews were missing near the rear of the church, and Raul thought he saw burn marks on the stone floor where they had been. *Had there been a fire here? Was it during the Liberation protests?* For a moment, he wondered what kind of person would stoop to setting fire to a church.

Afterward, he approached Father Ryan as the man straightened the altar; he was an older man with tufts of white hair for eyebrows and deep blue eyes. Raul introduced himself and told the priest what he was doing in Detroit, and the Father asked many questions about their work and if they enjoyed the Youth Corps.

Raul told him about the confrontation with the Muslim men. The genial face of the older man nodded and slowly went from jovial to rigid. "God teaches us to turn the other cheek," he said.

"But why were they imposing their religion on us?"

Father Ryan sighed, as if this were a conversation he'd had many times over. "There was a time, not long ago, when I would have told you that they couldn't. The United States did not allow such things—they called it the separation of church and state. We also treated every religion equally. That all changed four years ago. After the Fall, things changed, not necessarily for the better. Detroit has always had a large Muslim community. Before the Fall, we lived in relative harmony. With Newmerica however, some communities have begun to inflict their religious beliefs on others. The government refuses to step in. Being Muslim means you are an oppressed religion, and the FedGov looks the other way when they overstep their bounds. The Catholic church is seen as a privileged religion which promotes racism and class distinctions."

"I'm Hispanic," Raul said. "How could my church be racist?"

"We are not," Father Ryan said. "We are all equal in God's eyes. The Ruling Council feels that we possess too much wealth and power, so they have taxed us and persecuted our practices. The truth is the first victim of oppressive governments. What had been tolerance, has become strife. You are not the first to tell me of such confrontations.

"Now, you, as a good Catholic, must endure the pressures of the Social Enforcers, as must I. Jesus bore a cross; we must bear others inflicting their beliefs upon us."

There was something noble in what Father Ryan told him that resonated with Raul. "What do I do if they come back and attempt to force us to follow their laws?"

The priest put his hand on Raul's shoulder and squeezed it. "Raul, you seem like a good young man and a good Christian. I cannot tell you what to do. The government has forbidden the church to weigh in on such matters. They would abolish us altogether if they believed they could get away with it. What I can tell you is this; there are times we must defend our faith."

"So we should fight them?"

He shook his head. "I'm not saying that. What I am saying is you must trust yourself and do what is right. The church believes that no one, even those of our faith, has the right to force their belief systems on another. We believe in the free choice of every person. The government will tell you the opposite of that, that people can make their own laws and inflict them on others as they deem appropriate. Your mortal soul will tell you what is the truth.

"I believe in our Lord and Savior. He is all knowing, and all forgiving. Trust in yourself Raul, trust in the word of God, and you will make the right choice at the right time." As he finished, he flashed a warm smile.

Raul thanked him and walked back by himself to the Troop camp. There were things that the Father had not said, crammed in between the words he had spoken. The FedGov and our church do not see eye-to-eye. In fact, to Raul, it seemed that they were on opposite sides of the fence when it came to SEs. The differences between what the church taught him and what the government did seemed strange. A part of him wondered if there would be a time when they clashed... and if they did, who would win?

Wheeling, West Virginia

Caylee got out of her car and stared at the flashing lights of the NSF vehicles all around the entrance to The Graveyard. She smirked at the way the cars had been parked. *Amateurs.* If anyone had a vehicle, they could get in or get out with just a few sharp turns. She refused to drive standard issue NSF vehicles—too slow for her, thanks to fears of high-speed chases and the weak-ass green engines. *A cop car is supposed to be fast and heavy duty... to hell with emissions and concerns that perps would get hurt in a chase.*

Caylee shook her head as she approached the gate. A pair of officers asked for ID, which she held up. One eyed her carefully, almost scornfully.

"No offense, but this is a little outside your jurisdiction," he said.

"From the looks of it, it's outside your competency," she said walking past him.

The Graveyard was a disturbing place, even in the early morning hours. The grass had been mowed but that was at least a month ago. It was wet from the morning rain. To some, from a distance, it looked like a cemetery with unusually large markers.

In reality, these were statues. After Liberation the Ruling Council felt that destroying the monuments to old America's past might spurn more resistance. Their solution was to put them in The Graveyard. Its formal name was the United States Tribute Gardens. There were statues of former Presidents, soldiers, countless Confederate statues, either torn down by mobs or removed after the United States had fallen and Newmerica was born. Caylee looked at them as she walked through and saw the damage that had been done to them, the faint outlines of old graffiti sand-blasted off. She could see BLM and ANTIFA tags and symbols sprayed in several spots where the cleaning had failed. Streaks of rust and tarnish stained some stones. She walked past the statue of Thomas Jefferson, ripped from its former memorial in the District. Someone had painted his face black and despite scrubbing efforts, it clung to the bronze. *How the mighty have fallen.* The old Jefferson memorial had been converted to the Clinton Peace Monument a year ago after the former President's death.

A few statues came with their pedestals of stone, but some simply stood on dull granite blocks, having been violently removed from their original mounts. *This is not a tribute to anything... it is the dumping ground for history.* The Ruling Council had ordered the creation of the 'Tribute Gardens' so they could wash their hands of the old monuments without having been labeled as demolishers of art. Putting them there, in the middle of bum-fuck West Virginia, was a convenient solution to a centuries-old problem. It made the Council look benevolent and caring, when in reality, they were simply hiding symbols they had grown to hate.

Caylee had been monitoring NSF reports, looking for the proverbial needle in a haystack for anything that pointed to the Sons of Liberty movement. There were a few seemingly random assassinations—usually of Social Enforcement, but those could easily be attributed to some overly brave civilian that somehow had managed to keep his or her rifle and was out for revenge. No, she knew that the SOL wanted to do something that could not be ignored, something that would provoke a response on the part of the administration. This mass killing, this fit their MO.

NSF detectives were good, but they came from a pure policing background usually. She was an operative, and that was a different animal altogether. Operatives all had some sort of Special Forces background. They didn't think like police—they were more devious, a bit more cunning, always more ruthless. She had been a Ranger in the Army right after the Liberation, one of the few women to ever pass the program, then transferred to military police. Caylee understood how the police thought and went past that. If she didn't get the answers she was looking for, well, she was an operative. NSF Operatives like her could beat it out of someone if they had to. Officially, operatives didn't exist, but everyone knew they did.

As she rounded a massive battered statue of Theodore Roosevelt, she came to where the crime scene technicians were gathered. Tied to the statues they stood in front of were the bodies of fifteen individuals. Most had their throats cut and she could see the bruises many bore on their faces. They were tired up, arms extended, with cheap old rope... something that would be hard to trace. The techs were getting up on ladders, carefully scanning the bodies and the statues for evidence. She looked at them, strung up on the statues as if they were crucified.

She spotted someone she assumed was the lead detective and walked briskly over to him; her feet were already wet from the grass. He eyed her with total disregard until she flashed her badge. "Spec Ops," he said turning to face her with a little more respect. "An honest to God Operative. I thought you folks were myths."

"It is best that you continue to," she said. "It's how we prefer it."

"I'm surprised you'd be involved in something like this."

"Call it a hunch," she said coolly. "You would be surprised the things we are involved with. What do you have so far?"

"Two different cells of SE from the look of it. One was a team that went off the grid from Lexington, Kentucky about two weeks ago. The other was a small group that patrolled the Graveyard here, you know, looking for anyone visiting so they could be investigated. We have two with gunshot wounds, the rest had their throats cut."

"Blood pools here?"

He shook his head. "The rain was pretty hard last night. We found a spot about twenty yards that way," he pointed past the statues to the right. "It looks like that's where they took out the locals.

So the Kentucky team were killed elsewhere. "Cameras?"

He shook his head. "They had hidden ones around here, you know, just to catch anyone that decided to pay their respects. All are missing from what we can tell."

The Graveyard had long been bait to lure in individuals opposed to the Newmerica government. Anyone who came to the site was logged and got less-than-friendly visits from their local SE Team. It was a pilgrimage for some, coming to see the inflammatory statues that had been taken down during the Liberation. She was sure some were just innocent people coming to see the icons of the past, but others, well they were radical "Alt" people. It was best to track them all. "Is it possible that someone from Lexington visited here, got roughed up by their locals, and decided to get a little revenge?"

The detective shrugged. "I had the same thought. We are still combing the records, but nothing jumps out, not in the last two years. Before that the records are a little spotty."

That was the problem with the Social Enforcers as she saw them; they were sloppy. Professionals understood the need for paper trails and good documentation. These former ANTIFA-kids preferred to grab a club or rock and just start chucking. *Sooner or later, we are going to have to put an end to having two policing forces out there.*

"There's more," the detective said grimly. "When we ID'd the first victim, we sent someone over to his house. His family had been murdered as well. We're still tracking down the rest, but it looks like someone made this *very* personal. Killing children... I can't wait to get my hands on these bastards!"

She said nothing but did nod, mostly to appear polite. The tactic was far from new. During the Liberation, ANTIFA and the other revolutionaries had done the same thing to police officers' families. It had shaken the law enforcement community to its very core. Many officers put their loved ones in hiding, while others refused to go back on patrol. *Now these tactics are being used against us.* She knew that no one would say it out loud, but the phrase that came to her mind was, 'Karma's a bitch.' *We established the rules to the game; now they are using them against us.*

Caylee watched as two officers carefully lowered one of the victims. She walked over, disregarding the glares she got from the NSF officers there. The one that was lowered had a gunshot wound. The entry was in his left chest; the exit was nearly his whole back. *Hollow-point— probably reinforced tip for penetrating. This short asshole never stood a chance.*

As one officer carefully used his gloved hand to open the bloody shirt collar, she saw that someone had carved the initials 'NSF!' on the victim's chest. "Sir," the officer called as the detective came over and squatted down to look at it.

Caylee looked at it as well, but with a jaded eye. The detective rose and turned to her. "Someone is sending a message."

She nodded. "They are at that, detective."

"You think it was one of our jobs?" he asked coyly.

"No. We are supposed to think so. And when the SE leadership get ahold of the report, and they will too, they will raise holy hell with NSF over it… claiming it was a hit on two of their teams. It wasn't us though."

"How do you know?"

"Because if it was, one of my people would have done it and we are not so sloppy."

He glanced around at the dead bodies hanging from the dull, green, bronze statues. "This seems professional to me. And pretty deliberate."

"Oh, it's deliberate all right. And there's a message here; just not the one you think. Someone is trying to assign guilt for their crimes to the NSF. It's a red herring."

"What's the message then?"

Caylee looked up for a long moment at one of the bodies, a young woman, her matted wet blonde hair obscuring her face. Her black buttoned shirt was opened and her faded UCLA tee shirt was visible under the wet, soaked bloodstain where her throat had been cut. She was close to the same age as Caylee, but they were worlds apart.

"The message is that the Sons of Liberty are back."

"The SOL?" the detective asked. "They were taken down years ago. How do you get that from this?"

She looked up at him. "It has all the hallmarks of one of their jobs. I remember seeing something like this before, a long time ago, back after the Liberation. Pull up the report on the incident outside of Cleveland—labeled 'Mentor-on-the-Lake.' I'm pretty sure that was it. Same hallmarks, right down to carving NSF on the bodies. They wanted to stir up a shitstorm back then, and for a few weeks, they did. I can't prove that this was the SOL, but it *feels* right." Instinct, she knew, was a big part of her success. *They did this, or someone tied to them.* We kept the Mentor-on-the-Lake stuff under wraps; the media played along because they didn't want to stoke the flames between the NSF and the SE.

"How do you know?"

"Because," she said reaching for her phone. "If I was them, this is what I would have done. I'd like you to shoot me over everything you have on these people, where they were from, anything that might help me lock down who they were pushing the wrong way. No media; tell them it is black-level shit. If they complain, give them the Secretary's number."

"The press is already here. I've kept them back."

"Secure their gear," she replied. "Kick them out. Remind them what happens if they don't cooperate. If they have a complaint, tell them to take it up with the Truth Reconciliation Committee." The media sided with the administration; they had little choice. They had incited the Liberation with their manipulation of information during the last election. Any pretense that they were going to buck the FedGov and run a story that was bad was quickly squelched. Their hands were as dirty as anyone's. Now, if they wanted a story out, it had to be cleared by the TRC—which was little more than a government censorship organization. *They know their place... and those that don't are long gone.*

The detective gave her a thumbs up. The SE team had messed with the wrong people and paid the ultimate price. *Whoever did this planned it out. They didn't just kill an SE team; they brought them here, killed the team here, and hung them all up for us to find. They covered their tracks. This wasn't retribution; this was a highly orchestrated event.*

Caylee knew she was on the right track. *If I can track down the leadership of the Sons, I can get to the President and finish my mission.*

CHAPTER 5

"Action against one is action against all."

Wheaton, Illinois

Arthur Forrest died on a Monday. He did not die alone; Andy was at his side when it happened. He had called for a nurse but none came, not until it was too late. His father had been a low priority patient, part of their ranking system for care. Andy understood, but it didn't make it any easier for him, not in those last few moments when he heard the gravelly rumble in his father's breath. *What the Social Enforcement Teams and Social Quarantine Camp couldn't do, the federal hospital system had finally accomplished.* It wasn't entirely their fault; he knew that the cancer was consuming his father. Their lack of response when he finally coded… that was the icing on the cake.

Karen didn't answer the call Andy made to her, so he left her a message. His father had given him a list of people to call in the event of his death. Most expressed their sorrow, offered their condolences. In terms of the funeral, most stammered and became evasive when he told them when it was. His one neighbor, Mrs. Klandry, said she wished that she could come, but she was fearful. Social Enforcers had gone around his neighborhood when he moved it and had told his new neighbors that associating with him might come with a price. Their intimidation tactics worked. Just showing up might draw unwanted attention, and many were fearful. *They are all older people, all afraid of the SE Teams suddenly targeting them.* He understood, but it did not make his duties any easier.

There was someone that wasn't on his father's list, Dick Farmer, the man that had helped him conceal the package. There were two Richard Farmers in Newmerica, based on the quick search that he did. He was about to call one, but hesitated. *What if they are monitoring my phone?* He waited until he was at the funeral parlor and, feigning a dead battery, borrowed the funeral director's phone to make the call.

The voice that came back to him sounded ancient, creaky. "Is this Dick Farmer?"

"Yes," it said slowly. "Who is this?"

"This is Andy Forrest. My father was Arthur Forrest."

There was a pause. "Yes."

"Well, did you know my father?"

Another long pause, almost to the point where he thought the call had been dropped. "I did at that."

"He passed away two days ago."

This time the voice came back with a sigh and quick response. "I'm damned sorry to hear that. Your dad was a good man."

"Thank you," Andy said, fumbling for how to approach the subject without being direct. "I know this is going to sound weird. My dad said you might be able to help me."

"He did, eh?" the man said. "Best not to say anything else. Tell me where you are at. I'll come there. I probably can't make the service, but tell me where I can find you." Andy gave him his address, unsure what to expect. A part of him hoped that his father had exaggerated what he had told him, that it was a fanciful story concocted out of the cocktail of drugs he was on. In some respects that made more sense than a tale of a mysterious package covertly hidden in a forbidden place.

Karen arrived, alone, wearing a black suit befitting the people she worked for and her mood. Andy made eye contact with her when she arrived, but that was it. Just the two of them showed for their father's funeral, standing ten feet apart, both looking at the open coffin. Each time he glanced at his father's face, he felt his body sag a little.

A minister came in and said a rambling jumble of words… at least that was what it sounded like. The Forrests were not a deeply religious family. Karen crossed her arms as he spoke, almost in defiance. As Andy watched her, he understood. The administration had been targeting religious institutions in the last two years or so, removing their tax-exempt status and claiming that some were 'radicalized' against the government. His father had commented that it was no surprise. "They have to remove anything that questions the administration's values or lack of morals." Andy had come to appreciate his father's wisdom more now that he was gone.

When the minister finished, Andy made his last trip to the casket. He wanted to say something to his father, but the words didn't come. A mix of sadness and anger swept him as he stood there, almost paralyzed in thought. As he finished, he turned and she was standing there, defiant, glaring at him.

"Karen," was all he could muster in that moment.

"I suppose I should chip in on this."

"I don't need or want your money," he replied flatly.

"Maybe you should. You've lost your job."

In that moment two thoughts surfaced. *She's been tracking me.* It was quickly followed by: *Did she have anything to do with me being fired?* He knew she was dark and cruel, but now he saw her for what she was. An enemy. "I'll get by."

For a moment she said nothing and he hoped that she might just go away. Instead, she took a half-step closer to him. "I may be able to help."

"I don't need help."

"You may need more than you realize." Andy heard the tone. This was a threat. Before he could respond, his sister continued. "Did Dad tell you anything before he died?"

"He told me a lot of things." He looked at her like a fish might stare at a looming shark. "Why?"

"Dad had some past associates Andy, criminals really. They have possession of some subversive material that the FedGov wants back. If Dad told you where it was, well, I might be able to assist you in getting your job back."

He eyed her carefully, slowly, recognizing the danger she represented. There was no doubt now that she'd had a hand in his being let go. If anything, it confirmed that what his father had taught him was true. As his eyes fell on hers, he realized that he no longer had a sister. Their father was the only thing that had connected the two of them, and he was dead. When Dad died, so did any bond between brother and sister. "I have no idea what in the hell you are talking about," he said firmly, summoning everything he could from his junior high school play in terms of acting.

"That's too bad. Without that, there's not much I can do."

"I don't want you to do anything for me, *ever*." The venom rose in his mouth as he spoke.

"I always knew you were not as smart as you liked to believe," she said. "If you happen to remember something, you know how to get ahold of me." She pivoted with nearly military precision and walked away, leaving him alone with his father.

He went back to his apartment, not remembering a single step of that trip home. At some point in the quiet, dark room, he shuffled off to bed. It was more of a controlled collapse. He hadn't even taken off his suit—it didn't seem to matter. Time was a blur to Andy Forrest. The only thing that was clear was the mental image of his sister and her threatening words.

Waking up mid-morning, he had a half-cup of coffee. He peeled off the suit and put on running shorts. When he opened the door, a small paper note drifted like a feather down to the floor. He glanced down the hall both ways and picked it up. "Bus stop at Gamon and Elm." Stuffing the tiny note into his shorts pocket, he stepped out and began his jog. Now, at least, he had somewhere to run to.

When he arrived at the bus stop, he was wet with sweat, despite the uncommonly cool morning air. Winter had made one more last surge before spring could emerge. An old man sat there, hunched over slightly, with a big, white bushy mustache and black and red Stormy Kromer hat with its ear flaps tied up. Andy sat down with a space between them, drawing in the cold air as he breathed heavily from the run.

"Hello, Mister Forrest," the man said never looking at him. Andy recognized the gravelly voice.

He opened his mouth to respond, but the man cut him off. "Don't say anything, don't look at me. Chances are they have eyes on you."

"You sound paranoid," he said, looking forward across the street as a handful of cars passed.

"I have good reason to be. You might want to take it up yourself," he said with a slight chuckle.

"I'll take that as good advice." He paused and glanced around as casually as he could. With Mr. Farmer's words, he felt invisible eyes staring at him from everywhere when he arrived at the bus stop—the CVS across the street, the cars driving by. The government's digital billboard on the outside of the building flashed the message of the morning, "Putting yourself first is putting everyone last." It flashed in bright red lettering on the glowing white background. Every time he read the latest message it was frustrating. *What's so wrong with trying to be the best?* He kept his thoughts to himself. Saying such things out loud was risky, even among friends. With all of the incentives out there for people to turn in friends and family members for infractions, smart people kept quiet.

He regained his focus in a millisecond. "So you helped my father?"

"I did. We were good friends. He needed someone to do some of the heavy work. I may look old, but I'm still pretty damned strong. It had to be hidden in a way that no one would bother it. We did it when they finished their God-damned blasting."

"Where?"

"Borglum built it, but it never got used. He called it the Hall of Records. Typical government job; they cut the funding and it never got finished. If you want to fuck something up, you let the government do it. That's the one constant in the universe. It should be there. The whole site is off-limits after they screwed up their demo job. They don't like images that might get people fired up against them. I can draw you a map of how to get there. You may need some help."

"What is it that I'm looking for?"

"In the back of the tunnel. I made it look like a pile of rubble. It's under that."

"No," Andy corrected himself. "I mean, what is it?"

Dick Farmer shrugged. "He never told me. All he said was that it was important. He and Brummer didn't want it to fall into the hands of the mob. Of course, now those mobs are calling the shots."

"Can you come with me?"

Farmer shook his head. "Got the shit beat out of me in one of their Social Quarantine Camps—broke both my hips. According to them I am an 'insurrectionist,' at least that was their justification. The arthritis makes the hike out of question." Andy could hear the bitterness in his voice as he spoke of the injury. *Like Dad, they have taken a lot from this man.*

"I—I don't know if I can do this alone."

"I did some digging. Chances are pretty good they are watching you. I would just slow you down," he said, never making eye contact with him. "Sure as hell don't trust your sister."

"I don't *have* a sister anymore."

The older man shook his head. "I understand. Look, I still have a few connections. Let me reach out, see if I can get you some help."

"The Sons?" he asked in a low whisper.

"Damned right," he said with a grin of pride rising to his face. "We went so deep they thought they got us all. The ones they caught, your dad and me, well, they figured they broke us. Quarantine my ass. They squeezed us for names. Neither of us ever broke."

"I appreciate any help you can get me."

"We'll need a code word. If help comes, they will use it against you. They are devious fucks. If someone else shows up and they don't know the word, play dumb. You can't trust anyone Andy, especially folks in the administration. They will try and trick it out of you if they can. I've seen them do it before. They were a bunch of punk-ass anarchists, but they got crafty as all-shit."

"Okay," he said pausing. "What about 'Nightingale?'"

"That works for me," Dick Farmer replied. He paused and sighed, the thin white wisp of condensation in the air streamed out from under his mustache. "You know, I always figured that it would be like the Civil War. State against state, city against city, brother versus brother. We were sort of prepared for that. These fuckers, they came in and took us down from within, starting at the top. Their riots made us turn against each other. The media fed it all, just for the ratings. The old Democratic Party funded and helped them, only to find themselves almost cut out of the FedGov. Dipshits!" There was a longing in his voice, as if he wished that the revolution had been more a traditional war. Andy glanced at him from the side and saw the same expression his father used to have—a mix of frustration and lost hopes.

"Thank you for helping me," Andy finally said.

"Do me a favor?"

"Put the screws to them. I have no idea what your daddy put up there, but it was important. Whatever it is, use it. Make them pay." With those words, Dick Farmer rose and walked away, leaving Andy on the bus stop bench.

Falls Church, Virginia

Charli held the steering wheel tightly. It was still a beast to handle but no worse than when she trained on the President's limousine, code-named the Stagecoach. Driving the armored car was like trying to swim with someone on your back. It was slow and sluggish, especially loaded down as much as it was. Things were not made easier with the extra padding and the five-point safety harness she had to wear. The air conditioning in the armored car hadn't worked since the first Bush administration. Just maneuvering it made her wet with sweat.

In a few minutes the discomfort wouldn't matter.

One thing for sure, Jack Desmond knew how to ask for a favor. The building that was her target was impressive, a shimmering tribute to the ego of the architect and the arrogance of the administration. Greenish mirrored glass, sweeping lines reaching up fifteen stories tall. What was invisible was the lab facilities that extended four stories under the structure, labs dedicated to tracking down 'enemies of the people.' To the casual observer, the building looked like any other office building that ringed the District, innocuous and oddly sinister. Anyone passing it would think it was probably some government contractor's office, some company making its money off of the government teat.

It was a brilliant day; the sky was bright blue and only a few clouds were present. Charli looked at it and knew it would look good on the newscast that night, if the administration allowed it to be on. It would be a story that would be hard to ignore, even for the government-controlled media. So much was suppressed nowadays it wouldn't have surprised her if they didn't run the story.

Since Jack Desmond had tracked her down, she had been experiencing a strange feeling—a tinge of happiness, almost comfort. He had fulfilled his promise to introduce her to 'the successor' as they called him and she was convinced he was the real-deal. That was part of her recovered bit of joy. There might just be a chance to set things right, or at least start on that road. Desmond hadn't hesitated to cash in his favor for her.

The other part that fueled her rediscovered purpose was the strategy that Jack had laid out. "If we fight them directly, in a stand-up fight, we will lose. We lost before," he pointed out. "They want that kind of confrontation; it's easier for them and the numbers are on their side for the time being. They defunded a lot of police work, but combined all of the departments into the NSF. As such, the key is to get them fighting each other." Charli liked the sound of that. She was quick to volunteer, and had gotten this assignment. It had taken a few weeks to perfect, weeks of planning and preparation that were about to pay off.

The National Support Force offices and labs were housed in the pristine building looming in front of her. As Charli turned the heavy vehicle into the parking area, she saw the emblazoned golden eagle and the Latin phrase under it: "Tutor of Licentia."

"Protectors of liberty my ass!" she spat, turning the Brinks armored car slowly into a visitor parking spot. She even hated their name—the National Security Force. They refused to call it what it was, a militant police force, one she had been in during her self-imposed exile. 'Security' had a softer, kinder feeling to it. Pablum for the masses.

Charli looked at the building and noted the barriers that were in place, cement filled steel posts that lined the sidewalk. Everything as it had been on her few walk-through trips that she had done to reconnoiter the area. *Good, I don't need any surprises.* She stared in the oversized rearview mirror on the door and watched as the four posts lowered into their holes to allow her access.

It had taken a fake work order and a flirtatious look from her light blue eyes to get the guards to lower the security barrier in front of the building. She had told them that she was there to pick up the employee ATM just outside of the cafeteria and needed to back the armored car up so she could load it. No one questioned her or double-checked the work order. They scanned her FedGov ID and it had cleared, a testimony to the cost of the fake ID she carried. When the dust settled and they recovered the data, it would lead them to Kentucky, just as she and Jack had planned. The ID had only been part of the ruse. The advantage of being compact, blonde, well-built, and manipulative, was that you could often convince men to do what you want. *Their reliance on their technology is a weakness we can exploit.*

One of the black-shirted guards had suggested using the loading dock, but she had pointed out that she was alone and the ATM was going to be heavy to lug all the way through the building. "It would be easier if you allowed me to drive around front." They should have stopped her, but what risk was presented by an armored car driven by a pretty young woman? Chivalry, stupidity, and thinking with their crotches rather than their brains got the best of the guards.

The armored car had been purchased in a junkyard in Dumfries, Virginia and had been carefully repainted and repaired to look operational. Every identification marking on it had been meticulously ground or ripped off the vehicle. Several other modifications had been made to turn it into a machine of destruction, including welding the side doors shut to help channel the force of the expected blast.

Charli put it in reverse and slowly, carefully backed the armored car up to the glass façade of the building. Working the wheel like a pro, she angled the rear of the vehicle into the precise spot that Jack had described. To anyone looking, it appeared to be an armored car backing up to make a pick-up. Angle was important. The rear of the armored car was loaded with high explosives and the study of the building had told the SOL the right way to bring it down. Once she was good with the angle, Charli moved towards the edge of the barrier, pulling away from the building so that she could build up speed.

The lobby glass was bound to be bullet-proof laminate, tough stuff. It was resistant to shattering but hitting it with the blunt-force trauma of a loaded armored car at full speed in reverse was not something that the designers had taken into account. To make it even easier, the bumper of the armored car had some well-placed small steel spikes jutting out a few inches. Painted black, the same color as the heavy bumper, no one would notice them, but when they hit the glass, they would help in punching through.

She tightened her safety harness and put on the helmet that was next to her seat. In the pedestrian side, pushed down on the floor and covered with plastic tarp was the body of a young woman. They would be looking in the debris for the driver, and she had the perfect one for them. When they ran the victim's DNA, she would come up as a member of a Kentucky Social Enforcement Team. The NSF investigators would take it as an attack, somehow linked to the bodies that Jack and his people had left in West Virginia. Of course it would take a while to get that DNA tested, since she was taking out one of their primary laboratories in the attack.

Charli put the armored car in reverse as her foot hovered over the gas-pedal. She allowed herself a moment to check the rear-view mirrors one more time. Then, she jammed her foot all the way down and braced her body for the inevitable impact.

There was a bump, a crash, and the grinding of metal, all in the same second. The armored car backed right into the lobby, through the security station and toppled the metal detectors and sniffers. As the vehicle rocked into the lobby, she hit the brake and checked her position. From everywhere people were scurrying for cover, not sure of what had happened. Charli pulled the helmet off and tossed it on the seat. The two jugs of homemade napalm on the floor of the car sloshed and spilled. When the armored vehicle went off, it would be difficult for anyone digging through the rubble to find the remains.

She hit the red toggle Jack had put on the dashboard. There was a pop from behind her as the rear doors of the armored car blew open with the small charges. Charli pulled the emergency brake to lock the wheels in place.

Almost casually she opened the door and grabbed the blocks from her seat. She kicked them in the path of the two front tires as people scrambled across the broken glass, still stunned by what had happened. Hitting the security station had worked well. Charli saw an arm poking out of the rubble and she knew the guards were out of commission. The smell of dust and a whiff of smoke stung at her nostrils as she moved. She threw a wheel chock in front of the driver's side front tire, for added stopping, though the bits of masonry and terrazzo laying everywhere would likely do just fine.

Reaching up into the car, she hit the second toggle, the green one, on the dash. There was an audible beep from the car which she could barely hear over the loud screech of the building's fire alarm. The clock was running, and so was she. She ran out through the hole the Brink's car had made in the lobby, coughing a little as she sucked in dust caused by her crash. Someone called out to her, "Hey!" but she ignored it. The confusion wasn't going to last long, so she had to make the most of it.

When she hit the parking lot, she broke into a full sprint.

Then came the roar.

Explosives, in the hands of professionals, were incredibly potent and the experts that the SOL had at their disposal were consummate artisans in their craft. With over two tons of military-grade demolitions in the armored car, the blast went off with incredible power. The big rear doors of the armored car were wide-open, giving the force of the explosion a place to go, a natural channel for the released raw energy. It went off like a massive shotgun, a shaped charge of deadly destructive force. The blast ripped into the central structure of the office building, devouring the bank of elevators in the first millisecond and stretching to the far southwest corner. Along with the thunder-like rumble of the explosion, the sound of breaking glass filled Charli's ears as every window on the first six floors erupted. The echo of the explosion boomed off of other nearby buildings as did the shattering of some of their windows.

Normally a car bomb, even a large one of this sort, would have been insufficient to take down the building. Because of the angle and the fact that the central core of the office building had been gutted by the blast, the entire structure was suddenly in jeopardy. She stopped for a moment between vehicles, aware for the first time that car alarms all around her were going off from the explosive force. Jack and the explosives experts the SOL had assembled had explained to her what was going to happen next but regardless of that, it still amazed her.

The weight of the office tower was compromised with the loss of the lobby level of the central tower which supported the first three floors. In the heart of the building the weight was suddenly thrust to the outer walls which were not designed for that kind of extreme stress. Starting with the lobby, the building dropped down, straight down, like a pile-driver slamming home. The sudden crush of weight of the upper floors hit the subterranean lab levels and pancaked them.

Charli had been in middle-school when the World Trade Center was taken down by terrorists. When that had happened, she remembered the rolling clouds of dust and debris. This was different. The NSF offices and labs simply seemed to disappear downward as the structure fell in on itself. There was some dust and smoke, but for the most part it appeared that the building disappeared into a hole in the ground. It was fast, much quicker than she had expected. It was far more satisfying than she could have thought. There was a sense of pride in what she did, and a certain grimness. *The NSF has so much blood on its hands... the organization deserves this, if not the individuals.*

There was another emotion, one of exhilaration. For the last four years she had been hiding, going out of the way to avoid attracting attention. Charli had embraced the fear that she might be caught at any moment and harbored no illusions as to what the NSF would do to her if they did apprehend her. With the explosion, she felt strangely alive again. The excitement she felt was not born of fear but energized with action.

Charli dropped down between two parked cars and tore off the uniform that bore the embroidered Brinks logo and doused it with a bottle of liquid she had in her shorts pocket. She doused the pants and shirt and tossed the plastic squeeze bottle on them. A touch of her lighter caught it on fire and she kicked it under the car. With any luck the car would burn as well, further destroying the evidence.

Rising, she ran away from the blast, glancing over her shoulder from time to time. It took a while, but finally a pillar of smoke rose from the hole as flames devoured whatever was left of the lab facility. She didn't look back at the destruction she had unleashed. She knew the image would eat at her for years to come.

CHAPTER 6

"History owes us."

Detroit, Michigan

Raul Lopez looked out at where he and his crew had been working and could not help but feel a sense of pride. Half of the massive old factory had been cleared, right down to the foundation. Brick-by-brick it had been dismantled, recovering the useful material and hauling off the rest. Further up the block, several old apartment buildings were being dismantled by another Youth Corps squad, though they had not progressed at the speed of his team.

It had been hard work, but there had been benefits. He had never before had muscles like this. There was a sense of pride, not just in himself but in Newmerica. Only here could someone come up from nothing to have a place in society. It helped that his Youth Corps leader, Avalon Winston, made a point of recognizing everyone's contributions during the nightly talks. It wasn't all about hard work either. The Corps offered history, social studies, even hygiene classes. He learned more in those sessions than he had in high school.

Summer had come and it had been warmer than usual. He had been surprised at how humid Michigan could be. You had thunderclouds one minute, then walls of rain flooded the streets, then the sun came out and the air was thick as soup. His sinuses had been clogged for weeks because of the climate, but the hard work had made them more tolerable.

Since they reached the half-way point early, Troop Leader Winston had given them the afternoon off. Raul had gone for a walk, using the time to explore the area. From what he had been told, Detroit had been experiencing a resurgence up to the time of the Liberation. Those that fought against the FedGov had used that struggle to stage right-wing riots that had left many areas of Detroit in shambles. He saw first hand, gutted buildings that were little more than shells, businesses with broken windows, long abandoned. There wasn't a lot to see other than at one time, this had been a thriving community. *It was a shame that those who fought against the Liberation had done this.* Now he understood why so many had to be sent for social quarantine. *They caused all of this; what was it called, urban decay?*

When he returned from his stroll, Paco and several of his friends were there. Paco coddled a cardboard package in his lap. From it, he pulled out a beer. "Here you go, Raul!" he said, tossing it to him.

Raul had tried beer before, but not in a long time. He opened the can with a hiss and put it to his lips. Rarely had anything in his life tasted so good. The fact that it was very cold helped. Raul didn't gulp it; he held on to the can to savor it as long as he could before Paco handed it to another member of the squad.

"Where did you get this?" Raul asked.

"I had to walk nearly three miles. There were a lot of stores, but none of them carried alcohol," Paco replied. "Very strange for such a large city."

"It is those Enforcers," Julian said as he sat down on a cement block and cracked open his can of beer. "They are Muslim. Their religion does not permit alcohol. I'm sure they put pressure on the store owners."

Carter, one of the few young white members of the troop, spoke up with his heavy southern drawl. "Sounds like a religion I wouldn't wanna be a part of." There were chuckles from the gathered young men.

Shin, a slender Asian man in the troop spoke up in a solemn tone. "I don't understand why the FedGov allows them. They act like bullies or some sort of gang."

The voice of Troop Leader Winston came from behind them as he strolled up. At first, Raul was worried that they would be in trouble for the beer, but instead, Avalon answered his question. "They are here because they were part of the Liberation—a big part. Their peaceful protests were useful. The Alt-Righters that came out to counter-protest made it easier for us to identify and remove them from society. Now the SEs play an important role in our country. They help us keep people aligned to our principles of Newmerica. The NSF can't be everywhere and their justice is slow. The Social Enforcement Teams—they deal with people that just can't help themselves when it comes to following the rules. They make sure that people know their role in society... that they don't say or do things that would offend or hurt others."

Paco hesitatingly held up a beer for Winston who took it and smiled as he cracked back the pull tab. For the first time, Raul saw Avalon relax. Carter spoke up. "I remember the riots. My family was pretty scared."

"Peaceful protests," corrected the Troop Leader. "You can't call them riots because it isn't correct."

"Right," the southern boy said. "They set fire to a courthouse in my county—and the police station. Killed the sheriff's daughter, too."

Avalon shook his head. "Remember, that was the Alt-Right and their thugs that did those acts," he corrected. "The SE protestors were marching for good causes. The only people that committed acts of violence were those that were perpetuating the old system of hate and oppression."

Paco weighed in. "The lady down the hall, she turned in the family across the hall from us. They had a flag they hadn't surrendered."

As Winston took a sip of the cold beer, the condensation dripped onto his leg. "Good thing they did. That's the mark of a good citizen. People think you can hide things like that. That old flag was a problem. It represented centuries of persecution and wars. That's why you can't find one of those flags anywhere. The tech-leaders helped us track down every image and purge them. Things like that led to the incentive system. There are lots of good incentives for people to do the right thing and turn in violators."

Paco nodded. "*Si*. They were able to buy a new refrigerator with their reward." Raul listened and understood all too well. His own mother was in a store once and had seen a man with a pistol in his belt. She had gotten almost $300 for calling in and reporting him. The incentives were a good thing. They helped people be their own police, and they got rewarded for it.

Ramon, a beefy, dark-skinned youth who rarely spoke up, chimed in. "Is it true that they shipped people off to camps? I saw them take away a whole family in my hood. Word was, they were refusing to vote. The SEs came in and put them in a van and we never saw them again."

Avalon shook his head. "No one went to camps. The stories of these so-called camps are lies, told by the traitors. The social quarantine centers are nice places, put in place to protect those that refused to follow the new order of things."

"Have you ever seen one?" Raul asked.

"No, but I have seen videos from several as part of my training. One had a big swimming pool and a tennis court. The stories of those places being concentration camps, well, they are just plain lies. People go there so they can learn why their old thinking is wrong. A lot of the old-timers, they refused to see the racism inherent in each one of us. By sending them there, they are taught the truths that the old government hid from them. Remember, 'Association is guilt,'" he added, quoting one of the FedGov's many slogans.

Raul took a long drink of his beer but did not respond. That was not what he heard. The rumors were that they were *campos de concentración*. Yes, the nightly vid-casts liked to say they were more like resorts, but it struck him strange that of the people he knew that were taken away few ever seemed to come back. The ones that did, they were not the same— and no one talked to them out of fear of being turned in themselves— fear that they wouldn't come back, would have their possessions hauled off in government trucks, or be removed by other family members who refused to speak with anyone. As much as he trusted Avalon Winston, Raul questioned if he *really* knew what the centers were like. His mother had always told him that rumors were often based on tiny truths. Raul knew enough to keep his darker questions to himself.

Paco spoke up. "Troop leader, where do you come from?" It was a good question. For all of his sharing of politics and philosophy, Avalon Winston rarely told them about his personal life.

The taller man took a long drink of his beer, tossing it into the recycle dumpster nearby with a loud clang. "Me? I come from Seattle—back where it all started. I graduated from UCLA, but was working a tech-slave job in Seattle before coming here."

Seattle—that was where the Liberation had begun. "Were you ANTIFA?" Raul asked. It was a question akin to, 'Did you fight in the war?'"

He shook his head. "I wish I had been. I was just a tech worker at the time. When it all went down, we decided to organize our own little group—me and some good friends. We were SE before there was SE. Social Justice, that's what we were all about. We went out at night, mostly into the suburbs—you know, helping redistribute the wealth." He smiled when he talked, his voice hinting at the pride he felt.

"Did you see action?" Paco pressed.

"A little," he said. "The Seattle police had been impotent for years. If you didn't have a gun, they generally didn't respond. One night though, we hit the house of one of our managers, a guy that had been profiting off of our hard work for two years. He must have had some pull because the cops showed up with a bit of an attitude."

"What happened?" Raul asked.

"They caught us right at the front door, bright lights and all. One of our guys threw a brick, hit that racist bastard down in the first throw, right in the forehead. He just dropped, out cold. Well, they fired, but all they had was rubber in their guns. We rushed them. I got hit three times—let me tell you, it hurt like a bitch. We overpowered them, beat the shit out of the two that didn't run, set fire to their cruiser," his grin grew as he described the night, his eyes drifting out over where the factory had been.

"Sounds like a good time," Carter said grinning.

"It was," Winston replied. "Nothing really came of it other than us sending a message to the rich. There were a lot of us sneaking out at night, fighting the good fight our way. I like to think we contributed to the effort." He then seemed to remember where he was and turned to them. "Look, you earned your day off. Have some fun, but stay close." With that, the Troop Leader walked away.

Raul watched him saunter off and one thought came to his mind. Avalon had been so flip about his story… but what happened to the police? *They were just doing their job and were set upon and beaten.* Yes, police from that time were known racists, but it seemed a bit extreme. Raul said nothing, but held the cool beer in his hands, staring at the top of the can in silence. His mother had always taught him that there were two sides of every argument. *Am I only getting half of the story?*

Falls Church, Virginia

The remains of the building were still smoldering, even after two days of rescue and recovery efforts. There was little that looked like it had been a structure. The building was a massive mound of debris, crushed, jumbled, and smashed. A few steel beams jutted skyward as grave markers for the NSF people that had died in the blast. A thin haze of dust of obliterated concrete hung in the air, clinging to her straight black hair. The smell that stung at her nostrils was like that of burning plastic, thick with dust and a hint of ozone.

The National Secretary of the NSF had come to the bombing sight to appear to be concerned. She had learned long ago that perception was everything in politics, and appearing there, in her pristine black suit, looking out with sadness over the debris field, made for a powerful image in the news and on the net. She knew that people were taking photos and videos of her, and she gave them what they wanted to see, a deeply upset and mournful expression.

The Secretary bent down and picked up a handful of the powdery substance, then let it fall. Someone did this to *her* agency. Thanks to the work of the Truth Reconciliation Committee, the story had been one of a gas leak, but she knew the truth… this was a deliberate attack. *Who would dare come at us directly?* The resistance groups had all but been squashed, except for the Sons of Liberty which had raised its ugly head; but this… *this is beyond anything they ever tried.* The Proud Boys, the Michigan Militia, the Rangers, the Lawmen, the Boogaloo Boys; they had all been eradicated years ago.

The Special Agent in Charge, Velma Truman, came up beside her as the Secretary dusted off her hands. "What is the current body count?"

"Nine hundred and eighty-two unaccounted for," Truman responded.

"And the vehicle that did this?"

"Buried still, though a team has reached it. We found a body inside."

"Run the DNA through the National Registry." The registry had been a byproduct of the pandemic. The FedGov took a sample from anyone that got the vaccine. It was supposed to be for tracking purposes, to make sure that the cure didn't have an adverse effect on someone because of genetic traits. The Secretary and the NSF had long realized the power of having access to 90% of the population's DNA. Technically, she was not supposed to access the registry, but technicalities didn't win revolutions.

"I have. It came back to one Judith Sorrento of New Jersey. She is second in command of an SE unit operating out of Newark, the Booker Bois."

The Social Enforcers! Perfect! She had hoped to spark tensions between the organizations and now it seemed to be working. Yes, it had cost the lives of 982 officers and investigators, but it was a tangible act that could be tied to them. *This is the way a horrible situation can be turned around and made into something useful.* "Madame Secretary," the olive-skinned Truman spoke up. "This Judith Sorrento went missing a week ago. We have not been able to extract the body for testing, but it is possible that her body was planted in the vehicle to throw us off."

The Secretary ignored the cautionary words. "What do you know about the vehicle?"

"Not much yet. From the recovered security footage, it looked like a typical ATM delivery. Whoever built the bomb knew what they were doing. The blast force was channeled right into the central support structure of the building. The only kind of people that know how to use explosives like that are trained professionals—former military. Ms. Sorrento didn't have the background for that. Nor have we found any reason for her to launch such an attack. These people knew exactly how to use that bomb to take down this structure. It is way beyond the capability of the Booker Bois."

"Thank you, SAC Truman," the Secretary said smoothly, turning from the rubble to face the shorter, stockier agent. *Truman is doing her job, but I need to control this information. It is only useful to me if the SEs are implicated.* "Your investigation is now coded Black. You will share nothing of your findings with anyone other than me directly. Any theories you might develop, those stay between us. Everything is eyes only. Understood?"

"Yes, ma'am," she replied.

"Good. If this information got in the wrong hands, it might be misinterpreted. We don't want that. I will deal with the political implications. Your job is to get the data." Truman nodded and the Secretary turned to the massive mound of rubble in front of her. *I will determine how this information is interpreted and who sees it, and when.*

She knew she should feel more for the loss of the NSF staff in the attack, but her efforts were concentrated on not allowing a smile to reach her lips. *Someone out there is playing into my hands, helping me along. When the dust settles, I can easily deal with them. For now, letting this rest at the feet of the Director of Social Enforcement works well for my long-term objective.*

Lexington, Kentucky

Caylee walked into the garage and was bombarded by the sounds of power equipment and the pounding of metal by hammers. It was a five-bay operation, and she immediately assessed that ten people were working in the shop—nine men and one woman that could be easily confused for a male. The smell of oil and antifreeze hung in the air like an invisible fog, mingling with the sweat of the employees. Tools were everywhere on the filthy workbenches, and she made a quick mental note of the ones that could be used as weapons. In her mind, her egress was already plotted if things went south.

"Hey," a beefy man in oil-stained, gray coveralls called, "We don't allow customers in the bay. I'm afraid you'll have to leave."

"I'm not a customer," she yelled back.

"I don't care," he said, taking a few steps toward her. "You ain't allowed here."

Her mind sized him up, not as a threat, but as a potential target. Muscular, slight paunch, mostly upper body strength from what she could see. *Body blows are not going to work with this guy; you have to go for the head.* "I'm looking for a Mister Buck James."

"Who wants to know?" the man asked.

She pulled out her NSF badge and flashed it. "I have a few questions."

The man, whose sewn-on oval name badge said, "Frank," was clearly unimpressed. *He's misjudging me, which is a good thing.* He turned slowly and called out in the bay. "Hey Buck, you got a cop here to see you." Three of the men working stopped to watch as a larger man emerged, wiping his filthy hands on a filthier rag. He had black hair, a thick mustache, and a brow that had a tiny scar on it… matching the description in his file. A small smear of black grease shimmered on his cheek. "What do you want?" he said as he stood next to Frank.

"I have a few questions you should be able to help me with. That's all."

"About what?"

"Perhaps we could go somewhere a little more private," she said as two more of the workers put their tools down and started walking over. The cacophony of sound in the shop seemed to drop off.

"I want to ask you something about the Black Hats," she said.

"If you're NSF, I've got nothing to say to you," he replied flatly. For her it was the same old story – the SEs didn't speak with the NSF, a throwback to the ANTIFA days.

"We had nothing to do with your squad being killed."

"That isn't what I heard," Buck replied. "Two of my cousins are still warm in the ground thanks to the NSF."

"You didn't go that night," Caylee pressed on.

"I was sick," Buck spat back. "You can be sure if I was there, none of that shit would have gone down."

"Right," she said with a flip tone. "Regardless, your squad went to meet with someone. I would very much like to know who it was."

Buck James eyed her. She knew he was sizing her up, likely not seeing her as much of a threat. She only stood five foot six, and her choice of clothing did not reveal her strength. She could see in his eyes that he felt he could take her. "The SE will handle this," he said.

"Look. I need the name of the person you were going to meet. Now I can try and appeal to you, tell you I want to bring the man to justice. You'll just say something stupid in response, try to provoke me because you think I'm no threat to you. We will get harsh and you will walk away, your buddies patting you on the back for being an arrogant prick to a cute NSF operative. But the problem is, Buck, you have misread this situation and me. I need the name of whom your Black Hats went to meet. If you don't tell me, I will beat it out of you." Her threat was blunt, with little emotion in her words.

Buck chuckled, feeling all the eyes in the shop falling on him. Stepping towards her, he grinned broadly. "I'd like to see you try."

Caylee moved, not towards him, but to his left, putting herself next to a workbench of tools and her prey. Her hands moved out from her body and she lowered her stance. "Last chance dickhead."

The provocation had the desired effect. He balled his fist, reeling it back to throw a devastating punch as he lunged at her. In Caylee's mind, she saw it coming a mile away. She grabbed a set of metal pinchers off of the workbench as she dove low, feet first, narrowly shooting between his legs. His punch went awry as he ducked, trying to see where she went.

Kicking hard and spinning, she swung the tool as he rose and tried to turn to face her, catching him right below his ear, shattering the think bone of his skull there. Buck cried out, staggering back a step, blood coming from where she had cut the skin.

She did not pause, but continued to move, landing a hard kick to his knee. She didn't hear a bone breaking, but she knew he was in agony… knees were not designed to bend sideways. Dropping to his functional knee she wheeled the tool around again, connecting with the brow above his eye. It didn't break bone, but tore skin blinding him with his own gore as he fell backwards onto the shop floor.

Like a spider-monkey she sprang up, landing on his chest with both knees just below the rib cage, knocking the wind from his lungs. Panic filled Buck James's one visible eye as he struggled to breathe.

She opened the big set of metal snips, which had a sharpened edge to pinch off metal parts. She pinched it hard on his nose, they looked up. Several of the workers were grabbing tools and heading towards her, no doubt dazed at the speed and audacity of her assault. She glared at them. "Ah ah ha," she warned. "Take one step more and your buddy here loses his nose." Her threat worked. The other members of the shop stood in place.

Buck was in agony as he finally got his wind again, gasping, spitting blood. "What the fuck?"

"The name Mister James," she said with a calm degree of formality.

"You're crazy!"

"No. I'm just very good at what I do," she replied. "The name—and what do you know about him?"

"Raymond," he said as the blood from his temple ran down his now reddened face and began to puddle on the filthy floor of the garage. "Mike Raymond. He was a delivery driver. We got word that he was recruiting. We set him up. We didn't know he was one of yours."

"He wasn't," she replied, keeping the pinch on his nose. "Like I said, the NSF had nothing to do with your crime."

Buck moaned under her. "Who was he recruiting for?"

"The SOL—the Sons of Liberty," Buck replied. "That's what we heard. We were going to round all of them up. That was the plan."

Caylee released the pinch on his nose and slowly slid off of him, rising to her full height. James tried to stand, but the damage to his knee made him recoil. One of his coworkers moved in and helped him to his feet.

Her trained eyes swept the others and saw that the threat had diminished. She tossed the tool onto the workbench. "Thank you for your cooperation, Mister James," she said, pivoting perfectly and walking away.

A truck driver... good cover. Mobile, difficult to track. These SE rednecks had no reason to suspect they were walking into a trap, which made it a near-perfect setup. *This Mike Raymond, or whoever he really was, played to their overconfidence.* She already knew that the bar where it was supposed to have taken place had burned to the ground that night—no doubt the action of the SOL.

It wasn't a lot to work with, but a start. *By now he's gotten a new identity. He would not return to trucking because he knows we will look to that. I need to find his vehicle; that will tell me where he was last.*

CHAPTER 7

"Putting one first is putting all last."

Little Rock, Arkansas

Helping Charli behind him with a pull, Rupport Bishop climbed up into the tractor-trailer he was hauling and closed the big door behind them. Locking it from the inside, he turned on the interior lights. To the casual observer, it was dull. A mostly empty trailer was about ten percent filled with boxes at the back. He gestured to Charli who gave him a puzzled look. "Where's your CP, *Rupport?*"

Jack Desmond smiled, removed his prosthetic nose, and walked to the back. There was no more need for the disguise and the persona of Rupport Bishop.

The tall wall of boxes loomed over him. Some were filled; that was part of the deception. The rest were fake, concealing a small, six-foot space where Jack did his work. A false wall of cardboard. He moved aside two large, empty boxes and entered with Charli following.

The Bishop identity was an old one that he used from time to time and after the affair in Lexington, it was clear he needed to assume a new persona. The Secret Service had created several false IDs for catastrophic situations, which was how he and Charli had managed to avoid capture up to this point. They had used their old IDs to get new Federal IDs, part of Newmerica's means of keeping citizens trackable. On paper, Rupport was a good-old boy, a community college dropout who drifted between low-paying jobs and unemployment before he became an independent trucker. A new, short beard and prosthetic nose helped him avoid facial recognition systems. Staying moving was important and one of the key factors to his success at evading the NSF thus far.

There were three small stools and a desk with laptops on it, all hardwired to a small satellite dish that was hidden in a false compartment on the roof of the tractor trailer. Charli grabbed a seat and swung a leg over it and he took another. "Congratulations on the bombing, Charli," he said with a thin smile. He had watched the media coverage, how the FedGov was attempting to spin that it had been a gas explosion. What he heard from his operatives on the street was that few people were buying that given the devastation. *Good, make them lie, then let the conspiracy theorists do some of the work for us. Anyone looking at that rubble will think back to the 9-11 attacks and know that this was not a bad gas regulator.*

She nodded, not returning the grin. "I killed close to a thousand people," she said flatly. "If you don't mind, I don't feel like celebrating."

"I know it was hard," Jack replied, putting his hand on her shoulder. "You are saving lives down the road and that's what counts. The struggle that's coming is going to be a bloody-damned affair. The only way that I get through it is to remember those we worked with that died during their fucking Liberation. Lined up and shot, or beaten to death by the mobs in the streets." His own bitterness and anger tinged his words as he spoke.

"I know," she said. "I think about the night of the Fall, and the days that followed. They went after my parents, trying to find me. The only way that it worked was for everyone to believe that I was already dead." Jack could tell that a part of her was dead.

"You never told me what happened that night, with you and the President," he said in a low voice.

She stared intently into his eyes, into his soul. "No, I didn't. And I don't want to either. Not yet." *She blames herself for something... his death perhaps? Maybe something else.*

"Fair enough," he said removing his hand from her shoulder.

"You said I could meet the successor," Charli reminded him.

"And you will. Just not now. He stays on the move and so do I."

"I'm surprised they haven't started tracking you," she returned.

Jack allowed himself a wry grin in response. "The NSF and the FedGov have a lot of weaknesses. One is their reliance on technology.

Back when we were in the Service, we used tech as a tool to do our jobs. They are dependent on it; they let the technology do the thinking for them. Every technology, however, has weaknesses. You saw that at Falls Church. You took out a multi-million-dollar security camera system with a paintball gun. Low tech can beat high-tech if it is done right.

"They have the technology companies doing their dirty work for them. So when we need to coordinate and communicate, we go low."

"How?"

"One way is to use newspapers. We take out ad space for legitimate companies and insert key phrases or graphics. They don't show up on the searches that the technocrats run trying to track us down. In fact, the majority of our stuff isn't online at all. Cells know what days to check the papers and what ads to look for based on a list of advertisers we maintain and change regularly.

"That doesn't mean that we don't use email and social media, but we hide what we do in advertisements—usually in graphic images. They are harder to search and even harder to interpret. It has taken us a few years to perfect the system, but it works and so far, their best and brightest don't seem to have a clue."

Charli nodded. "I hate to say it, but that's brilliant."

"Thanks," Jack replied. "We use live couriers too, sending messages by word of mouth. It is a little slow at times, but impervious to tech. I have one cell that uses printed t-shirts with Newmerica slogans as a means of sending messages based on the colors, fonts, and slogans used."

She said nothing for a moment, then crossed her arms. "What's the plan Jack? You are a plan-guy."

Desmond grinned, soaking in how she cut to the chase. "Yours wasn't the only op we were running against the NSF's investigative capability. We had a team infiltrate the NSF facilities down at Quantico... you know, the old FBI labs and training center. They killed and impersonated a team of HVAC employees who were slated to do maintenance. That got them access to most of the campus, including the leadership offices down there."

"To do what?"

"Ricin," Jack said. "Nasty poison that comes from castor beans. It takes some skills to process it, but as it turns out, there's a lot of people that want to give the NSF and the administration a big, old shit-burger. We refined the stuff to a very fine powder and put it in their ventilation system."

"They have bio-sensors," Charli replied.

"Which are part of the HVAC system. Our team disabled them. As we speak, almost half of the campus is either dead or dying. They can treat the lesser cases, but I assure you, no one is going back to work anytime soon. The buildings are contaminated. The best-case scenario is they can't open them for nine months. In the meantime, their laboratory equipment, all of their evidence in storage, everything there is adulterated with ricin."

"They can still enlist other labs, contract them to do the work," she countered.

"They can… but they don't have the experience or expertise. Between your attack and this one, we have hamstrung the NSF investigative capability."

Charli's brow tightened in thought as she looked at him. "Clearly that's not everything."

"We have an active campaign that's pitting Social Enforcement against the NSF. Why should we have all of the fun? We have staged some incidents that put them at each other's throats. Retaliation has started between the two groups and we intend to foster that into outright fighting."

"It's a good idea," she conceded. "But can it be sustained?"

"It can. Look, their entire structure of governing is on finding enemies and crushing them. All we are doing is channeling that so that they fight each other. It's their nature. Revolutions are like that. For a short time, the revolutionaries rise to power; then they start to turn against themselves. All we are doing is prodding that along. They will react with their only real implement of action, violence. The local Social Enforcement teams operate under their own free-will as it is. They are constantly searching for enemies. All the SOL did was give them one—the NSF."

Charli nodded once, slowly. "It might work. Then what?"

"We are coming up on the five-year anniversary of their beloved 'Liberation.' They are planning a big-ass celebration in the District and across the country. The Ruling Council is going to announce a new

Constitutional Convention and free elections. They are going to play it up that they are giving the power back to the people, but we all know that in reality, they are going to ratify what they have done... try to legitimatize it. It is my intent to disrupt that event. We will use that event to expose the Ruling Council for their corruption. We will let the whole world see that the United States still exists in the hearts and minds of its people. On live TV, we will show the world that there is a true successor to the Presidency. That will give them hope."

"You'll trigger a civil war," she said solemnly.

Jack nodded quickly. "We don't have a choice. They took us out in a *coup d'etat*. The people never got the chance to fight for what they believed in. They woke up one day and found out that the President was captured, that the White House and Capitol had fallen, and that a new government was running the country. They were stunned and afraid. With some progressives in Congress embracing the mob openly, it was hard to tell what had transpired.

"The Ruling Council has been using that fear ever since to control and manipulate the masses. They learned that during the pandemic. The media has played along... God knows how much blood they have on their hands. The Sons of Liberty will give people the truth—that they can rise up and fight the tyrants, just like our ancestors did."

Jack could see it in Charli's face, an appreciation for the plan. *She's actually struggling to hold back her enthusiasm.* Her understanding gave him renewed strength as well. She said in a light tone of voice, "It sure as hell beats being a beat-cop in the San Jose NSF."

He smiled. "Yes, it does."

"So," she paused for a moment, moving her hands to her hips. "What do you need me to do?"

"There's a few ops where I could use you," Jack said, tapping one of the notebook computers to pull up a file.

"If you don't mind," Charli said. "No more mass killings for a while."

"Keeping you up at night?"

She shook her head. "No Jack. I'm worried that I will start to like it." Her simple sentence opened up a wave of emotion from Charli that he had never experienced. *She means it.*

Jack had more assignments than people, and while many assignments required someone with Charli's skills, he also could tell that she needed something easy, something light. As he scrolled through the list of open items, he spied one that jumped out at him.

"This sounds right up your alley, Charli. I got a message two days ago from one of the old-timers in the SOL, back before they were purged. He claims that a son of another operative in Illinois has inherited some sort of package when his father died. The guy is hot from what I have learned—the local and national SE are watching him."

"What's the package?"

"Unknown," Jack replied. "The target's father was a shooter in the SOL back after the Fall. He had some pretty good connections, too. I don't know what is in that package, but if he went to the trouble of hiding it, it might be something we can use. If nothing else, his son is in trouble and probably doesn't know it yet."

"So, you want me to bring this guy in?"

Jack flinched slightly. "Go get him and get whatever this thing is that his father hid."

"He's hot, eh?" she said.

"I'll dump you what data I have. Yeah. The sad part is that the poor guy has no idea about it."

"You want me to risk my life on a complete unknown?" Charli's concern was real.

"Charli, the FedGov doesn't care what it does to people. Oh sure, it claims it cares, but you and I know different. Yes, it would be easy to ignore this, but we are not them. We are better than they are. More importantly, we don't abandon our own. That's what separates us. They would sell each other out in a heartbeat. We don't—we have a shred of honor.

"So go and get this guy. Find out what his father hid. Bring him and whatever it is back."

That seemed to be enough for Charli. "Alright. At least I'm not killing people. Does this sap have a name?"

"Forrest—Andrew Forrest. Take care of him. He's a legacy—but in the dark."

"Marvelous."

Wheaton, Illinois

Andy pulled his car around the corner from his father's house, only to see no less than four vehicles in the driveway and street. Milling around the front door were men and women wearing black clothing and tactical gear, heavily armed. Cautiously he parked his car and slowly got out.

One man took four massive steps towards him, weapon at the ready. "Who are you?"

"I'm Andy Forrest," he said, making sure the man could see his hands. "What's going on?"

The man patted him down. Once he hit his wallet, he pulled it out, looked at it, and tossed it back to Andy, who fumbled trying to catch it. He bent over and picked it up as the man toggled his shoulder-mike. "It's the son."

"What's going on here?" Andy asked in as non-threatening a manner as possible.

"SE business," the man replied, stepping out of his way. He gestured for Andy to proceed. *They are ransacking Dad's house. What in the hell is going on?*

When he climbed the steps to the porch, the answer greeted him at the door. *Karen.* Her beefy arms were crossed. She wore the bulky black tactical gear of the other thugs from the local Social Enforcement team. The coldness in her gaze told Andy that she was holding all of the cards. "Karen, what's happening?"

"We are searching Dad's house," she replied. "What does it look like?"

"You can't just come in here and do this, Karen. Dad left the house and the contents to me in the will." Behind her, through the open door he saw several black-glad gooks dumping the contents of drawers onto the floor, then tossing them aside.

"I can and I did."

"Don't you need a warrant or something?" He realized the folly of what he said as soon as the words came across his lips. It happened from time-to-time—Oldthink, that's what the FedGov called it—when you accidentally referenced something from before the rise of Newmerica.

Karen grinned. "We are the SE. We are not bound by stupid laws and paperwork. If you have a complaint, go find the NSF and tell them.

Good luck in getting them out here though. The best you can hope is for a mediator to come and that mediator is going to side with us. In the meantime, I suggest that you stay out of our way and let us finish our job."

It was no bluff and Andy knew it. The SE teams operated beyond the law… hell, they *were* the law in many cases. They acted arbitrarily and with little oversight. "What are you looking for? Can I at least ask that?"

"Why don't you tell me?" his sister replied in an icy tone.

"I don't know what you're talking about." There was no way to sound more sincere.

"I wish I could believe you, Andy. If it is here, we will find it, so you might as well tell me where it is. If not, we will take this place down to the studs." As if to make her point, Andy could hear the sound of pounding in one of the back rooms, like a hammer punching through wallboard. Each thud hurt him emotionally. This was not their childhood home. His father lost their house after his detainment. He had been forced into this place, having lost almost everything. Now, Karen and her people were destroying it, one hammer-blow at a time.

He stood there, unemployed, listening to them destroy the only thing of value his father had left him. *No, not the only thing!* For a moment he considered telling her about the mysterious package his father had mentioned. *I could hand her the map that Mr. Farmer gave me, and it would all be over. I could go about my life and Karen could go grab whatever is hidden in South Dakota.* The temptation was real, but he buried it quickly. Giving in to Karen would only prove that she was right. *Dad left it to me, not her, because he trusted me.* As he glanced at her face, he knew that he did not want her to have the satisfaction of winning.

"Since I have no idea what you're looking for, then that's what you'll have to do," Andy said. "Rip it apart. It's just a building and stuff. It only proves that you never cared for Dad at all, Karen. That's what this is really about. It's about you having daddy issues. You ran off to be a mob enforcer and sent our father to a concentration camp. You sold him to the SE so you could get ahead. Go on, destroy everything inside. I don't care. It won't get you a thing, certainly not a bit of closure for the guilt you must feel. Neither of us knows what it is you're actually looking for, or if it exists in the first place. You want to take your final bit of revenge on Dad for whatever you think it is he did to you? Go for it. I won't be a part of it!"

He saw the rage rise in her face as it turned cherry-red. He prepared for her words in response, but instead, Karen balled her fist and swung at him. Andy saw it coming and mostly moved out of the way; only the end of his chin made contact with her fingers. It stung, but he smiled when he started rubbing it. *That got to her!*

Almost immediately two other men came out of the house, and stood with Karen. "Is there a problem?" one of them asked. A punch from this man was going to hurt... badly. Andy held his words in check.

Karen's fury had not faded; it showed in her bulging eyes. "No. My brother was just leaving."

Andy stood up as Karen wheeled about, flinging open the door to the house and leaving him with the two thugs on the porch. Andy looked at them and saw that they were more than ready to end the fight that he had started. There was no need. Karen's punch had told him everything, confirming thoughts that he had been holding for years. *I was right to think she had sold out Dad. She did it for her own gain... classic Karen.*

"Perhaps you should leave," the larger of the two men said, brushing his hand back across his ebony shaved head. "Or better yet, we can make you leave."

"Good idea," Andy said. He had scored one emotional victory on his sister. There was no point in pushing a bad situation. Still rubbing his jaw, he turned and started back towards his car. He ignored the sound of breaking glass behind him from within the depths of the house. *Rip it apart. What you are looking for isn't there. I don't know what it is, but I sure as hell will make sure you never see it, Karen.*

CHAPTER 8

"Tolerance is prosperity."

Detroit, Michigan

Raul was moving a wheelbarrow filled with recovered cement blocks when he heard the commotion and saw the other young men and women running. He went over to the huddle of people and was stunned when he saw Paco there, his shirt drenched in his own blood. Raul saw the cut above his eye. It was so deep he saw the white of the bone underneath. He had a bruise on his cheek and one eye was starting to swell shut. Paco was staggering, breathing hard, held up by the others of the Troop.

The Troop Leader Avalon Winston showed up and quickly helped Paco to one of the ATVs and sped off, presumably for a hospital. The other members of the Troop stood around, almost in a daze. "What happened?" one of them, a lanky younger girl, asked.

"He said he was jumped by the Muslims," another boy, Ufray, replied. "Them boys were lucky it wasn't me. I'd have been all over them!" His bravado seemed over the top.

It made no sense. Paco was not a big person; he was no threat to anyone. He was quiet. Why attack him? It slowly came to Raul that those might be the very reasons. *They are bullies, these SEs. They go after the weak.*

Troop Leader Winston returned that night alone. He gathered them around the nightly fire in the middle of the old factory. "I want you all to know what happened. Paco is fine. They say he has a slight concussion, but he will be back with us soon. It looked a lot worse than it was and I think we all know that despite his size, Paco is tough." There were nods of agreement.

"He was attacked by the SE team from Dearborn that came here a few weeks ago. He says that they told him we're violating their religious law."

"Did you talk to the police?" Julian asked.

"The NSF was informed," the Troop Leader replied. There was something in his choice of words that made Raul wonder if they were going to actually *do* anything. *You can't just have gangs of people wandering around and beating people up.*

"It is important that we not provoke these people," Winston said. "If you are confronted by them, run, don't fight. If you are going outside of our designated work zone, I advise taking someone along with you." There were murmurs among the troop at the options being offered. *This is supposed to be a free country—but we must travel in groups or risk being attacked.* It all felt wrong to Raul. He remembered what his mother had told him about being raised in Mexico under the heels of the cartels. It was the same thing, senseless violence and innocent victims. *She came here to avoid all of that; now it seems the same problem exists here in Newmerica.*

If there was any person he could talk to outside of the troop, it was Father Ryan. He had a way of taking things that were confusing and making them simple. That evening he asked Ufray to accompany him to the church. The lanky young man went along but declined going in with him. "I'll hang here, man."

"You might be safer inside," Raul offered.

"In a church? Me? I don't think so." There was an actual hint of fear in the young man's words. *Something in his past perhaps?*

When Raul entered, he found Father Ryan in the process of putting out the altar candles. The worshippers were gone for the evening and when he saw Raul, he flashed a big smile. "Ah Raul! What brings you here at this hour?"

"I would like to pray for my friend Paco," he said. Then Raul opened up. He told the father everything that had happened. Father Ryan took it all in, then knelt with him at the altar, saying a prayer in Latin for Paco. It was not long, but it helped Raul.

"Why do they do this, Father?" Raul said as he finished crossing himself. "Paco was just walking. They beat him for no reason. Why did they do it? Why would God let that happen?"

Father Ryan nodded once, seeming to understand. "This is a question for the ages, Raul. People are always asking me why God allows good people to get cancer, or allows bad people to prosper. God gives us self-determination—the ability to choose our own path in life. Some individuals give into temptation and sin. Rather than honor the Lord, they seek power. They get their power from oppressing the weak. It makes them feel strong to cause others to feel bad.

"Your friend Paco did not deserve what happened to him, I have no doubt of that. If he is a friend of yours, I know him to be a good man. These people believe that Allah allows them to inflict pain on others in his name. To them, you and your troop represent a threat because you do not believe what they do. So, they use violence to achieve their ends. They intend for you to leave. Individually, it makes them feel powerful. Together, they tell themselves that their actions are justified by their religion."

"It is not right," Raul said bowing his head in thought. "The innocent should not suffer, not needlessly. We should be allowed to go our way, and they go theirs. It makes no sense for them to hurt Paco or anyone."

"I agree with you, Raul," Ryan replied. "But our country has changed. While the government demands diversity, it often squelches those that want it. Those in power have used the divisions between us, by race, and religion, to keep us apart—keep us fighting. It is wrong."

"What can be done about it, Father?" he asked, raising his head and locking gazes with the older man.

"There are times when men should turn the other cheek. There are times when that action only results in more harm. I do not advocate violence, but I know it is often required to preserve peace. They have been pushing Sharia law in a number of neighborhoods. Those that comply are taken under their protection. Those that don't are punished."

"It is wrong to force your religion on other people."

"Right and wrong are difficult concepts when we have lost our moral center. I do know this though, when good men do nothing, evil prevails."

"So, I should fight if I must?"

"Raul, it is not my role to tell you what to do or not do. It is my duty to the church to help you find the right answer in yourself. The Bible tells us to face evil with good. In the last few years, I find myself turning to Ephesians, 6:12 'For we do not wrestle against flesh and blood, but against the rulers, against the authorities, against the cosmic powers over this present darkness, against the spiritual forces of evil in the heavenly places.' The battle is not with these people that attacked your friend; it is with the system that allows such violence to happen unabated."

Raul rose to his feet as did Father Ryan. "Trust yourself, Raul. And trust the word of God." As he left the church, Ufray walked up to him. "You get the answers you were looking for man?"

Raul paused. "I'm not sure," he said with full honesty. His mind went to Paco and the blood he saw. *None of this should be happening. It is all wrong.*

The District

The Secretary of the National Support Force did not like having to make the trip to meet with the Chief of Social Enforcement. To her, it was a mark of disrespect. After all, she controlled a legitimate police force, backed by law. Her counterpart was a person that controlled mobs. *Having me come to him for a meeting is his way of sending me a signal regarding the pecking order between us.*

She was politely ushered into his office and he greeted her, not with a handshake, but a smile. "It is a distinct pleasure, Alex," he said with a familiarity that she resented. He gestured to the seat opposite his behind the desk and she slid into it. "I was hoping the two of us could talk privately about some of the reports I am seeing."

Her eyes fell on the small party pin he wore, shimmering bronze. She wore the same pin. Only certain people wore the pins, those that had backed the Liberation from the start. The quarter-sized pins were thick, copper in color, shimmering—forged from the melting down of the Liberty Bell. It had been a symbol of 1776, the great lie about the founding of the old United States. Newmerica did not hold onto such corrupt myths. The pin was another reminder from him to her, that they were equals in his mind.

"I am always willing to help a member of the party," she said coolly as he took his seat. His ebony skinned face was all smiles, but she was not lulled into a feeling that this was going to be pleasant. *He demanded we have a face-to-face. Demanded… of me!*

"There have been a few, shall I say, 'incidents,' between our two organizations in recent weeks. The most disturbing is finding several bodies of my murdered brothers and sisters in West Virginia."

"I am well aware of that incident," she said. "Let me assure you, the NSF had nothing to do with those murders."

"That," he said, leaning back in his leather padded chair, "is a little hard to believe. Two of the victims had NSF carved on their bodies."

She frowned slightly. "I know. We didn't do it."

"How do you know?"

"Because if I had authorized it, my people wouldn't have left such a blatant clue," she said, gathering herself mentally. "And while we are on it, perhaps you can explain what happened in Falls Church?"

"What are you talking about?"

"We had a body in the truck-bomb that was used on a facility of my people. That DNA was from a woman out of one of your New Jersey SE groups."

"My people had nothing to do with that attack!" he snapped.

"That may or may not be the case," she said. "The investigation is still ongoing."

"I resent your implication that my people had anything to do with that attack."

"Quit trying to change the subject, Alex. This isn't about your wild-ass accusations; it's about a bunch of my people being killed and marked up by the NSF."

You know what your problem is, Doug?" she said, using the shortened version of his name as he had done with her.

"No, Alex," he replied, "But I'm sure you are more than willing to point it out to me."

"You aren't professionals. Your people are sloppy. You went after the wrong people, tried to intimidate them, and they fought back. My people didn't kill your team. Whoever did it has played you as much as they did them. You were misled to think that the NSF had something to do with this. We didn't. Plain and simple."

"Need I remind you, Secretary," he said firmly in response. "What you call *sloppy*, I call effective. My people led the Liberation. Many of your people were the corrupt police that led us to mass protests. Our methods may be unorthodox to someone such as you, who was a politician when this went down, but they worked. You wouldn't have the position you do right now if it wasn't for *my* people."

His arrogance was as thick as his sweaty neck. She kept her composure and continued. "I am not disrespecting your role in the Liberation. But we have an investigation underway right now tracking down the domestic terrorists that were behind this. Your people were victims, but they are also in the way."

"So I've heard. What is this operative you have out there? Caylee Leatrom?"

The Secretary did not let her face betray a shred of emotion. "The special operations program is a myth, spread by conspiracy theorists."

"Is it?" he said with confidence. "In Lexington, this operative of yours, Leatrom, beat up one of my people in a field interrogation. Remember our little conversation about that?"

"Of course, I remember your allegations," she said. The fact that somehow he had obtained Caylee's name was deeply disturbing. Part of what made Spec Ops work was that they didn't exist; they were invisible. He had called her a week ago hot about Caylee. "As I told you then, I have no knowledge of what you're speaking about," she replied, letting the lie flow smoothly off of her lips, as if it were the truth.

"Don't feed me that bullshit," he replied. "I'm not some member of the media who lives on whatever little tid-bit flows from your mouth. I know you."

She leaned forward across the desk. "How I run the NSF is my business, Doug," she fired back. "We have been butting heads for years now. The country can't have two police forces out there operating, investigating the same things. It's counterproductive."

"How can you say you are running an investigation when you are clearly suspects in the crime?"

"Easy. We didn't commit the crime."

His eyes widened as he leaned over the desk slightly, close enough for her to smell his cologne. "Alex, you need to get it into that pretty head of yours. I am done putting up with your stonewalling and BS. I wanted you to hear it from me first. I am going to ask the Congress to open an investigation into the NSF and its handling of the murder of my people. It's time that we peel back what you're doing there. Perhaps a little oversight might help motivate you to find these killers, if it wasn't your people."

There it was, the threat. The Secretary soaked it in for a moment. Was there a real threat? *No. We didn't commit these crimes.* But an investigation would be messy. She had kept the operative program secret thus far, but it was bound to come out once Congress started hauling people up to the Hill for testimony.

Worse yet, it would tell the entire nation that the Sons of Liberty were out there—still a threat. It would confirm that they had not been utterly destroyed, as was promised, years ago. This move will embolden our enemies. There were other groups out there, resistance to the new normal. The gun advocates, 2A, were still lurking in the shadows, striking from time to time when her people showed up to confiscate illegal weapons. United We Stand; a determined militia group with followers in five states had attacked NSF precincts in the past. ALM—All Lives Matter had counter-rioted just a year ago. There were others, who were out there, waiting for a sign of weakness… the kind of signal that a congressional investigation would initiate.

This was a power-play. She had been expecting it for some time and was more than prepared. Now it was all laid bare. *He will use these investigations to push for the same thing I want, the combining of our two organizations. Only he wants to be the one on top.* "Doug, you will have to do what you have to do," she said rising to her feet. "But know this. If you come after me, I will be forced to do the same with you. Being the Secretary of the NSF gives me access to a lot of data and intel. Most of the members of Congress have things they would like to keep hidden, as do you. If you put me on the stand to roast me for political gain, I will come out swinging."

Her words struck home. "What do you mean?"

"Oh, I think you know," she replied. "Your little love-nest up in Maryland, for example. I am sure your wife and the rest of the nation would be thrilled to know where you are spending two nights a week.

Then again, what do I know… maybe you have an open relationship. Maybe she encourages you to have an affair."

"You wouldn't dare," he growled, rising to his feet.

"Bring it on, Doug," she said. "You know me. I worked my ass off for this position. I have kept the administration and party in power. Come at me if you want. If you think I'm afraid of Congress, you've misjudged me. I served in Congress. They have almost zero real power. When you do decide to come after me, be prepared for the storm that follows… and I *will* bring the lighting."

"You have cops," he snapped back. "I have an army."

"I have an organization," she said, glaring at him. "You have a mob."

"My 'mob' brought down the government. ANTIFA and the other groups working together to topple the government. We took down the old Congress. My people, not yours, took the White House."

"And then what happened?" she replied. "You couldn't maintain order. No matter what, the people want order, they want structure. You promised all sorts of things you couldn't deliver. When you started facing real opposition, you were begging for the NSF to bail your ass out—and we did. Now you just want to plant a knife in my back… after all I've done for you."

"You and I both know that the administration isn't served by having two organizations at cross-purposes, Alex. Before you do anything rash or stupid, think about what you would be unleashing."

She pivoted in place and left before he could respond, slamming the door behind her. *He will do it regardless. He's in this deep already. He has already met with members of Congress and the Senate and has lined them up, otherwise he wouldn't be so bold in telling me what he planned. The personal threat won't scare him either. If he cared about his wife, he wouldn't have cheated on her to begin with.*

For her, there was only one viable strategy for dealing with such a person. Strike first, and strike hard. *His mistake was telling me what he had in mind.* She had already planned to make a move against the SE's leadership. Now Douglas Farraday was forcing her hand. That was why she had chosen Operative Leatrom in the first place. She knew Caylee would step on toes, that was her style. *Everything is falling into place, just sooner than I had thought.*

Brookings, South Dakota

Caylee Leatrom stood firmly on the back of Richard Farmer, flexing his arm, wrist, and fingers backward. "Tell me who you met with," she commanded, pushing his face hard into the pea gravel alongside the country road where she had overtaken him. Farmer's face ground into the roadside and turned red with pain and anger.

Her attempts to track the Sons of Liberty team that had killed the Black Hats had run into two dead ends. One thing: what little evidence had been recovered from the crime scene had not been tested. When she pressed the matter, she had been told that there had been a bioweapon attack at Quantico, taking out their facilities. Combined with the loss in Falls Church, the normally respondent National Support Force was now in a quagmire.

The second thing slowing her down was the lack of leads. When the SOL had struck, they had done so with brutal efficiency. She had some camera footage from security cams, but most were blurry images, mostly obscured, impossible to enhance even if the labs were available.

Faced with dead ends, she pivoted—beginning to look at former members of the SOL and their activities. Those that had come through the Social Quarantine Camps had been monitored carefully over the years. Most rarely left home thanks to the threats and intimidation of the Social Enforcers.

That had been the case with Richard Farmer, too. Then, suddenly, he took a trip… in violation of his travel prohibition that had been part of his sentence. She had been able to reconstruct parts of his journey with surveillance footage. One, from a parking lot camera at a CVS in Wheaton, Illinois, showed him having a conversation with a man on a bus bench. The angle of the camera didn't give her a view of his face.

"I told you, I don't know who he is. I've never seen him. We just had a casual conversation. I was in town for a funeral."

She twisted his arm hard and felt him cry out under her. "After I break this wrist, then your arm, I start on the other side. Then your legs. After that, I start to work on parts of you that won't grow back when I'm done with them. So, let's get to the point. You violated the terms of your release to travel across the country for a funeral, which you missed. You knew you were going to miss it, but you went anyway—which is highly suspicious. The only person you met with was, according to you, a complete stranger. Do you really think I will fall for that?"

He fought back, they all do, though at his age, in his 50s, she had been surprised at his vigor. They twist and squirm, but the angle is working against them. She had seen it a dozen times before. A car approached from the distance and slowed when she was seen holding Farmer down. The window slid down and a man called out to her. "Do you need help?"

She held up her ID and badge, "NSF business," she replied nudging with her head to indicate that he should continue on. The sight of the badge was all it took and the driver hit the gas and left. That was one of the few things about affiliation in the NSF that worked to her advantage; the fear they evoked. She once more turned her attention to the man under her heel.

"I've told you the truth," Farmer replied through heavy breaths of pain. "An old colleague died. I went to pay my respects."

"By colleague, you mean member of your terrorist organization," she corrected.

Farmer seemed to muster a morsel of resolve. "We were not terrorists. You were the ones that overthrew the government and killed innocent people to take power. We just had the balls to fight back when everyone else cowered." Those words made her twist his wrist sharply again. She had heard it all before from dozens of different criminals.

"I need you to focus Mister Farmer. The image I showed you, who is he? Give me a name, tell me where he is, and you can limp out of here alive." It was a lie, but offering her victim some sliver of hope worked in such interrogations.

Farmer did something she hadn't expected. He laughed.

"Did I say something funny?"

"You're torturing an old man," he said. "You don't have shit. If you're wasting time on me, that means whatever it is you're trying to find out, you don't have a fucking thing."

She cranked his wrist again, right up to the breaking point, but not past that. "I have plenty. The SOL is planning something. I know they have the President. You're going to give me the next link in this chain."

He grinned, despite what she was doing to him. "You arrested the President and he ended up dead in *your* custody. You are chasing a ghost."

"Am I? I am trying to prevent the death of innocent people. Tell me what I want to know. Who was it you met with in Illinois?"

"Innocent... pah," he spat through the ripples of pain. "Look at the blood you and the Ruling Council have on your hands. You're just a tool. You do their dirty work so they have some deniability. I know you; I know the type."

There was a sting in his words, a mental barb that struck her. I do have blood on my hands, but for the right reason. Caylee ignored that, suppressed it deep down in the part of her brain where she could deal with it later. Now... now there was a task to be done, a mission to complete, a target to find and take out. Our footage showed you talking to this man at the bus stop for five minutes," she said. "You don't look stupid enough to be a man that would talk to strangers. Especially when you are in a strange city, violating your parole. That's a sure-fire way to get someone to report you to the Social Enforcers, and I *know* you don't want that. Just tell me who he is and where I can find him."

"I don't know what you're talking about," he said as she twisted his wrist a little harder, to give him focus. "And if I did, I wouldn't tell you. They locked me up in one of those concentration camps of yours for two years; broke both of my hips. I watched your people torture friends of mine. I know what you have planned. If you think a broken arm or hand is going to make me squeal, you are a fool." The defiance in his voice was crisp and clear.

"The problem I have is that I believe you," Caylee said. She twisted hard and heard a snap, feeling the break in her palm Richard Farmer wailed in agony as she dropped his limp arm, letting him try and move it.

"It looks like you will need someone else to tie your shoes for a while," she said, reaching down for his other hand. He fought her, trying to use it to push up, but she grabbed it like the professional that she was and whipped it behind his back where she stood.

The burly man fumbled with his limp and shattered wrist, moaning in pain as he moved it to his side, then up by his face, as if he were looking at it. She knew it was causing him excruciating pain, but they did that sometimes, moved the broken limbs despite the warnings their bodies gave them. Then, suddenly, he stopped moving—stopped resisting. Caylee knew something was wrong. Flexing her arms and upper body, she turned him over. Farmer had a grin on his face, and looked to be frothing at the mouth.

Shit! She reached for his jaw to pry it open and Famer chuckled. "Ohhh," he groaned, but then continued, ". . . say can you see…" then went limp, dropping his head onto the side of the road with a dull thud. There was no point in checking his pulse, she knew the feeling of death in her hands.

I'm getting sloppy. I should have flipped his pockets, not just patted them down. Richard Famer had cheated her by popping a suicide pill. It was a maneuver she had not counted on, not this time. She wanted to kick her own ass for a moment. This was not some homespun terrorist organization she was after. Most of those types would have folded quickly under her 'intense interrogation' techniques. *I should have known better.* The Sons of Liberty had always shown sophistication in their work, but this took things to a new level. Her only saving grace? She had been right to look at the older members.

Caylee pulled out her phone and replanted her foot on the torso of the dead man. "This is 875. I need a cleanup crew at these coordinates." She hit the small button on her phone which transmitted her location. Looking down at the body of Richard Famer, his grin annoyed her. *You took your secrets with you old man, but not for long.*

As she waited for the large, black panel NSF van to arrive and pick up the body and all trace evidence, she contemplated her investigation. The SOL was not behaving as she had expected. There was some intelligence behind what they were doing. No media had covered the bioattack at Quantico, but she had gotten word of it all the same. The entire staff was hospitalized, and many had already died. Cases that were being investigated were on hold for months now, their evidence being contaminated with ricin. Combined with the bombing of the labs and offices in Falls Church, the NSF found itself suddenly hamstrung.

There had been destruction of a data center in Landover, Maryland that they used for their NSFCloud hosting. The fire was of a 'suspicious nature,' which Caylee interpreted as arson. For a week or so their files had been off-line, then reloaded to a facility in Utah. While backups were loaded and the secured cloud reestablished, there were gaps, things that had not gotten backed up. Some of it she attributed to the use of FedGov contractors being sloppy, but there was a concern that the loss of data had been deliberate. *They are fighting a war against us, and so far, they are winning.*

The NSF van pulled up next to her, flashlights hitting Richard Farmer's body and her. Caylee flashed her badge and a small team of four moved over to the body and began to bag it. One of them came over to her after looking at the foam in the corner of Farmer's mouth. "What happened?"

"Poison. Tell our folks I want a full analysis made of it."

The technician chuckled. "Good luck with that. We haven't gotten anything through for weeks."

Caylee stepped off into the darkness at the side of the road where her car was parked, preferring the shadows rather than being part of the cleanup. One tech dug out Farmer's keys and started his car. When they were done, there wouldn't be a sign that anything had happened alongside the road. One car that came by was saved, but the passenger was too afraid to even look. *That's right, nothing to see here.*

As she stood next to her car, her phone chirped. It was odd because very few people had her number. This one came in simply as 'The Secretary' and Caylee rolled her eyes before she answered.

"Agent Leatrom," the cool professional voice flitted into her ear. "I take it you did not have much luck."

She's monitoring me. That was an annoyance that she had gotten used to in the NSF but rarely tolerated. This was one of those instances where she had to accept it. "I ran into a complication, Madam Secretary."

"We all have our crosses to bear," she said back. "Apparently you are one of mine."

"Secretary?"

"I paid a visit to the Chief of Social Enforcement today. I would be underplaying it to tell you that there's a lot of tension right now between NSF and the SEs. They think we are putting the squeeze on them. The Chief is planning a few tricks of his own."

"This is what the SOL wants," Caylee said. "That was why they carved our initials on the bodies in West Virginia."

"Yes, as we suspected," the Secretary said. "Of course, it doesn't help me at all that he had a report from Kentucky about your little interrogation and investigation there." Her voice dropped an octave as she spoke, hinting at the gravity.

"You don't keep me on the payroll because you like how I work, Madam Secretary," Caylee said. "You keep me here because I get results."

"Agreed. Matters are more complicated than you realize. We found some DNA in the truck bomb from Falls Church and it matched a Social Enforcer related to one of the victims found in West Virginia. Her physical profile matches that of the alleged driver. It looks like it was a suicide bombing." There was a hesitancy, a pause in the Secretary's voice.

"But…" Caylee probed.

"Wheel chocks. We had a survivor say he saw the driver put wheel chocks in front of the tires to prevent the vehicle from moving when the bomb went off."

"Did this person you found have expertise in explosives?"

"No."

"Madam Secretary, whoever set off that bomb knew what they were doing. They understood the complexities of not just mixing high explosives, but how to direct the force of the blast where it would compromise the entire building and bring it down. This isn't the work of some redneck from Kentucky out for revenge… and anyone just wanting revenge wouldn't kill themselves."

"We are thinking along the same lines," the Secretary replied. "Which points to an enemy that is sophisticated and that sophistication is dangerous. In the meantime, I have people that are looking at the same evidence and saying it is a power play by the Chief of Social Enforcement. Needless to say, tensions are high between the two organizations right now. I need you to be careful about the toes you stomp on. There are larger implications in your actions, more than usual. The Chief of SE knew your name, which was no small task on its own. That means they will be looking for you."

Fuck me blind! This hasn't happened in a long time. Part of my job is to be unknown. They'll be looking for me, which complicates things. "Understood. I appreciate the heads up."

"You are right about one thing, Agent Leatrom, you *do* get results, even if they are unintended. Did you garner anything from your target?"

"Confirmation," she said. "I know now I'm on the right path. The old guy popped a pill rather than sing on his friends."

"That is unfortunate," was all the Secretary replied.

"Yes, but the fact that he had the pill and took it tells me my hunch was right, he *was* meeting with someone, someone he was willing to die rather than reveal."

"That doesn't give you much to work with."

"It gives me a starting point Madam Secretary."

"Which is?"

"Wheaton, Illinois." Caylee had never been there, but the sound of the place convinced her it was some dull Midwestern city, the kind of place where nothing exciting ever happens.

CHAPTER 9

"People are data."

Wheaton, Illinois

Charli Kazinski saw the SE surveillance team before they could get eyes on her. They were parked out front in a beat-up Buick mini-SUV, eating burgers as they sat there. She knew they were not with the NSF because their teams were much more discreet. Training and competence did that. An NSF Team would be spread out all over the area, everything from lawn mowing crews to ladies walking their poodles. The Social Enforcers were wannabes. Everything they learned about surveillance and special operations they got from *Grand Theft Auto*, *Assassins Creed*, *Call of Duty* and reruns of a half-dozen different cop shows, who all got it wrong. The punk-ass kids grew up, but their skills had not gotten better. Her time posing as an NSF officer had taught her a lot about 'the competition,' in the SE.

Charli knew how to conduct surveillance; it came as part of the job when she was in the Secret Service. You had to do a lot when the President visited some city or plant to do a KTB (Kiss the Baby) event. She found an apartment across from her target's that was vacant and discreetly popped the lock. Almost immediately she knew why the place hadn't rented; the stink of old cat urine, forever embedded in the carpet, made her gag for a moment. She pushed down that feeling in her gut... she had a job to do.

From her perch, she could see the SEs in their grade three, black tactical gear, ransacking Andrew Forrest's place. They did so with the subtlety of a charging water buffalo. Rather than go through his desk drawers, they unceremoniously dumped them on the floor, using their feet to kick the contents about. His closet contents were thrown about on the faux wood floor while they used hammers to knock holes in the walls.

She slid behind the horizontal blinds sending a ripple of dank dust into the air. From her vantage point, her well-trained eyes swept the scene, drinking in every detail. Whatever it was that this Andrew Forrest had, the Social Enforcers hadn't found it yet. It had to be important for them to go to this much effort. That begged the question as to what it was. Jack didn't know. He only hinted that it had to be a big deal. She was a little worried. *If they were going through this much effort, with no results, it was a matter of time before they'd grab this Forrest and try some old-fashioned brutality to get their answers.* The SEs were clumsy, unsophisticated, but brutal. *If they beat the shit out of him, it will be hard as hell for me to approach him.* Charli hated playing cleanup to someone else's clusterfuck.

Jack hadn't given her much beyond a name and a code phrase to let the guy know she was not a threat. Charli did her own covert digging and the two words she used to describe Andrew Forrest were *wholly unremarkable.* He had been a change manager in one of the Big Three accounting firms, pimping their consulting services. As part of the Great Reformation, a lot of jobs were being sent overseas, deemed 'unworthy' of Newmerica, and Forrest had been one of the people that architected such moves. It was a rotten job, and she hoped that he was better off without it. They had fired him when he had overextended his leave to be with this father. Given the nature of his job, she had to wonder if he felt better no longer doing it.

Andrew's father—now *he* was someone. A tenured history professor at what was now Sojourner Truth University. He had been one of the insiders in the last rendition of the Sons of Liberty. The man had connections, a lot of them, not just in academia but in the old government. He had written some brilliant articles on the violent overthrow of the United States, copies of which were now almost impossible to find. He had paid the price for voicing himself. The Social Enforcers had ruined his life, forcing the university to fire him. That wasn't enough. He had been shipped off for several years to a Social Quarantine Camp. Those records were impossible to get, but Charli had heard stories and rumors about what happened there. Andrew's dad had fought the good fight, only to be labeled as a threat to Newmerica and imprisoned without a trial. Now Arthur Forrest was dead and the SEs were trashing his son's place.

She checked again with her digital optics enhancer, getting a good look both at the team on the ground and in the apartment. They were not going to find it there, not the way they were going about it. Whatever it was this Forrest-guy had, he wouldn't have been stupid enough to keep it in his apartment. As she watched them pull a dresser away from the wall to smash a hole there, she shook her head. *This guy is definitely not going to get his security deposit back.*

Charli had used a colleague's userID and password to log on to the NSFCloud and pull up everything she could find on her target. Most of it was boring. He had two parking tickets in the last few years, but nothing else. Andrew had been under surveillance at the same time his father had been investigated for being in the SOL, but nothing had come of it. If Andrew had been in the SOL, there certainly was no evidence of it. The man was almost invisible digitally. Sure, he had bank accounts and credit cards, but there was nothing that attracted attention. Forrest was a nobody; a nobody that the SE had a hard-on for. Too bad the SE didn't share their intelligence data.

Her digging into Andrew Forrest had immediately surfaced his only other sibling, Karen Forrester and she lit up her notebook like a Christmas tree. She had changed her last name after her father's transfer to a social quarantine facility. She was a Social Enforcer, the same people that had crushed her father's ability to make a living. *Talk about daddy issues. What kind of a bitch turns on their own father?* The answer was Karen Forrester. She embodied what the SE loved, someone with a moral ambiguity who put their cause above all else.

Karen Forrester was, at best, a mid-level flunky in the jumbled mess that made up the SE organization structure. That had always been their problem. ANTIFA and other radical groups had been organized so much at the cell level that when they became a *defacto* social policing force, they couldn't agree on structure. Charli had never met Karen Forrester and despite that she already despised her. *How much of your soul do you have to sell to disown your family?*

Her eyes swept the area around the exterior of Andrew's apartment. With the tensions between the SEs and the NSF, if the SE was interested in this guy, the NSF might be as well. That was the problem with competing organizations having overlapping responsibilities. She had experienced it a lot as a member of the Secret Service before the Fall. DC had over a dozen police agencies within its borders during that period. All had been rolled into the NSF now, which should have made things more streamlined—but she knew better. It made for a confusing array of bureaucracy. Add in the Social Enforcers, and there was a feeling of competition between the organizations. Charli liked that. *Let them beat the shit out of each other.*

Down the street she saw Andrew Forrest appear. He was unremarkable. Black hair, at least two weeks overdue for a haircut. He was a fit man; that showed as he walked; there was no wobble of body fat. He wore round eyeglasses that made him look like a professor more than a consultant. His pace was slow, down the middle of the sidewalk.

Deep down she had hoped he would show up after the SEs were done trashing his apartment. It would make contacting him easier. As he came into view, she saw the open doors to the car where the surveillance team was operating. *Shit… they're going to confront him right on the street!* Charli knew that if they took him into custody, it would be hard as hell to break him out. Breaking away from the window she cleared the room in three strides and started for the stairs.

Wheaton, Illinois

Andy hated days like this, where there was warm, humid air but gray-purple clouds blocked any hint of the sun. Spring storms came from this, a byproduct of living in proximity to Lake Michigan. In winter you got lake-effect snow; in the spring you got the rains. On days like this, you could taste the moisture in the air, it was so thick. He hoped that he would reach his apartment before the clouds rolled in.

He had spent three days attempting to clean up his father's place, sleeping there on the largest piece of carpeting that hadn't been cut to shreds. Despite the carnage that Karen's goons had wrought, it still had the same smell as when his dad was there, that strange mix of old man and mustiness. Sleeping over there reminded him of his father and of better times.

He had met with the realtor and had been told that she could not list the house as-is. Andy suspected that there was more going on than what she was telling him. Yes, they had gutted several rooms with sledgehammers, but it was repairable. The clue had come when the realtor, a perky young woman named Lori, had told him that *no one* would list his father's house. That meant that the property had been tagged in some way. No doubt the SEs were doing it to put more pressure on him.

Andy had called his employer to talk about coming back, but they too had blocked him. "We don't want trouble with the SEs," had been the line human resources had given him. *I haven't done anything wrong, but I'm being treated like a pariah.* That told him that whatever was in the mysterious package was important. *Otherwise, why would they put the financial pinch on me like this?*

He had been tempted to call Dick Farmer, if nothing else, to make sure he had gotten home alright. In some respects, Farmer was the last living connection to his father. Andy had been waiting for some sort of contact, per his conversation with Dick, but none had come. Anxiety did that to him, it made him edgy, more prone to risks. Andy caught himself when that happened and kept his emotions in check.

Rounding the corner of his block he kept his focus not on what was ahead of him, but on the next section of sidewalk. As he got within 200 feet or so of his building's front door, he saw an older model Buick SUV. At first it was just a car parked by the side of the street, but he saw the doors open on both the driver's and passenger's sides and a man and a woman in black tactical gear got out. Andy stopped instantly as they both faced him, closing the distance.

"You're Andy Forrest," the large, male Social Enforcer said; his hand drifted down to the pistol that hugged his ample waist.

Andy took a cautious half-step back. "Yeah. Who are you?"

The female spoke up next, her voice rugged and worn, like a longtime chain-smoker. "I think you know who we are," she said arrogantly. "We've been sent to protect you. Come on over here. We can get you some place that is safe."

Andy understood his situation perfectly. A flash memory came to him of his father describing the night they had taken him away... the *mock-court*, a 'People's Tribunal,' that was the hallmark of the SE, along with the physical assaults he had endured. "There must be some sort of mistake," was all he could manage, taking another step back away from them.

"No mistake," the chunky man said. "Please, Andy, there are people out here that want to do you harm. We can protect you."

He paused for a moment, remembering his conversation with Dick Farmer. "Is that all you want to say to me?"

The man was confused. "We need to bring you in so you are safe."

Andy's eyes darted to his right and left and saw no one else coming. His flight instinct kicked in. He bolted with every bit of speed he could muster. As a runner, who was in excellent shape, his body felt as if it were suddenly filled with an energy drink. The moist air roared past his ears as he heard a cigarette girl calling, "Stop!"

Fearing the shock of a taser, he dodged a half-step to the left, then back to the right. He heard a 'zziitt' noise where he had been on the last dodge, as the taser wires fired into empty space. Andy's strides were long, eloquent, based on years of running. He continued to erratically dodge as he ran, swinging around the corner of the block, past a gas station as the two SEs called out for people to, "Stop him!"

He bounded into the street, just barely avoiding a car that did not see him coming. The blare of the horn was lost behind him as he ran. When he came around a panel van, he stopped for a moment to get his bearings and plan his next move. Then, over the roar of blood in his ears, he heard the footsteps of the running SEs hot on his tail.

Andy knew his neighborhood and chose a long alleyway. Darting around the corner and into the alley, he poured on the speed. He wasn't worried about the larger male; the toxic combination of donuts and couch time in mom's basement ruled him out as a threat. It was the female that had him concerned. As he splashed through a puddle in the shadows of the alley, he heard her call out, "Stop or I *will* shoot!"

In his youth he had played paintball several times, before it had been banned as an unacceptable pastime by the FedGov. *Fire away*, he thought, grinning broadly. It was hard enough to hit someone that was running if you were standing still, let alone if you also were running.

Still, when he heard the crack of the gun behind him, he instinctively ducked his head, as if he could dodge the bullet. There was a crunch and a light, metallic pinging noise off to his far right, no doubt a ricochet, a sound he chose to ignore. His ears filled with the pounding of his heart. Another shot followed; this one seemed to hit nothing but air.

Bursting out of the alley, he ran to the right. Suddenly, he heard the roar of a car engine and the squeal of tires as a green sedan came to a stop, almost right in front of him with a jerking lurch. *Shit, there's more of them!*

The pair scrambled to get out of their car, to get on their feet and to come after him. One was black, big, muscular. The driver was white, skinny, with a four-day beard. "Hey—stop!" the driver called out, fumbling for his pistol. Andy darted to the left and continued to sprint.

There was another shot, far behind him, echoing off the nearby buildings. Andy knew enough to break up their line of fire, to dart between two cars and turn hard right, down another street. His legs were on fire as they pumped, but he felt confident. None of his pursuers looked athletic enough to give chase. To confirm that, he heard the car doors slam and the squeal of the tires as the engine roared.

Spying the parking lot, he tore through it, hoping that if they were pursuing in a vehicle, it would break them off. Maneuvering between cars slowed him, but he was hopeful and more daring. Bursting out the other side of the parking lot, he came onto the sidewalk and ran. Behind him he heard the squeal of tires and the roar of an older car engine.

Andy turned his head for a millisecond to look behind him, seeing the car. Then his world went wild. His left foot hit a crack in the sidewalk and—for a moment—he was airborne, flailing his arms out in front of him, turning his head back around.

The concrete hit him hard; his hands felt hot from the skidding and shredding of his skin. His knees throbbed as they hit the ground. Andy scrambled madly, to get up, but fumbled, halfway to standing. As he rose, he saw the woman that had been chasing him, wheezing heavily, holding a gun on him. "Hold it right there, Forrest," she said between heavy breaths. "Running only made things worse for you." Behind him he heard the doors fly open and the sound of the other two pursuers lunging out of the vehicle.

His hands rose slowly as he got to his feet, his breath ragged from the sprint. Sweat stung at the corners of his eyes as he stood up and faced the woman. He could make out every detail on her olive-skinned face. She was young, too young to have taken part in the so-called Liberation. The pistol was small and her hands were shaking slightly, no doubt from the adrenaline.

Another car pulled up and the chunky man sprang out. Andy wanted to laugh as he lumbered into action. "Dewey—I've got this," the woman with a gun said. He considered bolting again, but the gun on him and possibly four SE operatives in close proximity made common sense override his urge. *They've got me... I'm fucked.* He glanced over at his right hand and saw where he had scraped it on the pavement. A single drop of blood fell from his right palm as he calmed his breathing and regained his composure.

Then he saw her... a figure running toward his small gathering. Dressed in running gear, she was almost a blur, blonde hair whipping as she sprinted. The SE folks didn't see her as she charged in. Andy didn't move, transfixed by the charging woman.

She plowed into the chunky man from behind, grabbing the back of his head and slamming it into the car door window, which he shattered. He went down really hard and fast, with no grace, like a dropped sack of potatoes. The woman darted around as the SE agents suddenly realized there was a new threat.

The woman went over the hood of the car and did a flying kick-leap onto the large, black SE operative, hitting him on the backside of his left knee, buckling the leg. Her elbow slammed down on his thick neck and he began to gurgle as he fell, grasping at his throat for air.

Andy took a step away from the woman with the gun on him. She was not sure what to do, keep with her target, or deal with the new threat. She caught his movement and angled the gun toward him as a warning.

The wiry hipster SE fired a shot from his side of the car, opposite from where the stranger had just taken down his partner. He missed, but the shot allowed Andy to take another half-step away. The mysterious new woman charged at the man, grabbing his right arm with the gun, hitting him in his left eye with her elbow. He reeled and dropped as she snapped his wrist, loud enough for Andy to hear the cracking of the bone; then she took his pistol. She fired at him, turned and fired a shot into the large black operative that had started to pull himself up, gasping for air. Blood sprayed from that shot, splattering into the street as the man dropped.

The SE with the gun on Andy was between them, unsure what to do. The other female rushed her, putting the gun to her temple. To her credit, the SE kept her gun on Andy. "Drop it," the mystery woman said. "You drop yours or I kill him." Andy saw the open barrel of the pistol aimed at him and suddenly realized that the odds in this game he found himself in had suddenly increased.

Wheaton, Illinois

None of this had gone down the way Charli had planned. She had hoped to intersect Andrew Forrest before he got home. The SE presence had not been anticipated, not in the strength she had seen. What they lacked in training and experience, they made up for in numbers. When Andy ran, he was a lot faster than she had anticipated. After losing sight of him, she did the next best thing—follow his pursuers.

Charli held the pistol to the woman's temple. "I warn you," the SE said. "I will kill him." Charli's senses were alive, and in her mind, she could see the entire scene. It was as if she could calculate the movements and actions that were around her. Forrest looked at the gun focused on him, but slowly made eye contact with her. *Good. Watch me.* She jerked her head to the side and down. Andrew Forrest made a very slow nod, hardly discernable.

"Okay," Charli said, slowly pulling the gun an inch off of the temple of the woman that she stood behind.

"Drop it!" the woman snapped.

Charli kept her eyes on Andy as she lowered the gun, but still held it. "Alright, I'm putting it down." The moment she had it pointing down, she mouthed the word, 'now' and fired.

Andy jumped in the direction she had nodded. Her first shot went in just above the right knee of the SE operative, through her shin, and into her foot.

The operative fired in response, but Andy was already moving. The woman tried to turn, but her leg gave way under her and she twisted and collapsed at the same time. Charli angled her gun for a shot and put it in the heart of the woman. Her gun went spinning across the concrete sidewalk right in front of Forrest.

The operative collapsed dead at her feet and Charli stepped over her victim's legs and closer to the man she was trying to save. Looking up she saw Andrew Forrest holding the pistol of the SE operative up, nervously pointing it in her direction.

"We need to get out of here," she said.

Forrest rose to his full height, keeping the gun trained on her. "I'm not going anywhere with you," he said. "This could all be a setup."

She glanced down at the dead operative as a pool of blood began to flow from under her body. "Seriously?"

"I don't know you," he said taking a step back away from her.

Charli put her pistol into her pocket and held her hands up. "I was sent to protect you."

"I don't know who you are," he said firmly, taking another step.

Oh shit, he's going to bolt, Charli thought.

"Nightingale," she said coolly. She had been given the code phrase by Jack Desmond.

For a moment, Andrew Forrest said nothing. He stared at her blankly. Then he lowered his pistol. "Okay," he said taking a long gulp of air. "Where are we going?"

CHAPTER 10

"Achievement is no one failing."

Salina, Kansas

J ack Desmond sat in the cab of his pickup truck and studied the people as they walked along South Santa Fe Avenue at the Walnut Street intersection. He had chosen this location for several reasons. There was a lack of security cameras covering the streets. His rented pickup was perfectly parked in a blind spot that ran for nearly three blocks. Jack had organized a series of late-night entries into the buildings and businesses surrounding the area and had disabled or destroyed their exterior and interior cameras that faced the street. One was left on, and thanks to a tab of Vaseline on the lens, it would give a pretty blurry image when the NSF finally confiscated the footage.

Desmond had also taken the precaution of blinding or disabling most of the cameras on his escape route. An airsoft rifle was an effective and remarkably quiet weapon in such efforts. A dollop of mud on the license plates helped too. The NSF would eventually piece together enough footage to ID the truck, and would find that it was rented, paid for with a credit card from a fictitious person. He almost grinned at the man-hours and frustration that he was generating.

Next to him sat Parker Pyle, the son of an SOL leader who had volunteered for the op. He was the right height, and with a little padding, the right build. "This makeup and stuff is hot as hell," he muttered.

"You look just like him," Jack said proudly. "Well, like him with five years age piled on."

"Thanks," Parker replied. "You sure this is going to work?"

"I'm right here, ready to rock. You go out, go into the deli, get a soda and leave. Let a few people see you. Remember, no conversation. You look like him, but they will start taking pictures and recording videos, and we don't want them doing a voiceprint analysis. In and out. Make sure they see you." The deli didn't have meat—they only got it on Tuesdays and it was gone shortly after it came in—part of the "Fair Food" rationing act... another sin that the Ruling Council would have to answer for someday.

"Got it."

"Keep those contact fingertips in place. Touch a few things, leave a fake print or two. We want the NSF to run the prints and get partials," Jack said.

"I have it," Parker replied. "Keep the motor running."

Jack watched as Pyle slid out of his seat and closed the door behind him. He walked with an amble, just as they had practiced, going down the sidewalk a quarter of a block, then turning into the deli. A few minutes later he came out, a bottle of Pepsi in his right hand, heading back to the truck. Behind him he saw a woman coming out of the deli, waving at Parker.

He got in and Jack leisurely pulled out onto Santa Fe and headed north. "Can I take this shit off?"

"No," Jack replied. "Not yet. We might get picked up by a camera in the city, and we want them to get some degree of confirmation. His own prosthetic nose and chin itched as well, so he knew how Parker felt.

Once outside of town the pair removed all of the cosmetic rubber. Jack took it to a spot alongside the road and threw it in Mulberry Creek below. He shook Parker's hand. "Good work."

"The one lady got a picture of me. She said she voted for me."

"Good," he grinned. "She will talk, share stuff on social media—and the NSF will blanket this place.

"Why here?" Parker said getting back in the truck.

"Why not?" Jack said with a grin. "He would not be hiding out in Florida or New York. They have spotted him once already... now they will have this. I want them wasting time, chasing ghosts of dead presidents, worrying that he might still be out there and expose their fake death of the man. Since the Fall, they have had the upper hand. Everything has gone their way. Now they will wonder if they slipped up.

"We've strained their investigative capability already, which will add to their angst. I have a few other surprises planned that will rattle their cages."

"Isn't that just going to piss them off?"

Jack shook his head as he wheeled the truck through a left turn. On the other side of the road, some distance away, was one of the Growth Opportunity Centers, a twisted name for an unemployment office. The line was at least a hundred people long. Some wore suits, some wore filthy clothing. He hated seeing the lines, but they were everywhere. The economics of Newmerica squashed working people in favor of those that didn't. It was far easier to take reparations or growth credits than it was to hold down a job, especially with all of the profit-crushing regulations. He pushed his thoughts of their plight out of his mind for the moment.

"Yes. It always makes them waste resources. You have to know, I've been living on the run for almost five years. I know what stress can do to a person or a group. It messes with your thinking. You make bad decisions because paranoia is governing you. They will spend a lot of effort trying to figure out why the President is here or preventing word of it from leaking out. They will eventually piece together that it was all fake, but that will only make them more nervous. That bitch that runs the NSF will be up late at night trying to figure out what our play is."

"And what is our play?"

"Restoration," Jack said. In one word he summed up what was needed.

"Can it be done?"

"If people believe it, then it can be."

"How do you do that?"

Jack grinned. "Parker, when they took us down, we didn't see it coming. They played off of our divisiveness. They took us down by pitting us against each other. They used the media to manipulate us. If we do the same thing, we can hit them just as hard." The truck hit a pothole and bounced for a moment.

"It's easy to plot the overthrow of a government. Holding onto power, that takes finesse and skill. They don't have it, and no one has been willing to challenge them, up until now."

Jack drove for nearly an hour, dropping off his accomplice at his car that was parked behind an abandoned gas station in the middle of nowhere. About a mile from his own vehicle, he parked the rental truck in a low depression he had scouted out in advance. Taking a gas can out from the rear, he dosed the vehicle's interior and exterior, leaving a trail of gas some 15 feet away. From there, he lit the gas-fuse, engulfing the vehicle in a ball of fire that sent a black plume rising skyward. There would be no DNA to recover from this vehicle, and he had chosen the isolated location to ensure its complete destruction.

He climbed into his own car and took off, heading north. They will pursue this sighting out of fear and that gave him some satisfaction. Fear was their lifeblood; it was what gave them strength to rise to power in the first place. It had started with the fear of the pandemic, then fear of riots, then fear of reprisals. *They love to inflict fear, now let them have a dose of it themselves. Let them wonder if the President is alive, what he is up to, how he evaded them for so long. Their fear will get them to turn on each other eventually.* Jack was fully prepared to feed that paranoia as well. *The more they focus on this, the more we can advance our own cause—the restoration.*

Wheaton, Illinois

Caylee sat at the bus bench across from the CVS; this was where she had seen footage of Richard Farmer with an unidentified person. She was not looking for any specific evidence, but she sat there trying to get into the head of Farmer. It was a gloomy day, light purple clouds blocking the sun. The air was humid, not warm or cold, just damp. The government-sponsored digital board flashed the day's slogan, "Your neighbor may be the problem," in large, red, scrolling letters.

The man he had sat on the bench with was young—which ruled him out for being an old crony from his days in the Sons of Liberty. Farmer had come to Wheaton for a funeral that he had missed. Her analysis had quickly narrowed that down to one Arthur Forrest. His rap sheet was less than spectacular, but entertaining. He had been locked away for being the leader of a cell for the SOL. A former college professor. His daughter, Karen, held a field post with Social Enforcement. That was intriguing to Caylee. She had changed her last name to Forrester after her father's release from social quarantine. *I bet their Christmas gatherings were entertaining as all hell.* Arthur Forrest never named names, even after being sent to social quarantine for two and a half years. While SE's files on him were mostly obscured for her access, she was able to piece together that he had been an almost ideal prisoner. She also saw notes of medical reports for injuries, which experience told her came from beatings at the Social Quarantine Camp. Forrest had died of cancer. *He had to be who Farmer had come to pay respects to.*

Caylee had tried to pry open more information on Arthur Forrest, but the SE had locks on almost anything. She looked at an old photo of him and saw what appeared to be a kindly, old college professor, short, less-than-imposing. Looks could be deceiving, she knew that, but he did not strike her as the domestic terrorist type. He had spoken out against the Liberation… that had been his crime. The SE targeted him, as they loved to do, ruined his career, his family, everything. It was then that he became a member and leader of the Sons of Liberty. *The SE took a man voicing his opinion, and turned him into a terror leader.* The irony was not lost on her.

He had a son, Andrew Jackson Forrest. His first and middle names would have been troublesome. The SE had 'encouraged' blacklisted people named after historical figures to change their names. Andrew hadn't. He was a chip off of the old man's block.

As she sat on the bench, she pulled up her iPad and swept through his files. No real trouble with the law. The SEs had an AI tag on him— Active Investigation. *Bingo.* She pulled up his image and compared it side-by-side with the grainy footage from the bench, the mystery man next to Richard Farmer. With a few quick stabs of her fingertips, she ran a comparison. An 89% match. So, Farmer had met with the son right where she was sitting.

Caylee Leatrom knew enough not to leap to conclusions; she had to think things through. Could it have been a simple conversation? Perhaps he wanted to share a story about their time together in the SOL. He had missed the funeral; perhaps he was just apologizing for that.

The trained detective in her shook that off. Why meet here? He must have suspected that Andy was being monitored at home. If it was a simply condolence discussion, why did Farmer take his own life? No, the conversation was something more than two men sharing their sorrow. He was telling him something, sharing information.

Could Andrew Forrest be a threat? As she tabbed through his file on her iPad, she doubted it. Where his father had been in the military, Andrew had gone to college. He lacked cyber or terror-related skills. He had never even taken self-defense classes, didn't previously own a firearm. She returned to his image and looked at his face. This is not a terror leader, not unless we make him one.

He did have one thing, the secret that Richard Farmer had shared with him. She shut down her iPad and put it in the messenger bag beside her. There was no doubt that she was not wasting her time. She had to penetrate the Sons of Liberty and find her target, the Traitor-President. Richard Farmer's suicide was proof that the Sons were alive and she knew they were active—she had seen that in West Virginia.

For long minutes she sat on the bench, contemplating her next move. I need to find Andrew Forrest. If Farmer would not talk, perhaps he could be persuaded. The local SE had him tagged as an AI, that would complicate matters. She knew his address was only a few blocks away. She left the bench and began the walk. As she moved, her mind went over everything she knew, making sure she had not overlooked something obvious. The SOL was being bold, daring; she had seen that with the dead left in West Virginia. Could Andrew Forrest be following his father's footsteps? He didn't look like the type, but what she had seen was data, not the man.

When she came to his apartment building, she noticed an SE surveillance team parked out front. They looked like a man and a woman sitting in an unimaginative sedan, the kind of car a middle-aged family man might buy. She noticed that the man behind the wheel was smoking. On the ground, near the driver's door, were several cigarette butts. They had been there a while.

There were other SEs floating around, she was sure of it. That didn't faze her in the least. She made her way to the apartment building and used her badge to get the security guard to let her in. She took the elevator to the fourth floor. It was not a plush building, nor was it a dive. Forrest had been a fairly successful consultant before he lost his job… thanks to a less-than-discreet inquiry by the SE with his employer. She had seen that in the data she had access to. That was all it took. When Social Enforcement started asking questions, most companies would rather terminate their people than deal with possible repercussions. *They probably told the guy he lost his job for some minor infraction.*

She walked down the long hallway to apartment 15 and knocked on the door. It opened quickly, but it wasn't Andrew Forrest that greeted her, it was a chunky woman with a round face. "May I help you?"

Caylee knew the face—it was that of Andrew Forrest's sister, Karen. She held out her badge. "NSF. I'd like to speak with Mister Forrest if he's available."

The woman looked at the badge, unimpressed. "He's not here right now."

"Do you know when he'll be back?"

"What is this in regards to?" the portly woman asked.

"That is NSF business."

"This is an active SE investigation," she said, pulling out her own badge and flashing it arrogantly. "We have this well in-hand."

Caylee leaned forward and saw two SE operatives in the room, dumping the contents of a desk drawer on the floor. "Yes, I can see you are being quite efficient," she said with a slight smirk. "Regardless of your investigation, I need to speak with Mister Forrest."

"You can talk to him when we are done," she said defiantly.

"Look," Caylee said. "I don't want to mess up whatever this—" she waved her hand at the room, which was obviously being trashed, "is. I just need to talk to him for a few minutes. I'm sure we can work this out."

"I told you," Andrew's sister said in a stern tone. "We have this taken care of." She stepped back a half-step into the apartment and began to close the door in Caylee's face. Leatrom jammed her foot in the way, preventing the door from shutting. She hit it hard with her shoulder, knocking it back into the larger woman's face.

"I don't want any problems," Caylee said through gritted teeth. "But the NSF does not fall under the SE's authority."

Red anger rose into the chubby cheeks of Karen Forrester. Behind her the other two agents dropped what they were doing and walked toward the door. "You are interfering with our work," she said angrily. "What's your name?"

"Caylee Leatrom," she said. "Though I can tell you, if you think you can apply pressure to me, you are sadly mistaken."

"Well Miss Leatrom," Karen continued. "If you don't leave now, I will have five more agents up here and we will physically remove you. What do you think of that?"

A part of Caylee wanted her to try. From where she stood, the SE operatives were hardly a threat. *Is this a situation I want to push? Andrew isn't here, so even if I beat the shit out of them, it doesn't get me any closer to what I need.* Another part of her wanted to punch the chubby woman, just for the fun of it.

She stepped away from the door. "Very well. This isn't over."

"Oh," Karen Forrester said. "I think it is." She shut the door and Caylee heard the deadbolt click into place.

She left the building, standing outside for a few minutes, trying to think about where Andrew Forrest might be. Her phone chirped and she saw that it was the Secretary. "This is Leatrom," she said as she answered the call.

"You're in Illinois," the Secretary said, not asking but stating it. "Any luck?"

"A little. I'm following on a lead that will get me closer to the SOL."

"Good. For now, I need you in Salina, Kansas."

"A problem?"

"A sighting of your primary target."

"In Salina, Kansas," she restated. What would the Traitor-President be doing in Kansas?

"The info is already in your folder in the NSFCloud," the Secretary said. "I want you to put a lid on things there. Whether it is accurate or not, we don't want rumors floating around."

"Understood."

"And operative Leatrom, if you *do* find him, you know what to do."

Caylee nodded. "Yes, Madam Secretary. I understand completely. No loose ends."

Detroit, Michigan

Raul Lopez was the most popular person in his Youth Corps troop. A box had come from his mother. Not only had she sent him a letter, she had sent him homemade cookies, a jar of her salsa, a small loaf of zucchini bread, several new pairs of socks, and an assortment of candies. Just opening the box made him long for her.

He loved working in the Youth Corps. He certainly had never been this physically fit in his entire life. The corps gave him training, too. He had learned to use a cutting torch and a jackhammer as part of his work to dismantle an old abandoned factory—skills that he could use elsewhere later in life. While the Youth Corps had been his surrogate family, nothing could replace his mother in his heart.

They were on a late-afternoon break, sitting in what had been some sort of conference room or office in the factory. Most of the building had already been dismantled by the Corps, taken apart by hand. Much of the brick and steel could be repurposed or recycled. The office—now little more than a room with faded, chipped, blue paint covered with graffiti and a floor with peeling tiles—was one of the few places they could assemble.

The others gathered around as he opened the box, practically salivating at the contents therein. One reached for the candy, only to have Raul slap his hand jokingly. The candy was the easiest to share. He opened the small box of chocolates and passed them around, taking two for himself. While the food was good in the corps, it had been a long time since he had tasted chocolate.

Paco had been badly injured in the assault by the SE, but was back with the troop and slowly healing. The stitches on his head left a nasty scar. His cheek was swollen, even after all of this time. He took a piece of candy and said, "*Gracias,*" which spurred the others to thank him as well.

Looking up he saw Troop Leader, Avalon Winston, standing off to his side, smiling. Someone handed him a piece of chocolate, which he took with thanks to Raul. "Take a good look at Raul," he said. "He's a good citizen. He received a gift from home and he could have kept it to himself, but he didn't. He shared it. When he had a lot, he gave to those that didn't. That was one of the reasons why we fought the Liberation. There were people out there that had a lot. They got what they had from the hard work and sweat of those less fortunate who were forced to work for them. They profited and lived lives of greed while people who worked for them had almost nothing. 'Equity is fairness,' that's what we are told and it is as right today as it was then." Winston unwrapped the candy and popped it in his mouth.

Raul had heard the justification before. There were many reasons that the Liberation had been waged. One was to bring about equality and fairness. The rich had been stripped of their wealth and it had been redistributed to others. Did it improve lives? Raul struggled with that. Most of the money that the poor got didn't seem to change their lot in life. What it did was give them more money to buy stuff. Stuff, he had come to learn, did not bring about happiness or prosperity. It was just stuff.

The other reason was the tyranny of the Traitor-President. Even speaking his name was banned; that's how bad he was. His injustices and crimes were many. Like most tyrants, he had met his fate awaiting trial in prison. Another justification was the rampant racism in society… especially the police. The federalization of the police into the NSF had solved one part of that—where reparations solved the rest.

What Raul struggled with was basic: How had these injustices been allowed to go on for so long? It made no sense to him. If these were indeed problems, who had allowed them to fester for so long and why? How did money solve inequalities? His mother had lived in the same apartment for years, and she still had to go and work. Raul wondered if such changes really helped the people they were intended to help, or did others benefit?

Winston pointed to the loaf of zucchini bread in the box and nodded to Raul. He understood… he wanted him to share that as well. It was one of his favorite things his mother cooked. This was something that he did not want to share, but he felt the stares of the rest of the troops fall on him as he held the loaf in the box.

Sharing it was the right thing to do. At the same time, this was something special. He could imagine his mother baking it, the smells of the spices filling the kitchen. The memories alone made his mouth water. Looking up at Troop Leader Winston, he got a single nod, telling him what he had to do.

"This is my favorite thing my *madre* bakes," he said unwrapping it. He could smell the spices as soon as the loaf was exposed to the air.

He pulled out a knife and cut himself the end of the loaf, a large enough piece to savor. He struggled with reluctance as he handed it to the greedy hands of the rest of the troop. The loaf made its way around the circle, shrinking with each person that cut themselves a slice. When it came back to him, there was only a single slice left, which he clutched as if it were found treasure.

Winston bent over, leaning in front of Raul's face. "I know that wasn't easy Raul. What you did makes me proud." His words made him feel somewhat better. He coddled the jar of salsa that his mother sent, intent on not sharing that as well.

A few minutes went by and the troop leader moved to the doorway. "Alright then, everyone thank Raul for being a good person and sharing his wealth." The young men and women rose and obeyed, thanking him. Suddenly there was a whoomphing sound, a loud roar, from where they had been working. The troop froze in place; this was a sound they had not heard before. Even Troop Leader Winston was frozen in place for a moment.

Looking out across the now-stripped factory floor, Raul and the others saw a plume of black smoke rising in the distance, in the area they had been working. He set the box down and joined the others as they ran to see what was on fire.

The troop had a Bobcat, a tiny excavator, to help with moving the heavy debris from their deconstruction efforts. The white and red machine was fully engulfed in flames, as if someone had soaked it in gasoline and set it on fire. For a moment everyone stood staring, the heat from the fire warming their faces as they looked in shock.

"Get some extinguishers," Winston called. The troop scrambled searching for them. Five were found and began to dose the fire. Raul hooked up a hose, which helped. It took the better part of an hour to fully extinguish the flames. When they were done, the charred and blackened Bobcat was still steaming wisps of white smoke into the air.

"How did that happen?" Julia said. "None of us were even around it."

Paco, sullen-faced, looked at the smoldering wreck, then turned to the troop. "It was that SE group, the one that beat me. They did it."

Troop Leader Winston held his hands out. "Now, we don't know that."

"Yes, we do," Paco said. "Look at where that's burned. The scoop is not flammable, but it's on fire. Someone soaked this in gasoline and set it on fire." There were murmurs of agreement. "It was those followers of Islam."

"We should do something," Arvella added. "They can't just come over here and beat us and burn our stuff."

Winston saw the anger rising in his troop and tried to smother it. "Someone set this on fire, but we don't know who."

"Let's call in the NSF," Jacob said. "They will investigate it."

Raul knew differently. There was a divide between the NSF and the SE. Everyone knew about it. They won't investigate it because it's messy… it's about religion. Father Ryan had told him about the rift, how religious freedoms were often oppressed by the administration and how law enforcement did not like getting pulled into religious issues. The government thought that religion was part of the problem in the country; it contributed to the need for the Liberation. Getting them involved would not make things better. "You can call," Raul said. "They will do nothing." *We are on our own.*

"Without the Bobcat, some of the jobs are going to take days," Arvella said.

"Can't these people be talked to?" Jacob asked.

Winston took control of them with a soothing tone of voice. "We don't know if they did it. I had hoped they would leave us alone. I will go over and talk with them. In the meantime, I will call the NSF and file a report. Since we didn't see who did it, chances are pretty good they will let it drop, but it is worth filing the report anyway. For today, let us get this cleaned up and make sure that the rest of our equipment is secure."

Raul put his box down, out of the way, and went to shut off the water to the hose he had been using. On his way back from the spigot, he came upon the troop leader. "We should post some of us on guard tonight," he said grimly.

Winston nodded in response. "Not a bad idea."

INTERLUDE

J ack Desmond watched the images unfolding in the White House above him from the security of the Service's Emergency Response Center. The battle on the lawn of the White House had been brutal, but they came in waves of humanity to storm the building. Some brought pick axes, others sledge hammers. To the casual observer, it looked like a mob, but Jack had been trained by the best in the Secret Service. This was organized. They had teams. They had an objective. *They won't get him. He's in the EOC, safe and secure with Charli.* If anyone was stupid enough to go after the President, they would have to deal with Charli Kazinski. She was the best on the detail, maybe the best Secret Service ever on the presidential detail.

The counter assault team was waging its own war on the main level of the White House. He could not hear their gunfire, but we could see the muzzle flashes on one of the monitors. The rioters were returning fire, shotguns destroying the décor and riddling the armored counter assault team with potentially deadly pellets. Fireworks were set off, Roman candles and mortars, intended for the outdoors, fired in the hallways. Drapes went up in flames as did numerous pieces of art. The fireworks were far beyond annoying… the flames filled the rooms and corridors with smoke. They were augmented with Molotov cocktails. Body armor could stop bullets, but was nearly useless against burning gasoline. One lucky hit splashed three members of the counter assault team, forcing them to break ranks and duck and roll.

Jack's jaw ached as he watched the monitors. "Why isn't the fire suppression system on?" he asked.

Special Agent Drake Barker sat at the ERC's main board. "I took it off line."

"Why in the hell would you do that?"

He spun in his seat, his service weapon in front of him. "Don't even think it, sir," he said.

Jack was stunned. He had known Drake Barker for a year since being posted to the White House detail. He seemed to be a bright guy, level headed. Now he sat with his gun drawn. Barker's eyes were wide, his nostrils flared with excitement.

"Your weapon," Barker said, nodding to his shoulder holster.

Betrayed. How many others in the detail are working with ANTIFA? His mind raced at the thought that one of their own had flipped. Jack opened his jacket slowly, exposing the holster. "How could you, Drake?"

"How can you defend such a criminal?" he spat back. "He stole two elections from the people. He has stomped on people's rights. He's a racist, a white supremacist. Everyone knows it."

"You're a fucking traitor," Jack said, studying Barker, his stance, the angle of his gun. *He is younger. We are only two yards apart. He's faster than me. I need a distraction. If I can get his aim off, I can still take him.* In his mind he knew right where to hit the man to disable him, but could it happen with a sucking chest wound?

"I'm a patriot!" he proclaimed. "I've already disabled the access controls and re-tasked the counter-sniper squads. Once we have neutralized the counter attack team, we will move on the EOC and extract the bastard… dead or alive."

Jack used his right hand to slowly move towards his pistol. As he got closer, Drake moved his pistol more aggressively in his direction. "Don't try anything stupid, Jack."

Desmond looked at his weapon, and he knew that Barker's eyes would follow his. He knew that his weapon was a threat, but not the only one. His left hand shifted to his belt, to the remote control on his belt. Only the Secretary had it, it was something that Barker no doubt did not think of.

As he touched his pistol handle with this right hand, his left triggered the ERC emergency alarm for the unauthorized intruder. It was a simple button, a remote. A klaxon sounded as did a red flashing light. Drake Barker's eyes darted to the warning. "What the—" Barker's aim went off as his body turned.

Jack pulled his gun, raising it before Barker could re-aim. Jack fired, hitting him in the left shoulder. Barker spun in the office chair under the impact, his own shot ricocheting off behind him. His ears roared as he lunged at the younger man, firing another shot that hit the left side of his target's head, tearing off a chunk of his ear. Barker dropped his gun, grabbing at the grazing wound that sprayed blood from the side of his head.

Jack grabbed Barker's gun and tossed it. He wanted to shoot the younger agent right in his heart. Kill him. That wasn't the way. *I'm a federal officer—I need to do my job.* Instead, he throat-punched the bleeding man hard, cutting off his windpipe.

Barker dropped to the raised tile floor with a thud, whimpering and gasping for air. Jack went to the main controls. What he saw stunned him. The security systems had been disabled. He tried to reopen the access controls, but they had been encrypted. Jack shut off the unauthorized intruder alert.

He turned to the man at his feet. "God damn it, Barker, what's the code?"

Barker got his breath in a gurgling surge of air. "I'll *never* tell you. He's fucked... and so are you. You're all going down tonight," he groaned. "Your family is dead if you fight back."

"What?"

Barker chuckled. "We have a team on your family. An insurance policy. If I don't get out of here alive, they are dead." He winced in pain, sweat drenching him on the floor. "You've already lost Jack; you just don't realize it yet."

There had been instances of ANTIFA targeting police officers' families. The Secret Service considered itself safe from that. Their screening process would have protected the identities of agents. Obviously, that had failed; the bleeding man that taunted him was proof. His thoughts of his wife and child flooded him, but he pushed them back into the dark recesses of his mind. *I have a goddamn job to do. Then I can go and save them.*

Jack stared at the screen; his face was hot with anger, and adrenaline filled his ears with a roar. He grabbed the mike and opened a line to the Emergency Operations Center. "Rabbit, this is Slingshot. Tunnel access is open on this end and I can't close it. Bad guys are heading your way. Kick on your systems." He paused, knowing that the elevator deterrents would only buy them time, not prevent the inevitable. "I am authorizing Snap-count. Say again, Snap-count. Rabbit, run, get out of there while you can."

There was no response from the EOC. Jack glared down at the wounded agent bleeding on the white tiles, smearing the floor as he writhed there. Glancing at the few working monitors, he saw that the counter attack team was being driven back through the smoke-filled corridors. Fireworks meant for celebrations were being fired as weapons. He saw one rioter with an AR-15 raise his gun and blast the camera—the screen went white.

I can't do anything else here. I have to get home. I have to save my family. He stepped over the fallen body of Drake Barker and donned his body armor.

Washington DC

So many movies portrayed an elaborate secret series of tunnels under the White House that it almost seemed cliché. They always seemed so big on film that they made people in the know chuckle out loud in the theaters when they played. Such elaborate tunnels were the things of myth, perpetuated by urban legend.

In reality, the purpose of having a bunker deep under the White House was to avoid having tunnels that could be accessed. The tunnels that did exist were not for human passage as much as they were for pipes, electrical lines, communications, etc. They were dark, narrow, and in many places had to be traversed on your hands and knees. They were deliberately difficult, with several steel barriers and sensors. No one could enter such tunnels without triggering alarms. The locks were inaccessible for anyone trying to break in. For Secret Service Lieutenant Charli Kazinski, crawling through the darkness was not difficult, but for the President, a man past his prime physically, it was a challenge.

She had gotten word from Jack Desmond before he went offline; trouble was coming. She could wait it out in the Emergency Operations Center… that was what protocol required. Protocol had never anticipated the White House falling to a siege situation, not like this. If Jack had told her to go, that was what she was going to do, to hell with procedure.

There were four other agents in the EOC with her. "Here's the word from upstairs—Snap-count." Everyone knew how grave the situation was with that code phrase: Evacuate the President. She had them break out their personal gear. Normal duty in the EOC allowed agents to bring a change of clothing. One agent had donated a hoodie and sweat pants that were approximately the size of the President. She had told him to put them on and he gave her a stern sideways glance, then complied. The hoodie helped conceal his face. A Washington Nationals ball cap solved the problem of his trademark hair style. The sneakers another agent provided were a bit big on him, but they helped further mask his identity. Another agent gave the President reflective sunglasses, which further hid his face.

U.S. Army Major Dan Swanson hovered nearby. Swanson held the President's emergency satchel, the nuclear football, the device that allowed the President to launch America's nuclear missiles. Swanson was in his 40s, white and black crew cut hair, no-nonsense. He glanced down at his uniform, then at Charli. "What about me?"

"Snap-count calls for one agent—to avoid drawing attention," she replied.

"Agent Kazinski, where he goes, I go," Swanson replied. There was resolve in his voice that told her not to push the issue.

"Ditch the uniform, Major," she said. Swanson did. Another pair of sweat pants were offered, and he put them on along with his white tee shirt. Even stripped down, he looked like a military officer.

The President stirred, looking at how he was dressed. "You've got me decked out like an old rapper. What's the plan Charli?" he asked after he put the clothing on.

"Sir," she said firmly. "The tunnel security should hold, but the call from upstairs is that we shouldn't count on it. "We have a plan, a last ditch of sorts, called Snap-count. I'm taking you out by the utilities tunnel. It isn't easy, but that was the call we got. These agents will hold them as long as they can. We go out, low profile, get you someplace safe." She reached into her pocket to make sure she had the keys to the tunnel security gates.

"I thought there weren't any tunnels down here."

"Technically there aren't. These are utility corridors. It's a tight squeeze, but we mapped it out a few years ago, just in case we had to use them. One run takes us to an access point on the Metro Orange Line near the Farragut station. The rioters should be concentrated around the White House and Capitol. If we are lucky, I can get you out of the city."

"I think I should try the Pentagon again."

"Sir, with all due respect, they are hanging us out to dry," she said, having heard their prior conversation. If the Director gave me the Snap-count order, that means I need to get you out of here."

He nodded glumly. "I never thought it would come to this."

"None of us did," she said.

Major Swanson, still clinging to the brown leather satchel, moved to her side. He took his sidearm and slid it into the waistband of his pants. She made eye contact with the officer who gave her a firm nod.

"Now then, let's get you out of here, sir," she said.

CHAPTER 11

"Doing nothing is something."

Aurora, Illinois

A ndy followed the short woman that had saved him. She parked the vehicle and got out. She hadn't spoken to him in two hours and as the sun began to set, he wondered what her plan was. They had driven to a shady part of Aurora, Illinois, a place of tiny Sears 1940s houses that had been run down, and some were burned out. As they came up to the chain-link fence that surrounded the freight yard, she moved to a place along the fence and pushed an opening that had been cut there. *She did this ahead of time… she planned on us coming here.* The woman held the fence back on one side and gestured for him to go through. It wasn't easy, one pant leg caught on a barb of the fence and tore at the waist of his pants slightly, but Andy ignored it.

"So, what is our plan?" he whispered as the two of them ducked, moving into the yard, hovering next to a steel roll flatcar.

"We hop one of the trains out of the city," she said in a low tone. "We need some distance between us and the local SEs. By now they will have alerted teams all over the state."

Andy was afraid. He had been chased and shot at. Now he was with a stranger planning to hop on a train like a hobo in some 1930s movie. He had a lot of questions, but the young woman was intent on her work. She made her way to a box car and used a small pair of cutters she pulled from her backpack to cut the seal. With a hard tug she cracked open the door enough to see that it was filled with boxes. Silently, she moved to the next one, with the same results.

Then came a voice… a low whisper, "Over here." On the next track over, a door was cracked open and a hand gestured for them to come. She went, with Andy right behind her. The hand reached down and helped them up. He was an older man, perhaps the same age that Andy's father had been. The air around him smelled of old sweat. His face had a thick, curly, grayish beard. As they entered, he closed the door behind them.

The woman produced a small light, which she turned on. The boxcar was half-filled with cardboard containers. The other half was empty. The woman that saved him seemed to size up the old man, eyeing him from top to bottom. "Thanks," Andy said, extending his hand. The old man's grip was tight and firm. "People gotta help each other these days."

His compatriot nodded. "We appreciate it. Where's this heading?"

"South," he said. "If the bills of lading are correct. Where are you going?"

"South," she replied, moving over to a bare spot and lowering herself to the floor.

Andy moved next to her and looked at the older man. "I'm Andy," he said, holding out his hand. The man shook it.

She extended her hand as well to the stranger. "I'm… Charli." There was a hesitancy in her voice, as if she weren't entirely sure who she was. *There is a story with her… a reason she hesitated.* He was happy that he finally knew her name. Even on the long car ride he had kept silent, constantly checking the mirrors to make sure they hadn't been followed. "And you are?" Charli asked.

"Robert," he said proudly, sitting down with them, moving her light between them as if it were a campfire. "You must be new at this. When you pop those seals, you have to bend them back around or the yardmaster will spot them and think someone's trying to steal stuff."

"Good tip," she replied. "I've done this a few times. I guess I've been lucky so far."

"Who's after you two?" Robert asked.

"Wha… what makes you think anyone is after us?" Andy asked nervously.

Robert grinned. "It doesn't mean shit to me, but I know people that ride the rails. You two aren't those types. That means you want out of town without those fucking Social Enforcers laying into you, or the NSF. Forgive my prying, but if we are riding together, I need to know if I have to worry about getting my skull caved in."

Charli flashed a small smile, the first he had ever seen on her. "We aren't the murder-hobo types. We've had a run in with one of the local SE groups. Really, it was just a misunderstanding. My boyfriend here." She put her hand on Andy's shoulder, "He decked one of them pretty hard. You know how they are. They trashed our pad, smashed everything. We figured we'd move on." Andrew marveled at her, how she wove such a lie off the top of her head. He would have fumbled and made mistakes. The way she talked, he actually could picture those events happening—it was so natural. *Where did she learn to think that fast on her feet?*

Robert smiled. "You don't have to tell me about Social Enforcers. I was a high school teacher, social studies. When the fucking 'Liberation' happened, they came at me with a lot of changes to my curriculum. Some of the stuff was pure bullshit. They were literally changing the country's history. I was too stubborn for my own good. I told them I wouldn't teach the kids things I knew were wrong." He dipped his head and sighed heavily, pausing in memories. "Then I made a big mistake."

"And that was?" Charli asked.

"One kid asked about the flag. It was right after the Ruling Council had purged it. Just owning a flag was a high crime. I had one, left over from my father's funeral. He was in the Army. I knew I was supposed to turn it in, but it was my dad's. So when the kid asked about the flag, I brought it to class, you know, to explain the symbols on it, the stars, the stripes." His voice trailed off for a moment, lost in memory.

"One of them turned you in, didn't they?" Charli asked.

Robert nodded. "I was stupid."

"You were doing your job," Andy said. "You were a teacher. They wanted to learn."

He wiped a tear from his right eye onto the dirty sleeve of his flannel shirt. "The SEs came and got me the next day. They took my father's flag and burned it on my front lawn… an example, I guess, for anyone else out there. Behind closed doors it was more personal, more vicious." The memories seemed to swell in him as he spoke. His voice became clearer, angrier.

"They rough you up?" Andy asked.

"They burned my house down," he said flatly. "They pressured the school to fire me. It didn't take much. Nobody in the school district wanted trouble, so they fired me. They scared my wife to the point that she took our daughter and disappeared on me. Everywhere I got a job, they followed me, hounding the schools that would hire me. Now, I'm tagged in their system as a risky employee. I can't work and it will be a cold day in hell before I accept their reparations or welfare." He paused as the anger rose in his face, reddening his round cheeks.

"So now I travel. I get odd jobs, enough to get by. Sooner or later my past catches up with me and I'm on the streets again. Those fuckers won't let me go. They claim I'm a 'corrupt element' in society. All I wanted to do is teach kids and do it right."

Charli bowed her head for a moment, then raised it, looking into his eyes. "They will pay for what they did, eventually."

"Will they?" Robert countered. "Hitler was in power for twelve years. They have been in power for almost five. He was one person. There's no single head to this snake. Their Ruling Council doesn't give people a single person to take out. They were smart about that. We don't have one enemy for people to rally against."

Andy understood. His father had said almost the same thing to him. "The tighter they squeeze, the more resistance they will face. My dad told me that."

"He might be right," Robert said. "How many have to suffer in the meantime? How many lives must be destroyed before people take back what is ours?"

"They can't take away our spirit," Andy said firmly. "They can't take away hope. Dad used to say that hope isn't a strategy. He also said that hope was the key to bringing them down. This system they have created is not sustainable. It will come down at some point like a house of cards."

"Your dad sounds like a hell of a guy."

"He was," Andy said. "He was a teacher, like you. They sent him off for social quarantine. They labeled him a terrorist, simply because he believed in freedom."

Robert nodded and the freight car lurched as the train slowly started out from the yard. The boxcar's rattling and rumbling and sounds of things shifting was surprisingly loud. "I've ridden this line before. You have six hours or so before we stop. If you pull apart some of the boxes, you can make a mattress of sorts out of the cardboard. It isn't much, but better than sleeping on the floor." He got up and moved off into the darkness, away from the light.

Charli wasted no time, tearing open a large cardboard box that held a dining room set, which was more like a giant wooden puzzle. "This is yours," she said, and put another large piece down next to it. She moved the flashlight between the two of them.

"I don't know if I can sleep," Andy said.

"Try," she replied, using her backpack as a pillow, carefully pulling out one of the pistols and putting it on the cardboard next to her hand. "When we stop, we'll get off and get our bearings."

"Where are we going?"

She looked at him as he lay down, the flashlight between the two of them. "That is up to you. I just wanted to get out of whatever net the SEs were throwing up to catch us."

He was confused and she clearly could see it in his face. She continued in a low tone, so that Robert couldn't hear. "Look. I was told that your dad was a big-wig in the Sons of Liberty in the day. We got word that your father left you a package. I was given the mission of extracting you if it got hot and helping you recover that package."

"How do you know it's not back in Wheaton?"

"Is it?"

Andy shook his head.

"You see, I know the SEs tossed your dad's place and yours. While they were rooting around for it at your apartment, I was watching them. That tells me that it isn't with you."

It made sense. "How did you know they were going to take me in?"

"I didn't. I just watched them. When they made their move, I decided to get you out of there."

"Why does everyone think this package is so important?"

She shrugged her shoulders as she lay on the makeshift bedding. "You tell me."

"I don't even know what it is," he sputtered. "Dad and a friend of his,

Richard Farmer, they hid it after the Fall."

"Farmer thought enough of you to get word to us."

"Who is *us*?"

She said nothing for a moment. "The Sons of Liberty never really got wiped out, no matter how hard the FedGov tried. As it turns out, it's hard to destroy an idea. A former colleague reached out and pulled me into their organization."

"Where did you work before all of this?"

Her jaw set slightly at that query. "I'd rather not talk about it."

"Sorry," Andy said. Her past was clearly an issue with her. "What is the SOL up to?"

"I don't have all of the details," she said. "The less people know, the better, I guess. What I do know is that they have a plan, one that will put the screws to the administration. For me, that's enough."

He wasn't sure if he believed her or if Charli was holding something back. "Look. It's not enough for me. Until a few weeks ago I had a job, my dad was alive, and I had a life. It wasn't great, but I had one. My dad died, my sister turned out to be every bit the asshole I always thought she was; I've had his house and my apartment trashed; I was in a fight with the SE who wanted to take me in, and everyone seems interested in some package that none of us knows what is in it. Every question I ask you, you seem deliberately evasive about. I get it. We all have our burdens. My life is at risk. I've lost everything. I don't have a family, a home, or anything else. I'm not some counterrevolutionary. I'm just a guy."

Charli said nothing as he stopped and drew a long breath. Her eyes looked across the space between them as if she were studying him, judging him. As her short hair fell across the backpack she was using as a pillow, she lay silent. Finally, she drew a deep breath. "I've been playing at being other people for so long, I've forgotten what it's like to be myself," she said. "You've been through some shit, I'll give that to you. So have I." Charli paused, as if gathering her thoughts. "You want the truth?"

"Yeah. I think I do."

She breathed out a long sigh. "You remember the night of the Fall. I was assigned to the personal protection unit for the President. I was a Lieutenant in the Secret Service."

Andy said nothing for two seconds. "You were?"

"Yup."

"How did you get away? I mean, they captured him at the White House."

"They didn't."

Andy was stunned. "He got out?"

Charli closed her eyes for a moment, then nodded. "We did."

"But I saw pictures of him in prison—and of them hauling his body out on a gurney after his heart attack."

"A farce. A production. You have to remember, Hollywood was a big backer of the Fall. They wanted his blood, too. When he didn't surface, they presumed he was dead but didn't want to deal with people thinking he might be alive out there. It was all a show, designed to satisfy the radicals and to send a ripple of fear into everyone else. CGI, doctored photos—the whole shooting match. With him dead and presented to the public, the President of the United States, who could really feel safe? Who would dare oppose them?"

Andy stirred on his piece of cardboard. "So he's alive?"

She shook her head and her cheeks seemed to draw in. "No. It was… complicated."

Andy understood. The Secret Service was supposed to protect the leadership, and she had failed. It clearly hit her hard. He wanted to know the details, but he also saw the pain the memories brought her—it showed as wrinkles on her brow and the way she diverted her eyes.

"What happened to you?"

"I had access to some fake identities. I went into hiding. As one of the people that was with the President, I'm a wanted person. After all, if I talked, their little sideshow would be exposed. I knew that if they found me, I was as good as dead. So I became other people. I took on new identities. I hid in plain sight, twice working for the NSF after it was formed."

"Why did you stop?"

"An old friend, my Director, he had joined up with the SOL. He told me something… something that gave me hope."

"Which was?"

Charli cracked a thin grin. "There's a successor out there. A legitimate and rightful person who legally is in the line to be President."

"If that's true—"

"It means that all of this bullshit can be brought down around them. They have had their day; they have ruined the lives of a lot of people. It's all been fun and games for them. The armed mobs won and their anarchy became the rule of law. Well, all of that changes if there's a legal successor. My former Director, he has a plan to kick off a restoration... kind of a rebooting of America."

Andy paused. "It will be civil war. You know that."

"'The tree of freedom must occasionally be fertilized with the blood of patriots,'" she said, quoting Thomas Jefferson. "There will be a fight— but there should have been one last time. They overthrew the government with relative ease, helped out by the opposition party, who the crazies turned on as well. It was so fast, there was no time for conservatives to organize. This time around they will have to fight people who are fed up with their BS. This time the people that love the country will take it back. Their *cause* has fallen apart. We have hurt them, badly. They are afraid. Otherwise, they wouldn't come after you."

"I'm no threat."

"They don't know that. You know why? When you have illegally seized power, you start to see everyone as a threat. That makes everyone a target. You said you are not a counterrevolutionary. I call bullshit. We *all* are Andy. We are Americans. It is part of who we are. Revolution is in our nature. Hell, it might be genetic. We want our freedom, we demand our rights. We believe in something greater than us individually. That was what spawned the Fall. ANTIFA and BLM didn't call themselves domestic terrorists; they called themselves 'patriots.' You are a freedom fighter, whether you know it or not."

Her words hit home. It was strange hearing that kind of talk not coming from his father. *Dad knew that the spirit of the people could not be squashed. He was right.* Charli validated that. He knew what they had to do. They had to recover the package his father had hidden.

As the rail car swayed slightly, Charli switched the light off. "Tomorrow we will get our bearings, come up with a plan."

"I know where it is," Andy said slowly. "But to get there, we have to go where we are not allowed."

Charli's voice in the darkness came back to him. "I've spent the last four years in places where I am not allowed. Where is it?"

"South Dakota," Andy replied, closing his eyes. "We're going to Mount Rushmore."

"Of course it is," she said sarcastically. "Alright," she replied. "Get some sleep. We are going to need it."

Salina, Kansas

"You can understand my skepticism, Caylee" said Mrs. Mannheim as the woman put a cup of fresh coffee in front of her.

"I'm telling you, it was the President of the United States," she said proudly. "Just as plain as day. You saw my photograph of him."

Caylee looked about the small kitchen; her eyes fell on the tiny, wall-mounted, display rack with a collection of Hummel figurines, then back to the round-faced, middle-aged woman she had come to visit. "Yes, your photograph did get my attention," she said, slowly lifting the coffee and breathing in its aroma before taking a fast sip. As she sat it down, she watched Mannheim's face carefully.

She had been trained in lie detection. People did things when they tried to conceal or mislead. There were gestures, the way they held their eyes, a dozen or more ways to spot it. "Did you see where he went after he purchased the bottle of Coke?"

Mannheim shook her head. "I did see him walking down the street, south on Walnut." Her eyes didn't drift up or down as she spoke.

"Did you see him get into a vehicle?"

She shook her head. "No. I was so surprised, I just waved to him as he walked away."

"You waved to him?"

"Well, yes. I mean, he *was* the President. How often do you see that?"

"He died in prison of a heart attack," Caylee said. "You must have seen it."

Mrs. Mannheim nodded. "I did. We all did. But you saw the picture. Don't you think it was him?"

Caylee shook her head slightly. "How could it be him, Mrs. Mannheim? He's dead."

"Well, you can't believe everything that's broadcast on the news," the woman said. "Maybe someone made a mistake. Maybe the government got the wrong person. Maybe he had a body-double. I have heard that some famous people do that. They hire someone to take their place."

"Don't you think that the authorities would have tracked down someone like that?" Caylee offered, taking another sip of coffee.

"Well, they must have missed something. Because there he was, right on the streets of Salina, in broad daylight." Caylee looked for any indication that the woman was being deceptive, but there were none of the tell-tale signs. *She believes what she's telling me.*

"Well, we have taken the image down," Caylee said. "We have also removed it from your device."

Her words seemed to puzzle Mrs. Mannheim, who cocked her head slightly to the side. "You've removed my picture?"

"Yes," Caylee said, putting the coffee back on the table. "Obviously you are not to speak of this to anyone. If anyone asks you about it, you will tell them that you met with someone in the NSF and that you were mistaken; it was a man that happened to *look* like the Traitor-President."

"But my picture—"

Caylee cut her off. "Mrs. Mannheim. We cannot have people spreading false rumors that a traitor has somehow escaped justice. I'm sure you understand. Such talk would create possible problems. As such, we require your silence and compliance on this matter."

She looked dejected and somewhat saddened as she nodded. Caylee understood. That photo had made her a minor celebrity in her tiny circle of friends.

"If I may?" the woman asked.

"Yes?"

"Well, you *did* take that picture. Doesn't that qualify me for some reparation points of some sort?"

There it is… compliance. Bought and paid for by the administration's reparation policy. "You know, Mrs. Mannheim, normally it wouldn't. But you seem like an upstanding citizen, someone that realizes the risks of spreading false information. I believe I will initiate a request on your behalf, contingent of course on your doing exactly what I said."

The woman shook her head and beamed. "Oh, thank you officer. You know, I don't think I got your name."

"No," Caylee said. "You didn't."

A few minutes later she stood at her car where one of the local NSF detectives met her. His name was Thomas Ferguson, and he was a cops-cop; she could see it in the way he carried himself. Such men were old-school, they did the necessary hard work. Some of the newer, non-legacy, recruits to the NSF were punk kids. They went through checklists, but didn't go much further. "This loose end has been tied up. What did you find?"

The older Ferguson rubbed his clean-shaven face and on the light breeze, she could smell his cheap Axe cologne. "I had a crew pull every bit of footage within four blocks of the deli. Strangely enough, most of the cameras were out of order. The bits we got didn't help much. We switched to road-signal cameras, but a lot of those near the area had been disabled."

"Disabled?"

"Deliberately damaged," Two with pellet rifles, three with paintballs. Another six were knocked out of alignment."

She paused. "Paintballs?"

"Yeah, why?" he said, lowering his notepad for a moment.

"We saw the same thing in Tysons Corner."

"You think they're connected?"

"What are the odds that no security footage picked up this guy, who happens to look like a dead President—in broad daylight, in the middle of a city? Seems a bit far-fetched to me. It's like someone deliberately blacked out the security information."

"Why? I mean, if it was someone who knew that the former President was going to be seen, why block it out? Having a lot of footage would only make the case stronger that he was alive, right?" the detective asked.

"They wanted him to be seen, but the folks with him didn't want us to be able to trace him." *If this was deliberate, it was a well-organized effort. They thought this through, planned it well. This is not the action of amateurs.* Caylee liked the thought of that. This was an opponent that was worthy of her skills and talent. This was someone that presented a challenge.

"On a lark, I went through our drone footage for parking control. They aren't great cameras, but I did get a sweep of the street a few minutes after Mrs. Mannheim had her little encounter."

"You found something?"

"I did." He handed her his iPad. "Red truck. Look at the bumper, it's a rental. It was on the street at the time. Now, we have tracked down almost everyone in that area. Two of them said they saw a red truck parked six spots down from the deli at the time that our target was seen."

Caylee studied the grainy image. "The license plate is obscured."

"Yeah. We got two letters and a number. I tracked down the rental company. They rented forty-three of these make and model trucks in the state that day. With that partial license tag, I narrowed it to two, both rented well outside of the city. One was unaccounted for, until last night."

"Go on…"

"One was found about an hour from here, in a gully, burned to a crisp." He took back the iPad and pulled up the image of the burned truck.

Caylee looked at it, then back at Detective Ferguson. "Good work, Detective."

"Just doing my job. So, what does this tell us?"

"If we presume our fake President left in the truck, we can assume they didn't want any checks for DNA. Otherwise, why burn the truck? They pre-planned this encounter, taking out the cameras in advance. They didn't want us to have a lot of evidence in our hands, just enough to get our attention. They *controlled* this entire situation, from top to bottom."

"We lifted damn near 260 prints from the case where this guy got his Coke. I've dumped them to your file. The word I've gotten is that the lab's backlog is weeks after some incident at Quantico. You're an operative; you can probably bump up the order."

Caylee nodded, handing him back his iPad. *I can—and will.* "These guys are polished, whoever they are. They have access to some state-of-the-art thinking, too," she said.

"They aren't locals then. We keep a pretty tight tab on the locals that would have this kind of expertise. That means they have already moved on. No point in loitering in the area."

"Right," Caylee said. "We have control of the image and we've taken it down. We will need to get to everyone that saw that image, tell them it was false and not to spread any rumors that will land them in trouble."

"I've got a team of folks good with social tagging. We will put a lid on it."

"Even with that," she said. "Someone will pick up on it and try to get it to the media. People love conspiracy theories and this plays to that. If any locals do pick it up, make sure our spokesmen play it off as a bad prank. Let them know we don't take this seriously because we know the traitor is dead, but that people who spread such misinformation are subject to investigation. That should scare the snail-snot out of them."

"Most of the local media would clear this with us in advance anyway," Ferguson said. "They don't want trouble with the NSF or the TRC."

Caylee crossed her arms and gave him a single nod of approval. We are being played. Whoever it is has some serious balls to mess with the NSF. In her mind, everything was strangely connected—right down to the attacks at Quantico and Tysons Corners. *They're building up to something; something big.*

The sightings of the Traitor-President were deeply disturbing because they were puzzle pieces that didn't seem to fit the picture. *Our first sighting was in Gettysburg. There was one near Nashville as well. Now this one in Kansas. Almost five years and no one sees him, and now we have sightings. That can't be a coincidence.*

Her analytical thinking kicked in. *Why appear in public? If you have been able to hide this long, why risk stepping out where you will be seen? Why would you risk it?*

You wouldn't. There was something else in play here. She could feel it. As she stepped out of the elevator, she put her phone in her pocket. *I can't ignore going to Kansas to follow up on this. I can put out feelers on this Andrew Forrest in the meantime.* Her gut told her that getting to the Sons of Liberty leadership was the key to finding the former President. *Someone wanted to keep Mister Forrest out of the hands of the Social Enforcers, someone with the same skills I possess. That has to be the SOL or someone of that caliber. Why protect him if he didn't have something they needed? What was it that the SEs had not been able to find?*

Caylee Leatrom had more questions than answers as she reached her car. There would be plenty of time to think it over on the flight to

Kansas. If the traitor President was alive, she would find him. If not, she would find who was trying to perpetuate the illusion that was still out there—and why they were doing it.

I won't find my answers here. I need to penetrate the Sons of Liberty. They're driving this bus. If I can find this Andrew Forrest, find out why the SEs were after him, that's a good starting place.

And when I do figure this out, I'll take them all down.

CHAPTER 12

Outside of Bluffdale, Utah

The Utah Data Center, codenamed Bumblehive, was secure on many fronts. It was built mostly out in the open, making the approach to the facility difficult without detection. There were rings of security fences and sensors which made approach within a half-mile of the facility nearly impossible. Much of the facility was underground.

Jack Desmond loved the impossible. He saw it as a challenge. When the NSA had been folded into the NSF, he knew that Bumblehive was where the NSF's often-taunted security cloud was housed. Hitting the NSF facility in Maryland all but guaranteed that the NSFCloud would be hosted in Utah, and with good reason. The facility was a fortress, with its own security force. Taking down the facility would further cripple operatives in the field. Their investigative data would be inaccessible. It would leave many in the NSF blind.

But how to take down such a big facility without launching a massive assault? It had been a problem he had tasked to a handful of members of the Sons of Liberty. Their plan was remarkably simple.

The farm of computers at Bumblehive generated a great deal of heat. The facility had two chiller plants and twelve cooling towers. If these were disabled, even for a short period of time, the NSF would have to start taking down servers, cutting agents off from data. The facility also had four power buildings for channeling the massive electricity into the facility. These, too, were points of vulnerability. The genius engineers, being lazy, had put the power centers next to the chilling units to save time moving between the two for maintenance.

If the cooling towers were taken down, there was a company already contracted to provide mobile systems as backup. They were in Salt Lake City. The first step was to infiltrate the mobile units, planting hundreds of pounds of high explosive in them. Once they reached capacity, the explosives were set to detonate. The explosion of the mobile units would take out the power centers as well. Those facilities were custom built, nearly impossible to replace on short notice. *Typical fucking government job,* Jack thought when he had reviewed the plan the team had come up with.

The plan was simple. Cripple the chilling units, wait for the backups to arrive, blow them up and take out the power centers. Bumblehive would be unable to share its precious intelligence data for weeks, if not months.

Jack moved alongside the strike team as they broke out the drones. They had been purchased commercially, untraceable. They had been high-end drones, the kind used in media production. Rather than carrying heavy cameras, they were equipped with explosives and detonators. Four would be used on each chiller plant, targeting the plant and the cooling towers. One drone was equipped with white phosphorous so as to cause massive heat damage, the kind that would prohibit simple hardware swap-outs of the damaged equipment. With a range of three miles, they could come in low, rise up over the fence, and hit the facility before anyone could respond. His team had done dry runs in Colorado with fairly good luck... now came the real test.

"We're ready to go Skipper," said former Navy SEAL Travis Cullen. Travis's father had been one of the founding members of the Sons of Liberty after the Fall. His father was a Gulf War vet and the newly formed NSF had labeled him a 'gun nut.' With the ATF rolled into their jurisdiction, the desire to confiscate his weapons gave the NSF the justification they needed to move in on him. It was Ruby Ridge all over again, only this time with overwhelming firepower. The authorities had surrounded his cabin in the woods of Washington State and had blasted it apart with enough gun fire to level a city block. A staggering number of such gun roundups took place. Jack saw it for what it was—legally justified murder. They called his old man a crazy and killed him. Desmond still remembered the footage of the authorities hauling out the elder Cullen's guns and his body in a blood-soaked stretcher. The media sang high praise to the efforts, saying that Adam Cullen was a danger to society. They said he was planning a mass shooting event—a lie, but one the people ate up. Travis had been waiting, wanting revenge ever since.

"We get one run at this," Jack said to the eight operators. "We screw the pooch on this and they will tighten security to the point where we can't pull off anything."

"We've got it," Travis assured him.

Jack nodded. "Then light the bastards up." Twilight was coming as the sun set in the distance. They had less than half an hour of good visibility. Since Jack was poised to the west, the setting sun would blind anyone looking their direction. The winds were light, making piloting the drones somewhat easier.

The drones hummed to life, kicking up a lot of dust as each pilot checked their controls and the screen. Jack squinted and held his hand up to keep the dust from his eyes as they rose up and over the hill between the pilots and their targets. He moved behind Travis, who piloted one of the drones, watching the screen.

He was surprised how well the images came through as the drones shot across the flat desert ground. As they approached the rings of chain-link fence, they arced upward slightly—in one case just clearing the fence. Inside the compound they wasted no time finding their targets.

One by one they exploded. It took a few moments for the sound to echo over the hill and Jack watched as each screen flickered off. The booms bounced over his head.

"Alright, pack it up and get your asses in gear," Travis commanded. He drifted over to Jack with a big grin on his face. "Right now, they are back there trying to figure out what happened. In about 20 minutes their servers will start kicking off because of the heat."

Jack nodded. The Sons of Liberty had just struck another gut punch to the NSF, and tomorrow, when the backup coolers were brought in and powered up, things would get a lot worse.

Wheaton, Illinois

Caylee hated hospitals, especially the nationalized ones. The National Hospitals were not where she ever wanted to be treated, she paid more for insurance to avoid going to them. They reminded her of when her grandmother was dying. The smell of disinfectants, the dispassionate staff; it all came back to her every time she went to a hospital. This trip was necessary though. She had come to Wheaton, Illinois to track down the man that Richard Farmer had met with. The local NSF had reported that someone had assaulted four members of an SE team, killing one and putting two in the hospital. It was the kind of coincidence that caught her attention. While she did not hold Social Enforcers with any professional degree of respect, she also had to acknowledge that it was rare that someone could take down so many of them. *Who was their target?* That was the question that compelled her the most. She needed a connection to Richard Farmer, and now there was an incident with a botched SE operation.

She stood over the hospital bed and looked at the man before her. His face had several lacerations, with stitches holding pieces of his chubby cheeks together. His head was badly bruised, as was his right eye. He had suffered a concussion and a fracture of his skull—the result of his face being put through the window of a car door. Caylee tried to summon a smile, but failed miserably. "So then Mister Larson, how many people attacked your team?"

"Two, maybe three," he said. "It was hard to tell. It all happened pretty fast. They came at us all at once."

"I see," she said calmly, pulling out her phone. "Perhaps you can explain why the footage only showed one attacker that actually engaged with your team?" She hit the play arrow and the footage showed a short female slamming his head through the car window. The woman was a professional. Caylee had studied her moves and that much was obvious. She stopped the footage when the one victim was hit through the leg and foot.

"Well, I mean—"

"I get it, Mister Larson, you got your ass handed to you by a woman that you grossly underestimated. Your frail little male ego couldn't handle the fact that she got the better of your team almost single-handedly. It helped to tell your buddies in SE that you got taken out by a number of attackers to make up for your own failings and mistakes. After all, you wouldn't want them to think you are less of a man, would you?"

"That's not it. I—"

"You've already lied to the initial NSF officers in your report Mister Larson. You know that filing a false report is a federal crime. You could be facing some serious time in jail. I'm sure those scars on your face will turn off some of the men there, but most of them don't care about your face. They are interested in other parts of your body."

His face reddened; she knew she had struck pay dirt. Men could be big and tough all day long. They loved putting up a rugged exterior. Mention prison and the possibilities and horrors there, most would crumble... especially someone as doughy as Larson. "Look. I'm sorry. I may have been mistaken. It all happened so fast."

"Who was the female?" she asked in a sterner tone of voice.

"We don't know. We didn't think our target was working with anyone. We had tossed his place. The guy was a nobody. She came at us like a fucking ninja."

Caylee could not argue against that. *What that means is that they underestimated their target.* "Tell me about the man, the one you were trying to pick up?"

"Forrest? The guy's dad was in the SOL back in the day. His sister is a District Director for the Midwest. We were told that his old man gave him something, something that we needed to recover."

"What was it?"

He shook his head against the pillow. "We don't know. We were told we would probably know it when we saw it. His old man died a while back. We trashed his place, nada. So, we went for his apartment, but we got nothing. His PC had nothing on it of use—our guys scoured the drive. When he showed up, we thought we should take him in. You know, a little kick-in-the-crotch interrogation. He bolted but we cornered him. Then *she* showed up."

"Forrest's full name?"

"Andrew Jackson Forrest," Larson said.

Andrew Jackson... with that name combo he would have ended up on an SE list no matter what. President Jackson had owned slaves. Part of the purge that took place was the removal of such names in public, and private. Individuals like Forrest would have received an "encouragement" letter about the risks of living with that name—a threat. "I will want a copy of his file," she said flatly.

"We don't… I mean, the SE doesn't share our intel with the NSF."

Caylee flashed a fake smile, if only for a moment. "That is true, normally. But this isn't normal. You lied to our officer when you called for us to come in and help you out after you got your asses ambushed. Since we got pulled in, that makes this an official NSF investigation. Neither of us wants you flagged for falsifying testimony, so you are going to provide me your file on this Andrew Forrest."

"I'm going to need to talk to my superiors. I mean, I need permission for this sort of thing."

"No, you are not going to ask permission. We are way past that Mister Larson. I need that data to catch this female and your Mister Forrest. You will shoot me the data, or this plays out as follows: I will slap the cuffs on you right now. I will make sure your data gets buried, so that you can spend a few nights in jail before they put you on the street again. You will need to hire an attorney; I'm sure you mom will front you the money. This will drag out for a long time. I hear that the SE tosses liabilities, and that is what I will turn you into. A former SE has a hard time out there without cover. You've probably stepped on a lot of toes over the years, roughed up some people that will love to hear you are on the street without protection. Oh, and when this is over, you *will* be going to jail. Or you shoot me the damned file. In reality, the choice is simple, but yours to make."

Larson nodded. She handed him her phone so he could log in. His chubby little fingers shook nervously as he keyed in his access. It took a full two minutes for him to dump the data to his phone. She tried to copy the information to the NSFCloud, but got a string of error messages. *I must have some sort of a signal issue.*

"You see," she said taking the device back and checking to see if the material was there. "Now then, where is this PC you recovered?"

"In our evidence locker," he said. "You can't get in there. I mean, our district office has pretty tight security. Besides, like I said, it was wiped."

The SE didn't have the kinds of tech resources that Caylee did in the

NSF. "I understand. I was just curious."

"I don't want any trouble," he said, almost pleading.

"Your name will likely never appear in my report Mister Larsen. Needless to say, telling anyone about this would not be a prudent move on your part."

"Don't worry," he gulped. "I don't want to talk about this ever again."

"That's the spirit," she said. Caylee saw him for what he was, pathetic and weak. The Social Enforcers were a mix of high school bullies and pitiful punks that wanted to *be* bullies. The SE gave them a feeling of protection and power, a dangerous mix with those of weak hearts or minds. Larson would never talk about their conversation because, deep down, he was afraid. The same organization that gave him power would sell him out in a heartbeat, and he knew that. He would go from enforcement to target. That was how they worked. It was a dysfunctional organization that lured in the weak and made them strong. She did not even offer him a wish of getting better because she didn't care if he healed or recovered.

Larson might talk to his superiors, thinking it would help him. It didn't matter to Caylee. She had his data.

Chicago, Illinois

The Greater Chicago Social Enforcement branch was headquartered in a building on Ogden Avenue in what had been a police precinct building before the Liberation. The brick building had been one of those overrun by protesters and taken over later by the SE. Once the dust had settled, they had done a fairly crappy job of maintaining the structure. The once-well-groomed flower planters had overgrown into a nest of weeds. Spray-painted BLM and other tags had never been fully removed and still showed. They had taken the precinct over, but had not taken over responsibility for maintaining the building.

Caylee watched people coming and going from the building for a day. There didn't seem to be any real security per se. She had come up with two plans for getting Andrew Forrest's PC. One was to infiltrate the building. Normally she would have pulled up the plans, but there were issues with the NSFCloud, a problem with a data center. She couldn't get a straight answer, but from the sound of it, the NSFCloud was going to be inaccessible for a while. That meant going in blind. That didn't intimidate her, but it was a complication.

The other option was to go in and ask for the PC. With the right amount of bravado and some character acting on her part, it should be easy. Counting on their incompetence, she went with that plan. Donning a black shirt and black jeans, he made sure her firm cleavage was showing enough to distract anyone from remembering too many other details about her appearance. She then walked in as if she belonged there, going up to the front desk.

"Hi—I'm Meredith from Regional," she said with her best Midwestern accent.

"Hi," the skinny twenty-something kid behind the desk replied. "Can I help you?"

"I was sent to pick up a PC—the violator's name was Andrew Forrest."

"Do you have a case reference number?"

She shook her head. "No, they just told me to come down and get it. I honestly thought you'd have it up here waiting for me."

The black-shirted kid looked around under the desk. "Sorry, I don't have anything."

"Great," Caylee replied, rolling her eyes. "I drove for four hours from Indy to get here and now I have to go back without it. They are going to ream me when I get back." It was, as she referred to it, her damsel-in-distress persona.

"Well, I guess I could go back and see if I can find it," he said.

"Could you? That would be fantastic," she said.

"Give me a minute," he said taking off for the bowels of the dimly lit building. She knew the risks. Someone might call Indianapolis and be told they didn't send anyone. That was easy to bluff past too, she was prepared. One thing she relied on was the incompetency of any bureaucracy, and the Social Enforcers were laden with a poorly run one. After a few minutes, the young man came back with a PC in his arms. "Sorry it took so long; it is a mess back there sometimes."

"Oh, I know; you should see our evidence cage," she said. "Do you need to have me sign for it?"

He fumbled, looking for the right ledger. "Yeah, if you don't mind."

He looked at the evidence tag on the PC and jotted it down. Caylee signed as Meredith with a false ID number. "You're great," she said to him as she grabbed the PC. "Next time I'm up, maybe we could grab something to eat."

He got up and opened the door for her. "That would be great Meredith," he said grinning broadly.

She got the PC strapped into the passenger seat of her car and took off, knowing that it was likely that they would never figure out what had happened to their precious evidence.

CHAPTER 13

"Truth is more tangible than facts."

Detroit, Michigan

hree days had passed since the arson destruction of their Bobcat excavator. Raul found himself constantly pausing during his work, looking around for any sign of the attackers. Their last attack had been done near the end of the day, but in broad daylight. They were not afraid of the troop, that much was clear. Ufray joked that Raul was being overly paranoid, that these were bullies and little more. Still, he was nervous. At night, he slept with a club he had made from a scrap piece of lumber that had been salvaged. The others in the troops did the same thing, including Ufray.

The troop leader had tried to engage the National Support Force police, but it seemed like a waste of time. They came out, looked at the fire damage, and gave him a report for insurance purposes. When one of the troops asked him if they would take action, Winston shook his head. "They said we didn't see anyone do it, so all we have is speculation."

Paco had the cot next to him. "If the NSF is not going to do anything, we should leave," he said.

Raul winced. "Our work is nearly done. In a few weeks we will be moved, maybe away from Detroit altogether. We have done good work here on this reclamation. I would hate for us to go before we are done."

Paco pointed to the scar on his head. "You would feel differently if you had experienced these people the way I did." It was hard to argue against that point.

"The troop leader has told national about this. If they felt we were in danger, they would have pulled us out."

"These enforcers," Paco said. "They are not going to rest until we are gone or dead."

Raul struggled with the thought that these were from the same organization he knew back home. Social Enforcers back in Alvarado had done a great deal of good. They protected citizens from the cartels bringing their drugs in. They had been active in the community. When someone stepped out of line, they did not use brute force, but protests and gentle persuasion. That wasn't the case here in Detroit.

"They are religious people, but resort to violence," he said, laying his head on the small pillow on his cot, looking over at Paco a few feet away. "It makes no sense. Father Ryan preaches the gospels. I have talked to him about it and their Allah follows many of the same teachings as Christ. This group is different."

"We have to be prepared," Paco said, pulling out his club just enough for Raul to see it. "The world is full of people that don't think the way we do."

Raul drifted off to sleep. A noise jolted him awake. He sat up, then fumbled under his blanket for the handle of his club. Paco was already on his feet, armed and crouching. It was dark and the sounds were those of loud voices. There were several people talking—no, yelling at each other. He could hear Troop Leader Winston's voice. As he slid on his work boots, the others of the troops began to wake up.

One irate voice rang out louder than the rest, a deep booming voice with an accent that seemed Middle Eastern. "You are to leave… tonight!"

The voices seemed to be coming from the area of the old factory parking lot outside, and from the light coming from there, several cars must have pulled up. The young troop members were drawn to the light like moths to a flame.

"Please," Winston said. "I understand your concerns. I was a social justice warrior myself. We can work this out."

"You are *nothing* like us," the voice roared. Raul moved closer, finally coming to a half-removed wall. From there, he could see the group. There were six of them, male, older than the young men and women of the Youth Corps. They wore light brown and tan robes, which seemed to shimmer almost white in the headlights of the three cars that had pulled in. All of the men were bearded, dark skinned, and from what he could see of their faces, furious.

"We will be out of here soon," the troop leader pleaded.

"You will leave now," the leader of the SE group said, closing the distance between the two of them. "You will leave or we will make you."

Raul moved with the rest of the troop alongside of Winston, which prompted the SEs to close the gap as well. They were so close that Raul could smell the men across from him. They reeked of some spice, some food, something he was unfamiliar with. It was not body odor, or if it was, it was from something he had eaten, pungent and foreign to his nostrils.

Looking at the man in front of him, he saw the raw anger in his face. His black beard glistened with sweat, his eyes were wide, his brow wrinkled. Raul clenched the club in his hand tight. Glancing over at Winston, he saw something he had not seen before with the troop leader… fear.

"We have just a little work to complete; then we will move on," he said calmly.

The larger man across from the troop leader responded with a violent shove, which pushed Winston back three feet. "You leave tonight, all of you!" his dark eyes swept the Youth Corps workers.

Winston rallied and resumed his place. "We have every right to be here. The FedGov sent us here."

"You have only the rights we give you!" the leader of the party said. "You are infidels. You have ignored our warnings. There is a price for such arrogance."

Raul was two people down from Winston. The dark man reached down into his robe and pulled out a gun. In that moment, everything seemed to speed up for Raul. He saw the gun and saw the flash. Everything became a blur as the troop leader was knocked backwards. Raul sprang for the extended arm with the gun as the two lines of people collided with each other. Paco, next to him and between him and the man with the gun charged forward, using his club like a battering ram on the stomach of the man in front of him.

Raul went past Paco and swung his club up over his head and

down at the extended arm with the gun. He hit it just at the elbow and heard a cracking sound of breaking bones. The man lost his grip on the gun, dropping it, grunting in pain. On his backswing, Raul caught his opponent's cheek with the club, twisting his head hard to the side.

Sounds jumbled in his ears as he dove for the gun. He had never held one before and it was heavier than he expected. He turned to the man that had shot the troop leader and used both hands to steady the weapon. Jerking the trigger, the gun roared and the larger man flew back, blood spraying like a mist in the headlights of their vehicles. The gun kicked hard, harder than he had imagined, almost flying from his hand.

Raul did not think, he acted. The man Paco had hit slammed his friend with a brick on the side of his head. Raul swung the gun around and fired again. This time he controlled the kick of the weapon as the bullet hit the man in the neck, dropping him instantly. He wheeled again at one of the robed men wielding a piece of pipe and fired, missing.

It seemed in that instant that every eye fell on him and the gun. The robed men seemed to realize that things had turned, and they dove for cover, running towards their vehicles. Raul turned to one car and fired between the headlights that glared at him. He heard a 'thwack' of the bullet on the windshield and the strange Arabic shouts of the men as they climbed into the cars. He didn't know what to do; he simply pointed the pistol in their direction and kept squeezing the trigger. A ricochet snapped and zinged as he fired. Raul fired over and over, until the gun stopped firing.

The cars roared away, burning rubber in the night. Trembling, he lowered the gun and looked around. Three of the Youth Corps were down. Two of the attackers lay dead; their robes were soaked in blood. The head of the one he hit in the neck was twisted at a strange angle, its mouth open as if it were screaming into the darkness. *What have I done?* His entire body quaked and he felt like he was going to vomit.

Paco got up, blood flowing from where he had been hit in his hair. His friend moved to the fallen form of the troop leader, and Raul followed. Avalon Winston was pale and shaking, his eyes unable to focus, looking up at the stars. His stomach had been hit with the bullet that had started the brawl, and his yellow t-shirt bearing the logo of the Youth Corps was soaked crimson with gore. Raul knelt next to him, the gun still in his right hand. As he glanced down at it, he saw tiny droplets of blood on the gun and his wrist.

"I don't understand…" Winston said. "I was one of them… this can't happen to me. We were going to leave. We were on the same side—"

Then his shaking stopped. His eyes did not close, but stared off into the night.

Raul felt the tears run down his cheeks and he sniffled slightly. Somehow, he rose to his feet and all the eyes of the troop fell on him. "They will come back," Julian said. "We should call for the NSF."

"Man," Paco said, glancing down at the gun still in his hands. "You didn't have a choice. They would have killed us all."

Raul looked at the gun. He wanted to drop it, but couldn't. It was as if it were attached to his hand. His mind was racing with thoughts. *How would I explain to my mother what happened? They will arrest me. I have committed a sin!*

The last one registered with him… *Father Ryan.* He would understand. Raul turned to Paco. "It isn't safe here. We need to go to the church. The padre will protect us. We can call the NSF from there."

Chicago, Illinois

It was late at night at the NSF Chicago Field Office. Caylee hovered behind Andersen Bane, the tech working on the hard drive she had brought in. In many respects, he was the antithesis of her. Where she was a honed weapon, he was a geek. He had thick glasses and a wiry frame that told her he would not last more than a few minutes in a fight—if he had ever actually been in one. When she had flashed her badge at him, he actually took a moment to study it before reluctantly agreeing to work late. He had kept the office dark, which was fine by her. Only a lone desk lamp and the white light from the massive array of three monitors provided an illumination.

The SEs had not found anything on Andrew Forrest's hard drive, but they were not the NSF. They had said it had been wiped. You didn't try and nuke a hard drive unless you were hiding something. From what she had been told by the Special Agent in Charge in Chicago, Bane was their best cyber-tech.

"Got it," he said. "Your perp was pretty good. He used a proprietary tool to scramble his drive. Those are hard to pop; I mean there are lot of them and each does it a different way. So, what I did was run a level three deconstruct algorithm that assumed that he—"

She cut him off. "I honestly don't care how you did it, Mister Bane. What have you found?"

He shrugged. "Well, not a lot. There's files here, but most are related to his job and are old."

"His browser history?"

"Well, he's not into porn, which frankly is a relief," Andersen said. "I had this guy a few weeks ago that had to have had the biggest collection of horse-porn I have—"

"What did he search for in the last two weeks?" she said, cutting him off again.

"Right," Bane replied, squinting at his screen and leaning towards it slightly. His fingers danced on the keyboard as he read the data in the monitor. "Not a lot really. He hit some job sites, did some searches for open consultant positions. I can pull them up if you want."

"No," she said, leaning towards the screen herself. "What else have you got?"

For a moment, Andersen said nothing as his eyes processed the stream of words in front of him. "Hmm, that's odd."

"What do you have?"

He pointed at a line on the screen. "He ran a search for Mount Rushmore."

That was odd. References to the location had been purged from the web by the alliance of tech companies that had supported the Liberation. It had been deemed a discretion and had been destroyed, the land returned to the native tribes in the region. All that the world ever was allowed to see of the sight was the demolition of the faces of the tainted Presidents there. It had been a half-assed use of explosives but it sent a clear message—the icons of the past were no longer permitted.

"I thought you couldn't search for that?"

"True," Bane replied. "But he looked up where it was located—not a search on Mount Rushmore itself."

"When was the date?" Bane rattled it off. *Two days after Famer and Forrest met in front of the CVS.*

"Does that mean anything to you Operative Leatrom?"

I was in Brookings, South Dakota with Richard Farmer. This is not the case of Forrest looking up this man—they had already met. There was only one good reason to look up a location that was banned. "Yes," Caylee replied. "It is telling me where I have to go next."

She patted Bane on the shoulder. "Good work."

"Thanks," he replied.

If Forrest is heading for South Dakota, so am I.

Detroit, Michigan

Raul and the rest of the troop arrived at the old Catholic church out of breath from running. They had called the NSF, but then fled, fearing that their attackers might return. Raul ran up the wide steps and banged on the door of the church. He waited, but heard nothing for a minute. Then he pounded again.

The door opened and Father Ryan filled the doorway. "Raul, what is the meaning of this?"

"We need your help."

The priest looked out at the small gathering of young people and motioned for them to come in. He closed the door of the church, sliding the deadbolt in place. "Raul, what happened?'

For a moment, Raul hesitated. He deeply respected the priest, and feared that his actions might ruin that relationship. Reaching into his jean's beltline, he pulled out the gun and handed it to Father Ryan. "We were attacked. They killed our troop leader. We fought with them. I took the gun from one of them… Father… I shot two of them." Tears streamed down his face as he spoke.

Ryan looked at him, taking the gun and setting it on the nearest pew. He then hugged Raul. "Do not worry my son."

"I killed them Father," he sobbed.

"What you did was self-defense," Ryan said, releasing him and setting him down on the pew as the others huddled in around them. He looked around at them. "Some of you are hurt. There is a first aid kit in the rectory, through that door," he pointed, "down the hall to the right. Get cleaned up."

"What do I do Father?" Raul asked as half of the troop left.

"Raul, did you start this? Did you provoke this?"

He shook his head, wiping his nose on his sleeve. "No. We had clubs, but they attacked us first."

Father Ryan nodded. "It will be your word against theirs," he said firmly. "And they are social enforcers. I know these people—they have been attempting to inflict their Sharia law in our neighborhoods. It won't take them long to figure out where you have gone."

Raul looked around the church. It seemed so big, so empty. How can we possibly be safe here? "We should move then. They shouldn't bring violence to a place of worship."

"Where can you go, if not here?" the priest asked. "Is there anyone you can call in the Youth Corps?"

"I don't know," Raul shook his head. The only one that dealt with the Youth Corps leadership was Avalon Winston, and he lay dead in a parking lot. The loneliness crept in even more.

"I will try and reach out to them, see if they can help. In the meantime, you will remain here. I will grant you sanctuary. You will be under my protection and that of the Holy Mother."

Raul was thankful, but afraid. "Father, these men, they will not respect this place or you. If they come, they come with hate and guns."

Father Ryan only smiled. "The Book of Peter tells us that the good shepherd is one that protects his flock. You are my flock, and I am your overseer; I am your example. I will protect you my son, all of you," he said sweeping the small gathering that had come with Raul. "Your safety is my responsibility. You shall have sanctuary in these walls."

Raul felt a surge of relief in that moment. "What will happen now Father?"

"Violence," Ryan said with resolve in his voice. "They have mastered it well. For now, we are safe here. They would not suspect you coming here. They will lash out; it is the way of the SE."

"I feel terrible," Raul moaned.

"God tests us Raul," the father said. "He only gives us tests that he knows we have the strength to overcome. Everything is part of the Lord's plan. He would not have given you this burden if he did not think you strong enough to overcome it."

Raul said nothing in response but gave a nervous nod. *My whole life is changed now. I never should have pulled that trigger. If they find me, they will kill me, just as they did with Avalon. If this is part of God's plan, I wish I understood it.*

CHAPTER 14

"Comfort Equals Compliance."

Keystone, South Dakota

Charli climbed down from the semi-truck rig, Andy right behind her. "Thanks for the lift," she said. The evening air was brisk, not biting as it had been in the winter. The sunset over the Black Hills was earlier than she had expected. In the distance Charli could make out thin purple streaks of clouds on the western horizon, just above the orange sky of the setting sun.

"You know," the driver called back. "They've got a shower in there if you want to get cleaned up." He nodded in the direction of the truck stop.

Keystone was a wide spot on the road. When Mount Rushmore had been a tourist spot, the town had thrived. Now many of the businesses were boarded up, with graffiti spray-painted on the weathered plywood. Adding to the economic misery was the shutdown of the Keystone XL pipeline right after the Fall. Outside of town there were lots filled with rusting construction equipment and construction metal. The Ruling Council felt that it was better for the environment to shut down the pipeline, putting thousands without jobs. It had been a crushing blow to towns like Keystone.

The Keystone Truck Stop was a two-story building with a vast parking lot. Only two tractor-trailers were parked there. Charli understood the hint he was giving them. They had been living in the same clothing for several days. She couldn't detect their body odor, but others probably couldn't ignore it. "Thanks," she offered. The trucker, named Dale, headed in while she and Andy waited outside in the cool evening air.

"You think he's trying to tell us something?" Andy said with a bit of sarcasm.

"I think we may be a little ripe." Her trained eyes swept the outside of the truck stop for cameras. They were there, but older models. Given the isolated location, there was a good chance they would not be wired up to the net for monitoring by the NSF. *I hate taking the risk of being spotted, but we need to get some food and get cleaned up.* "I think this place may be safe," Charli said leading the way in.

Once inside she motioned to the single shower area. Pulling some clothing from her backpack, she motioned to the shopping area. "I'll get cleaned up first. You go and get us some clothing. No credit cards. Pay cash only." He nodded and left and she went into the shower.

The tiles were yellowish by design. The bamboo mat was designed to keep you from slipping but had a slick feel to it. It didn't matter as the warm water flowed over her. There were pump dispensers for some sort of shampoo and soap, which she embraced. She had grabbed a towel from the pile and dried herself and the shower, per the small sign on the outside of the shower. When she reached the lower right side of her torso, she came across the scar from the bullet she had taken. The bullet hole itself had a scab of dry skin on it and she felt behind her where the incision had been made. It was a reminder of the worst night of her life, and every time she touched, it the memories rushed forward again.

Charli paused to rinse out her underwear, wring it tightly and wrap it in a paper towel to dry as much as possible. Her sweat pants were old from when she had been posing as an NSF officer, Angel Frisosky. They were dark blue with a faded white NSF logo on the right thigh. A shower and change of clothing felt great. She slid one of her two handguns into the sweatband of the pants, letting her shirt fall over it. Her hoodie, while dirty, would still have to suffice for the time being.

Their journey across the country had been slow but careful. They would be looking for Andy after the incident in Illinois. The judicious use of rail cars and hitchhiking helped keep him off the grid. The SEs and NSF would be looking for her too by now, but that didn't worry her. *I've been able to avoid them up to this point.*

Charli's life had been one of avoiding people. She only socialized enough to avoid raising suspicion since the Fall. Every conversation with her had been careful and calculated. *I knew something they didn't—what happened to the President after the White House fell. If they were willing to fake his death; my murder would be a cake walk.*

Andy was different. He had engaged her in conversation, or at least tried to. Years of living in the shadows had taught her to shut down such efforts. Bit by bit he was getting her to talk. It felt good to Charli, somehow right. Andy was a normal person who had led a normal life. Now he was caught up in something way over his head. *I knew what I was signing up for in the Secret Service. This poor guy just had his father die and his whole world came down around him.* Charli didn't feel sorry for him; she merely appreciated his situation.

As she tossed the wet towels into the bin, she ran a brush through her hair, which fought back with vigor despite its short length. This mission had not turned out at all like she had expected. *I thought I was getting a milk run, something easy. Instead, I have had to take down an SE team and extract someone from a hostile situation. Now I'm off on some sort of Indiana Jones thing, and neither of us knows what we are looking for.*

Jack Desmond owed her for this and for everything else. He would deliver too. While she had her secrets from the night of the Fall, Jack's were more public. They had gone after law enforcement's families during the Fall. ANTIFA and its now SE-thugs thought it was a great way to pressure officers to stand down. It worked in many cases. In some cases, it was simple slaughter of innocent people. *When this is over, he promised to introduce me to the successor... he owes me that much.*

Walking through the small truck stop, she came to Andy who had a pair of overpriced generic blue jeans for her. "I guessed on the size," he said. She looked at them. "Not bad. I will roll up the legs and cuff them." He had a bulky sweatshirt for her as well as a fresh t-shirt, which she stuffed into her backpack. "My turn," he said walking to the back of the restaurant.

Charli checked the eating area. Two other people were there, sitting at a counter that had probably been there for decades. There weren't any visible cameras, but that didn't mean she was safe. The ancient waitress came over and asked what she wanted to drink. She went with water rather than anything containing caffeine. They had a long hike ahead of them.

The waitress brought over the check. Caylee eyed it and asked, "Is cash okay?"

She smiled. "We still take cash," she said. Since the pandemic, the government and business had been pushing people to use credit cards for even the most mundane purchases. Myths were spun up about a shortage of coins, a shortage of bills, but in reality, it was a means of tracking people and everything they purchased. Big Tech had encouraged this and used the data to feed the FedGov. In some cities, cash had been banned, but was still accepted and such purchases were treated as black market by the NSF. Caylee didn't want to have to use one of her many stolen credit cards if she didn't have to. *The less to trace the better.* She handed her two Obama's, forty dollars, which just covered the inflationary price of their meal.

Andy returned in a few minutes, shaven, his hair still wet. They ordered breakfast for dinner and sat for a long time saying nothing. When the food came Andy devoured his meal; she ate slowly, choosing to savor every bite. He finally shattered the silence. "Is this normal?"

"What?"

"This," he gestured with his eyes, sweeping the room. "I was a consultant. I traveled a lot. I certainly never ended up in a place like this. Is this how you have been living since, well, you know?"

Charli smiled slightly. "You were raised in a bubble, Andy. But for what it's worth, we all were. No, I didn't live in places like this," she said, sweeping the diner with her eyes to make sure no one was in earshot. "I had to adopt new identities, take on new jobs. We had a set of pristine false IDs ready for this kind of thing, but none of us expected to ever have to use them. I chose to be a fugitive that was hiding in plain sight. For a long time, until I got sucked back into this, I was working in the NSF as an officer."

"They didn't find you?" She could see the look of amazement on his face.

"Like I said, I hid where they never thought to look—in their own ranks. Hiding in plain sight is sometimes the best move." There was a hint of pride in what she accomplished; Charli was not ashamed of it.

"That had to be hard on you. When they federalized law enforcement the way they did. These were organizations you worked with, I presume. They had become the strong arm for the Ruling Council."

"That was easier than the crap they pulled up to that point," Charli said, taking another small bite of her pancake. "The media barely covered it, but the mobs came after our families. It was a form of extortion—"Do what we say or your loved ones get killed." There were a lot of murders of law enforcement friends and relatives to pressure them to stand down."

"I remember bits and pieces of that," he said, resting his elbows on the table. "The reporters made it sound like it was a few isolated incidents."

"That's because that played to their narrative," she replied. "They wanted the rioters and the anarchists to come across as peaceful. That's why you didn't see much footage of them dragging Secret Service people out of the White House and shooting them in the heads. It happened, but the media gave the people a story that wouldn't upset them, one that made the mobs look like innocent protesters."

Andy leaned back. "My dad talked to me about this, but I was in denial, I guess. I was so focused on him being sent off to a Social Quarantine Camp; I didn't think about the big picture."

"That's how they worked," Charli said as she used her fork to play with a small bit of pancake that she pushed around on the plate. "We lost sight of the big picture. We were told so much disinformation that it was impossible to know what was real and what was fake news."

Andy paused for a moment, taking a long sip of water. "They said my dad died of cancer. I know that is what killed his body. I was there. I also know that the SEs took something from him in that camp. He wasn't the same when he came back. They took a bit of his soul there. They had done things to him. He never got to see this through, whatever it was. He was not the same man that left. I like to think he wanted me to go and find this thing he hid."

"He gave you no idea what it was?"

"None. He told me that a friend of his, an Abel Brummer, got it out of DC the night of the Fall. I tried to look the guy up, but he died three years ago. He worked in the FedGov, I know that much. Whatever it was, Dad thought it important enough to hide in the most obscure place on the planet."

Charli wondered what it could be as well, and as much as she had a good imagination, it was hard to picture what it was. "Well, we are going to a forbidden place. Since they trashed the monument, the area has been banned. I guess the administration doesn't like it when people post pictures of their dirty deeds. The monument was a symbol for a lot of people. When they broadcast the destruction, it led to counter-rioting. All that did was give them an excuse to round up anyone they tagged as undesirable. Still, they have patrols up there, Native Americans. I'm guessing they have cameras, good electronic security too. It will be a slow go once we get close."

"Our target is behind Lincoln's head," Andy said. There was supposed to be a vault built there; they called it the Hall of Records. They tunneled out a lot of it, but never finished the job. Dad and Mister Farmer buried the package in the back of the tunnel chamber and piled up debris to block the entrance."

"We'll need gloves," she said. "Water—some protein bars, and blankets. If we can get some nylon rope, that might help. I want a can of spray paint too. If we get caught, we can always claim we were up there to graffiti the place."

"We should be able to get that stuff easily. How do we get near the site?"

Charli held up her thumb. "We'll hitch a ride and bail a ways from the monument site. It's a long haul up there. Unfortunately, I don't have a map. They have taken all of that stuff off the web, to discourage people from sneaking up there."

Andy nodded. "Let me try." He waved for the old waitress. She came over and flashed a fake grin. "What do you need, honey?"

"Isn't this place pretty close to where Mount Rushmore used to be?" he asked innocently.

She nodded. "The place is banned now though... a federal felony charge if they catch you up there."

"Oh, I don't want to go up," Andy said. "The last thing I need is trouble with the NSF. I just couldn't find anything on the web about the place, not even a map or a picture. I was curious. My dad went there before it came down and I wondered how big the park was back then."

"I have a whole bunch of the National Parks Service brochures on the place tucked away in the office. They had a map on the back of them. The Park Service made me take them down after they blew up the damn place. I didn't have the heart to toss them. Let me go and grab you one."

"Thank you *so* much," Andy said as she left. He looked over at Charli and his grin widened.

"You know Andy, you might just have a taste for this kind of life," she said.

Palo-Alto, California

Jack Desmond watched as the Palo-Alto NSF bomb squad approached the heavy-duty vehicle at the start of their morning shift. He was on top of a building almost two blocks away, squinting through the binoculars as they got near it. He hated the thought of killing or injuring law enforcement officers, but tempered that thought with what they were now, the strong arm of the FedGov. These were no longer his comrades in arms, his brothers and sisters. They had been turned into a modern-day Gestapo. The NSF enforced the will of the Ruling Council, just as much as the SEs did.

As the bomb squad got close to the vehicle, one member noticed the spray-painted tag one of his people had put on the rear of the big van. SE Rulez! He could see a female officer pointing to it and the others looking at it, one shaking his head. It was at the start of their shift and he knew they were going to have to report it. He couldn't hear them, but in his mind, he could hear the complaining over the paperwork that the graffiti would cause them. The graffiti was useful. When the job was over, it would drive yet another wedge between the SE and the NSF. Misdirection. It was the key to any good operation.

The bomb had been planted in the middle of the night, courtesy of former Navy SEAL, Travis Cullen. The defunding of the police only paid for the bomb squad during the daylight hours. They had cut back on their parking expenses by parking police vehicles on the street behind the station. Jack had driven a truck next to the vehicle and parked for less than three minutes. One of his people had dropped out of the truck from a hatch he had put there, planted the bomb, and had never even been seen. Later that night, another volunteer had done the tagging.

One of the officers led a German Shepherd on a leash, letting the dog into the back of the truck. Oddly, the thought that the dog was going to die hurt Jack more than the deaths of the officers. He and his family had a dog years ago. To Jack, the dog was as much a part of his family as he was. *They took Pepper away from me during the Fall. They took everything away from me.* His mind conjured up the smell of burnt fur and a wave of emotion swept over him. He considered, for just a moment, not setting the device off. He knew he had to though.

As the officers climbed into the truck, Jack held the detonator in his hand and squeezed the trigger. There was a flash, and a moment later a 'whomp' as the vehicle filled with flames, blasting out the windows and raining glass on the street. A black ball of smoke rose skyward and opened up like a flower, spreading out.

One of the officers tumbled out of the vehicle, on fire, but alive enough to roll on the ground. Nearby officers coming out of the station rushed over, desperately trying to help the officer. Jack knew if he had planted a second bomb, he could have taken out a lot more of the NSF officers, but that was not the plan. *We only need to hamstring their ability to search for a bomb. We are not at war, not yet.*

He gathered himself, dusting the dirt from the rooftop. He made his way to the far corner of the building he had used for his perch and began to climb down. The fire department sirens blared more loudly as they grew closer. When he reached the ground, Jack got into one of the cars his team had appropriated and took off. A tear ran down his cheek as he thought about the death of the dog.

The District

The Secretary of the NSF scrolled through the list that she had ordered compiled. One hundred and eighty-eight names. Each name was one of the key leaders of Social Enforcement. These were the true leaders, the most vocal commanders of SE. Removing the 188 people would cripple the organization from the top down. The organization would be gutted, weak, vulnerable. *Mine for the taking.* Looking at the list it seemed so simple. Kill the people on this list and the SE would be paralyzed. She could assume command and roll them into her NSF. *No more competing for resources, no more competing, no more working against each other.* The efficiency was appealing. The increase of her power was seductive.

I will control an army that rivals the military.

And all that stood between her and that power was 188 names on a list.

It was a pitifully easy decision for her, one she had made long before the list had been compiled. The continuation of the SE as an entity would eventually lead to internal strife. The SE and NSF had been sparring for years. Now, fueled by the Sons of Liberty, the two organizations were clashing everywhere. Despite the media keeping a lid on some of the incidents, word spread. SE squads had assaulted her officers in six states. She had not shackled her NSF in retaliating. If anything, the SOL was helping her, escalating the strife between the organizations.

Of course, there were those on the Ruling Council that would call her out for her blatant power grab. They would be worried about what the public might think. Others might fear that with that kind of power, she could control the council. In her mind, that had been one of the downfalls of the Liberation, the formation of the Ruling Council. So many voices, so much internal bickering. Every little faction wanted to be heard, considered, acknowledged. She would smooth the debate by leveraging the information she had gathered on the council members. Having access to their data, their searches on the internet, who they met with, surveillance audio and video recordings, it was easy to assemble blackmailable material for more than half. Ultimately, she was sure she could assure their rubber-stamping the downfall of the SE.

Timing would be critical as well. It would be better to do it right before the fifth anniversary celebrations. The Council would not want anything to disrupt the celebration, and would be more likely to downplay the change of leadership.

There were risks; every good plan had them. The recent sightings of the Traitor-President made her nervous. There was always a risk that he was still alive, but in over four years, no one had found a trace of him. Suddenly he had appeared twice on surveillance vids. If anyone from the old chain of command was still alive, it would be a risk. The Speaker of the House had tried to join the revolt during the Liberation at the last minute, only to find herself beaten to death by the mob that stormed the Capitol. There had been some sweet justice in that for the Secretary, the two of them rarely agreed on anything. The traitor's Secretary of

State had been killed in his house when liberators had overwhelmed his security. The Vice President had died in his limo, his charred remains verified by DNA tests.

She had one of her top operatives in pursuit of the ghost of the Traitor-President. Of course, they had to tell Caylee Leatrom that the President had not died in jail as the public believed. That had turned Leatrom into a liability. Once she completed the mission, another team would take her out. No loose ends. Too many people as it was knew that the traitor had not passed away in custody. Of course, once she had full control of the NSF and the SE, she could tie up those loose ends as well.

Everything was going exactly as she wanted. Now it was a matter of days, if not hours, before she had what she desired. With a new Constitutional Convention being announced on the fifth anniversary, her future would be cemented in history. Looking down at the list she couldn't help but smile. One-hundred-and-eighty-eight people stood between her and the destiny she knew she deserved. *It is far too easy...*

Her phone rang and she picked it up. "Madam Secretary," the voice of her Midwest Operations Director Daniel Fey, came over crisp and clear. "We have a *situation* in Detroit."

"What is it Derek?"

"Riots have broken out. Fairly substantial ones."

"I assume these are SE teams and not the general public," she replied curtly.

"Correct. There was some violence with a Youth Corps team... some SEs were killed. The details are sketchy at this point, some blurry phone footage of a kid with a gun shooting someone. It has gotten a bit out of hand. They have burned a neighborhood that was primarily Hispanic. The fundamentalists and the Chaldean SEs have gone on a rampage."

The Secretary paused, soaking in the information. *It really is a gift from heaven, proof that Ferraday can't control his people. I didn't even have to stage this incident. Douglas is serving it up to me on a platter. It's perfect.* "Well, we can't have innocent people losing their homes and businesses because of an unconfirmed incident, now can we?"

"No, Madam Secretary."

"Order your forces in to restore order."

"Madam," Fey said firmly. "Things are likely to get out of control.

Some of these groups are pretty heavily armed. I'm reluctant to send our people into a bloodbath."

"We can't have that," the Secretary she said smoothly. "Our people are authorized to use Level Five force but only if we are attacked or fired upon. I won't have our people slaughtered because the local SEs can't keep their people in line." It was partially true. She was counting on the SEs to start the violence. Level Five was the highest amount of force that could be applied. They had dropped the words, 'deadly force' long ago. Level Five was so much more appealing with the media and had tested well in focus groups.

"Very well. If this brews up more, we are going to need reinforcements," Fey added. "The Islamic community here is fairly large, the biggest outside of the Middle East."

"Pull in from Toledo and Cleveland if you have to," she said. "Whatever we have to do to preserve law and order."

"Understood," he replied. "Given the size of these protests though, I'm not sure Level Five is going to cut it."

"Understood," she said. *Let them have their fun. Let it look like the SEs can't control their own people.*

She lowered the receiver and grinned. *Even the timing is right. I don't need much more of a pretext to execute my plan.* Reaching over to the laptop, she shut down the list. *The price of 188 lives is nothing compared to the future of Newmerica.*

CHAPTER 15

*"Everyone is owed. Everyone has suffered.
Reparations set things right!"*

Plankinton, South Dakota

aylee pulled into the gas station and put her Green Deal! ration card in the reader so she could pump fuel. It was one of the few perks of working for the FedGov; you didn't have the tight rationing that the rest of Newmerica had to deal with.

The NSF scans had picked up an image that was an 82% match for Andrew Forrest. He had been seen in a truck stop in Keystone, South Dakota the day before. It was four hours away by car. It didn't take a rocket scientist for her to see that he was near the old Mount Rushmore site or the Black Hills. Further, he had an accomplice. Her face didn't come up on the queries, which made her fascinating to Caylee. *Why in the hell would they be going to Mount Rushmore?* It struck her as the perfect place for the SOL to assemble, a place representing America's twisted past, banned, isolated. *I'll start there, pull in resources as I need them.*

The small pickup that had been following her used the gas station across the street. She had noticed the tail about fifty miles ago but had taken no action. Whoever was following her was good. There were several times they drifted off, out of sight, and she had almost chalked the incident up to professional paranoia. Then, every so often, she would catch a glimpse of the vehicle in her rear-view mirror. The fact that they disappeared for thirty minutes at a time meant a drone was likely observing her as well. She eyed the old short-bed Ford, painted red with rusty quarter panels with a bit of respect. *They are discreet and well equipped; I will give them that much.*

The reflection of headlights behind them had shown two occupants to the vehicle. She did not directly look at them as they fueled up at the BP station across the street from her, but caught glimpses of them. A man and a woman, late twenties was her guess. The flannel shirts they wore over their faded t-shirts was a nice touch. Untucked, they could easily conceal a bulge that was a knife or gun. He wore a ball cap; she had her dishwater blonde hair pulled back in a short ponytail.

Caylee loved a good puzzle and this was one. Her first assumption was that she had somehow exposed herself to the SOL and that they were trailing her. It didn't seem likely; Leatrom was good at covering her trail. She wasn't sure where she had exposed her cover, but it was the option that made the most sense. The possible use of a drone showed some sophistication she wouldn't have expected from the SOL, but perhaps they had upped their game.

As she finished fueling, she accepted the realization that her tail had to be dealt with. There was no question of that in her mind. If it was the Sons of Liberty following her, she could flip the tables and capture them. Caylee realized that proceeding west on I-90 would not give her the proper environment to effect a capture. According to her GPS which she checked before starting the car, Old Highway 16 ran parallel to the interstate. It was rural with areas where she could exercise her skills without pesky civilian involvement.

She pulled out casually and made her way through the small town of Plankinton onto the two-lane highway. The area was flat—wide open space, with a dotting of trees every mile or so. On both sides of the road were ditches, less for water run off than for snow in the winter. She checked her rear-view mirror and could barely see the red truck, at least a mile back if not more.

Whoever they were, they were keeping their distance, avoiding suspicion. Twilight was setting in and the sun, partially hidden by the clouds, shimmered orange in her face as she switched to her sunglasses. Good, the sunlight will blind them a little as well. She carefully planned her next steps once she had put Plankinton many miles behind her.

She accelerated, gunning the engine as she came up over a long shallow rise in the ground. It was mostly to give her distance which, in her mind, gave her time. The contour of the road and her acceleration took her out of the line of sight with her pursuers. She jammed the brakes, skidding along the side of the road. Caylee angled the car towards the ditch, getting one tire right to the edge of the drainage ditch. In a fluid motion she opened her door, got out, slammed the door shut, and rolled across the road into the other ditch opposite of her car. It was muddy, but she ignored it, moving back down the road, towards Plankinton, crawling, her gun at the ready.

The truck came up fast and she was fairly certain that they had not seen her cross the road. Seeing her car at the edge of the ditch, with skid marks, the driver slowed down, pulling off the road. Both of them got out, both drew weapons and assumed a tactical stance, going low, making themselves smaller targets. These were not the actions of good Samaritans—confirming her suspicion that she was being tailed by people with harmful intent. Caylee instinctively knew what they were thinking. Had she lost control of the vehicle? Was she still inside? The drawn weapons meant they were suspicious but fully intended to finish the job, if it was indeed an accident.

The young male approached the vehicle from the roadside, keeping low, while his partner moved into the ditch. Both had their guns drawn, arms extended, like professionals. The male held up a hand and made a fist, then waved it to the left, a tactical signal for her to move along the front of the vehicle as he passed the back, angling for the driver's side door. *They are pros. Ex-military, maybe former police.*

Caylee had to even the odds, she knew that much. The male was the obvious choice. His partner was in a muddy ditch, limiting her movement, hemming her in. She rose just enough in the ditch to rest her arms on the ground, still concealed by the grass at the edge of the ditch. Taking careful aim, she fired. The shot hit him in the upper left chest. In a spray of crimson, he flew back. His face contorted in pain and he aimed his gun from the ground, firing three shots rapidly. Leatrom felt a sting on her left upper arm and her body tugged from the hit. She ignored the pain and aimed slowly, meticulously, and fired again, hitting him in the throat. It wasn't personal; this was a matter of life and death.

Glancing over she saw that the shot had grazed her, not bad—no artery—but the moment she saw it, the pain escalated. *This will have to wait. The job isn't done.*

Caylee kept low, her gun in front of her, gritting her teeth as her upper arm throbbed. *I know what she's thinking right now… 'oh fuck!' and 'where in the hell is she?'* From the ground level, she could see under her vehicle. Some of the view was obscured by the tires, but she could see through. With the sun setting, that would change soon, but Caylee had no intention of this standoff dragging on.

She saw the woman, huddled in front of the car on her knees. Without hesitation she aimed at the knees and fired two shots. There was a scream as the woman dropped all of the way into the ditch, out of her line of sight. "God damn it!" she cried. "Hold your fire." She threw her gun into the middle of the highway.

"You pull yourself out into the road," Caylee commanded.

"You shot my knee to shit!" the woman called in anguish.

Consider yourself lucky. "Crawl out!"

There were anguished groans as the woman used her elbows to crawl out into the street. "Arms extended, face down on the pavement!" Caylee ordered. The woman complied.

Leatrom rose slowly at first, then moved in on the wounded woman. She zip-tied her hands behind her and frisked her, finding a knife in her sock and an ankle holster with a small .22 automatic, and a secured cell phone, which she took. One of her bullets had gone through the woman's left knee and out the back, leaving a hole and her jeans soaked in blood. Rolling her victim over with an audible moan, Caylee double-checked her for anything else that might prove to be dangerous. "I'll bleed out if you don't take me to a hospital."

"I don't care." Caylee continued to pat the woman down. On her belt, under the flannel shirt, she found a badge. NSF. Not just NSF—this woman was on Operative, just like her. *What the hell?* She didn't betray her shock and simply tucked the badge into her own pocket and rolled the woman over. Her victim moaned.

"You're NSF?" she asked.

"Yes," her victim said through gritted teeth. "God damn it… that hurts."

Caylee looked at the wound and the expanding red stain on her jean.

"From what I see, you have just a few minutes before you go into shock. I can tie you off with a tourniquet; that will help. We are about fifteen miles from town. That might allow you to get back. Then again, I can let you bleed out here and die."

"What do you want?"

"Why are you following me?"

"We had *orders* to tail you. Once you completed your mission, we had orders to bring you in."

"That's a lie," she said flatly. "You came at my vehicle with drawn weapons. You don't do that if your job is to simply follow a target." She paused for a moment. "We are both operatives. I will give you some degree of professional courtesy and not step on your wound to make it hurt more. So, then, let me ask, who gave you the orders?"

"You have to tie my leg off. I'm getting dizzy."

A wicked smile rose to Caylee's face. "I bet you are. I can see the sweat on your forehead too. Shock is coming—then death. Tick-tock, tick-tock. Who sent you here?"

"Director Dorne. It was a red-level op."

Burke Dorne was cold and heartless, but he had no reason to want Caylee dead, at least none that she could think of. *Dorne wouldn't take a healthy shit without permission. He would have only done this kind of action with authorization.* Red-level. That meant that the Secretary had authorized it. *What the hell? That bitch sent a team to assassinate me.* She stood over her once-former comrade, looking down at her devoid of emotion or sympathy. *A minute ago, you and your partner were planning to kill me, and now you ask for my help.*

"You've got to tie off my wound!" the injured operative wailed.

Caylee ignored her and went over to their truck. There were a pair of backpacks there, which she took. She glanced in one of them and saw an NSF iPad inside. She briskly walked back to the woman on the pavement. "Your passcode," she demanded.

"I'm dying," she said, her voice bordering on panic, her breath getting rapid. "This is murder. We are both operatives."

"Yes, we are. And you were going to kill me. You *do* see the irony of you asking for my mercy, don't you? I can help you, but I need something from you. Once more, passcode," Caylee repeated flatly. *Yes, you are on operative, one sent to assassinate me. We do not share any special bond or code. This has become about survival. My own people sent someone to kill me.* She was angry, frustrated, and confused—but none of that came through her voice.

"872ABA," the operative said between quick breaths.

Caylee repeated it and started to walk away, towards her car. "You can't leave me like this!" she called.

"You're right, I can't." Caylee Leatrom turned, raised her pistol and fired, obliterating the woman's face in a spray of crimson. Checking to make sure there were no headlights coming in either direction, she dragged the bodies into her car and started it, letting it coast into the ditch. She pulled a small can of lighter fluid from her own bag and sprayed the bodies and the interior of the vehicle. The keys to the truck had been harder to find; the male had them hooked to his belt rather than in his pocket. Then, with a flick of her lighter, she set the car ablaze.

Her mind processed the events carefully at this point. The burned bodies would throw off the NSF. Caylee would have to lose any IDs she had that she had generated with the NSF—they would be tracking her. She tossed a number of them into the flames, keeping only her badge since she had pulled the chip from it a long time ago. *It will take some time for them to figure out who was in the car and try to piece together how fucked up their op had gone. More assets would be assigned, better ones.*

"No loose ends," she muttered as she went to the beat-up red truck and tossed in the backpacks.

Detroit, Michigan

Raul watched the television in Father Ryan's rectory in horror as the neighborhood called Southeast in Detroit roared in flames. Rioters beat people in the streets. From what he had learned, the community had been called Mexicantown for decades, but had been renamed in the reformation period after the Liberation. Now it was being burned and the citizens living there were being beaten by angry Social Enforcement mobs.

The riots had not been limited to that community. The Arabic SEs had rioted and looted in upscale Royal Oak and Birmingham as well, knocking out business storefronts and taking what they wanted. All along

Eight Mile Road, the dividing line between Detroit and the suburbs, fires raged. The NSF was bringing in forces to restore order, and there had been clashes with the police as a result.

The protesters held massive banners and signs, many calling for Sharia Law, others calling for justice... others simply saying, "Spics must leave!" The signs were not crudely done as he would have expected; these were professionally made, printed, as if they were prepared in advance. Most unnerving was that the news media had a short musical intro for the riots, and already had a logo, the black outline of the empty Renaissance Center downtown Detroit, with red and orange flames in the background. It struck Raul as if they were marketing the violence, packaging it for the public. *Did they have this prepared in advance, just in case riots happened? Or did the media know that this was coming?*

Many protesters carried riot shields and clubs. Others held items that looked menacing, but were hidden in the darkness. The scrolling newsfeed at the bottom of the screen read, "22 killed so far in the second night of riots..." Then came the video, the one played every few minutes. It was a blurry cell phone image of Raul firing a gun. Each time it came up his stomach knotted a little bit more.

"That isn't how it happened," Paco said. "They edited down to just show you shooting. That isn't all of it." His friend was trying to sooth his nerves, but it wasn't working. *I did pull the trigger. I killed those men.*

"They do that," Father Ryan said from behind him. "It is the way that the SEs work. They always film what they are doing, then release the parts that fit the story they want people to see."

"It is wrong," Julia said. "It is lying with pictures."

"Of course, it is," Father Ryan said. "They don't care though. To them, they need to justify their actions. Showing that video does that."

Raul's stomach pitched again and he felt he wanted to throw up. Father Ryan must have sensed it. He walked over and shut off the TV. "I think we've seen enough of that."

"It's all my fault," Raul said, unable to look the priest in the eyes. "I caused this."

The priest put his hand on Raul's shoulders as he stood next to him. "That's not true. You were protecting yourself and your friends. You had no choice."

"I shot two people."

Ryan nodded and closed his eyes for a moment of silent prayer. "Raul, you did. And you are atoning for that. You didn't have a choice, I believe that. These people…" he gestured at the blank TV screen as if the images were still there, "they have been looking for a reason to riot. They came after you and your friends. They took the life of your Troop leader. They might very well have killed all of you to cover up their crimes."

Raul nodded. Ryan's words helped, but the guilt hung onto him as if he were draped in a wet blanket. It pulled him down, made it hard to move. *My mother will never understand.* He was thankful that the image the newscasters were using was so blurry that no one could identify him… not yet at least.

Outside of the church there was the sound of people starting to gather. Several of the Youth Corps went to the windows, opening the blinds a bit to see what was happening outside. Julia called from her spot at one of the windows. "There are people starting to gather outside. They're dressed like those men that attacked us." In the distance, far off, the echo of a gunshot bounced against the windows of the rectory, rattling the panes of glass.

Father Ryan moved to the venetian blinds and peered out into the night. "It looks like we may need to leave."

"If we go out there," Paco said. "They will kill us for sure Father!"

Ryan shook his head. "I have a van in the garage. You will get inside and no one can see you. We will drive out of here."

"Aren't we safe here?" Raul asked. "This is a church. They won't attack a place of God."

Father Ryan's face gave him the answer he didn't want to hear. "These people *will* attack and burn a church Raul," he assured him grimly. "Religion is a threat to the SEs because they cannot control it and it provides people with moral guidance rather than the morals that the government wishes to impose. They have taken away our authority, burned our buildings, all aimed at breaking our will. The SEs and the FedGov don't realize that when they do that, it only makes us stronger."

"Even if we can get out Father, where will we go?" Julian asked nervously from the window.

"I have friends," Father Ryan said. "People that can get you somewhere away from here, somewhere safe."

"I wish we could just go home," Paco replied.

"We need to get you away from here," Father Ryan replied. "After that, well, that is up to you." He went into the kitchen of the small rectory and began pulling cans of food off of the shelves, putting them in recyclable carry bags. He instructed Julian to put the case of water in the back of the van. Paco was told to gather blankets from the hall closet while Raul helped him pack the food. As they filled the third bag, Raul looked up to the older man. "How long will we be gone."

"I don't know," Father Ryan said. "Brother Fenton will take over services for me here. I need to make sure that you are safe."

In the dark and closed garage, the father organized the young people, having them lie in the back of the van flag. He covered them with blankets, and several boxes, mostly empty, were placed on top of them. Several grocery bags of cans were gently placed on them as well, aimed less at comfort, and serving as camouflage. Nine of them lay together and on top of each other. Paco's shoes were near Raul's head, and the stink from his feet was strong, but not enough to distract him from the fear he felt. "No one is to move or speak or anything. Trust in God—he will see us through this." Raul lay in the middle of the group, next to Paco and Julian. Their arms touched and it was hot under the blankets, but no one shifted. He was afraid to even breathe.

He heard the garage door rumble and rattle open and the van pulled out slowly. The sounds from the street suddenly were loud and ominously nearby. The boxes thrown on top of them shifted slightly as the van dipped down the driveway to the street. Then came the pounding on the side of the vehicle. There were curses, pure rage, from the crowd in the street.

Father Ryan must have lowered his window, because one voice came through clear. "Where are you going?"

"Taking food to the elderly," Ryan said to the voice. Raul saw the flickers of flashlights shimmer through the blanket. His body went rigid. *If they find us, they will kill us.* "I do this every Saturday night," the father added with an almost happy lilt to his voice. "You are welcome to search the van." Those words made Raul start to sweat.

The pause seemed long and with each beat of his heart, he thought the rear doors to the van would fly open. There were voices in a foreign language that sounded harsh and crisp. Finally, he heard the man speak to the father through the window. "Go about your business," he commanded. Father Ryan thanked him and the van lurched slightly into motion.

For a long time, no one spoke. The occasional distant gunshot banged off as the van seemed to move faster. After an hour, the father slowed the vehicle, making a series of turns, finally coming to a stop. "It's okay. We are out of the city."

Raul got up slowly, as did the other youth in the back, tripping over the boxes as the rear door of the van opened. The cool night air hit his sweat-soaked skin and he felt chilled, but Raul could not complain. He saw they were parked in front of a two-story house, far from any neighbors or other prying eyes. "Where are we Father?" Paco asked.

"Monroe," he said. "Downriver, far from the city." His words added a surge of relief. Raul had been so proud of working in Detroit for the Youth Corps; now he saw the city as dangerous, violent, filled with hate. The porch light came on and a man and woman emerged. They were middle aged, both wearing sweaters and jeans. They approached Father Ryan and the woman hugged him. The priest spoke with them out of earshot of Raul and the others. The conversation went on for long minutes, and Raul worried that there might be a problem. Ryan had not called anyone—not that he had seen. *We have just shown up on their doorstep. Hopefully they will not turn us out into the night.*

They spoke for long minutes, with the father pointing at them, and the man crossed his arms as he listened carefully. The auburn-haired woman, perfectly outlined by the porch light, stepped away from the conversation and motioned for them to come closer. "Come inside. We will get you settled for the night." Raul started to walk with the others, but Father Ryan motioned for him to join him and the man.

"Raul, this is Peter," he said. "He and his wife Ruth are going to help you and the others."

"*Gracias,*" Raul replied, extending his hand. Peter took it and shook it. "It sounds like you have been through a lot Raul," Peter said.

"Yes," he managed.

"We will take care of you and get you to safety," he said.

"Thank you."

Father Ryan put his hand on Raul's shoulder, pressing hard "Peter and I were speaking about this, Raul. Peter will arrange to get the others back to the Youth Corps. It has to be done carefully. The NSF and the SEs are looking for them. We need to make sure that they get back to the right authorities so there is no retribution. You understand, don't you?"

The realization hit Raul. Ryan was talking about the others, not about him. "What happens to me?"

Peter stepped forward, uncrossing his arms. "Raul, we have seen it time and time again with these incidents. Justice is not fair or balanced. We've been following the riots. If you are turned over to the FedGov, there will be a trial. Politicians will get involved. They will want to hang these riots on someone; they will want someone to blame. Those SEs out of Dearborn will want blood. If we turn you over to the Youth Corps, the father and I fear what would happen to you."

"So, I should go home?"

"No," Peter said. "The others will tell the authorities what happened, but after that, you will be a wanted man. Your home will be under surveillance."

"But I only was protecting my friends!" Raul said.

"Of course you were," Father Ryan said. "But this is not about justice. It is about public opinion. The media has already painted you as a killer."

This is wrong! I only did what I had to protect my friends. "It isn't fair!"

"Nor is it right," Ryan said. "After the Fall, it has ceased to be about what is right. Right and wrong are subject to the politicians and the media."

"And they are one and the same," Peter added.

"Where will I go then?" Raul said.

It was Peter who spoke next. "We have friends that can help you Raul. I am going to get you to them while Ruth takes care of getting the others some place safe."

He liked the sound of that, but fear still ate at the edges of his mind. "Who are these friends?"

"They are the Sons of Liberty."

Ryan offered a wry smile. "Raul, they are not terrorists any more than you are a murderer. Think carefully. The media took a video of you and made you a criminal. That is what they did with the SOL. These were not terrorists until the government started hunting them down and sending them off for social quarantine. They were patriots who refused to accept the overthrow of the government as legal."

His words hit Raul hard. Things like that had been said before; he remembered one of his uncles saying the same thing. At the time it had no meaning. The news told him that the Sons of Liberty were bad people. It was easier to believe that than it was to question it. Now, though, he was living that nightmare himself. *If I had done nothing, I would be dead; so would the others. I did nothing wrong and they have made me a killer. If they could do that to me, they could do it to others.*

In that moment, his world seemed to collapse. *What else have they lied about? They manipulate people… good people… into doing bad things.* He remembered the sound of the jingle that the media had played at the start of every report on the riot. It was as if it were planned, orchestrated. His body sagged under the realization that the government took part in such grand lies. *Have we all been misled?* They have told us that the Liberation was necessary. But was it? Every bit of what he accepted as the truth in his life seemed to melt away. Raul questioned them all. His skin got warm again as he tried to cope with the confusion, and the utter sense of betrayal that consumed him there in the darkness.

"Are you alight Raul?" Father Ryan asked.

"I… it just… they have made me a criminal. They must have done the same with the Sons of Liberty."

The priest nodded. "Not just you Raul. They have painted many others as criminals as well, including our sacred church. The Newmerica government seeks to eradicate us as well, and will if they are allowed to. Groups like the Sons of Liberty, the Red Flags, The Honor Boys— they are the ones refusing to let the administration rewrite our history and reset our morals. People still remember things before Newmerica. Many people are not ashamed of our past; they cherish it. I came to learn that what defines our future is our past. You don't erase it, you don't change it to fit an agenda, you build off of it. Some of that is nostalgia but a lot of it is the feeling that we stood for something more; that we were a culture that others aspired to. Yes, we made mistakes in the past, but those mistakes didn't define us; they guided us to better decisions. Newmerica's Ruling Council, they think the way to fix the present is to rewrite or erase the past. When they do that, they lose part of their souls."

"I will be giving up my life," Raul said. "The Youth Corps was like family for me. Now I have to walk away from it."

Peter took a half-step closer. "I understand. Before the Fall, I had a great job, I made a lot of money. My job was like a second family. I saw some of those people more than I did my wife and kids. They drove my company to leave the country with their taxes, redistribution of the wealth, and regulations. They took that all from me too. For a long time, I struggled to find something that would fill that gap in my life, something to replace that family they had blown apart. The SOL, that gave me something like it—only better. It gave me a sense of purpose."

"Raul, you see, the thing that makes a good family is not all of your friends. What makes a good family is *you*," Father Ryan said.

"I will never see them again?" he asked, glancing over at the house.

"Don't say that," the priest said. None of us knows what the future will bring. But your association with them will make things hard on them, and I know you don't want that."

Peter rejoined the talk. "I like to believe that we have reached the bottom and can only climb up from here. There will be hard times, of that I am sure. Never? No, I refuse to believe that. But for you to return to the life you had before will require hard work and sacrifice. Things will have to change. You can be a part of that change, a part of a new family."

The thought of leaving his friends pained him deeply. The fear of what the NSF or SEs would do if they caught him was overpowering though. He had heard stories of camps where people were sent, of places where torture was done. It didn't matter if it was true or not, the fear was there regardless of what he tried to tell himself. *If I don't go, Paco and Julia and others will all suffer because of what I did.*

"Alright," he said nodding quickly. "Enough people are in trouble because of what I did."

Peter and the father smiled. "You've made the right choice," Father Ryan said.

"More importantly," Peter added, "*you* made the choice. In the last few years, the government has made choices for all of us, whether we liked it or not. This is yours Raul, you own it. It was your decision, and I think it is a good one."

"I'm frightened," he confessed.

Father Ryan smiled. "You will not walk this path alone. I will go with you."

Suddenly there was a burst of hope. "You will?"

"I'm a man of God. It is my duty to see to your safety."

CHAPTER 16

"Data is Reality."

Keystone, South Dakota

The Mount Rushmore gates were closed, rusty from no maintenance, and chained shut. That prevented vehicles from entering the facility, but it was easy enough for Charli and Andy to walk around them. The parking lot had weeds grown up through it, most brown and dead from the harsh winter.

Charli found an old trail cam and moved to disable it until she saw the brown streak of a corroded battery drizzled down its side. The Newmerica government had put security in place but hadn't maintained it. The threat of security was enough to keep people away. They walked past the visitor center, its windows long ago broken out. The pathways were covered with bits of plastic litter, with grass and weeds taking over.

As they stepped out into the grand viewing area, Andy looked up and saw what was left of the once great monument. Memories of the night when they had tried to blow it up came rushing back. George Washington's visage was missing cheeks and his chin was cracked. Teddy Roosevelt was almost unrecognizable, the black mark from the explosion scarring all that remained—his forehead. Thomas Jefferson had not only been blown up, leaving half of his face as rubble far below, but red paint was dumped on what remained. Abraham Lincoln was missing his nose and most of his beard. His hairline had been blown apart as well, leaving a massive chunk of granite that ran down into his forehead.

The image of the destroyed monuments sucked the life out of him for a moment. Staring up at them, he tried to remember what they had looked like before, when his father had brought the family there to see them. Karen would be happy to see them like this. Andy knew his father had seen the damage and for a moment, he knew exactly how his father felt. *A part of me wants to cry... seeing it like this.* The elder Forrest had come with Dick Farmer and had hidden something up there, behind Lincoln's temple, in the Hall of Records.

Charli stood at his side, staring at the defaced monument, saying nothing for a long time. "We took all of this for granted." Andy turned to her and they locked gazes. "I never saw it before all of this. I always assumed it would be there, that I had plenty of time to see it. It was hard to imagine that people had so much hate in them to try and destroy it."

"They couldn't even get that right," Andy said, glancing back at the defaced edifice. "They didn't destroy it. They ruined it. A bunch of mindless amateurs. When they realized they'd screwed up, they simply made it illegal to come up here or to post this picture on the web. Like everything else they didn't like, they erased it."

The corners of Charli's mouth raised slightly. "No, they didn't. This isn't about a monument. This is our history—it is an ideal. You can't erase that. That is where they made their biggest mistake. They think it is about statues and books. It's not. It's about what is in your heart. I think that scares them. They know that America really isn't dead; they have just smothered it with their bullshit. That is why they are fucking dictators, why they have SEs running around ruining people's lives. They know that the idea of our country still exists."

"It's a hike to get up there," Andy said looking at the old map that he had gotten at the truck stop. "The Hall of Records was never open to the public. There's a maintenance road that leads up there. That's our best bet."

Charli eyed him. "Are you up for this?"

He nodded nervously. This was not a question of his physical capabilities, but how he felt. "Dad wanted this... he wanted me to recover whatever it was he left up there. I don't know what it is, but I know I need to find it, touch it." He paused and felt a blush rise to his cheeks. "I know that probably sounds stupid."

She shook her head and put her hand on his forearm. "No, it doesn't."

She gave the monument a quick glance again. "We need to get moving. We probably won't get up there until twilight."

Jersey City, New Jersey

Jack Desmond sat on a graffiti marked park bench in Liberty Park looking over the Hudson to Manhattan, cradling his cup of caffeine. A black woman, a little younger than him, took up a seat on the same bench, a space between them. Her hair was short, topped by a ball cap with a Mets logo. Jack knew she had been a Yankees fan, back when they were called the Yankees. Social justice "reformation" had made the owners change the name to the NY Defenders. Even wearing the old logo was illegal. It marked you for the SE to target. Wearing a Mets hat was a covert symbol of civil defiance, one that the FedGov hadn't picked up on yet. Jack eyed her carefully, looking out over the bridge of his cosmetic nose, then turning back to the city. "Well Valerie, you look well."

Valerie Turner had been a Commissioner in the New York Police Department at the time of the Fall. She, and most of her leadership, had paid a high price after the mobs had taken control of the government. The police had been defunded, putting numerous officers out of work, including Turner. That wasn't enough. The local Social Enforcers felt that the officers and their families needed to be targeted, 'payback for years of abuse of power.' Despite being black, she was painted as a racist, 'a betrayer to her people.' It was a convenient label that the SEs used for people of color that did not adhere to their political views. They tormented her husband and children, protesting in front of her house day and night, broadcasting all night long, shining lights in their windows. They hounded her husband Desmond at work, getting him fired. Her children were followed to school, threatened with each step they took. It was too much for her son Zack. After three weeks of harassment and threats, he cut his wrists in the bathtub and died. Jack knew her from his days with the Secret Service and had maintained contact with her. After the death of her son, she no longer wanted peace and quiet. She wanted justice.

"As do you," she said not making eye contact."

"So, what do you think?"

She cracked a thin smile. "When you first told me your idea, I thought it was nuts. I ran it by some of my tech people. It's doable, but there will be breakage."

Jack took a long sip of his latte. "I always assumed there would be breakage," he said calmly. Turner nodded. "ABC broadcasts out of the city, but the signal is relayed here to Jersey. NBC TV and radio are out of 30 Rock still, and CBS is downtown as well. National broadcasts go out from here to the local affiliates for distribution globally."

"That's what our insiders told us. We need one studio for the broadcast; the others will get the feeds from here in Jersey. What one do you recommend?"

"Easiest and safest in-and-out would be CBS," she said. "Getting out of Manhattan will be tricky, but we can set up some teams to usher you out. Once you're off the island, you'll be hard as shit to track."

"How tight are the studios?"

"Studio and booth security is a joke—renta-cops, only a few actually armed. I assume that one or two will try something stupid, hence my comment on breakage. No one has ever tried this kind of thing before, so they have no plan for it. We go in with teams, secure the booths and the transmitters. Taking them is easy. Chances are they won't go off the air. What I can't guarantee you is that the local affiliates won't cut the signals once they realize it's going down."

"They won't," Jack said confidently. "That kind of decision requires authority, and getting that takes time. We don't need long—a few minutes."

"New York's finest will not let you down," Valerie assured him.

"Can your people get out once they get in?" Jack asked.

She chuckled. "The hard part is getting them out without doing damage along the way. Some of my former officers lost family members to the SEs. Not like me; they went after them, beating and killing. They have been waiting for this kind of chance, an opportunity to strike back."

"I don't want suicide missions," Jack cautioned. "This is the start. We will need your people over the long haul."

"They aren't *my* people anymore," she said with a long sigh. "We've been whittling away at some of the SE teams in the city, but it's less organized than you might think. These people played by the rules for years and got burned. Most of them are running dark. The rules no longer apply—the bad guys showed us that."

It was a sentiment that Jack found hard to deny. He had lost everything during the Fall, his home, his family, his career, everything. *When they take everything from you, they make you either subservient or the greatest threat ever.* He embraced the latter. They had taken away his life and given him new purpose, new meaning. *These Social Enforcers took good, peaceful people and pushed them too far. Now they will pay the price for their arrogance.*

"When does this go down?" Turner asked.

"Shortly," he replied. "For security's sake, I'm not putting the date out there. Your folks will have a day or two's notice at best. Is that going to be a problem?"

She shook her head, staring off longingly at Manhattan in the distance. "No. Most were excited to get the call. I was a little surprised that you were in cahoots with the Sons of Liberty though. I mean, those guys disappeared three years ago."

Jack took another long sip of his latte as a jet roared overhead, outbound from Newark International Airport. Frightened pigeons were sent scattering to other parts of the park. There had been a time when he and his wife would take their kids to the parks around Washington DC. Now such places were for clandestine meetings. He looked around and cringed at the tipped over garbage cans, the litter caught in spring's tall, and unmown grasses.

"Everyone thinks that the Sons of Liberty is an organization. It's not. Up until a few years ago, you could have an organization of people that were opposed to the government. When you are structured, they can come for you. ANTIFA got that much right. Without a body, you struggle to bring it down. What was it they used to say, "It's just an idea?'

"When the new group formed after the Fall, they had an organization and it cost them. The SEs and the NSF tore them apart. We learned a lot from our enemies."

"So, no structure?" Valerie asked.

"None. Not in the conventional sense. No target for the NSF or SEs to go after. There's no head to the snake, not yet anyway. We also learned that it is much easier to be a rebellious faction taking down the government than it is to be a government trying to protect its power. When they overthrew the government, they *became* the government.

Yes, they suppressed resistance, but the tighter they squeeze, the more people want to rise up against them. The FedGov can't even say our name—they use our initials to identify us."

Jack paused for a moment, then continued. "They taught us how they think, what their tactics are, how they operate. The showed us what worked. They weren't brilliant. They didn't have a grand plan when they had their little coup. It had the benefit of never having been tried. Many of the old-guard members of Congress that secretly supported them ended up swinging at the end of long ropes when it was over. They won because we never thought it could happen here. Now we know differently. They changed the rules of the game. We have now mastered those rules and will flip the tables on them."

She turned to him, locking her gaze. "That's bigger than the Army. It takes more than an understanding to topple people like them. They control the military, Jack. They nationalized the police force and control it. They've got muscle."

"Their control of the military is paper thin. Granted, the DoD stood down during the Fall. Not everyone in their ranks felt that was a good decision. We have a lot of contacts in the military now who realize they backed the wrong horse. They helped those fuckfaces get into power and got their budgets slashed, redistributed to welfare programs. Word I've got is that they are more than a little pissed at the Ruling Council.

"And the NSF—sure, their operatives are die-hards, but the rank and file hate how all of this has played out. You and I both know that a lot of police stayed on with the NSF to support their families. There isn't a great deal of loyalty there from the old guard. They have added a lot of true believers to their cause, but they have pussified the training for officers. While the newbies are loyal, they aren't trained to deal with real resistance. You've seen it Val. Showing up at an active shooter scene with a sociologist, a field psychiatrist, and a counselor hasn't played out very well."

Turner chuckled. "You know what you get with that scenario? A lot of dead social workers."

"No shit," Jack said. "They will follow orders at first. We intend to give them something to make them question if they are on the right side of things. A lot of them are going to stand down, I think. Some will side with us. They are tired of seeing cops killed because they can't defend themselves."

"Jack, we've known each other a long time," she said with an almost motherly tone. "You don't have to do this. You did your job. You can walk away from this."

He took the cap off of his latte and dumped it on the tall grass surrounding the bench. "I think we both know that isn't going to happen, Val. They brought this down on themselves. This isn't only about revenge for me. It's about what is right. Most of the country has sat on its collective asses and allowed them to seize power. They didn't have that right, no matter how much they change history to justify what they did. It's bigger than me."

She paused, seeming to take in his face with her deep brown eyes. "I had to raise it; you know me. There's going to be blood with what comes. If I didn't ask, I wasn't being a good friend."

A grin flickered to Jack Desmond's face. "You're right. There's going to be blood. The tree of freedom demands it from time to time."

Keystone, South Dakota

Caylee Leatrom sat in her vehicle and reviewed what she had found on Operative Tori Bell's secured NSF iPad. By now, police and fire had put out the flames in her car and were desperately trying to identify the two bodies. Caylee had been thorough though, stripping the male operative of his ID as well. It would take time, and she needed it.

The orders were there, on the iPad, Red Level. "The Secretary hereby authorizes Zipline against Agent Caylee Angelina Leatrom. Operative 504. Agent Leatrom is working an op. It is desired that she complete that mission before Zipline is completed, but this is not required." Zipline was a terminate order. It went on to explain that Caylee had been involved with several incidents with various SE teams that had led to a national escalation of tensions between the two organizations. "Further, she had no authorization to execute these tasks and had done so as a rogue agent."

I call bullshit. The Secretary had authorized her to undertake the measures she did; in fact, she had not stopped her at all. It was a setup, plain and simple. *I'm being made the fall-guy for something else.*

That galled her. She had been loyal and dedicated to the NSF. *I've done their dirty work for years. I've cleaned up messes that the Secretary and Dorne were responsible for. Now they send assassins after me.* Rage peaked in her brain and she did nothing to calm it for a long time. Her mind went everywhere in her inner-fury, questioning everything. It was rare that Zipline protocols were used, and she couldn't remember them ever being used against an operative before. *I haven't crossed any lines that I haven't crossed before. There's something more in play here, something I am not seeing.*

She wondered if it was the mission that she was on, trying to find the SOL leadership to see if the President was indeed still alive. That made some sense. *I know something that probably only a handful of people still alive do; I know that the President wasn't apprehended and died in jail.* In fact, only a few people knew that his death had been staged, a CGI-fest for the angry mobs. *How many of them had been Ziplined over the years?* Why send her out looking for him, then send someone to terminate her?

Bit by bit her anger subsided like a receding tide. There had to be more to it than just her knowledge about the Traitor-President. Her secrecy had always been ensured. *I'm missing pieces to this puzzle.* There was a possible source, the Secretary of the NSF. Caylee gave thought to penetrating NSF's private security and getting to her directly, squeezing it out of the black-haired harpy. While those thoughts made her happy, she knew that by the time she was on her way, they would be alerted. The odds would get stacked against her. While she was confident in her skills, she also knew not to push a bad situation, regardless of the temptation.

Torturing her immediate supervisor, Burke Dorne, had much more appeal but faced the same risks. It would be a matter of hours before NSF figured out that their two operatives were the charred remains in her car.

Analytical thinking prevailed over the lust for vengeance. She eyed the phone that she had taken from the female, Operative Bell. It could be traced, but they had no reason to, yet. Taking it out, she keyed in the access code that Bell had given her before her head had exploded. There was one person that could give her answers. She dialed the number of the Secretary, and then pulled out the plastic wrapper of the energy bar she had just eaten. Putting the phone on speaker, she waited for a pickup.

"Operative Bell," came the crisp voice of the Secretary.

Caylee crumbled the plastic wrapper continuously to simulate static as she changed the tone of her voice. "Madam Secretary. The mission is concluded."

"Excellent," the Secretary replied. "Was Operative Leatrom able to complete her mission?"

"Unknown. She spotted us and we had to engage her before learning if she was through."

"Understood," the Secretary replied. "It is unfortunate that she turned against the party. She had become a risk that could no longer be tolerated." The Secretary was sending a message to the operative she thought was Bell. *This could happen to you too.*

"I would like you to stage the body, if at all possible, to make it look as if one of the local SE teams was responsible for her death."

Is that what this is about? "Madam?" she asked, crumbling the wrapper faster near the microphone of the phone. The thought of her body being used that way didn't disturb her as much as it should have. What bothered her was that she was being used. It's like those dead SEs in West Virginia at the Graveyard.

"Carve something on her body or leave something that will point to the SE," she clarified. "It is important for another op we have in play that this appear to be an SE hit. Understood?"

"Yes, Madam Secretary," Caylee said. She would mutilate my body to point the fingers at the SE. *She is planning something, I can feel it.* "I will handle that."

"Very good. It is never easy when one of our own turns traitor. At least we can put her body to good use."

"I will take care of it," Caylee replied coolly.

"You've served me well Operative Bell. When you are back in the District, I have another operation in mind for you."

"I will see you soon then," she replied, hanging up. She pulled a tracking chip off the back of the iPad and the one off the phone, stuffing them into the bumpers of two of the trucks at the truck stop. It was always easier to let someone else mislead the enemy—and the NSF was now her enemy.

She entered the small diner area and took a booth in the corner. Her mind raced at the thoughts of the SE being blamed for her death. It hit her. *I was set up from the start. The mission—that was secondary. This was all about me locking horns with the SE. The Secretary knew I would step on a few feet with the SE while looking into the Sons of Liberty. Her death was going to be attributed to the SE.*

If she called for my termination, that means something else is going on, something I'm not privy to. She's planning something with the SE, something big. I was a pawn. She was going to use me to stir things up, then leverage my death to take some sort of action in response. Caylee pondered what it could be. Tensions between the two organizations had been growing with each passing year. The Secretary was a known power broker in the District. She had started as a wet-behind-the-years Congresswoman who had fed the hate that had led to the Liberation. When other members of Congress had been arrested and killed, she had managed to emerge unscathed in the purge, in control of the NSF. She had built her own army with the NSF, and the operatives were her special forces. The Secretary did not do things in half-measures. *Whatever it is she's planning, it is big. Big enough for her to be willing to take out her best operative.* The thought that she had been played, that she was nothing more than an expendable tool, ate at Caylee, searing her soul.

An operative lifestyle demanded few connections. Caylee did not have true friends to fall back on. *Now that they are after me, what little family I had will be under surveillance.* She did not have people she could trust to fall back on. *My life is dispensable to the NSF now.* Loneliness was something she had not felt for years, but it hit her hard as she tried to mentally process the twist of events.

The waitress came over and Caylee ordered some coffee and a hamburger, barely paying attention to the woman. *I need a plan. Right now, I'm adrift. Without a plan, I'm vulnerable—I'm forced to play defense.* She knew her strengths were not in defending, but in being on the offense. In her mind, the options broke down simply. One: She could assume a new identity and blend in, fly under the radar. The problem was that sooner or later, they would find her. The NSF could strike when she least expected it, even years from now. Two: She could take her skills to the District and kill the Secretary. Caylee always believed that vengeance is good for the soul. *They will be expecting this kind of play on my part, making it very difficult.*

The third option was one that was more complicated, but offered a better chance of survival. *The enemy of my enemy is my potential ally.* If the SOL wants to wage war against the administration, why not fight for them? *I have a lot to offer, not to mention that I have done a lot of highly illegal work for the party over the years... murders, assassinations, arson, sabotage. That information alone is worth something to the enemies of the state.*

The choice was simple—option three, the execution: That was an entirely different matter. She needed to make contact with the SOL. They would be suspicious, and rightfully so. Convincing them that she was something other than a counterintelligence asset would be the hardest part. *Hopefully I can do it before they decide to kill me.* She immediately downloaded her personal files from the NSFCloud, dumping them down a burner phone she carried in her backpack. They would cut off her access soon, so she had taken what she could get. The information she had, details of ops, signed authorizations, all would be potential bargaining chips.

Her targets were heading for Mount Rushmore—though why they were was beyond her imagination. She shut off Operative Bell's phone and cradled the coffee the waitress delivered. When she came back, she held her order pad in her hand and she had a big smile on her face. "Hon, you look like you've been rode hard and put to bed wet. What can I get you to eat?" Caylee ordered the breakfast platter, despite the fact that it was afternoon.

The waitress turned to go and put in the order, but Caylee called her back. "Excuse me. If I remember right, isn't Mount Rushmore around here?" she asked innocently.

The waitress beamed. "It was. It all but killed Keystone when they... well, you know."

"You wouldn't happen to have a map to the site? I love old historic stuff like that," she said in an almost sing-song tone.

The waitress chuckled. "That's strange. Nobody has asked for one in well over two years. Now you and another couple do it a day or so apart. What are the odds of that?"

Someone else? A couple! "Really. Someone else asked?"

"A guy and his girl. They were here yesterday. Let me get your order in and I'll dig out one of those old brochures with a map." The waitress left and Caylee Leatrom grinned broadly.

CHAPTER 17

"Wealth is Weakness... Wealth is a Cancer."

Keystone, South Dakota

Andy reached the entrance to the Hall of Records first. The sun was setting in the distance and the breeze near the top of the monument was stronger, a bit chilly. The area leading to it was a narrow cut, stone trail ending behind Lincoln's head. There was an area that had been carved out, a low platform. The tunnel leading to the Hall of Records ran further back and down into Mount Rushmore. It was blocked by a pile of broken and blasted stones. In the large flat area was a steel safe of some sort, blown apart with explosives and left open.

"What is that?" Charli said pointing to the safe.

Andy eyed it carefully. "When the builder of Mount Rushmore conceived of this place, it was intended to hold our historical documents. He intended that people would come here, see the monument, and visit this vault to see our most prized national documents. Congress cut the funding. Construction was already underway though, a typical government project. Rather than fill it in, they installed a safe in the back of the Hall of Records with a copy of the Declaration of Independence and the Constitution. From the looks of it, the SEs decided to haul it out and destroy those copies." He eyed the smashed safe and the tiny bits of teak wood that had once held the contents. From the damage to the safe, it was clear that substantial explosives had been used.

Charli looked over at the opening of the vault. "It looks sealed up," she said. Only the header and exterior casings of the vault were visible.

The rest was filled in with head-sized pieces of stone piled up to block the entrance to the downward sloping tunnel. "Dad and Mr. Farmer piled the rocks there to deter people from getting in." Andy walked near the obstruction and eyed it. Memories of his father flickered to the forefront of his mind, if only for a few seconds. *What were you putting up here, Dad? What could be so damned important to get you to come to South Dakota?*

Charli stood next to him, pulling a flashlight out of her knapsack and turning it on. She propped it up on the blasted safe so that it shone on the pile. "We may as well get started." Walking to the mound, she grabbed the top stone and pulled it free, tossing it to the side. Andy joined her, pulling the rocks down one at a time, throwing them on the carved out flat area. It took the better part of an hour to clear it enough to enter.

She handed him the flashlight and he shined it down the tunnel. The tunnel itself was ten feet across. The walls had small holes, thousands of them, where drills had been used to chisel out the opening. It was crude, unfinished, almost like a dark mine shaft. Andy climbed over the remaining rocks, followed by Charli, and entered.

The tunnel ran back and downward some seventy-five feet where it opened to a larger room. They stepped down the slight incline as Andy angled the flashlight around. Occasional bits and pieces of broken stone lay about, but for the most part, the tunnel itself was remarkably well preserved. When they reached the end, the tunnel opened into a large chamber, even more crudely cut out than the passage that led to it. The ceiling was tall, nearly fifteen feet in height. The room itself ran perpendicular to the tunnel that intersected it, extending to fifty feet on either long side, some twenty-five feet deep. Uneven carving channels from the stone masons that had cut it made for a rutted surface to walk on. The end of the drill holes under the light of the flashlight gave the room an almost beehive appearance.

The flashlight caught a pile of stones in the corner and Andy could not help but smile. *There it is, just as Mr. Farmer had said.* He walked over to it and paused for a moment. "So that's it?" Charli asked from his side.

"Yeah," he said with a sigh. "We traveled halfway across the country to get here," Andy replied, staring at the rocks in the far corner.

"Andy," Charli said after a moment. "Don't you think we should find out what it is?"

He nodded in response, stepping forward and starting to remove the melon-sized stones while Charli held the flashlight. It took a few minutes, but at the bottom of the mound, he saw it—a metallic case and tube, sealed in plastic, covered with stone dust. With a flick of his hand, he wiped away the majority of the dust and pulled out the large case and tube. He pulled off the plastic covering, billowing more fine gray powder in the air, enough to make him cough. The case was marked, "National Museum of the United States Marine Corps." The tube was hefty, thick aluminum, painted black and hermetically sealed tape covered the end that opened. It bore a single marking etched into the large cap lid. "Property NARA."

Charli stood at his side. "NARA?"

"National Archives and Records Administration," he said. As he shifted the tube in his hands, he could feel something inside it.

He turned to her but said nothing... he could muster no words. She seemed to understand. "Go ahead. Open them. We've come this far."

Removing his sweatshirt, he put it on the uneven stone floor and used it to cushion his knees . He started with the large case. It was sealed along one of the long, narrow ends, protected from the atmosphere. It took a strong tug, but he peeled back the archival seal tape and unsnapped the case. There was something inside, cloth, wrapped in a thick plastic zipper case, the kind used to protect artifacts. He pulled it out and immediately saw that it was an American flag, an old one, stained slightly with age. He could see that the red and white stripes were frayed slightly. He didn't unzip the case, but instead saw a piece of paper in it. "Shine the light on this," he said, tipping the flag.

The small inserted paper simply read, "Mount Surbachi flag, on loan, NARA."

As he read the words the package seemed to grow heavier. "What is Mount Surbachi?" Charli asked.

"Iwo Jima. The famous flag raising. You know, the Marine Corps... World War II. This is that flag," he said. It had been a long time since he had seen a flag, let alone one of such historical significance.

He glanced over at Charli who reached out to touch it. "It has been so long since I saw one. They removed all of the images when they outlawed it. Now and then it pops up on the internet, but only until the fuckfaced censors in Silicon Valley take it down." Her touch was light, with reverence.

Andy, slid it back into the case carefully and re-latched it shut. Turning to the tube, he removed the sealing tape around the lid with a snap, and unscrewed it. Extracting it from the long tube required tipping it slightly so the contents shifted down to where he could grasp them. Inside were two wrapped documents. They were heavy, heavier than normal paper, and large. Pulling them free, he could unroll the first one just enough to make out the inked script. "We the People… was larger, bolder than the other text. He stopped unrolling it the moment he realized what it was. "Oh Christ," he muttered.

Charli had seen it as well. "Is that… ?"

Andy nodded. The next document he kept in plastic as well, unrolling it enough to make out, "In Congress, July 4, 1776," at the top. "I don't believe it."

"These are the originals?" Charli asked in astonishment.

Andy groped for words. "They were destroyed right after the Fall," he muttered, carefully returning the Constitution and Declaration of Independence to the tube. "Dad said that some guy named Abel Brummer got them out during the riots. He must have worked at the National Archives."

"The ones we saw burned on TV," Charli said. "He swapped out fakes and saved the real ones."

Andy had a swell of pride for his father. Dad had helped save these precious artifacts. The mobs had burned them in front of the National Archives—the ANTIFA-led mob had created a bonfire and had filmed them being thrown into the flames. It had infuriated Andy at the time, as it had many Americans. The rage and anger could not bring back what had been destroyed though. No, that task had been left to his father, Mr. Farmer, and the mysterious Abel Brummer. Three men had saved this bit of America. Andy tightened the top of the tube. "That or they lied," Andy said.

"They do that a lot," another voice said from the entrance to the Hall of Records. Charli's flashlight dropped and Andy heard her gun clear the holster as she dropped to a firing stance. In the dim light, he could make out a lean young woman, short-cropped blonde hair, her hands in the air but a gun slung in a shoulder holster.

"Who are you?" Andy demanded.

"An interested party," Caylee Leatrom replied.

Philadelphia, Pennsylvania

Raul and Father Ryan had left after a few hours of sleep and had driven into the night in the old church van. Raul sat in the passenger seat of the van and the priest had put on the AM news station from Detroit, WJR, which talked about the street closures from the riots the night before. People were being advised in several neighborhoods to shelter in place. There were other riots according to the radio, in Toledo, Cleveland, and Chicago—protesters claiming that Muslim rights had been violated. Raul scowled when he heard that. *Now I am responsible for problems everywhere.*

The priest seemed to be able to read his mind. "Raul, don't let it get to you son. This is how the Social Enforcers operation works. They take little things and make them bigger. It makes them feel more important. They thrive on seeing themselves as the oppressed, when in reality, they are the problem."

According to the news, there was no word as to who the shooter was that had started the rioting, but the authorities said it was only a matter of time before he was identified. That was chilling to Raul, and Father Ryan must have sensed it—he turned the radio off.

"Father, I thought that the Sons of Liberty had been wiped out," Raul said.

Ryan nodded as he maintained his focus on the driving. "We almost were. They rounded up most of the leadership and sent them off to Social Quarantine Camps. A lot of them died there. Those that came out, well, they were broken both mentally and emotionally. We learned the mistake. We had given the NSF a target, and they were effective at taking out targets. As such, the Sons became more hidden. We learned to attack from the shadows and not make a big splash that would draw attention. The key is to not give the enemy a name or face to go after. Besides, the FedGov declared us wiped out. So, when they did think we were back, they couldn't very well tell the public that."

It strangely made sense to him. It also told him much more. The Ruling Council of Newmerica lied to the people. It misled them. The media was behind it too. Things he barely considered thinking about a few weeks ago were suddenly starting to come together, like the pieces of a massive jigsaw puzzle. The problem was, he didn't fully understand what the image was in the puzzle that he was trying to complete. It was a mass of confusion... but each piece made it more real, more tangible.

They drove past one of the Newmerica digital slogan billboards which flashed, "Saying something is as important as doing something." Then it flashed a blurry image of Raul holding a pistol, the one that was on the media. "Wanted. Contact 911 if you know this individual." He slumped slightly in his seat.

"Don't worry, Raul," Ryan said. "They didn't get your face in that image."

"It is only a matter of time," Raul said glumly. "I'm wearing a Youth Corps t-shirt in that image. Eventually they will learn who I am. No one will be safe."

"You don't know that Raul," the priest said. "Worrying about the future will not help. We are going to get you to some people that can help you." As he spoke, he turned off the Pennsylvania Turnpike onto the exit, sliding through the EZ Pass lanes.

It was clear to Raul that Father Ryan knew where he was going. He made his way through the city, into what had been an industrial complex decades ago. It reminded Raul of the factory that he had been working to demolish. The buildings were brick and steel, defiant, rusting, covered with graffiti. The windows were little more than a few shards of glass that had been missed with rocks over the years. Boston ivy engulfed some of the walls, as if the earth itself were attempting to reach out, grab the structures and pull them down.

The van stopped in front of a chain-link gate and a man wearing a denim jacket came out, giving both of them an icy stare, then opening the gate with a squeal that only rusted metal could generate. The van entered, hitting two deep potholes slowly, one after another. The gate closed behind them as the van turned, entering a dark old warehouse. As soon as it was inside, the massive barn doors rattled and rumbled closed.

Father Ryan opened his door and Raul did the same. There were six men and women moving in around the van. Some had guns, holstered at their hips. One heavily tattooed woman had a knife strapped to her thick thigh. The knife looked as if it could cut down a tree.

"I didn't think I'd see you again, *padre*," one man said with a thick Puerto Rican accent, grasping Ryan's hand firmly with both of his and shaking it. He had short, curly black hair, a dark complexion and wore a red bandana around his neck.

"It is good to see you again Jayden," the Father said. "This is the one I told you about. This is Raul," he gestured to Raul and the man seemed to eye him from head to toe. "Raul, this is Jayden."

Raul slowly extended his hand, but the man did not settle for that. He pulled Raul in tight and gave him a quick hug. "If the *padre* brought you here, then you are part of us now."

"Who is us?" Raul asked.

The man swept his long lanky arm around at the others. "What you see is part of the Sons of Liberty, The Order of the Bell." He spoke with pride ringing in his words. "We number in the dozens. We fight for those that demand a restoration. We fight for those that cannot defend themselves. We fight against this lie called Newmerica." The small gathering nodded, smiled, and reached out to shake his hand or fist bump him. Raul responded in kind.

"Peter called us about your little problem," Jayden said. "It took a lot of courage to stand up to those SEs like you did. You were lucky to get out of there alive."

Raul felt ashamed of what he had done, but Jayden and the others clearly did not. Their approving nods of Jayden's words showed that. "I didn't want to hurt anyone."

"None of us *want* to," the tattooed lady spoke up. "We didn't ask for this fight. They brought it to us. What separates us from a lot of the country is we are willing to stand up against the SE and the NSF."

"We will take care of you, Raul," Jayden said. "You are one of us now. We are a family. Everyone here has been hurt or betrayed by the FedGov. Some of us have lost loved ones; others have had our lives taken from us by social justice warriors. That is what we share, our pain."

There was a sense of relief at the words he was hearing. "Thank you,

Jayden," he finally managed. "I'm not a fighter. I only fought to defend myself and my troop."

Jayden nodded. "We are not here to make you a killer. We won't ask you to do anything you are uncomfortable with. Some of our best people have never held a knife or gun; they help us in other ways. We will protect you, because we are family here. We will give you work to do so that you contribute your fair share to the cause. You will learn new skills, things that can help you get on in life, once we are all free again. This is fair, yes?"

Raul nodded. Oddly, it sounded very much like the Youth Corps to him. They had promised and delivered to him many of the same things. This was different though. The Sons of Liberty were in the shadows, where the Youth Corps was very public. He preferred the darkness now, especially with his blurry image plastered on billboards around the country. "Yes. That sounds great."

"Good!" Jayden said, putting his hand on Raul's back. "Then let me introduce you to your new kin…"

The District

The Secretary of the NSF looked at the plans that Director Dorne had created with a sense of pleasure. One hundred and eighty-eight assassinations were hard to coordinate. Some targets were bound to be out of position. Dorne estimated that in a worst-case scenario, some fourteen of them may survive what she was about to bring down on them. Still, they could and would be hunted down. This was not the time for half-measures. Per her instructions, it could be done in a matter of a few hours, leaving the Social Enforcement organization effectively decapitated, unable to prevent her next steps.

Her desk monitor chirped. "Director Dorne is here, Madam Secretary," her admin called from the outer office. "He says it is urgent."

"Send him in," she replied. *No doubt there is another wrinkle in our plans. Dorne tends to get a little overdramatic at minor hiccups.*

He stepped in, closing the door behind him. "Madam Secretary, we have a situation."

She gestured to the chair in front of her desk and he slid into it. "I just received word that Operatives Bell and Hoover are dead."

His words caught her off guard. "Impossible. I spoke to Bell personally a short time ago."

"That wasn't Bell," Dorne said. "She's been dead for a day or so."

"What in the hell are you talking about Burke?" she demanded.

"They were found in a burned-out vehicle," he said, red color rising in his cheeks and forehead. "Operative Leatrom's car. The local authorities thought it was some sort of accident. It took a while to get positive IDs on the bodies."

That means… "She's still alive."

"Yes ma'am," he replied.

In her mind she replayed the conversation. *I should have seen through that static in the background.* The realization was that she had confessed to her intended target that she had ordered her assassination. *There is no need for Dorne to know that.* "We need to mobilize additional assets. She is more of a liability than ever."

"I have already ordered that," Burke Dorne replied, taking out a handkerchief and wiping the sweat from his forehead. "Caylee Leatrom is dangerous. She will have figured out that we ordered her death and will take measures to get her, shall I say, extremely difficult. I know her, she's going to want revenge. As such, I have ordered operatives placed on our building and residences."

Those words hit the Secretary hard. *Would she actually try to extract vengeance?* She quickly came to the realization that it was a question she didn't want the answer to. *Of course she will come at us personally.* It was a thought that made her stomach knot. *With what we have in motion, I can't afford to have her unaccounted for.*

"We should be able to trace Operative Bell's devices. She called me from that phone."

"Traces are being run, but you have to remember that Leatrom knows our operating procedures. We pinged her phone tracker on a semi-truck in Kansas. Agent Bell's phone is showing in Denver and we have a team moving to intercept. Caylee wouldn't make the mistake of keeping those devices near her."

"What about satellites and drones? Surely we can use them to track her down."

"Our surveillance analysis has been slowed since the attack on

Bumblehive," Dorne replied. Gathering the data isn't a problem, but sifting through it requires CPUs that are still down. We lost a full third of the servers due to overheating."

"We are the largest police force in the world," she said through gritted teeth. "We are talking about finding a single person."

"Not just a person," Burke Dorne replied coldly. *"This is an operative."*

"That doesn't matter. She still has to be on the move. Get our checkpoints. I don't care if you have to shut down highways—I want her found, now! We are on the verge of launching our most critical and sensitive op since we came into existence. The last thing that I need is for a rogue agent to show up at the wrong time."

"She dumped down a local copy of her personal data file," Dorne said. "The copies on the server are encrypted and we are working to get through them, but our cyber team is at half capacity after that attack on their facilities in Maryland." The mention of that attack only stoked the rage she was trying to contain. Someone had disabled the water supply to the building, then set off over a dozen small fire bombs on the first and second floors. The staff had been trapped, many choking on toxic fumes from melting plastic and burned carpeting. All fingers pointed to an SE-sponsored attack, but thus far they had denied involvement... *just like what happened at Quantico. There's no way that this is the SOL. They never showed that level of sophistication before.*

The data that Caylee had taken was disturbing. "She has been part of almost every major op we have undertaken in the last four years," the Secretary said in a deepening tone of voice. *She has more guilt than anyone, but if that information somehow got public, there will be cries for investigations, Congressional hearings... all things that might disrupt my plans.* Would Leatrom go public? *What does she have to lose?*

The media could be controlled. Thank God we have the Truth Reconciliation Committee, but there was always a chance that some reporter might decide that the story should go out. It might make its way to some country that wouldn't suppress it. Congress... well, they were mostly impotent since the Liberation, but they loved to investigate, to hold hearings, to grill lesser people. They would overlook the context of the operations that Leatrom was involved with. The Secretary had stepped on a lot of toes over the last few years, and many people would be happy to see blood in the water with investigations and inquiries. *A lot of them would like to see me sent packing, in jail, or back tending bar. I can't afford to have them undermine everything I am putting in place. Not now, not when I'm so close.*

"Director Dorne," the Secretary said in her most frigid tone of voice. "You are responsible for bringing her in and containing this clusterfuck. I don't have to remind you that if she causes trouble, your head will be on the chopping block before mine will. She reported to you after all. I'm sure you realize the implications of your name on many of those orders and memos that she may have."

His nervous nod meant that he had received the message… the threat. *Dorne will be a fall guy if Leatrom does go public.* "I understand completely, Madam Secretary. We both need to recognize that she *will* cause problems for us. It's in her nature to leave a wake when she passes. She may have taken those materials as insurance, leverage to make sure we don't make a move on her. Then again, she may weaponize the data."

"Either way, I want her eliminated," the Secretary replied.

"What about the upcoming operation?" Dorne pressed. "With Leatrom out there, should we defer it to a later date?"

"No!" she snapped. "She's one person. What we have planned for the SEs… that is a matter of national security. That operation goes on as planned.

CHAPTER 18

"Fear makes you brave."

Rehoboth, Delaware

Jack Dorne looked at the footage of the office building engulfed in flames as Sarah Carter of "The Frackers" pointed to the small notebook screen. "It went just as planned. Killing the water supply at the source allowed the fires to spread quickly. For all of their talk of being green, there were a lot of plastics and flammables in the building to feed the fire. The chains on the fire escape doors ensured maximum casualties." She shut the image off and closed the screen.

Sarah had been with the U.S. Marshal's Office in Pittsburgh as part of the DHS when the Fall had happened. Jack had known her from his time in the Secret Service. The Social Enforcers had gone after the Marshal's families to get them to stand down. Her husband had been beaten, not to death, but instead left brain damaged by some social justice warrior's baseball bat. He died a year before, and Jack made a point to be there for her. She had formed the Frackers as part of the Sons of Liberty with one expressed purpose—to bring pain to the FedGov for the agonizingly long death of her husband. Revenge was a powerful motivator, and her pain was one that Jack knew all too well.

The Frackers were a tough group. Their full name was the 'Fucking Frackers,' and they tagged their graffiti with an F2 symbol. Some were out of work steel workers; others were coal miners who had lost their jobs when Newmerica had deemed coal to be an enemy of the world and had closed the mines. The push for 'global economic prosperity' had left former Americans forced to live off of welfare. While some people enjoyed living off of the government teat, others, like the Frackers, did not. It galled them, humiliated them, and demeaned them. While the media and the FedGov claimed that the changes brought about a cleaner environment and more competition, it actually only pushed more people into groups like the Frackers. *Like so many, they are wanting a chance to strike back and take back what was theirs.*

Jack leaned back on the sofa in the house she had rented on Airbnb for their meeting. It was a party house, built for rental at the Rhoboth beach community. Five bedrooms, five bathrooms, cheap carpeting, disposable furniture. It was the kind of house that frat boys rented. Jack was thankful that he didn't have a UV light... he was sure that the walls, furniture and floor would paint a sickening story if he did.

"What do you think their losses were?" he asked of the fiery redhead from Kentucky who had led the attack on the NSF's cyber facility in southern Maryland.

"We took out a lot of them—we're estimating 40 to 50% of the staff, full loss on the hardware," she said proudly. "They have two other team facilities in the District; both have beefed up security. The damage has been done though. You can replace hardware easily enough. Replacing experienced staff? That takes time... a long time."

Jack smiled, not proudly, but with a sense of satisfaction. "You did good work. Let your Frackers know that we are pleased with their results." She grinned broadly at the compliment. "So where do we stand on their communications systems?"

Carter flopped down in an easy chair opposite of him. "Those are more challenging to target. DHS had a communications center in the Southeast of the District, on the old site of Saint Elizabeth's Hospital. Obviously, the NSF has that facility now. It is a brand-new complex, built for multiple layers of security—biometric, facial recognition, multiple layers of authentication. Getting in... well, we haven't found a way to crack that nut directly."

"No security is ever perfect. There has to be a crack we can exploit."

She grinned, almost wickedly. "The key is to not try. They have anticipated penetration through traditional means. Given our other attacks, security is tighter than ever. So, we don't try to get in. We get someone who already has access to do the job for us… without them knowing it."

Desmond leaned back. "What do you have in mind?"

"It's a government facility, which means they outsource everything. We need a way to kill and cripple the staff on a large scale. Our thought was that we would use their food service to lace their food and drink supplies with a slow acting poison. We don't have to penetrate the building; the vendor will bring the stuff in and serve it up to them for us."

Jack drank in the words carefully. There was a hint of brilliance to it. "So, they have a cafeteria?"

"Oh yes. And the Southeast has a remarkable lack of restaurants. Given all of the security, the staff hates leaving for lunch and having to queue up to get back in. The result: They eat in the cafeteria."

It has a hint of brilliance about it. "So, what do you need?"

"A slow-acting batrachotoxin would be best," she said. "That or ricin. Personally, I think we will want a mix of poisons, so we can overload the hospitals and have them struggling to identify the toxin they are fighting. We need to inject it into a wide range of the food supplies designated for use at the facility. We have watched; the vendor's staff is cleared for the building, but there is no protocol for testing incoming food. It gets wheeled in, cooked up, and served."

"What about their food prep facilities?"

Sarah's grin broadened. "Almost zero security. They do most of the prep off site in Suitland, Maryland. We can hit them there or at their warehouse. We lace a lot of different food sources, everything from salt shakers to injecting oranges and breads. The vendor prepares the food, not aware the stuff has poison in them. They deliver it for us. The staff eats and starts dropping a few hours later. It will take hours if not days for them to figure out where it came from, and when they do, the vendor will take the fall."

"What's the downside?"

"The vendor, General Food Services, has contracts with three other government agencies to provide the food. If we hit it at the warehouse, which I recommend, some of that food is bound to be delivered to other agencies as well. That means we are killing people we were not targeting."

Jack said nothing for a few minutes. When the Fall had happened, most government workers did not resist. Driven by their desire to keep their jobs, they embraced the Newmerica government. Rather than rise up and say, 'This is an illegal government coup!" they had played along. Some had downright savored it, having a dislike of the President. To Jack Desmond, there were no innocents in the old federal government. They were accomplices to the Fall.

"I will get you what you need," he said.

"So, it's authorized?"

Jack nodded. "Our enemies have shown they are willing to take extreme measures to achieve victory. They are willing to hurt innocent people to get what they want. In that respect, they have set the rules of this game. We need to learn from them. We need to fight at the same level they do."

Sarah's smile faded. "I understand."

"It's important that when they figure this out, the finger gets pointed to a local SE team. I want to leverage the tensions between the NSF and the SEs. The more we can nudge them into squabbling with each other, the better."

She paused, her eyes narrowed slightly in thought. "That's trickier than the deed itself. I guess we could leave a warning note or two in the boxes, little taunts signed off by the District SEs. 'Enjoy your lunch!' kind of thing."

"Perfect," he replied. "Do you think that the same approach, poisoning the food, can be used on a Social Enforcement team?"

"I don't see why not," she replied. "If anything, the SEs have sloppy security. Poisoning them would be a cake walk. It's a matter of targeting the right team."

Jack rose to his feet. "I want you to run surveillance on the SE teams in Newark and Pittsburgh. I want them hit too. Not at the same time. Let's wait a few days, then do it. Make it look like retaliation. I can get you some ricin from a different source—enough to throw off the investigators."

"Retribution," Sarah said slowly. "Yeah—my folks will love that shit."

"Like they say, 'Payback is a bitch,'" Jack replied.

Keystone, South Dakota

Charli kept her aim on the center mass of the woman that had entered the Hall of Records. "I don't mean any harm," her target said with remarkable calm.

"Take the gun out with your thumb and forefinger, real smooth, and drop it," Charli commanded.

The woman nodded once and moved slowly to comply. She lowered the pistol and dropped it. "For the record, I have one in a shin holster as well, right side," she said.

"Get it," Charli commanded Andy.

He looked at her and she could read his face perfectly, 'Who me?' He stepped cautiously toward the woman, careful to not get between Charli and the stranger. He knelt and lifted her jeans leg where he found the holster. Andy fumbled with the strap but finally got the gun out. He backed away, picking up the pistol the woman had already dropped on the rugged stone floor.

"Who are you?"

"Caylee Leatrom," she said firmly. "I was an operative of the NSF—sent to intercept you."

"Was?" Andy asked as he backed away.

"A few hours ago my relationship with the NSF came to an unplanned end, Mister Forrest," she said.

"You know who I am?"

"I do. My last mission was to try to track down sightings of the, eh, former President. It was believed that his appearance might be tied to the Sons of Liberty. Eventually, that led me to you. I had hoped you might be able to direct me to their leadership."

"Why do you say your relationship with the NSF is over?"

"It is," the muscular woman responded. "They sent two operatives to kill me. I guess just laying me off was out of the question." She smirked a little bit. *She seems awfully clam for someone with a gun leveled at them.* Charli refused to relax her stance. *If she is an operative, she is very dangerous, even without her guns.*

"If you ended your service with them, why did you follow us here?" Charli pressed.

Leatrom shrugged slightly. "Where else would I go? I can't go home, not that there's anything there for me. I killed the operatives that were after me, which means I'm more wanted than ever before. They will hunt me down. That left me with little in the way of options. I could either flee, try and hide, or turn the tables on them."

Andy spoke up. "What do you mean?"

"I'm an operative, Mr. Forrest. I do the dirty deeds that the government disavows. Over the last few years, I have done a lot of things that go beyond the law. That and I know certain truths, some of the secrets that the Secretary of the NSF won't want out. I came to the conclusion that my best chance at survival was to do the one thing they wouldn't expect, join the fight against them. The old saying is *the enemy of my enemy is my friend.* I doubt we can be friends, but I can't survive on my own, not for as long as I intend to live anyways. So, I come offering my services and information to the Sons of Liberty."

Charli chuckled. "And why should we believe you? You said it; you are an operative. Maybe this is a ploy to penetrate the leadership of the Sons, then turn us in, or kill everyone. You aren't exactly coming with a resume that says, 'trust me.'"

"Fair enough," Leatrom replied. "I presume you have access to polygraph equipment—you can test me. You can scan me for tracking devices or wires. I expect that you would want to. I would if I were in your shoes. If you want, you can put me in a cell and ignore me. If nothing else, I'd live longer than being out there in public with the entire NSF breathing down my neck."

Charli shot a quick glance at Andy who gave her a look of, 'I have no idea.'" *Neither do I,* she thought. Her gut instinct was to kill the operative right there and then. It was the easiest solution, the best short-term move. *What if she's telling the truth?* If that is the case, she may have intelligence information that could help Jack and the others. Bit by bit Charli came to realize that Leatrom may be more useful alive than dead. Still, she needed more.

"I should shoot you right now," she said firmly. "For all we know you have a strike team waiting outside, ready to ambush us."

"If that is the case, you are screwed, but not as bad as me," the woman arrogantly replied. She paused for a moment. "Look, there's no strike team out there yet. They *are* looking for me though. I ditched my truck in a lake, which should buy me some time, but they will begin to narrow their search for me—that much I can assure you."

"We could tie her up," Andy offered. Leave her here."

"Bad play, Mister Forrest," she countered. "I saw what was in those cases. If they managed to get that information out of me, they will come at you too."

"Again," Charli said, motioning with her gun slightly. "It makes more sense to kill you."

The operative did not look threatened. "I'm dead already. That was why I continued to track you down. The things I know—the things I can prove—they have made me a marked woman. The Secretary herself has ordered me terminated. Most of my identities are worthless now. No more safe houses. They will run me down, capture and kill me."

"If you're looking for pity…" Charli started

"I'm not. I'm stating facts. The things I know can shake things up. It puts the Secretary at risk—she knows that. I just think that you'd be stupid to kill me and miss the opportunity to shove a big fat wide-one up that bitch's ass."

Charli suppressed a grin. *I like the way she talks.* "You're not very good at this negotiation stuff," she replied instead.

"I'm on operative. I didn't negotiate as much as use brute force to get what I needed."

The former Secret Service Lieutenant eyed the woman carefully. *She could have simply come to the door and killed us. We didn't even see her there. Killing us wasn't her intent. She may be attempting to infiltrate Jack's organization. We can make sure that doesn't happen.* The temptation to inflict harm on the Secretary of the NSF was seductive to Charli. *She has turned the police into her private army. If this operative is telling the truth, she may have information that could harm her, perhaps ruin her.*

"I know what you are thinking," the operative said. "I could have simply shot the two of you from the doorway. You didn't hear me sneak in. You're wondering if the information I possess is worth the risk of taking me along with you."

"Pretty much," Charli admitted.

"You need to decide. As I said, I am wanted. They will come soon.

We need to be as far away from this place as possible when they do show."

Damn! Charli hated being pressed into making a decision. *This is above my pay grade. Jack can make the call as to whether she's telling us the truth or not. If she's lying, we can shoot her then. In the meantime, I will have to assume she's being honest.* Charli reached into her bag and pulled out a zip tie. She tossed it to Andy. "Bind her hands."

"So that's it?" Andy said. "We are bringing her with us?"

Charli nodded. "She's right—if she was here to kill us, she would have done it already. If she is betraying us... trying to get into the SOL, we can kill her at our leisure. In the meantime, if she is right, we need to get out of here. Grab her backpack and make sure she doesn't have anything in there that might be a tracker of some sort."

Andy walked over and wrapped the white zip cord around her hands. "You haven't done this before," the operative chided. "You need to make it tighter. I could get out of this without even trying." Andy looked at her and tightened it another inch. "Better," she said.

Andy started digging in the black backpack that the operative had. "Lots of ammo, knives, survival gear—some food—and one government iPad."

"I've pulled the tracking chip from it," Leatrom said. "Feel free to check. It has a dump of my files on it."

Andy locked gazes with Charli as if asking whether and how he could check. She shrugged it off. *I can check that later... now we need to get on the move.* "You take that and the flag," Charli said, holstering her weapon and picking up the operatives. "We need to get down and find a vehicle."

"You walked in?" Leatrom asked.

"Yes."

"I sunk my truck. That puts us on foot. Not good."

"We will get down from here and find a vehicle."

"I passed a lumber mill about three miles or so back towards town. There will be vehicles there," her prisoner offered.

Charli picked up the tube that held the Declaration of Independence and the Constitution. For a moment, she paused, realizing the value of what was in her hands. *Oddly enough, when this room was carved, it was supposed to hold these documents. It took a few decades, but they finally made it.*

Starting for the doorway, she turned back. "We're going to have to move quick."

"I never got your name," Operative Leatrom said.

"And you don't need it," Charli replied. *The less she knows at this stage… the better.*

CHAPTER 19

*"Every voice is equal unless it is the
voice of intolerance or division."*

Philadelphia, Pennsylvania

It took several days before Raul found himself able to fully relax. Jayden and the others had treated him as if he had been a part of their cell for a lifetime. They wanted to know everything about him, his family, and they shared their stories as well. Jayden taught him some self-defense moves, which he seemed to learn quite quickly. His favorite was when Jayden grabbed him from behind, wrapping his arms around him tightly. Raul learned to bend over quickly, grab one of Jayden's ankles, then snap back to a standing position—toppling them both over onto his attacker's back, breaking the hold.

Father Ryan had stayed for a few days, but then went back to Detroit. He said he didn't want to arouse suspicion by being gone so long. He assured Raul he would be returning soon. While he missed him, he became more comfortable with the others in the cell. The Father's departure forced him to engage more with the others.

One of the members of the group was a young woman, Sasha. During one meal, she shared how she had come to join the Sons. Her father had been a staunch supporter of the Second Amendment and had an impressive gun collection. He was not even a hunter, he just liked collecting and shooting guns. When the Ruling Council had banned the ownership of guns and forced a nationwide buy-back, he had refused. The NSF had come with an armored vehicle and a dozen officers in full tactical gear.

She had been hiding in the house, under a bed, but had seen it all. Her father held a gun, but never fired at the police as they busted down the door. They shot him... tore his body apart with bullets. Her mother had been arrested, taken away, and Sasha had been shuffled off to a foster home. Her mother had been painted as an unfit parent, raising her in a house with guns.

On the news, it was all about him being a radical, leading a 'stand-off' with the NSF, shooting at officers first. Sasha said it was all a lie, one she was still clearly bitter about. "I still remember some of them posing with his dead body, flashing gang signs. To them, it was a joke." Tears welled up in her eyes as she spoke.

She had run away and had lived on the streets for three months when Jayden and the others took her in. They had given her home and hope. Her mother had been sent off to a Social Quarantine Camp. "I don't know where she is or even if she's still alive."

Other members of the Order had stories that tore at him as well. Suddenly his own plight didn't seem quite as bad. Despite all of the hardships they had endured, they seemed happy. He had his own room in a nearby house, owned by one of the Order of the Bell. There was good food—even laughter. After a few days, he felt relaxed. The rioting had slowed to 'peaceful protests' in the streets... little more than armed mobs chanting and demanding justice. Raul allowed himself to think that it was going to blow over eventually.

At one point, he asked Jayden the name of the cell. "The name of our group comes from the Liberty Bell. It used to be housed in Philly. It was a symbol of freedom and of America, so it had to either be destroyed or corrupted. That's how these Newmericans work. They decided to destroy it. We have heard that they melted it down and made little souvenirs for the members of the Ruling Council—pins, ink pens, and things like that. I suppose they thought it funny or instructive—like when someone rubs a dog's nose in its shit to teach it a lesson." The last sentence came with anger as he spoke, raw, unfulfilled.

"They forget that the bell's inscription was a rallying cry to end slavery before the Civil War. They ignore history that is inconvenient to the story they want to tell. They took a symbol of freedom and liberty and melted it down to make jewelry for themselves. For me, it is a reminder of how corrupt and evil these people really are. Anything that doesn't fit their narrative has to be destroyed." Raul could see the anger and frustration in Jayden as he spoke about it.

He had seen images of statues being torn down and had been told by the media that the people they represented were bad. But a bell? *How could that be bad? If it represented Liberty, does that mean that the government was against Liberty?* Until a few weeks ago, his life had been so simple. He didn't have to think about things like the Liberty Bell. The media told him what to think, how to feel, and what actions he needed to take. *My whole life is different now.*

Near the end of his first week, Jayden pulled him aside, taking him into what had been an office for the warehouse. Raul took a seat in an old folding chair and Jayden took a chair, turned it backwards, and straddled it in front of him. "Is something wrong?"

Jayden nodded rapidly. "I am so sorry, Raul."

"What is it?" His thoughts went to his mother... to Paco and the others from his Troop. *Had they been found?*

"The Social Enforcers, the ones that killed your troop leader—they broke into the church where Father Ryan preached. They said they knew he had harbored you and the others."

"No," he said, barely able to form that word, let alone others. Images flashed in his mind of what they might have done. Violence and blood.

"They beat him," Jayden said, his face seeming to sag as he spoke. "Then they burned the church with him in it." Jayden dipped his own head for a moment to hide the hurt and anger on his own face.

The image of fire and the church where he prayed seemed to suck the air from him. His ears throbbed with the pounding of his heart. For a moment, he felt nervous to the point of panic. Jayden seemed to sense this. *What kind of monsters would burn a church?* He reached up and put his hand on Raul's shoulder. "Breathe my brother—breathe."

"They didn't have to kill him. He was just protecting me." *This is my fault... just like the death of that SE man that attacked us.*

Jayden squeezed his hand on Raul's shoulder. "The *padre* did what he had to do. He knew the risks associated with getting you and the others out, but he followed his heart and his faith, Raul. This is not about you. This is about them... the Social Enforcers. This is how they operate, with intimidation and violence. A lesser man than Father Ryan would have buckled and told them what they wanted to know. He believed in God and believed in you Raul."

Raul slowly got control of his emotions. He wanted to cry. The tears started to form, but he couldn't. He slid from sadness into anger almost instantly. "These people—they are inhuman."

"The government allows them to operate," Jayden said. "It is one of the ways they exert control. If you don't fall in line, the SEs come; they harass, intimidate, beat, or kill. If you fight back, they riot and loot. They use fear to force compliance. They claim to desire peace and coexistence, but in reality, they are oppressors. They bully and subjugate people into falling in line, the line they draw."

Raul's jaw set tighter with each word said by the leader of the Order of the Bell. "They killed a man of God. He never hurt anyone."

"It is in their nature," Jayden said, removing his hand from Raul's shoulder. "It doesn't matter that he was a priest or that the building they burned was a church. He didn't comply. He didn't buckle under. When you rule by violence, even a passive resistance cannot be tolerated. History has shown that over and over. Newmerica is a lie, built on a foundation of lies. Most citizens have no idea. They only want to get through their day. Many don't care, until the government comes after them." Jayden's voice rang not with rhetoric, but from experience; Raul could hear that in every word.

Jayden continued slowly, choosing his words deliberately. "When people come to power based on the blood of others, they eventually become more oppressive than the people they overthrew. I don't understand why it is, but it is the nature of people. They claim they are opposed to all of this—the things that they did to Father Ryan and others—but they allow it to happen. It is their way."

For long moments he said nothing. He dipped his head and wrapped his mind around the thoughts of fury boiling in him. Father Ryan had been an important voice in his life, even in the small time that he had known him. He had given his life for Raul to get him to the Sons of Liberty, where he would be safe. *His sacrifice should not be for nothing.*

As he raised his head, Jayden spoke again. "Are you alright Raul?"

He nodded, and wiped away the tears that never fully formed from his eyes. "I am," he replied, drawing a long, deep breath.

"Can I get you something?"

Raul's eyes bore into Jayden's. "All I want now is revenge. They must pay for what they did. They have ruined my life and taken my Troop Leader and my friend. They cannot be allowed to continue on and do this to other people."

Jayden rose to his feet and Raul did the same. "Then you are in the right place my brother. Because we are about to take the fight to them."

Raul Lopez felt warm, confident, more determined than ever before. He had regained something he had lost with the death of Avalon. Raul had a purpose. *I will make those that ruined my life and killed these people pay for what they have done.*

Iowa City, Iowa

Stealing a truck proved to be easier than Andy had expected. Charli knew how to hot wire one, which should have been more of a surprise than it was for him. Their 'accomplice' as Andy referred to Caylee Leatrom, had been quite passive. Still, as he sat in the back seat of the Chevy truck, he couldn't help but be worried about her and the rumors about operatives—that they were a cross between James Bond and Jack Reacher, a combination that he did not want to be on the receiving end of. Still, Leatrom was oddly calm, despite being zip-tied. She even offered suggestions to Charli while she hot-wired the truck.

Half-an-hour out from Mount Rushmore, a pair of black NSF helicopters roared over, heading towards the monument. It was dark, impossible to see them, but their roar of rotors overhead was evidence enough of their presence. Leatrom watched the dark night sky, staring intently at the blinking red lights on their tails as they zoomed into the distance. "They are looking for me," she said craning her head around to keep them in view. For a few moments, Andy thought it was a boast, her flaunting her ego. Slowly he realized she was likely telling the truth. No one countered her assertion.

The driving was long. Charli used different credit cards everywhere she went. She seemed to have a lot of them in her bag. Dinner consisted of junk food from a 7-Eleven, chips, soda, and sandwiches that were slightly soggy. Charli purchased a burner phone and used it to make several long calls out of earshot before tossing it in the bed of another truck to avoid tracking.

Andy didn't complain, he knew better. Oddly, this was a lifestyle he found himself slowly becoming accustomed to—being on the run, avoiding detection. It was a shared experience; he wasn't in it alone. Those days after his father died, he had felt the weight of the world on him. *If it wasn't for Charli, I would be under interrogation right now. Creature comforts are a small price to pay.* He hugged the case he carried tightly to his lap. Caylee commented, "You can relax. I'm not going to take it, Mister Forrest."

"I know. But the last man to touch it was my dad," Andy replied. "And you can call me Andy. Mister Forrest sounds too formal."

"A professional courtesy," Leatrom said. "In my profession, I've found that being respectful and formal sometimes helps. Some people appreciate such formality. Old habits die hard... Andy."

Leatrom turned to Charli who was driving. "If it is not asking too much, where are we going?"

"Someplace where we can validate your story. I'm not taking you to any key asset until I can authenticate what you say," she replied. That seemed to be enough for Caylee as she leaned back. Andy only caught glimpses of her as headlights hit them. She didn't seem nervous or concerned. The operative leaned her head to the side of the seat and closed her eyes. Andy doubted he could be so calm in the same circumstances. He couldn't sleep, though he tried.

As the sun rose, the vehicle reached the outskirts of Iowa City, Iowa. Charli checked her phone several times before turning off a series of side streets in the outskirts of the city. She finally stopped in front of a small, nondescript house. It was an older neighborhood, one dating back to WWII if not earlier. The houses had been refurbished, probably several times. It was quiet, except for a barking dog several doors down. Charli got out and opened the door for Caylee and led her up to the door. She wore the archival tube slung over her back, while Andy still carried the case.

A burley man with Asian features opened the door just before Charli could knock and motioned them in. The house had a smell to it, a mix of oatmeal cooking and spices Andy couldn't quite identify. The man led them to a dining room in the center of the home. Charli motioned to a chair at the head of the table and Leatrom sat in it.

No one spoke as the chunky man swept the operative with some sort of gray wand scanner. He nodded to Charli; then he pulled a large box from another chair where it had been sitting. Andy had never seen a polygraph machine, but knew this was one. He began hooking her up, then gave a nod to Charli. "Alright little girl, let's step outside and let him do his thing." Andy followed her out of the room and she closed the door behind them.

Charli stretched for a moment, then went into the small living room where she flopped down on the couch. She closed her eyes and was asleep in a matter of heartbeats. He took a seat in an easy chair opposite of her and, still clutching the case, did the same. Even a few minutes sleep would help and it consumed him quickly. In his mind he thought he was awake. He heard muffled voices. Andy's body sank into the seat as if it were slowly consuming him.

He was jarred awake with the large man's voice. "She passed." His eyes fought his urge to open them, a battle his consciousness finally won.

"Damn," Charli said.

Andy looked at her. "You sound disappointed."

"If she had failed, we could have simply killed her. Now I have to deal with her instead." This was the side of Charli he found himself oddly attracted to. She was more than willing and able to utilize violence to get what she wanted. He knew he should be afraid of that kind of behavior, but there was something very genuine in her that made it appealing.

"Polys can be beaten," the man said. "I got no indication of deception though. Usually when someone is good enough to beat the system, you get a hint of it. She believes she's telling us the truth."

Charli rose from her seat on the couch and stretched slightly. "Thanks, Curly," she said, shaking the man's beefy hand. He reached out and hugged her with his free arm. "We are brother and sister," he said. "Blue blood runs thick."

"You have a phone?" she asked. He handed her a battered old flip phone. Charli took it and marched down the hallway. Andy was left with Curly. "So, you know Charli, I guess?"

"Never met her before... not face-to-face," he said. "We are both law enforcement, or were. They painted us as criminals, went after our families. She kept in contact with me, as did her chief. It's all handled now in short calls and secret messages—but the brotherhood of blue is still out there. We're waiting for the right time."

"Time for what?" Andy asked.

Curley flashed a grin and a chuckle. "You are in this and you have no idea what is going down, do you?"

Andy shook his head as Curley continued. "Let's just say that some shit is going down. A lot of us had people and things taken from us. We were silenced. Not anymore. When you accuse people of stuff they didn't do, sooner or later, they start to feel obliged to do that stuff. That time is coming."

Andy was a little taken aback with the words. *Something is happening—something soon.* There had been a hint of that in things that Caylee Leatrom said too. He wondered what it could be, or if Leatrom was talking about something entirely different. *If something is going to happen, what is it?*

Charli returned after several minutes of muted conversation in the next room. "Curley, I'm going to need some ration cards."

He flashed her a smile. "No problem Little Girl," he said. He left the room and came back with a handful of cards. "Use once and toss 'em." Andy knew what the ration cards meant. More hours on the road.

"Got it," she replied. "Thanks for your help."

"Good luck with that one," he said nodding in Caylee's direction. Andy glanced over and thought he saw the operative crack a thin smile in response. "It has been a treat Mister Curley," she replied.

As they made their way to the car, he found himself admiring Caylee. *If it were me, I'd be worried about being shot in the head just to be rid of me. She seems calm... resolved.* As they got in the vehicle, Andy positioned the cases on the floor in the back seat next to where he sat. "Alright then, where to next?"

"To the top," Charli replied as she angled the car out onto the narrow street and accelerated.

CHAPTER 20

"The Individual Is the Enemy. Groups ensure prosperity!"

Culpeper, Virginia

The town of Culpeper consisted of a few blocks, two main streets, and the appearance of having been torn from reruns of the old sitcom, *The Andy Griffith Show*. Some of the buildings dated back to before the Civil War and all of them had a small-town charm. The two main streets were pitted with potholes that the Ruling Council swore would be fixed by their infrastructure spending bills. Aside from the run-down condition of a few buildings, there was an innocence about the place. Charli angled her car past Davis Street and turned into a backstreet parking lot. She admired Jack for picking interesting safe locations. This one's proximity to the District, only sixty miles away, did make her slightly edgy, but she understood the logic. *Sometimes the best place to hide is right on the enemy's doorstep.*

Some of the quaintness seemed to fade as she drove through town. Businesses were boarded up; others had been closed a long time; the faded signs in the windows harkened back to the Fall. One building had scorch marks from fire on the outside, charring the restaurant's façade. Graffiti of an up-thrust fist of the Newmerica flag had been crudely recreated in black spray paint. Charli found herself thankful that the small town didn't have one of the government's digital billboards flashing their slogans. *People forget that the revolution hit small towns just as much as the big ones—maybe harder.*

She, Andy and Caylee got out of the car and made their way after her to the old post office building. Charli carried the archival tube and her backpack, while Andy carried the flag in its bulky case. The boarded-up doors and windows showed the white paint burned black underneath, scars of some of the rioting that had taken place during the time of the Fall. The old building had been used by the county government, but had been shut down, never repaired, after the riots. At one time the stately white pillared building must have had quite a bit of charm. Now it sat in the late morning haze of Piedmont humidity. The abandoned building was a reminder of the dark side of the Fall.

The trio walked past the building to the back alley and made their way past long-uncollected trash bins to the rusty rear door. She knocked and the door opened. Three burly armed men, one in grease-stained blue coveralls greeted them. "He's waiting for you upstairs," he said with a low, southern drawl, pointing to the staircase. Charli said nothing as they went up the stairs.

Jack was there, no fake cosmetics, just Jack. She walked up to him and gestured. "Jack, this is Andy Forrest." Andy shook his hand, fumbling slightly with the case. "And this is our *guest*, Caylee Leatrom." The former operative nodded once as Jack eyed her from head to toe.

"And you are?" Leatrom asked.

"Your worst nightmare," he replied flatly, gesturing to several battered folding chairs in the office. The air still stung with the smell of burned wood with a hint of mildew. There were no windows, everything had been boarded up long ago. At the top of the stairs, the man in the coveralls came up, AR-15 in his hands.

"I'm not sure about that," Caylee said taking her seat. "I tend to give nightmares, not have them."

Jack turned to Andy, then Charli. "What did you recover, aside from Mister Forrest here?"

Charli pulled out the tube case she had been so protective of. "Be gentle—they are the originals," she said.

Jack took the tube over to a white plastic Costco folding table and gingerly pulled out the documents. As he unrolled them Charli could see his eyes open wide. "My God. They said they were destroyed."

"They say a lot of things," Caylee chimed in from her seat. "Lying has become easier than telling the people the truth. Then again, with politicians, it has always been that way."

Andy rose and walked over to Jack as the former Secret Service Director carefully rerolled and sealed the Declaration of Independence and the Constitution back in the tube. Andy slowly opened the other rectangular box and showed Jack the flag. "I take it this one is special?" Jack asked.

Andy nodded. "It's the one that was raised on Iwo Jima."

Jack reached out and delicately laid his hand on it, as if to confirm it was really there in front of him. "They destroyed all of them. Even the ones on the net get blocked or taken down the moment they appear." His gaze never lifted from the old flag as he talked, and Charli wondered if he was speaking to himself, or to those in the room. "They are so afraid of a symbol that they censor it, erase it from history." Removing his hand, Andy sealed the case.

The older man looked at Andy, then to Charli. "We can use these. They are powerful symbols. A lot of people resent that they can't even look at the image of our flag now, that the Truth Reconciliation Committee has ruled it a symbol of racism and hate. When you tell people they can't do something, they want to defy it. They know the truth… this isn't about hate; it's about rewriting our true heritage as a people."

Andy slightly stiffed at Jack's words and hugged the flag case. "These are artifacts. They are delicate… not something to be used. People have died to keep them safe. My dad, Mr. Farmer, Abel Brunner… they sacrificed their lives in many respects to make sure they were not destroyed."

The older man seemed to understand, allowing a thin smile, more than Charli had ever seen from him. "I know Andrew. We will treat them with respect. And for the record, many good people have died for what they stand for over the centuries. Your father was a smart man, protecting them. He didn't do that to hide them though. He must have known how important they were. People need symbols to stand behind. There are none more important than these." Jack's words were sincere, almost reverent. Andy relaxed his grip and nodded slightly.

Jack took a moment to gather his thoughts, then turned to face Charli. "Now then, we need to address the elephant in the room. Charli, from what Curly told me, this former operative wants to flip," he said, darting his eyes at Leatrom.

"I don't have much choice," Caylee replied. "It was either run until they found me, or fight. I tend not to avoid fights, especially when my life is on the line."

"We could kill you," Jack said, crossing his arms and making his shoulder holster jut out from his chest. "It would be easier for us than trusting you."

"You polygraphed me—zero deception. I came with my files—every dirty little operation that I have ever been on. If that stuff gets out, you will make the Secretary's life a living hell." As Caylee spoke, Charli pulled out the iPad that the operative had provided her. Jack glanced at it, flipping past two screens worth of data.

"I appreciate this," Jack said. "That doesn't mean I fully trust you."

"She's planning something," Caylee said. "The Secretary. Something big."

"What?" Charli asked.

Leatrom shrugged slowly. "I don't know for sure. I was ruffling the Social Enforcement's feathers in trying to track down the Sons of Liberty. That somehow seems to play into what she had planned."

Charli turned to Jack who said nothing for a moment, deep in thought. "Why were you after us?"

"We had sightings of the traitor—er, the former President. The folks in Silicon Valley said that there was a high probability that it could be linked to the SOL. My last mission was to get into the Sons and find out if indeed the President is still alive."

Charli dipped her head, averting her eyes for a moment. Memories from more than four years ago washed over her. The humid room suddenly seemed warm to her. She shuffled her stance. "He isn't," she said in a low tone of voice that surprised even her as she spoke. The eyes in the room fell on her. She could feel them stabbing at her.

"Well then," Caylee said. "Then I guess my being here is more an accident than anything."

"Accident," Jack added, "or luck."

"You trust her then?" Charli asked, slightly surprised. Despite the polygraph examination, she had her doubts about Caylee Leatrom. Some of it was her arrogance, that haughty tone of voice that the operative used. Part of it was pure professional caution. Charli understood intelligence operations, and that having a former enemy in your presence was a danger.

Jack could sense her resistance but smiled a touch more. "Charli, the worst enemy of an oppressive state is always the state itself. The more restrictive the government, the more dictatorial, the more it starts to rot from within. This operative—" he waved his hand towards Caylee, "is proof of that. They always turn on their own. It happened after the French Revolution as well. After a while of lopping off the heads of the royals and the rich, they started to turn on each other. From the sound of it, the Secretary turned on her." Caylee gave a lone nod in response.

"So just like that, you trust her?"

His head shook. "After what we have been through, I don't trust many people, and she isn't on that list yet. She gave us her only real bargaining chip—the information on her iPad. I want to look it over, see if I can corroborate some of what she has there. If I can, that's a big first step."

"I assumed it would go down like this," Caylee said. "I will give you the access code to my files," she said with an eerie calm in her voice. "You may kill me. I personally think it would be a waste of a good resource, but I understand if you do. The Secretary tried to kill me; that isn't something I take lightly. My choice in life was to live on the run, waiting for that sniper bullet to the back of my head, or to turn myself over to you."

Bit by bit Charli began to understand. *They used her. She was their tool. She did their dirty work, and in the end, they changed the rules of the game on her.* It was hard to look at Caylee as a victim, but she was. She had given them her loyalty and trust, and the reward for that was a death sentence. She couldn't quite muster feeling sorry for the operative she had brought in, but at the same time she did feel an understanding of her plight.

Charli pushed those thoughts aside. When Jack had sent her to Andy, it was supposed to have been a light mission—but it had turned into much more. And there was the matter of the promise. Jack had told her that a legal successor to the Presidency existed. The time had finally come for Charli to collect on that promise. Turning to Jack, she put her hands on her hips. "We had a deal," she said slowly.

Desmond looked back at her and nodded. "We did at that. He's outside of town, we have him in a farmhouse—way off the grid." Charli was surprised that he was that close. *Whatever it is that Jack has planned, it must be coming about soon if they are willing to risk having a successor so close to The District.* "I'll take you there," Jack continued. "But know this, he's going to have questions for you Charli."

"About?"

"The President."

Her eyes closed slowly for a moment as she felt the emotional gut-punch of his words. She didn't like thinking about the events that had taken place that night, the night of the Fall. When anyone brought it up, she dodged discussing it. It was a wound, both physical and mental, that had not healed. Picking at it only made it worse. She nodded a response, unable to grasp the words.

Jack turned to Andy. "I'd like to take those with me. For what we have planned, they will be useful," his eyes darted to the two artifacts.

Charli was surprised but Andy moved to block Jack's view. "They are not going out of my sight."

The corner of Jack's mouth rose in a half-smile. "Very well. You can come along with us."

Charli gestured to Caylee. "What about her?"

Walking in front of Leatrom, Jack paused. "She will stay here for now. He lowered himself to look her in the face. "I trust that you won't be any trouble."

"I don't have anywhere else to go," Caylee replied. "I would appreciate a chance to shower up and get some decent food."

Charli saw him nod. "More than reasonable. We will get all of you to a safe home we have nearby, give you a chance to clean up. I will run you out there tonight," he said locking gaze with Charli.

Cleveland, Ohio

Karen Forrester finished her shower and dragged a brush through her hair. There was no style to her haircut, which was a style all on its own. She did not use makeup; that was a sign of subservience to males—and Karen was against all such demonstrations of that type. Deodorant was one of the luxuries that she afforded herself. Hers had come from a home that her SE unit in Cleveland had raided. One of the few perks of her job was confiscation privileges. The cosmetics industry had struggled under the regulations and the costs of such luxuries were high. It was their own fault in her mind. *If they had not used chemicals that threatened the environment, they wouldn't have had regulations put on them.*

The entire affair with her brother Andy had boiled up as of yesterday evening. Someone had beat the SE team out of Chicago that had been investigating him. Several were dead; the rest had been hospitalized by a mysterious attacker that had come to her brother's defense. From what she saw on the grainy surveillance footage of the attack, this was no ordinary bystander jumping in to help her brother. This person had moves... the moves of a professional killer.

As she went to the kitchen and put an English muffin in the toaster, she wondered about Andy. He had always been headstrong... stupidly so. He got that from Dad. Her father had been an embarrassment to her, having been associated with the Sons of Liberty, sent off for social quarantine. Karen had been forced to change her name to put some distance between them. Andy was too close to their father. *What has he dragged you into Andy?*

Karen had been summoned to the District, no doubt to talk about her brother. *Thanks to you, I am once more getting my career tarnished by a family member.* She hated Andy for that and his stubbornness. *He has fallen in with some tough characters to wrack up that kind of body count. Then he goes black—no one has seen him.* The SE had set up check points all around the Chicago area but he hadn't surfaced. *He's smart, but not smart enough to slip past us—not on his own.* Andy Forrest was no longer Karen's brother; he was a hard-target fleeing the scene of a crime and avoiding an SE investigation.

Karen resented Andy and the relationship he was willing to have with her father. When the Great Reformation began, her father had spoken out openly against it, publishing several scathing editorials against the peaceful protests which he mislabeled as riots. She fell in love with what the protestors were striving for. Change had to be brought about with violence. That was what the forefathers had done against the British after all. Her father had come down on her hard, forbidding her to take part. Andy had been there right beside him. *I hated Andy's smug arrogance, his blindness to the corruption in our dad. Now look at what it's gotten you Andy. You're a fugitive from social justice. When we catch you, you'll understand why compliance is so important.*

She knew what would happen to him when he was taken into custody. Social Enforcement interrogations were intense, both physically and mentally. They had to be. Social non-conformity was a threat to Newmerica and had to be uprooted whenever it was found. *They will beat the shit out of him, starve him, work him over with the probes. If he had only told us what Father had hidden and where it was, none of that would be necessary.* Karen would be a part of it too, if only to persuade her brother to talk. Strangely, she was not dreading the role that she would play… she was looking forward to it.

This would not help her career in the SE at all, not unless she came out strong against Andy and those that he was working with. *Just like Dad, he's only thinking of himself, not how any of his actions might affect me.* Karen was convinced that she would have risen higher in the ranks of the SEs if her father had not been a member of a terrorist organization. Andy was following in her father's footsteps, doing the same sort of behavior. *Once more I have to shoulder the burden of the Forrest family.* This would be the last time Karen was going to see to that. *Andy won't see the light of day once we find him. They will lock him away for good.*

The toaster oven beeped and she opened it, gingerly pulling out the hot English muffin. Turning to the refrigerator, she was stunned to see someone standing there, in her kitchen, only a few feet away. The figure was wearing a skin-tight black bodysuit complete with a hood that obscured most of his face. She saw his eyes, brilliant green, staring right at her.

"Who in the—" Karen began. The figure jerked, and her words were cut off with a hot feeling that morphed instantly to pain at her throat. *Air… I can't breathe!* She dropped to her knees, her hands dropping the muffin and grasping at her throat. Panic engulfed Karen as she attempted to understand what was happening.

The figure moved. She saw his feet, shifting behind her. Some air got in through her damaged throat, but not nearly enough as she gasped. Then she felt it, something wrapped around her throat from behind—a wire. Her chubby fingers attempted to get between it and her skin, but failed as the wire was pulled tight.

Karen flexed her thick legs, trying to rise, but felt a wave of dizziness and warmth take control of her body. Her vision tunneled. *Why? Why was this happening? Who was this?*

Her last thoughts, as she writhed on the kitchen floor, was not of family or friends—but asking questions that she would never get answers to.

The District

Director Dorne had been keeping her posted as the counts had started coming in at midnight. The Secretary's NSF operatives were busy, whittling away the list of 188 leaders of the Social Enforcement organization around the country. Only four remained unaccounted for, and they would not last long—not with her operatives on their trail.

The director of the organization had tried to flee when he had seen his killer, or so Dorne had reported. He had slipped and fallen into his pool, making him an easy target for her operative. She had asked that his death be filmed and was looking forward to reviewing it personally. *I look forward to reviewing it. Douglas Ferraday was always so arrogant, and in the end, that brought him down.*

As her driver brought the car in front of the old post office in the District, where the Ruling Council met, she got out, made sure her suit was hanging just right, and headed in. Her NSF security for the building knew better than to ask for ID. She was merely ushered in.

It took several minutes to reach the Ruling Council chambers and when she entered, she could feel the eyes of everyone in the room fall on her. *They will have started to hear about it, rumors mostly, but they are wondering and they are afraid.*

She graciously took her seat and the doors to the chamber closed. "Alex," the chair of domestic affairs said. "There have been disturbing rumors."

"I'm aware," she said firmly, offering no hint of emotion. "It is my extreme displeasure to inform this body that the NSF recently detected a planned coup from the SE organization… a coup aimed at seizing control of the NSF under SE leadership." She paused and could see the looks of confusion and fear rise from her fellow council members.

"In order to suppress this, I ordered the NSF to take executive action against the SE leadership that was involved with this plot. They have, as of now, been neutralized and are no longer a threat to Newmerica or this council."

"Wait," barked the older chair of foreign affairs. "Are you telling me that the SE leadership is dead? Douglas too?"

"Dead sounds so horrible. I prefer to think the threat to our nation has been neutralized," she said matter-of-factly. "And yes, Douglas too. This was a corruption that went all of the way to the top. Not only that—I have seen evidence gathered by our signals intercept group that indicates he may have been planning to seize control of the entire Ruling Council. As such, I took action to prevent an ugly and damaging scandal, one that would have placed everything we have built at risk."

"How many people are we talking about?" Adam, the beady-eyed Director of Congressional affairs asked.

"Not that many," Alex answered, tossing her black hair back on one side. "Less than two hundred people."

"Two-hundred people?" Adam said in dismay. He was still smiling slightly, it was a quirk he had, that perpetual grin. "That is not a small number of people. People are going to notice two hundred citizens from the SE Director going missing. Where did you get that kind of authority?"

"I have had it all along," she answered. "You certainly didn't raise any concerns when the NSF took action at your bidding. I will grant you, two hundred people sounds like a lot, but they were spread all across the nation. No one will be able to connect them. To the public, it looks like some random people disappeared. Trust me, it will be forgotten. And if anyone does do some digging, we always have the Truth Reconciliation Committee on our side to help us control the media."

"What evidence do you have against these people?" the Chairman of the Joint Chiefs, a beefy Army general, asked.

"*Ample* evidence," she assured him. "As you are aware, I have reported to all of you in our recent meetings about the attacks on the NSF, aimed specifically at our investigative capabilities. Some of these were bioweapons, while others were weapons of mass destruction. I had a team investigating if it was the work of domestic terrorists, but have come to believe that, based on the evidence, it was the work of the SE organization in what could only be perceived as a coup attempt. I reviewed the evidence personally. In due time, I will make that available for your review, Ted." It was a deliberate use of his first name, not his rank. "I will have summary reports sent to you in the next few hours, all of you, for review." The Secretary paused, suppressing the urge to grin. She was unsure as to who had been striking at her organization, but whoever it was had given her the perfect reason to lay the blame at the feet of her political foes—Social Enforcement. *There will be plenty of time when the dust settles and I consolidate my power to search for the real perpetrators.*

"This is most disturbing, especially given the timing. In a few days we were going to announce the new Constitutional Convention on the anniversary of the Liberation and the new elections. Now we have this... this... insurrection," said the Council Chairman from the head of the lengthy oblong table where they sat. "I don't want anything that might distract from what we have planned."

"There will be no distraction," the Secretary assured him. *I won't tolerate it.*

"Who will lead the SE?" asked Barbara Collingsworth, a former congresswoman that now led the treasury in the Newmerica Administration.

"I will," the Secretary replied. "I have already prepared communications to that extent. I assure you, it is a temporary move, just to make sure that we have indeed suppressed this coup attempt." She said the words as if she believed them. *Once entrenched, I will have control and with that control, it will be impossible to extract me from that role.*

"This is most irregular," the Council Chairman said, shifting in his seat. "It might be more prudent to have someone else take control of the SE, someone fresh and new."

That did have her crack a slight smile. "The NSF just saved our country. It only makes sense that my organization assume temporary control of the SE. Bringing in someone new at this point would only introduce new instability to an already dangerous situation. We restored law and order after the Liberation. Now we are maintaining it."

"I'm a bit uncomfortable," the Chairman continued, "about this without seeing some of the evidence myself. I mean to say, there is no one here to defend the SEs. What we have is your word, Alex."

"I was unaware that my word was questionable," she replied.

"It's not that. I mean you authorized what amounts to executions of the SE leadership. That isn't something that people are going to take lightly."

"You want evidence," she reached into her briefcase and pulled out a folder. "I will show you, as the Chairman. Your eyes only." Rising to her feet, she marched over and put the folder in front of the chairman. He opened it slowly, glanced at the photographs one at a time, slowly, then closed it.

The Secretary hid her smile. The images of the Council Chairman had been taken by her surveillance team. *Daniel, you shouldn't have had sex with your babysitter.* He glanced up at her, the color draining from his pudgy face. *Yes, now you understand. I have dirt on everyone in this room in some form. Those I don't, I will have it made up. You won't raise a finger to stop me, because if you do, these images will get out.*

"I—I think I've seen enough," he said. "My apologies for doubting you Alex," he said, averting his gaze from hers.

She picked up the folder. "No harm Daniel. I think it is safe to say that neither of us wants this information to be made public."

"No, no we don't." The color did not return to his face.

The Secretary moved back to her seat and tucked away the folder. "We will need the appropriate communications to go out. I think we should position this as a move to streamline government. We don't need to mention the removal of the leadership of the SE at all. We can simply say that I am temporarily assuming leadership of the SE. My people are already cleaning up any loose ends. This was done all across the country, so there is very little for the media to connect. I believe we should position this as a *reorganization.*"

Rebecca Clarke, the head of the Truth Reconciliation Committee nodded. "We will need to position it properly, almost make it a non-event to the public. The less we say about it, the less people will pay attention to it. I can have my people start to work on approved media releases right away."

Alex flashed a wry smile. "I have taken the liberty of preparing drafts in advance of this… to make your job easier. I think you'll find that they are acceptable. I will email them to you when we are done here."

There were nervous nods around the table, except from the Chairman of the Joint Chiefs, whose red face revealed nothing to her. *He senses something isn't right, but knows enough not to cross me. That is all I need from him.*

As the Chairman raised the topic about the celebration of the Liberation, the Secretary leaned back in her seat and templed her fingers in front of her. Things had played out exactly as she had expected. Then again, reading her opposition had always been one of her strong suits. *I just became the most powerful person in the free world and the people that realize it are afraid of me and will say nothing. With the SE and the NSF under a unified command, we can finally give the country the peace that it deserves—by destroying anyone that opposes us.*

CHAPTER 21

"A danger to one is a danger to all."

Philadelphia, Pennsylvania

Raul had started to finally feel comfortable with his life as part of the Order of the Bell. The various members were fascinating. All seemed to have suffered under Newmerican rule, which he initially found odd. *Everything I was always taught was that Newmerica fixed all of the problems of the old country. The more I speak with these people, the more I understand that they have all lost something.* Clearly some people had benefited, but Raul realized there had been a price for their gain, a price paid for by others.

Sasha introduced him to Maria, a young girl whose family came from Puerto Rico. Maria's father had worked hard and had founded his own company that did importing from her home country to the U.S. One night the protesters from Social Enforcement had come to their house, busted down the door, and had taken him prisoner. His only crime was being a member of the party that was not in charge of the country. She struggled with Raul, telling how he was sent to a Social Quarantine Camp. The SEs had taken his company from him, claiming it belonged to the workers. In reality, they all lost their jobs as a result.

It didn't end there. Maria spoke of how the SEs had harassed her mother's place of work to the point where she had been fired. No one ever told Maria what happened to her father; he had simply been whisked away in the night and never returned. In a matter of months, they went from a prosperous lifestyle to living in a homeless shelter. One night, her mother was walking back to the shelter and had come across a 'peaceful protest,' by the local SE. Someone threw a brick hitting her in the head. She was taken to a National Hospital and had died during a five-hour wait to get into the emergency room. Her death left Maria on her own… that is until the Order had taken her in, giving her hope.

Her story moved Raul. *Why would they do what they did? What did society gain by ruining his business?* His image of the FedGov crumbled with every new relationship he forged. The story they told him of a new prosperity seemed to be a complete lie. *They have ruined lives to achieve their goals.*

Jayden taught classes at night, usually history. Raul was surprised at how different the classes were than the ones he had taken in school. America was not a horrible society before the overthrow of the government, which was what he had been taught. Not all of its accomplishments were the results of slavery or oppression. It was confusing to him at first, but Jayden explained that he was 'unlearning' what the FedGov had mandated be taught. You were taught one version so that they could justify the crimes they had committed for what they called, 'freedom.'

Reconciling the two versions of history was difficult at first, but after a few days it began to make sense. *It is about control. If you control what people think about their past, you can control them.* Learning the truth was somehow liberating. Newmerica was not the great saving revolution; it was the seizing of power. Yes, there was universal healthcare—but the price had been freedom. The police had become a brutal force, and the Social Enforcers were little more than mobs that took justice in their own hands.

Another member of the Order, Darius, trained members on self-defense and the use of firearms. A shooting range had been set up in the basement of an old warehouses so that the sound of gunfire would not travel. The gun scared him—he had been told his whole life that guns killed. The only time he had ever held one was to shoot the SEs that had attacked them, and the use of a pistol stirred those memories. The more he did it, however, the more comfortable he got, the safer he felt. Eventually gripping the pistol became familiar and even reassuring for him.

The rest of his time was his. He was free to leave the warehouse, but was encouraged to stay close. He walked around the abandoned factories and marveled at some of the massive steel machinery inside the buildings which were now long abandoned. The buildings reminded him of those in Detroit that they had been dismantling before his life was upended. *Years ago, these employed thousands of people, and now they rust and fall apart.* Jayden had told him how the jobs were deemed 'undesirable' and had been sent to other countries. It struck him as odd, since he thought that making things was something to be admired, not shunned. *Who made that decision, and why?*

One morning Jayden assembled the twenty-eight members of the Order in the warehouse. Raul could sense something was different. He had seen and met individual members, but never had they all come in at once. Jayden pulled up an old wooden wire spool and climbed on top so that everyone could see him.

"The time has finally come for us to show the world that we are not taking this coup quietly. The anniversary of the Fall is coming in a matter of days, and the Sons of Liberty are planning to crash their little party.

"Our group has been given an assignment as part of this payback, one that I think is very important. Axel," he called out to the lanky middle-aged black man in the group. "I think we are going to need you to cook up one of your special recipes. Something special."

The man nodded back slowly. "How big?"

"Very," Jayden replied. "We will need a vehicle to transport it in— something with reinforcement in the front that won't attract attention. We are going to need some transports too, something that will hold a few hundred people."

Darius spoke up. "I saw an old Army two-and-a-half tonner in the salvage yard a few days ago. They run on diesel so we will need the right ration cards, but those engines are pretty easy to work on. One of those should handle whatever Axel cooks up." Axel nodded silently in response.

Another woman spoke up. "My husband's old Ford is sitting around gathering dust since he's just collecting reparations at this point. Might as well put her to use."

"Perfect!" Jayden said with a broad smile on his face. "Now, each of you will have a special part in this plan. Everyone is important and critical. The lives of a lot of innocent people are going to be at risk and we don't want to hurt anyone we don't have to."

"What's the target Jayden?" The question came from someone that Raul didn't know.

"Valley Forge," he said solemnly. Darius whistled in response and the group broke into a murmur.

Raul leaned over to Sasha and whispered, "What's so special about Valley Forge?" He knew the reference to the camp outside of the city where George Washington and the Continental Army had lived during a bitter winter.

Sasha leaned in close. "It's a Social Quarantine Camp," she replied.

"I don't have to tell you," Jayden continued. "This is something that has not been tried. Some of us have friends and family that have gone into that place. We hope and pray they are still there. We are going to strike in coordination with other cells. We have been tasked with blowing our way in and getting the prisoners out."

Another man wearing a fatigue green jacket spoke up: "That place has gun towers."

Jayden nodded. "They do. But they built the place to keep the prisoners in, not for someone launching a prison break—not on the scale we are going to do it."

"Assuming we can pull it off—" an older man named David said. "What do we do with the folks we get out?"

"We will use our safe houses and this warehouse," Jayden replied. "We will need to start stockpiling food, fresh clothing, the essentials."

"We'll need portajohns," another man said. "We can hit some construction sites for those."

"Good call," Jayden said. "We have no idea about the condition of the people. Some have been behind the fence for years now."

"So how do we do this?" a female in coveralls asked. "The guards have to outnumber us. The minute the shit hits the fan, they will call for help. NSF will be all over us."

"Another cell is going to be keeping NSF busy," Jayden assured her. "A diversion. As for the guards, most of them are SEs. They are all talk, no action. Once a few of them drop, they will run. Those that don't, well, we will make them regret it."

The crowd seemed electrified with the information and Raul couldn't help feeling the same way. *This is something big and important.* He thought about Maria's father and wondered how many other people were suffering in concentration camps.

Jayden paused for a moment, then continued, "We need to plan this carefully. We owe them for what they did. We were named for the Liberty Bell, a symbol of freedom that they destroyed during the Fall. They hunted down the original members of the Sons of Liberty and tortured them in camps like this one. We are going to give them payback. I don't have all of the details, but we are part of a number of operations across the country.

"They think they are going to be celebrating their overthrow of the government. They are going to cheer at what they did to the President. They have a big party planned. We are going to ruin it for them. We are going to start to take it back. We are going to remind them that they have not crushed the spirit of our country."

Raul could not help himself; he joined in the cheer that followed.

Culpeper, Virginia

Caylee sat up in bed in the Red Roof Inn and watched the news broadcast. The room was far from comfortable, but she had stayed in worse in her career. It was dark, and a hint of cigarette smoke clung to the bedspread, carpet and drapes despite the sign saying, "No Smoking." She had two security people from the SOL with her, beefed-up rednecks with more firepower than brains, at least from what she could tell. One was named Hawk, the other, the one with the thick, twisted beard was Ray. They were far from threatening; in fact they were quite friendly, with Ray seeming to flirt with her. She told them they were not needed. "I'm an operative. I could kill you both before you ever clicked off your safeties."

Ray smiled. "We ain't keeping you here. We're here to protect you."

Shaking her head, she glared up at her guards. "Who do you think they will send in after me? Local NSF? No. They will send operatives—plural. Mister Ray, I want you to understand, if they come at me, you two won't even be speed bumps for them."

Ray chuckled in response. "That may be, but we are here and we are going to do our job." She admired his courage, or feared his stupidity. It was an even match.

CNN came on; the tiny Truth Reconciliation Committee, TRC-approved logo appeared in the corner. The lead story was about the growth of GDP and how the economy was starting to turn the corner. The next tiny bit flashed the image of the Secretary of the NSF and talked about her temporarily taking over the Social Enforcement nationally. "This action will save millions by streamlining operations—and is intended to be temporary." The newscasters went on to their next story. Caylee shut off the television.

"You see that story?" she asked of Hawk and Ray. Both nodded.

"That's it," she announced. "That was what she was planning."

"Who? The Secretary?" Ray asked.

"Yes. It makes sense now."

"You mean her taking over the SE?" Hawk asked.

"Yes." Her instincts were clear. *Of course, this was a power play.*

"How do you know?" Ray pressed.

She looked at both of them. "The government lies. You know that, right?"

This got firm head shakes from both men. "I used to provide covers for my ops. When the Truth Reconciliation Committee tells you something is a big deal, generally it isn't. When they tell you a story like this and play it off as nothing important, you can assume it is a big deal."

Ray settled on the dull green sofa, resting his AR-15 at his side. "Oddly enough little lady, that makes a shitload of sense."

"That bitch," Caylee cursed. "Don't you see what she's done?"

Hawk, the leaner of the two nodded. "She's combining the NSF and the SE."

"Exactly."

"Pretty ballsy move," Hawk commented.

"It gives her an army," she replied. *That's what this was all about from the beginning. It was never an investigation into the SOL. She turned me loose knowing I would stir the proverbial pot.* For a brief moment, Caylee had to give the Secretary respect. It was brilliant thinking on a level she had never fully anticipated. That realization was hard for her to admit, that she had been out-thought. *It won't happen again.*

Caylee stabbed the power button on the remote to shut the television off. "She used me—used me to stir up tensions with the Social Enforcers. It gave her some pretext to move against them."

"Does it matter?" Hawk asked.

"Of course it does," she snapped. "She used me."

Ray shook his head with her response. "Stop acting like this is all about you. You aren't alone little lady. Newmerica has been using all of us. We got played like a cheap fiddle. The media told us those protests were peaceful, that they weren't organized. They said ANTIFA wasn't a threat. Everyone suspected that they were funded by politicians, but we were told there were no connections. When they got more violent, we were told that *we* were the problem. It wasn't the radical left that was causing the violence. It was us. No matter how stupid that sounded, half the damn country believed it." He paused for a moment, dipping his head, gathering his thoughts.

"Then they overthrew the government. We all thought it was going to be temporary, that somehow sanity would take over. We watched when they wheeled out the dead President, and the message was received. If you are not with us, you'll be dead. He didn't die of a heart attack, he was Epsteined. People like you in the NSF backed that up. Your kind hunted us down. Anyone that spoke out was labeled a domestic terrorist or a dangerous racist. Silicon Valley told you about everyone that ever supported a conservative cause and you shipped them off to concentration camps and called it *social quarantine*. You told us we were experiencing a 'Great Reformation' but we only saw our rights being stomped on. Liberation? *Hell* no. What you did was a revolution against an elected government, simply because you didn't like the people in charge. That's why we call it the Fall, because that's exactly what it was.

"Every day they chipped away at our freedoms while at the same time telling us we never had it so good. They burned history books and tore down statues and shoved a new version of America down our throats… all the while telling us to smile and be happy with it."

"You act like you are something special, when in reality, you were part of the problem. You took our America from us. The people that you worked for, that bitch heading up the NSF, she was in Congress before all of this went down. She plotted and schemed from the start to tear down the government. Why is it a big surprise that she's as corrupt as the rest of them?"

Filtering out Ray's southern drawl, Caylee realized that he was right. *I was the enemy. I did things over the last few years thinking I was a good patriot, but in reality, I was a part of the bigger problem.* She always thought she was smarter than that, that she would have realized she was being used. The realization had been growing on her ever since she had killed the two operatives in South Dakota. Even she had to admit that when she saw the weathered and stained old flag that Andy Forrest had recovered, it had moved her. It wasn't only the allure of seeing something that was forbidden. It had stirred old memories in her, before the flag had been replaced and erased from history. *I can't deny it, there is a big of nostalgia... no... cherishing of the memories of the days before the Liberation.* She remembered one of the party slogans, "Nostalgia is dangerous." *Yes, it is, because it reminds you of how good we had it.*

Caylee eyed Ray and Hawk differently as she soaked in Ray's words. "I'm sorry," she said. It had been a long time since she had apologized and actually meant it. Her trademark snarkiness was not present in her words. "You must hate me for the things I did."

Hawk said nothing, but bowed his head to avoid looking at her. Ray shrugged. "I don't hate you. Hate doesn't get you anywhere I found. It just eats at you from the inside out. From the sound of it, you got played like the rest of us—just differently. You did what you thought was right at the time. The only difference is that now you are seeing it for what it was, oppression."

She glanced at him, standing before her in coveralls, a paunch, that rough beard, and was amazed at the contrast. "You don't look like a warrior poet Mister Ray, but clearly you are a philosopher."

He chuckled. "You can drop the 'mister,' it's Ray, Ray Jenkins. Don't let the appearance fool you, I was a deputy sheriff when the shit hit the fan four years ago. The NSF didn't want me because I was a member of the local Republican Party."

"Very well Ray," she said. "Regardless, you have wisdom, and in my experience that is something that is more valuable than intelligence, and short in supply. How did you become part of the Sons of Liberty?"

Both he and Hawk snorted a laugh. "The Sons? You talk about it like it's an organization. It's not. If it were, it would have been on your radar long before now. It is a feeling. It is patriotism. It's belief in what we once had, not what we have now. Hell, it's the American Dream. It's a *cause…* and causes are hard as hell to squash. Sure, there are organized groups, but we have learned to get around all the tech your former comrades in Big Tech use. We learned from the first time around. Stay under the radar and you can do a hell of a lot more damage to the system than if you are public. The Sons are everywhere, and nowhere. None of us know more than a few people in the cause."

Hawk spoke up. "You see, it's like this. We are a nation hidden within a nation. Some media used to call us the 'silent majority,' before they were taken out. There's a bit of truth in that. People like your former employer. They took our country from us. There were no elections, no referendum, they simply took it and told us we needed to be happy with it. Well, a lot of us weren't. We didn't acknowledge Newmerica. We are citizens of America. That's what the Sons of Liberty are. We are the secret nation that refused to die; one that the people never gave up on."

There was a hint of brilliance about it. *They learned that from ANTIFA—no structure, no targets. When we arrested the original members, we forced them to use our own tactics against us.* "It is brilliant, the way you have copied the opposition and upped it one."

"I didn't come up with it," Ray confessed. "But I am part of it. A lot of people are. It's not a secret society or a gang, it is a belief and a devotion to a county that still exists in our hearts."

There was a pause, a strange silence in the hotel room for a moment as Caylee wrestled with the thoughts running through her head. All seemed to come back to the same thing, the Secretary. *She needs to pay for what she did to me, what she is doing right now. She has staged a coup within the government. There needs to be a reckoning.*

Caylee dipped into her mental toolkit and came up with a simple solution. "I think I need to kill her."

Ray chuckled. "Who, the Secretary of the NSF?"

"You are whacked," Hawk added.

"I want justice—but the only justice that seems appropriate is to kill her."

"You can't," Hawk pressed.

"I assure you Mister Hawk, I am more than capable of doing so. Between my Army training and that which I got from the NSF, I am a killing machine. To turn a phrase, I make ninjas look like pussies. If I say I can kill her, rest assured, she is as good as dead."

"She will have a security force around her—people like you," Ray said. "She might very well expect you to show up. They will be prepared."

"There are ways around any security detail," Caylee countered. *It's a matter of planning and preparation. No system is perfect.*

Ray shook his head. "You are going about this all wrong."

"What do you mean?"

"If you kill her, they will put some other asshat in her chair. They are a bureaucracy. There's always someone else in the wings ready to step in, especially since she merged the police with the brown-shirt army of the SE. You kill her, and you give them a damn good reason to come after you even harder. Killing her takes care of the symptom, but leaves you with the cancer."

There was a ring of truth in his words that Caylee respected. "The key with these fuckers is to *hurt* them. They taught us that and it's a damned good lesson. The people they shipped off for social quarantine that came home were broken. We saw that and it intimidated a lot of people. If they had just been killed, no message would have been sent. The key here is not to kill her, but instead to *hurt* her ass. Make her suffer. Take away the thing she cherishes. Make her feel some pain. It doesn't have to be physical. The worse pains are the mental ones, the emotional ones. What you want to do is give her a lifetime of not being able to sleep at night."

"Ray's right," Hawk said. "You go off and kill her, well, she doesn't suffer. A bitch like that—you want her to constantly be worrying when the next axe will fall. You hurt her, hurt her bad, and that's better revenge."

They were both right. Death was too easy to administer. Not only would it be no challenge, but the Secretary would not suffer. Caylee allowed herself a grin as she came to the realization. *I have a lot of information that will embarrass the administration and hurt the Secretary.* The key was getting it out. The social media companies suppressed anything news-wise that wasn't cleared by the Truth Reconciliation

Committee. Things could go up on the web, but they had an army of young people that took them down almost as fast. *I need to find a way to circumvent all of that. A way to get my data on my former missions that will injure the government. She will know that I'm the one doing it, and it will be a constant reminder that I'm still out there and can continue to hurt her.*

"You both are right," she replied. "Murder, however slow, is too good for that bitch. She needs to feel pain. She used me and others like me to do her dirty work. Now the rest of the country needs to see what I have done and see that dirt on her hands as well. It will eat at her. If we do it slowly, and get it to enough people, she can't make people unsee it. She will always wonder what else I have and when it is coming out. I have to admit, I like the idea of being her constant nightmare. At the same time, I would like to feel her neck in my hands."

Ray took a step towards her. "That's what unites us. We have all suffered; some more than others. For a long time they have been inflicting pain on us. I've put up with it for almost five years. They took my job, my ability to provide for my family, and a bit of my dignity. They made me have to take reparations to squeak by. My wife left me, went back to her family. I don't blame her. I blame them. I swore I'd make them pay. I could kill them too, but I won't. That would make me like them. I *will* make them suffer though. I find ways to rebel a bit every day against the government they inflicted on me and mine. Every day I strike back, if only a little."

Hawk chimed in again. "That's what makes us Sons."

Caylee understood finally what she had been fighting against. *I traveled all across the nation looking for the Sons of Liberty, and they were all around me. It isn't a group, it's a belief. These people were not enemies of anyone other than the administration. They were not at all the monsters we made them out to be. WE were the monsters.* "This has been a most enlightening conversation Ray, Hawk."

"You get it now," Ray said.

"I do. You are not the Sons of Liberty. *We* are."

Ray flashed her a toothy smile.

Culpeper, Virginia

Andy was surprised when the paved road ended and turned to red clay and gravel. This was horse country. Every house they passed was a ranch of some sort, most had horses. They passed a winery that had been shuttered, no doubt the victim of the environmental taxes. The vines clung to the wiring, untended, overgrown. It was a waste. His father had warned that all of the new taxes would crush small businesses, and sadly he had been right. *Dad was right about almost everything. All that did was cost him... his freedom... his career... his family.*

They stopped at a house, a two-story structure, surrounded by wooden, black, plank fencing. As he got out of the car, he could hear the thunder of hooves, a spooked horse no doubt, not far from where the parked. The couple that greeted them at the door were in their 50s and welcomed them in as if they were expected dinner guests. The mysterious Jack went in first, followed by Charli, then Andy. It was a warm and inviting home, with knickknacks on the shelves in the dining room. The woman, who was introduced as Sherri, offered to get them a drink while her husband Dave greeted them with a hearty handshake.

Jack shook hands with the owners and then motioned for Charli and Andy to join him in the open kitchen/family room area. Charli entered first and seemed to freeze in place, so much so that Andy had to shift around her. His eyes followed Charli's and he was stunned at who rose from a La-Z-Boy recliner.

It was the Vice President.

He looked older than the memories Andy had, but the face was definitely his. The cheeks sagged slightly, as if he had lost weight. His hairline was still white, but further back on his pate. The VP's eyes looked weary, but the smile, the brilliant teeth, would be difficult to duplicate. Andy was stunned as he stepped forward and extended his hand. Andy put the cases down on the counter and shook it, his mouth hanging slightly open. Charli shook it as well, also seemingly stunned into silence.

"How is this possible?" Charli finally said as Jack cracked a smile. "They reported you dead."

"I wasn't in the limo. The Secret Service shifted me to a follow-up SUV at the last minute. I don't know if they misreported my death or if someone deliberately messed with their DNA results after the wreck and the fire. By then I had been moved to a safe location." The voice was oddly calming and reassuring to Andy. *It is him!*

"I remember you," he said nodding slightly to Charli. "You were the one they called 'Slingshot,' right?"

Charli nodded quickly in response. "I don't understand. If you have been alive, why haven't you spoken out? Called them out for lying about it?"

"It wasn't that easy. The military stood down when we needed them most. You were there. When they said they apprehended the President, then he was dead... well, I knew that if I surfaced, they'd do the same thing to me. So did my wife, God rest her soul. Timing was everything, but as long as I lived, I was the legitimate leader in the chain of command. I've been on the run ever since, waiting."

"For what?"

"My beloved wife. I couldn't make a move without risking her life. She passed a few months ago," he said pausing for a moment, averting his eyes. "I couldn't even attend the funeral. I knew they couldn't use her for leverage. My kids all got out of the country. I knew the time was right. The time to make the move was perfect."

"What move?" Charli asked.

The Vice President flashed a grin. "All in due time, Lieutenant," he said. "Jack here tells me that you were with the President that night. I would very much like to know what happened. At the risk of sounding like a conspiracy theorist, I don't buy into the heart-attack-in-jail BS they tried to force down our throats."

"It was all fake," Charli said firmly. "I was with him almost to the end. None of their story is true."

"Charli," the VP said, putting his hand on her shoulder. "I need to know what happened."

Her eyes closed for a moment and she drew a long breath. For almost five years she had been carrying a burden, a secret of what had happened to the President. She liked to think it was noble that she had never shared it. In reality, it hurt to go back to those memories. There was a feeling of failure on her part, a crushing guilt. *He* is *the Vice President—he has to know.* "Alright. I'll tell you."

CHAPTER 22

"Individual achievement hurts us all. Only together can we grow and thrive."

ALMOST FIVE YEARS EARLIER...
Dun Loring, Virginia

Getting out of riot-torn Washington DC had been easier than Charli expected. The metro was still running, mostly bringing in fresh rioters rather than being loaded with those leaving the city. She had come out in a Metro access tunnel after their flight from the Emergency Operations Center under the White House. In the chaos on the subway platforms, no one thought it odd that three people were coming out of the tunnel and climbing up off the tracks. Still, she kept herself at the ready. *If anyone recognizes him, this will go south quick.*

Her charge, the President, clearly had never ridden the Metro before and she had fumbled with her card to get him through the turnstile until she saw that most people were simply jumping it. Law and order were gone, evaporated into the darkness of the night. People were crying out, 'We've taken the White House!' and "Kill 'em all!" There was a frenzy to get where she had just come from, to the point that no one seemed to pay attention to her and Major Swanson as they boarded the nearly empty Metro car heading to Virginia.

"What's your plan?" Swanson whispered from the seat behind her.

"We need to get out of this area."

"Mount Weather?" he offered.

Mount Weather was the location of an Executive Branch emergency operations center. While run by FEMA, the military staffed the site. It had been designed for use in case of nuclear attack, a location where the President and his executive team could take shelter and ensure the continuance of the government. She considered it for a moment, especially since it was close, but hesitated. "No. No offense, but the military left us high and dry—and that means that some of their leadership are willing to back the people trying to kill us," Charli whispered back. She paused and swept the others in the Metro car to make sure no one was eavesdropping.

"Understood," Swanson said. "Then where to?"

"Out of Virginia. It's not safe here, too many hostiles," she said. There were no contingencies to work off of; no plan that the Secret Service had prepared. "My car is at Dun Loring. It will take them a while to penetrate the EOC under the White House and find out that we aren't there. We will head west, get to West Virginia. We need some time to plan."

The President, sitting next to her, leaned into the conversation. She could see her face reflected in the sunglasses they had given him as part of his disguise. "I need to get on the air, tell people what has happened. My supporters will rally to me."

"Understood sir," she said. "But right now, your safety is at risk. We need to get you out of harm's way. Then you can talk to anyone you want."

She could tell from the look on his face that the President wasn't happy with her words. When the Metro emerged from the tunnels at Ballston, Interstate 66 ran on both sides of the train tracks and in both directions, it was slow going. A passing Metro train heading into DC was filled to standing room only, with people carrying clubs, baseball bats, etc. They had protest signs, professionally printed from what she could tell. *This was organized and financed. This isn't some spur of the moment revolution.* That realization hit her hard. *The people behind this are playing for keeps and I am sitting next to the biggest target in the country.*

When the automated voice told them they had arrived at Dun Loring, Charli began to relax, if only a little. The trio exited the train and made their way to the escalator off of the platform. Her black Toyota Corolla was parked at the far end of a long line of cars. She kept one hand on the President, ushering him forward into the dimly lit parking lot with Major Swanson on his other side.

They reached the car and she pulled out her keys. Suddenly she heard footsteps off to her side. Turning, Charli saw a dark-skinned man holding a gun on them. "Hand over the keys, bitch," he said turning the gun sideways, gangster style.

"Look, we don't want any trouble," she said, shifting slightly to the side. *I need room between us. He's only a few yards away.* Her gun was tucked into the band of her sweatpants. Drawing and aiming was going to be risky, especially in the tight quarters between vehicles. She was already calculating the moves needed to pull it off, the result of years of training.

"Give me your fucking keys," he demanded, shaking the gun.

"You don't want to do this," the President said. She cringed. His voice was distinct, something she couldn't camouflage.

The black-clothed robber turned slowly to face the President as Charli's right hand drifted downward for the gun. "Look, here's the keys," she said, trying to get him to focus on her.

The robber seemed to be studying the President. "What the fuck... you... you're him!" he said, gesturing with this gun. Anger rose in his face as his jaw set. "Fuck you!"

Charli knew he was going to fire before he did. She pulled her gun and sprang forward to shield the President with her body. There was a pop as his gun fired, hitting her mid-flight. She fired a shot but missed as she and the President dropped to the ground.

Major Swanson fired his gun, also missing, and the shooter fired at him, two shots that hit his briefcase. Charli hit the vehicle parked next to hers, then slammed into the ground as she fired her second shot, hitting him from a low angle, where the robber's jaw connected to his head. The bullet went up and out the top of his head, spraying a splatter of crimson into the air. His limp body dropped to the ground next to her, his right arm trembling, even in death.

Skidding on the pavement hurt her left arm. Then came an almost electric shock of pain from her right torso. Glancing down she saw blood where the bullet had hit her. Charli cranked around, ignoring her own pain and saw the President leaning against her car door. He too had blood on him. The shot that had hit her must have gone through her and into him.

The Major moved in and began to apply pressure to the President's wounded midsection. "I'm okay... I'm okay," he said breathing in short pants.

Charli made her way to her knees and felt dizzy merely performing that motion. "We need to get him to a hospital," Swanson said. "Both of you."

She shook her head and realized that a cold sweat was coming on. "No. You take him there and the mobs will storm the place. We need to get him to a doctor outside of this area."

"Can you stand?" Swanson asked her.

She nodded. "Don't worry about me, get him in the car."

The next few moments were a blur in her memory. She remembered Swanson getting the President in the back seat and taking her keys. Somehow, she ended up in the back with the President leaning against her. For a few minutes she didn't remember anything, and then she saw they were on the highway, driving crazy fast. "You took the bullet for me," he said wearily as the car under Swanson's control, swerved around a pickup truck.

"I'm sorry you got hit, sir," she managed. She felt cold, wet with sweat, and glanced down and saw a sickening amount of blood soaking her pants and seat—both her blood and that of the man she had tried to save.

"My wife and family..." he moaned. "Are they okay?"

"I don't know sir," she said. "I'm sure they are." *Could anyone be sure? The White House was supposed to be impenetrable, and it had fallen.*

He shifted in his seat and groaned loudly. "I never knew it hurt so much to get shot."

"Me either, she said groggily. Her eyes closed slowly and she seemed to drift off. The sounds of the car on the road penetrated the mental fog of her agony, but all sense of time disappeared. Charli tried to talk but couldn't muster the energy to do so. The darkness took her completely.

A searing wave of pain stirred her to consciousness. Looking up she saw a brilliant florescent light and a masked doctor leaning over her, his almost bald head possessing only a few curly gray hairs. She was lying on her back, cold, disoriented. "You are going to be okay," he assured her.

"The President," she said. "Take care of him first."

"I did," the man said. "He's resting in the next room. I don't have a general anesthesia, so I will have to use a local," he said. Charli closed her eyes and once more the darkness overwhelmed her.

The next time she awoke she was on a bed in someone's house. Her lips were dry and cracked and her eyes felt caked with grime. Her body was a dead weight, resisting every effort to move. Each joint protested as she sat up enough to pull the covers down and look at the gauze wrapped around her wound.

Major Swanson entered wearing at least three days growth of beard. "How are you feeling?"

When she spoke her throat ached, but Charli ignored the pain. "The President?"

He lowered his head. "He's not good. It's an infection."

"Where are we?" She glanced at the window and the sun was shining brilliantly outside, hitting the branches of a hickory tree that had not yet released its dead fall leaves.

"Wheeling, West Virginia. I didn't take you to a hospital, but to a doctor's office. I explained our situation and he did the surgery there. It wasn't optimal, but the best I could do. He's put us up in his house."

"I need to check in—bring in some assets," she said.

"I don't think you can. Charli… the government… it's gone. They're holding most of Congress as prisoners at this point. The VP's limo was blown up—they are pretty sure he's dead. I contacted some colleagues at the Pentagon and they are looking for me after the football went off-line. The MPs have taken my family into 'protective custody.' There's no government or Secret Service for you to call. The mob is rounding up anyone associated with the President or his party. I saw the footage of them executing many of them right in front of the White House."

Fuck. Those were her friends. She hoped that Jack Desmond somehow got away, but a part of her doubted it.

"Am I okay?"

"Doc Davis said that the bullet destroyed your appendix and went through your large intestine before exiting out your back. You seem to be recovering well," Swanson said.

"I need to see him. He's my responsibility."

"You need to rest," he said.

"It's my duty," she said, gingerly attempting to move her legs. The pain from her wound and the aching of her legs made her instantly hot and uncomfortable. She winced as she put her feet on the wooden floor. The Major moved in beside her, helping her to stand. He led her carefully down the hallway to the door of another bedroom. Charli pushed the door open and saw the President on the bed.

His pallor was pale and he had a wet compress on his forehead. His hair, almost always pristine for the public, was a twisted mess that made him look balder… older. His face was red, redder than she had ever seen it, almost sunburned in appearance. Seated at his side was the doctor who had treated her. Major Swanson led her in and she lowered herself into the chair next to him. Charli reached out and took the President's hand in hers and it felt wet and cool to the touch.

"How is he?" she asked.

The doctor's face was devoid of emotion, which made her feel grim at the prognosis. "The bullet nicked a part of his intestine that I missed during surgery. He was recovering but I had to open him up again and the infection is fairly bad."

"Would it be better to have him in a hospital?" Charli asked softly, weighing her options.

"They would be giving him exactly what I am. I'm—I'm sorry," tears formed in the corners of his eyes as he spoke.

Charli held his hand for several hours before becoming lightheaded. *He's my charge—my responsibility. He should have his family here, not me.* Unconsciousness washed over Charli and she embraced it. A mix of nightmares and memories of the shooting haunted her.

She awoke to a cloudy day… a different day. *How long have I been out?* On the table next to her was a cup of water with a straw and she savored every slow drop.

Major Swanson entered her room slowly. "How are you today?" he asked in a low tone.

"Better," she said, shifting in the bed, every muscle and joint protesting. "How is he?"

Swanson bowed his head. "Charli, he died yesterday. You had passed out and we moved you back to your room. He left us a few hours later. He woke up, was in a lot of pain, then he drifted off."

I failed! She felt as if her body was shrinking under the sheets. Swanson continued, clearly sensing her mental anguish. "I'm so sorry to have to tell you. I wasn't sure what we should do. I arranged for his burial in an unmarked grave. We couldn't use an undertaker out of risk that word would get out. I thought it was best not to let the authorities know."

It was a good call on the major's part. *They wanted him dead. There's no point in letting them know they succeeded. I should have been there with him.* Guilt engulfed her, guilt and anguish. "You did the right thing," she finally forced herself to say.

"If it hadn't been for you, he would have died back in Virginia," Swanson said. "He even said that when he was conscious. He wanted me to give you his thanks."

"What I did didn't matter in the end, he died anyway," she scowled.

"It mattered to him. He had me write a letter to his wife, though I doubt I can get it to her anytime soon. She has been placed under arrest along with his sons and daughters. At least he got to tell them goodbye in writing."

"Has some order been restored?"

His jaw set slightly with her words. "No. The inmates are in charge, in some cases literally. Some militia groups have tried to step in between the police and the mobs, but all that results is more bloodshed. They have assembled special teams, roaming the streets with lists of names of the President's supporters. They are televising the entire thing, pulling people out of their houses, beating them."

"Lists?" *Where would they get lists like that?*

"The tech companies provided them. They are 'aiding in removing the scourge.' That's what they said. They were tracking every time someone clicked 'Like' or 'Dislike,' and now they are looking for the more vocal supporters. I have to believe that kangaroo courts will start soon too. The media has started to call it 'The Liberation,' but it feels like a *coup d'etat* to me."

Because that is what it is. This isn't America, not any more. The children have crawled out of their parent's basement and are trolling the streets looking for victims and calling it justice. "What about the police?"

"In some communities, these anarchists have gone after the families of officers. A lot of cops are not reporting for duty, staying home to protect their loved ones. The ones that are out there are not interfering much out of fear that they will be targeted next."

"What will you do?" she asked, desperately hoping to change the subject.

Swanson shook his head. "We were lucky. One of the shots that hit the football disabled the tracking mechanism so they can't follow me. I can't go home; they have my family under house arrest. If I show up anywhere, they will do just about anything to find out what happened to him. I need to hide, at least for the time being. It's probably best that I keep moving."

"A man without a country," she said, taking another short sip of the cool water.

"Just like you, I imagine," he said.

His words caught her off guard. *He's right. I have to disappear too. If they find me, they won't stop until they have dug him up out of the ground to verify he's dead.* Charli's sister would be a target by now which only added to her crushed feelings. *The Service was penetrated by them, they have our names and access to our personnel files. I'll need new IDs, a new life. I have to stay one step ahead of them.* The thought of being a fugitive tore at her. *I gave my whole to the Service. Now that is gone. The world is better off thinking I'm dead.*

"I want to see where he's buried," she said after a few long moments of thought.

"You need to get some strength back," he said.

"You're right," Charli replied. *There's no hurry. He's not going anywhere. And as long as the mob that took Washington over doesn't know for sure he's dead, his ghost will constantly haunt them.*

Culpeper, Virginia

Charli Kazinski finished her story with a long sigh. She had not told anyone the events of the night of the Fall or the President's ultimate death a few days later. It was a secret she bore, along with the scar on her abdomen, a nagging reminder of the events that unfolded. Every eye in the room was locked on her as she finished. Pausing for a moment, she wanted to cry, but pushed the tears down hard.

"I'm so sorry for all that you've been through," the Vice President said.

"Thank you, sir," she replied, fighting to keep her composure. "I haven't told anyone about what happened. Especially after they put his death photos and videos on the web. I knew it was a lie and that they would do anything to protect it."

"Sir," Jack said, turning to Andy. "This is Andrew Forrest. His father was in the Sons of Liberty and managed to save these items."

Andy stepped forward and held out the case and tube. The VP carefully opened them, first the documents, then the flag. He read the tag on the flag slowly, touching it with reverence. "These are the real-deal?"

Andy shook his head. "He and a friend hid them in a place he knew they'd be safe."

The VP handed them back. "If you don't mind, I'd like to use the flag at least."

"For what?" Andy asked.

Jack spoke up again. "The time has come to strike back. For almost five years our asses have been handed to us."

Charli loved hearing the passion in his voice. "Alright Jack. You fulfilled your promise. What's the big plan here?"

"We are going to hijack their anniversary event," Jack said. "We are going to swear in the VP as our President live, for the whole world to watch. We are going to hit them in so many different directions at once that they will not know where or how to react first. Then we take the fight to them and take back our nation."

Charli was stunned. "Is it even possible?"

"It is Charli," Jack replied, his voice ringing of confidence. "You've helped and not even known it. We have been slowly hamstringing the NSF, hitting their capability to do their job. That building you took down in Virginia—that hurt them bad. We're going to hit the Big Tech companies too, long enough for us to get the images and videos out on the net before anyone can censor them."

The Vice President rose to his feet. "They like to feel invulnerable. That's one of their many weaknesses. We've had time to plan this, time to prepare. You helped—that attack in Virginia crippled their labs and investigating capabilities. We are going to hurt them, show them to be the liars that they are. We will be showing the people they have disenfranchised that there is hope… that the America they knew is still alive. We are going to give them the one thing they haven't had much of—hope.

"It won't be easy. Regrettably, there will be bloodshed. We will have to fight dirty to win, but they have taught us how to do that. Millions feel the way we do. They have been seething, waiting for the right moment to rise up. We are going to provide that."

Charli rose to her feet. She had been in hiding for so long that the thought of being free again, assuming her identity and place in society, had almost been forgotten. She had suppressed those dreams in exchange for survival. *They are going to start the war that should have happened four years ago. We are long overdue.* "Count me in," she said firmly.

Andy nodded as well. "Me too."

Jack nodded, as if he were proud of them. "We still have work to do. The Secretary of the NSF taking control of the SEs is a wrinkle we hadn't planned on, though we were trying to stir the pot between the two organizations for some time now."

Charli crossed her arms. "She will move fast to consolidate power. We need to keep them off-balance, hopefully fighting each other and not noticing us."

"My thoughts exactly," Jack said. "We've got a lot to do and not a lot of time."

CHAPTER 23

*"Only trust information that is proven trustworthy—
look for the Truth Reconciliation Committee logo."*

Valley Forge, Pennsylvania

Raul could barely contain the nervous excitement at what he was doing. Most of his life he had followed orders. This was different. The Order of the Bell had several of the members, including him, performing surveillance on the Social Quarantine Camp. Armed with binoculars and a sketch pad, he settled in on a hill outside the camp and carefully drew the fence line and the towers. He made notes regarding how many people manned them, when they came and left, anything that might help. *I'm a spy now! I went from being a construction worker, to fugitive, to spy in a matter of weeks.*

He thought often of Father Ryan who had given his life to protect him. He often thought of his mother who would be worried about him, and about Paco and the other Youth Corps members. At night, when alone, he prayed that his friends and family were safe. He knew that his actions had put many people at risk and the subsequent rioting had cost lives. *I wish I had never pulled that trigger—that I had run instead.*

The camp was remarkably crude. The unpainted gray lumber that had been used for the fence and buildings was already showing signs of wear. Some buildings were painted. Those were the ones the guards went into. The razor wire that topped the chain link fence didn't look incredibly secure. There were no sidewalks, only muddy paths through the camp. A lone road led to the facility; at one time it had been the entrance to the national park. Outside the facility, some half-mile from the barracks, was a massive stone arch that had been built to commemorate the Colonial Army staying there. Now it was in a thicket of tall, overgrown grass and someone had climbed it to spray paint, "Camp #42," in black uneven letters. At ground level, barely visible through the grass was other graffiti… BLM and the symbol of the upturned fist. Raul could not help but think at one time this park had been beautiful. Now the unmown fields were filled with saplings, some five years old and a sea of weeds and grass as high as his waist.

The ground surrounding the camp for several hundred feet had been cleared, leaving dead tree stumps and tall grass and saplings. Beyond that though was a forest of trees. Crudely dug drainage ditches surrounded the fence line as well, not very deep, filled in with last year's dead leaves and growth.

The guards were armed, but many looked out of shape. There were remarkably few of them. *They must assume no one can escape.* He caught glimpses of the prisoners as well. Wearing worn, gray clothing and bright orange crocs, they moved slowly, ushered between buildings in lines, prodded by the guard's weapons. Most looked starved, their faces gaunt, their eye sockets dark. They were brought to a grassy area in the middle of the camp one building at a time, where they were allowed to stretch and get some sunlight. The men were unshaven, with ratty beards. Some barracks held women, their hair unwashed, their faces seemingly devoid of emotion. He didn't see any abuse by the guards, but it was not hard to imagine based on the people he saw there.

This was part of the country he had never heard about. Oh, there were rumors about such camps. It was said that the only people sent there were the threats to Newmerica. Now that Raul saw the people there, he realized they were no threat. Some were in their 50s. They were not terrorists, they couldn't be. Some walked with such a slow shamble it was impossible to see them as a danger to anyone. When he raised the topic with Sasha during breakfast one morning, she explained it simply. "They are not physical threats. The risk they pose is that they refuse to submit to the government. They speak out. They are here because their risk is what they think and believe."

At first, he was bewildered at what she said. *What kind of people lock up others because they think differently?* Raul knew the answer to that; it came to him slowly, eating away at his sleep at night. This was the same government that sanctioned Social Enforcement squads. The same government that allowed rampant rioting. The same government that allowed men like Father Ryan to be killed.

For hours he lay on the hilltop, nestled in the long pine needles and dead leaves, watching the camp. There were no external patrols. Jayden had been right. Everything seemed to be built to keep the prisoners in, rather than others out. He was there for several days, poised on different hills, making notes. He even came up with names for various guards— Lumpy, Stringbean, Tall-Hair, Redneck, Witch Hazel. He noted what cars they drove every day, when they arrived, went to the bathroom, everything.

As his day ended, he carefully and quietly hiked nearly three miles to get picked up by one of the Order's drivers and taken back. They drove him into the city to the warehouse. When he arrived he was taken to one of the offices where a table contained a full model of the camp, complete with cardboard buildings and crude fence lines made of some sort of fabric mesh that actually looked like chain link fencing from a distance. A lone florescent light hung over the model table, perfectly illuminating it. Each of the observers did the same thing Raul had done; they fed Jayden and the other leaders the information, and they recorded it carefully on a battered PC that was not connected to the net.

"So how do we do this?" Raul asked as he leaned over the model and studied it. "They have a lot of guns."

"Having guns and knowing how to use them right are two different things," Sasha said. "My father taught me that much."

Anthony, a tall, lean, black youth nodded. "Most of them guards is out of shape. Hell, the one Raul called Lumpy, I swear, that dude waddles when he walks." Everyone chuckled at his comment because it was so accurate. "These guys are not military or former cops. They are wannabes."

"They think they have the upper hand," Maria said as she surveyed the table from the side opposite Raul. "Arrogance is a weakness."

Jayden paced beside the length of the table diorama looking at it. "I learned from my four years in the army that you can get a lot done with distraction and misdirection." He pointed to the main entrance. "They have most of their firepower focused on the main gate. That's the one way in, on the main road."

"Yeah," Julius spoke up from Raul's left side. Two towers, open ground in front of them. Good field of fire. Anyone approaching that gate for a quarter of a mile is in full sight." He pointed to the terrain of the camp near the front gate.

Jayden smiled. "What we do is get the guards away from that gate."

"How?" Sasha asked.

"We take two vehicles, four-wheel drive, probably trucks. We use a piece of wood to run them at full speed and send them empty, right at the fence lines in two places at the rear of the camp. They should be enough to clear the drainage ditch and damage the fence enough to get inside. There won't be anyone driving, so chances are they will hit the barracks, but that should be enough to get the attention of every guard in there. We can have some teams in the woods fire off some roman candles and other fireworks from the far end of the camp, lots of noise. Let them think that's where an attack is coming from. They will run to the distraction."

"Then we hit the front gate?"

Jayden nodded. "Yes—a few minutes later, enough to get them sucked in by crashing at the other end of the camp. That leaves the towers with either no one or minimal guards. We use one of our big trucks, up-armored, to plow through the gates."

"The guards will return as soon as we do that," Maria said.

"Yes, they will, but we will be in the camp—and we will open up on them," Jayden replied coldly. "We will then have a team move in from the holes the vehicles make at the rear of the camp. They will find themselves surrounded. Some will fight, some will run, some will just surrender."

The realization was settling on Raul; *people are going to die doing this.* It should have bothered him, but oddly, it didn't.

Jayden continued. "We will bring guns for the prisoners and we will arm them. We load up and get out fast."

"What about the police?" Julius asked. "They are going to call 9-1-1 right after the fireworks start. I mean the place is isolated and all, but the cops are only a phone call away."

Jayden's grin broadened. "They didn't run any landlines to the camp. I checked with the Park Service records. That means they are using mobile phones. Two towers service that area. Before we spring the attack, we take out the towers. They will have phones, but no way to reach anyone.

"Once we get out of the camp, we split up our vehicles, everyone bringing some of the prisoners with them. We can use the Deuce-and-a-Half and the dump truck and another smaller vehicle. Once clear, we work our way back here. Not directly back. They will monitor traffic camera footage after the shit hits the fan. Everyone gets here by a different route."

It sounded simple, but something in the pit of Raul's stomach told him that it wasn't going to be a cakewalk. *You run a few trucks against the fence for a diversion; they take out the main gate. The problem is that such plans, no matter how good, often fail in the face of the enemy.* The thought of it nagged at him as he listened to the dialogue from the other members of the Order.

After several minutes of conversation, the group left the table and moved out into the warehouse proper where a late-night dinner was being prepared. Sasha sat across from him, tossing back her short black hair and saying a little prayer before she started. That alone would have been enough to make Raul smile.

"Are you nervous?" she asked between spoonfuls of stew, keeping her voice low so that only he would hear.

"A little," he said. "I shot two men that attacked us. I don't like the idea of killing anyone," he replied just above a whisper.

"No good person does," she replied, her eyes darting around to make sure no one was listening. But we are all called upon to do our part. My father was taken to one of these camps. Many of the people that go don't come back and those that do are never the same. They call it 'reeducation,' and 'reconciliation.' It's torture. They use pretty sounding names to cover up their crimes."

Raul had heard both of those words before and never equated them to the camps. "I keep telling myself that by going and doing this, we are saving lives."

"That's a good way to think of it," Maria replied. "Those people are being held there against their will. They have families and friends who do not know if they are even alive. We have to try. Someone has to do something. Why not us?"

Why not *us?* Raul considered that carefully. Everyone always hopes that someone else will step in and do the job that has to be done. It was easy to sit back and wait for someone else to do the hard work. If Father Ryan had done nothing, Raul knew he would be dead now, along with the rest of the Youth Corps that managed to escape Detroit. Did the priest regret his actions? *No, that was not the kind of man he was.*

Raul nodded to Maria's question. "I will do this because it's the right thing to do. Too much has been sacrificed to get me this far. I won't let that be for nothing."

Culpeper, Virginia

"She's a cunning bitch, I'll give her that," Jack Desmond said as Caylee finished laying out the coup that the Secretary of the NSF had pulled off. Jack and the others had just returned from their 'visit' with the Vice President to find a scowling Caylee Leatrom impatiently pacing around the Red Roof Inn hotel room. "Now she's more dangerous than ever." Jack stood in the Red Roof hotel room, his arms were crossed, his face wore a scornful expression. She's dangerous now... more than ever." He paused for a moment and thought about how he had tried to sow the seeds of tension between the NSF and the SEs. He couldn't help but chuckle.

"Something funny?" Charli asked.

"I may have actually helped her. We were framing the NSF for some actions against the Social Enforcers. We wanted them to turn on each other. I never expected it on this scale."

"The bodies in Wheeling at the Graveyard—that was you," Caylee said slowly as she pieced it together.

Jack nodded in response. "And others."

"I want her," Caylee said. "Not all of her, but a piece of her. She needs to suffer," she said casting a quick glance at Hawk and Ray who gave her a smile and a nod.

"The information you have... if we made it public, that would stir a shitstorm around her," Jack offered.

"Not enough," Caylee said defiantly. "She set me up, plain and simple. *Nobody* plays me as their pawn. "If you put out that information, the Truth Reconciliation Committee will say it's all BS. Yes, people will read it, but they will be told it's all lies. If we are going to hurt her, we have to do it in a way that is meaningful."

Justice and vengeance were concepts that Jack cloaked himself in. Often times they were all that gave him solace as he traveled across the country. The Sons of Liberty had been nearly eradicated when he had stepped in to fill that void. He didn't talk about those early months and never spoke of his family, with good reason. A part of him identified with the former operative sitting on the bed in the hotel room. *She gave everything to her job, a professional, and in the end, they have taken everything from her.*

"People like to think that the way you hurt powerful individuals is to take the power away from them. In some cases that's true. It depends on the person and the circumstances. If they have followers though, and determination, they will come back. People forget that Hitler tried to topple the government in the Beer Hall Putzch. They took everything from him and locked him up for nine months. He used that time in prison to write *Mein Kampf* and came back with even more resolve, wiser for the lesson.

Caylee thought hard about her enemy, her former leader. "She's only a threat because of the organization she runs. She holds onto power because she uses the data from Big Tech against her political foes. J. Edger Hoover did the same thing, and he only had a fraction of the information she has access to."

Charli rose from the hotel sofa to stand next to Jack whose brow only seemed to furrow in thought. "How do we cut her off from that kind of power?"

Jack paced several steps, back and forth. "There's a way." He paused. Caylee could see he was struggling with the concept. There was a pain there, hidden, obscured... but it was there. "We take a page from their rules. We do to them what they did to us."

Caylee looked at him. "What exactly do you have in mind?"

"A good dose of their own medicine," he replied.

"What exactly do you mean?" Charli asked. Jack paused for a moment. The memories were there in his mind, buried deep. They were in a place he hated to visit, a place that hurt him deeply every time he touched the memories. The plan that he had cobbled together and worked so hard for could go south. Jack Desmond came to grips with the fact that he might die for the cause he had devoted himself to.

Outside, he heard a barking dog in the distance—it ripped into his thoughts for a moment to the point where he winced slightly, as if in physical pain. *If I die, those memories die too. They are in this like me. There's no turning back for any of us. I'm asking people all across the country to potentially sacrifice everything for a dream. The least I can do is share my nightmares.*

ALMOST FIVE YEARS EARLIER...
Washington, DC

Jack Desmond waited kneeling on the floor of the elevator from the Emergency Response Center, keeping low; his service issued SIG Sauer P229 pistol was still holstered but accessible. *No, this requires something with a little more bite.* He braced his shoulder against the short, blocky black stock of the FN P90 submachine gun and waited for the doors to be pried open by the attackers. Drake Barker's betrayal had handed the White House to the attacking mob, but Jack had a mission... he had to get out. Barker's taunt was driving his actions... "Your family is dead if you fight back." *He's given them our personnel files. They are going to go after my family.* He had tried to use his cell phone but couldn't connect. *These rioters are overloading the local towers with their own shit. It's all part of their plan.*

The thought of abandoning his post galled him, but this was a scenario that no one had anticipated or even dreamed of, not on this scale at least. Charli had Excalibur, the President, and maintaining control of the White House was moot. His focus was on something he had not expected in this moment—protecting his family.

The door to the elevator cracked momentarily, then slid back shut. Jack knelt in one of the rear back corners of the elevator, his weapon at the ready. *Come on you assholes—open it.* He thought about his wife and daughters in Chevy Chase. Insurance policy... that's what he said. Barbara was smart. He had taught her and the girls how to shoot, but they had no idea of the harm that was headed their way. *I need to get to them, to save them.* He had no misgivings. His job was to protect the President, and he was in Charli's hands, hopefully safe. Now all that mattered was getting to his family, and that was not going to be easy.

The door was pried open again, this time with a crowbar. As it opened, Jack saw three men standing in front of it, wild eyes, grinning. He fired six rounds, controlled single shots, hitting all three. They didn't fly back like they did in the movies or TV, they simply twisted slightly and dropped as blood sprayed in the air behind him. His ears rang from the gunshots as he got to his feet. That was something else that TV always got wrong.

Gunshots rang off to his right, but no bullets flew his way. A haze from fires hung in the White House, and the lights flickered as the backup generators kicked on. He could see a lot of people, seemingly unorganized, opening doors and looking for would-be victims. One knocked over a small table in the hallway, pure vandalism. A trio of teens tore down one of the Presidential portraits as he climbed over the bodies of the men he had just shot. A group of younger people started to rush at him and he blasted away with perfect small bursts. The group leader's head exploded and the others dove for cover. They fired back, wild and wide of their target, the bullets hitting the wall next to him. Jack dove for an open office door, firing cover shots as he ran, jumping across the hall, slamming the door behind him. In the chaos, he was counting on their not seeing where he had gone.

In the room was a large man, rifling through the desk. He was donned in black clothing from his black headband to his black jeans. He saw Jack and Jack saw that his pistol was on the desk. They looked at each other, then at the gun. Jack pointed the deadly stub barrel of the FN P90 at the man. "Don't even fucking think about it," Jack growled. The hulking black man solely lifted his hands in the air.

The large man shook his head and arrogantly grinned. "You's Secret Service man. You ain't gonna shoot me."

Any other night and any other place, he was probably right. Desmond had always been a good officer, a man that played by the rules. Tonight, however, the rules meant nothing. Jack pulled the trigger once, sending a round into the man's groin. He doubled over with the loud pop. His hand found the gun on the desk and he fired. It was a chance shot, a desperate shot. Jack saw the flash and felt a shove and a stabbing pain on his right side. The hulking man lost his grip when he fired and fell over backwards with a barely audible thud thanks to the ringing in Jack's ears.

The pain was like a hot poker being stuck in his side. He checked his body armor and saw that it held. *He cracked one of my ribs, but it didn't penetrate.* It was small relief. He moved over to the man's body where the pool of blood was already forming on the wooden floor from where his bullet had hit his victim's crotch.

He set his assault weapon on the desk and bent over, pulling at the man's black turtleneck sweater. Each tug made his side throb. It took a lot to remove the garment, and each tug made him wince with agony. It hurt to pull it on, but wearing it allowed him to blend in with the people that were sacking the White House. With the oversized sweater covering his body armor, he looked more like one of the anarchists. He removed the sweat-soaked black bandana that the man wore and tied it over his own hair.

Grabbing his weapon, he unlocked the door and opened it. The hall was filling with more people who had overcome the defenses of the White House and were now tearing the place apart. It was tempting to open up full auto and mow them down, but that would not get him to his family. Jack moved into the crowd, holding the gun low so as not to draw attention. He moved through the West Wing, the ringing in his ears diminished as he heard the low muffled anger of the crowd all around him. There was a smashing sound, the shattering of glass or dishes. A pair of protesters held up the large painting of Thomas Jefferson and dragged their knives through it, destroying the artwork to the cheers of those in the hall. Gunshots fired off in other parts of the building, distant pops, a reminder of how dangerous his place of work had suddenly become.

Jack reached the outside through the Cross Hall, where the once luxurious red carpet on the stairs was being torn up by the rioters. The pain in his side throbbed as he made his way on the lawn. Glancing back, he saw smoke rising into the night from the East Wing, illuminated by the lights of the surrounding buildings. Hundreds of black-clothed people poured into the building, swarming like sharks on chum in the water. It seemed that everyone wanted to be a part of the destruction of the 'People's House.' Many were chanting, "Kill him!" and Jack prayed momentarily that Charli had managed to get away. Rage was all around him, the perfect cover.

Shuffling swiftly through the crowd, two blocks from the White House he came across a young George Washington student attempting to ride his scooter in the opposite direction. His school t-shirt was dark purple and he wore a black armband showing support for the rioters. Jack reached out and put his hand in front of the young man, whose long-braided hair waved as he stopped in at the H&M that had been sacked earlier by looters. "Hey dude, what's the deal?" he asked.

"Give me the bike," he said.

"Hey man… fuck off," the student replied.

Jack stuck the assault weapon barrel right above the student's Adam's Apple. "Get off now," he said in a growl.

"What the fuck?" Jack grabbed the man by his shirt and pulled him off the bike with a violent jerk, tossing him to the road. He gunned the engine and took off for home. Every bump on the Washington DC streets made his side throb with agony, but Jack didn't care. Drake Barker's words echoed in his mind. The night air stung his face and made his eyes water. Every few blocks another building was on fire, or he saw mobs looting another business. Sirens wailed over the district and the sound of helicopters bounced off the buildings around him.

As he wheeled around his block, his heart sank. He saw the row house he lived in engulfed in fire. Flames roared high into the night sky and a crowd surrounded his home. He stepped off the moving bike, letting it fall on the ground with a sickening, metallic grinding sound. He ran toward the front door.

Jack had never been exposed to a fire like this, the heat was overwhelming. His eyes darted through the crowd, hoping to see his wife and daughters. A form on the front stoop was dangerously close to the fire. Jack shielded his face and darted in, grabbing and pulling it away from the fire. The shooting pain in his side meant nothing. The sweater he had taken from the man he killed was smoldering from the heat as he reached the street. He stripped it off, tossing it on the grass.

The 'form' wasn't Barbara or one of the girls lying there. It was Pepper, his ever-faithful golden retriever. The dog had been shot; its hair singed by the flames. He could smell the aroma of the burned fur and it stung at his nostrils. Jack held onto Pepper, pulling the dog close, hugging her warm body in his arms, rocking as he held her tight. He then knew the truth; he had lost everything. *If the attackers would shoot his dog, what hope would his family have?* The roaring orange and yellow flames lapping into the sky were a funeral pyre. He couldn't think of Barbara, Jean or Jamie. All he could do was hold Pepper tight, ignoring the heat from what had been his home, his life.

His neighbor Jackson came over and knelt next to him. "A group of them showed up an hour ago. They ignored every other house, but threw Molotov cocktails at yours, front and back. We tried to put out the flames, but couldn't. When the dog came out, they shot her," Jackson said. The neighbor continued to talk but Jack couldn't hear anymore—not from the ringing in his ears but the overwhelming sorrow in his heart. The words were a blur. *They burned my family alive, just because of who I am. They took everything from me.* Tears streamed down his face as the flames soared high in the skies over Chevy Chase.

Culpeper, Virginia

Andy Forrest spoke up as Jack finished conveying the story of what he had experienced the night of the Fall. "If we do this, we are no better than they are."

"They have always counted on us taking the moral high-ground," Charli said. "They knew that we would not stoop to their level. That was why the people didn't rise up when they took our way of life. Sure, there were some fights back, like what went down in San Antonio, but we were caught off guard and everyone assumed someone else would fix it. Good people stood by refusing to get their hands dirty and do what it takes to win. It didn't get us anywhere but marched into camps or beaten into submission. Jack is right. This isn't the time for us to take half-measures. They need a dose of their own medicine. They need to experience the pain and fear that we have all suffered. Force is the only thing they understand, so I say we give it to them."

Caylee stood slowly, as if she were using the gesture to give herself time to gather her thoughts. "Mister Forrest, I was on the other side of this fight for the last few years. I assure you, we never stopped and considered the moral implications of our actions. It was the kind of thinking that made you hate yourself, so you simply didn't do it. That is what separates you from them. You know what you are doing is offensive and wrong. In the NSF, we saw the same actions as the means to an end."

"Do you feel different now?" Andy asked.

"The moment I realized that my own people were being sent to kill me... yes. It's one thing to be on the end administering what you call justice; it's another when you have a target painted on you. I have that target right now. Overnight I flipped from being an asset to a liability. It changes your perspective dramatically. It was that, or run until they ran me down.

"So I *do* feel that Mister Desmond's concept is sound. Moreover, I'm the right person to do it when it comes to taking the fight to the NSF. I will hurt the Secretary, let her feel the exact same fear she has inflicted on so many people."

Jack surveyed her face. *She was tracking us down. We were her targets only a few days ago. Now she's as much a victim as the rest of us. She lost her freedom, while the rest of us have lost more—but that doesn't diminish what she feels.* "If you do this Caylee, you do it in coordination with the rest of our plan—understood?"

Leatrom nodded once. "I've never been much of a 'cause' person. I worked in the NSF because it was a place where I could use my talents. We are in the same boat now. I agree, Mister Desmond."

Jack uncrossed his arms. "Then it's settled."

Andy appeared edgy. "I think I understand what we are doing. Caylee's part is one aspect of all of this. We are not just making a statement. The totality of what we are doing could lead to all-out civil war."

"What else is left to us?" Charli asked. "The government has literally become everything it swore we were. They take people into custody and lock them away without due process. They kill those that they see as threats. There is no more free speech. You can say what you want, but they then apply social justice and destroy your life and the lives of your loved ones. They overthrew the government rather than try to change it from within. If it takes a civil war to reverse that, well, I say, bring-it-the-fuck-on." She spoke with a deep passion in her voice, years of frustration and failure ringing in each word.

Andy nodded in response. "I had to say it out loud."

Jack cracked a thin smile. "I'm glad you did. One should never undertake something like this lightly. Lives are precious things."

Jack paused and drew a long, deep breath before continuing. "We have only a short period of time before the Ruling Council releases its glorious new plan for Newmerica." Sarcasm rang in his voice as he spoke. "They believe they have crushed their opposition, and now they will try to toss out what is left of the Constitution and come up with a new one that validates their tyranny.

"We have all suffered losses. That hasn't left us beaten. They have given us resolve. And shortly, they will learn exactly what that resolve can do. Most of the citizens out there ignore the crimes of the state, just as long as they get their reparations for turning in their neighbors. Others have kept as low a profile as possible out of fear of being the next target. Even more are out there, waiting for the right moment and reason to stand up against these bastards. Well, we are going to give them that moment; we are going to give them their chance to rise up."

.

CHAPTER 24

*"Are your neighbors being good citizens? If not, turn them
in for reparation points. The more points you have, the more
you earn. Surveillance is every person's responsibility."*

The Bronx, New York

Caylee's day had been busy already, having gotten off the plane at
JFK Airport and arriving at her second target site for the day. The
apartment building was remarkably plain as she walked past it to
survey any possible problems. Security cameras were present, but those
could be dealt with easily enough. At one time the apartment probably
had a door attendant, but those kinds of jobs were the first to bite the dust
after the Fall. Everyone had cut back jobs when the economy tanked.
They will pay the price for their decisions tonight.

When she returned to her rental car just a few doors down and across
from the main entrance, she rolled down the window and used a small
laser sighting device to zoom in on each camera, one at a time. Most
commercial laser sights were only enough to possibly pop a balloon, and
then it required some modifications. Hers was a military grade one, and
she had it modified several years earlier for this kind of mission.

The twilight setting sun in the city helped obscure her actions.
Aiming at each camera, she waited until she saw a wisp of smoke as the
green power light winked out. She hit the camera on the street corner as
well, just to be sure. As she emerged from the car, she appeared harmless,
which was the intent. Her plaid shawl concealed her guns and the Kevlar
she wore under her loose-fitting shirt. Making her way through the lobby,
she took the elevator up to the fifth floor.

The hallway was well lit, but she saw no sign of other surveillance
equipment. The carpet was a green color, some fancy pattern that

someone had thought neutrally tasteful, though it did nothing for her. Just in case, she hit a small remote control on her belt. It would generate a low impulse jamming signal that could mess up any nearby gear. Its range was fairly limited, but it would help for the things she couldn't see that might be tracking her.

Counting down the room numbers as she walked, she arrived at 511. She leaned forward slightly and knocked on the door. She heard sounds on the other side of the cream-colored door, no doubt someone looking through the peephole. Caylee grinned and waited as the door cracked open. The door guard chain strung taut. A man's face hovered in the crack near the chain. "May I help you?"

"You are Mister Cortez, correct?"

He nodded. "I'm Gabe. What can I do for you?"

"I'm a reporter with the *Times*," she said, still maintaining her grin. "I'd like to get your thoughts on the upcoming events tomorrow night— given your sister's position on the Ruling Council. You know, just a little fluff about what you think now that five years has come to pass… that kind of thing."

The black-haired man nodded. "Sure," he said closing the door enough to open the chain. The millisecond it closed, Caylee drew her Walther and as the door opened, she shoved it into the middle of his forehead, and took a step into the apartment.

Fear gripped him as his eyes crossed looking up at the gun barrel that dug into his flesh. Both hands feebly rose. "I—I—take whatever you want. Just don't shoot."

She used her left heel to kick the door closed behind her. "Are you alone?"

"Yes. Look, I don't want any trouble," he said, stumbling over each word as fear gripped him. It was a facial expression she had seen a dozen times before.

"What you want is irrelevant," she said as she pulled the trigger. He dropped with a thud on the hallway rug, and blood splattered on the walls beyond. Caylee quickly holstered her pistol, pulled out a rubber glove to use the doorknob to leave. Glancing back she looked at his dead body. *The hurting started earlier today. Now she will know that it is personal. Now your sister will feel true pain.*

Manhattan, New York

Charli sat next to the Vice President in the small flat over the comic book store right off of Broadway. The flat was shabbily furnished with much of its décor dating back to the last century. A musty aroma rose from the sofa every time someone on it moved. Charli didn't mind at all. She had been in worse places over the last four years.

Jack had given her old job back—protecting the leader of America. "You did an outstanding job four years ago," he had said. "No one else would have gotten him out of there." She wanted to protest. A part of her always felt she had failed, but Jack never saw it that way. "There's no better person on the planet that I trust more with the life of the VP." Charli resolved to herself that history would not repeat itself.

She was not alone. Andy had come along, hugging the archival cases they had recovered. Four others were present in the room, one from Virginia, the others Jack had brought in from another cell of the Sons of Liberty, presumably from the New York area. Jack had been going down to his truck, parked in a blind alley a block away, constantly monitoring messages.

"You're nervous," the VP said as she paced around the room.

"Cautious," Charli replied. "We are in the heart of liberalism."

"It's the last place they'd expect us to be," he assured her. "Besides, we both know that they think I'm dead."

"Relaxing isn't part of the job description," she replied.

He smiled at her. "I have been looking over my shoulder for five years as of tomorrow. Their social justice warriors tormented my family and drove my kids into exile. They use the word 'justice' but we all know that is a load of crap. They wanted revenge… revenge for things we had never done. I kept my family in the dark except for my wife. They had to think I'd died that night."

"So you waited," Charli said.

He nodded, his silvery hair unwavering. "If I had just emerged and spoken out, they would have arrested and killed me. I needed support, backing, especially when the military sold out my predecessor. When Jack found me, I was with some loyal supporters in Indiana, living in their basement. Together, we brought the Sons of Liberty back from the dead—recrafted it so that it could handle the storm that is about to come."

It should have never come to this… the Vice President hiding like a fugitive. She understood though. Jack must have pulled in more than a few favors to find him. *How would he know to have even looked?* That realization came to her somewhat slower. *You don't trust anything they tell you. With their Truth Reconciliation Committee, they determine what is reality and what is fiction.*

Andy leaned into their conversation. "My father was one of the originals in the Sons… until they hauled him off to one of their camps. He never broke, but the experience did something to him, something horrible. He was never the same after that."

"He wasn't alone," the Vice President said gloomily. "Big Tech gave them the lists, the names of everyone that had ever supported conservative thinking. They had been monitoring every click and every 'like' we ever made. They put together profiles and went after anyone that might be vocal. It wasn't enough to seize the government. They had to eradicate the opposition. What had been the Republican Party was gutted. Only a few made it out—those that turned on their ideals and sold themselves out. It's hard to blame them, with their families and colleagues held hostage. They were only kept around long enough to make the rest of us look like 'radical domestic terrorists.' I think those were their words. I'm sure your father was a good man whose only crime was that he stuck to his principles."

"It cost him everything in the end," Andy said. "Except these," he patted the archival cases.

"Well, tomorrow, we start to set things right," the Vice President said. "We've been on the defense for years. I haven't played a lot of sports over the years, but I learned a long time ago that I hate playing defense. The time has come for us to fight. The time has come for us to put them on the defense. Let's see how these bastards like it for a change."

The District

As the door to her office opened the Secretary of the NSF wiped the tears from her face, removing a smear of makeup and mascara with her tissue. The word had come that her mother had been found dead in her home in Florida. A cleaning woman had found her near the front door. It had been four months since she had last visited her. She had always been a source of support to the Secretary, and now she was gone.

It had been a grueling day, reviewing the speech that the Truth Reconciliation Committee had prepared for the next day's anniversary of the Liberation. Some people hated speeches, but she did not, not under normal circumstances. She had tried to call her brother Gabe, but he had not answered the phone; nor was he at work—so she sent some of her local NSF people to inform him of their mother's demise.

"Yes?" she asked of her aide who had interrupted her.

"Ma'am, you have a call on line one," the nervous assistant responded, the color draining from his face.

"I told you no interruptions," she growled.

"Madame Secretary," the aide said slowly. "I think you need to pick up this call." As he finished, he backed out of the doorway and closed the double doors behind him.

She snatched up the phone angrily and jabbed her finger at the lit button. "This is the Secretary," she snarled.

"This is Detective Reins with the NSF Bronx, madam," came back the older sounding white male voice on the other end of the line. "I was sent to deliver the message to your brother, Gabriel."

She said nothing for a moment. "Go on."

"Madam, I regret to inform you that when we arrived at his apartment, we had the superintendent open the door. We found your brother, dead."

She felt the life seem to drain from her face with those words. Her body felt like a dead weight in her thickly padded leather chair. *No! It can't be! Mom died this morning, now Gabe?* "How?"

"Gunshot wound to the head Madam Secretary. From what we can tell, it was at point blank range."

Execution style. Someone murdered him. Gabe had no enemies. He was harmless. "Do you have any footage… any witnesses?"

"No ma'am," Detective Reins replied. "The security cameras were disabled somehow. No one saw the perp enter or leave."

Her mind was an erupting volcano of chaotic thought. *Both dead on the same day! Was it a coincidence? Why would anyone kill them?* The loss of her family hit her hard; she even had trouble drawing a breath. Grief made her light-headed for a moment.

Slowly, methodically, she started to answer her own questions. *This*

couldn't be a coincidence. Someone did this. This was aimed at me!
"Detective," she said slowly. "I want you to contact the authorities in Miami that are investigating my mother's death. I want a full toxicology run on her. Her death might be tied to my brother's."

"Your mother died too?"

"Yes. Now get on it before they do anything stupid with her body. Contact the local airports and have them do facial recognition scans against our Red List targets. See if someone killed my mother and traveled to New York."

"I'm on it," Reins said. She slammed the receiver down and leaned over her desk, planting her elbows on the desktop and rubbing the back of her neck. *Who would want to do this to me?* Her immediate thoughts went to the Social Enforcement organization. *I just ordered their leadership laid waste. Is it possible that someone over there is retaliating for what we did?* As she tried to process the information, she began to discount them. *They are street thugs. They are organized, but if these deaths are connected, it has the mark of professionals. The SEs are anything but that. Besides, I just purged their leadership. Most of them are trembling in their boots.*

Who else could it be? Another member of the Ruling Council? It made sense. They all saw her as a threat, some more than others. *Most lack the balls for such an action, especially after what I have done, grabbing control of the SE.* Ever since she had been elected to Congress, she had stepped on toes to get ahead. She had been the master at manipulating the media. Her opponents had been beaten. Those that still lived, did so in fear of her.

That fear could have been enough to force someone to strike at her. This was professional—if they disabled the cameras at Gabe's apartment building, they were not amateurs. Various groups out there had an axe to grind. They hated her. The NSF had racked up a long list of enemies. For a few long moments, she tried to think about who could be striking out at her personally and realized that the list was far too long.

It was easier to discard the notion. *No one would dare to make such a move against me, not unless they were crazy.* For a few long moments, alone in her office, she began to think she was being paranoid. *Maybe it was a coincidence. No one would risk such an action against me. I have an army at my disposal. There would be no place for them to hide.*

She drew a long, deep breath and sat up. *Now I have two funerals to plan in the middle of all of these festivities.* The Secretary drew solace from one thought. *If we communicate this to the masses, it generates sympathy for me. On the heels of what I just pulled off with the SE, this couldn't have come at a better time. If nothing else, it will play well in the media; make people see me as more human.*

Manhattan, New York

Andy sat at one of the two dining chairs in the apartment where they had been huddled with the Vice President, eating cold pizza. He had always hoped to have a slice of authentic New York style pizza, but had never pictured it in this kind of setting, under these circumstances. Jack Desmond had been adamant about the group not using their phones out of fear of being tracked. The leader of the Sons of Liberty disappeared, sometimes for an hour or more.

He picked up on bits and pieces of things. Charli had told him all about Jack after her admission of what happened the night of the Fall. Jack had been Delta Force before joining the Secret Service. According to her, he had a long list of citations, many of which were for unofficial missions—the kinds of operations that the government never fully avowed took place. Jack himself admitted that the mobs had targeted his family, as they had with much of law enforcement's leadership. He hadn't just lost the White House the night of the Fall, he lost everything he held dear.

As Andy surveyed the room, he realized they all had dealt with loss as a result of the events almost five years earlier. It had cost him his sister and years of life with his father. His father had lost everything as a result of what the mobs had brought down on the nation. *Everyone in this room has suffered as a result of the Fall. We are told that the government supports the people, but it has become more oppressive than anything that had existed before. They pedal lies as the truth.* His father, in death, had beaten them though. He had saved several bits of old America from the rioters and looters. *I wonder if he realized how all of this would have come together.* With his father being an historian and member of the SOL, he liked to think it was somehow part of his father's grand plan.

There was a knock at the door and Charli, along with the others, immediately went for their weapons. He felt naked without a gun, despite not having much experience at shooting one. Jack entered and at his side were two large black men flanking a younger attractive woman. Her blonde hair was short, but somehow, as he saw her face, he remembered it being longer. He tried to place the face. Then it came to him.

It was the President's daughter! Andy dropped his pizza slice back into the box.

She was ushered into the room and the door was secured. The Vice President rose from the sofa and held his arms out. "I thought you were dead," she said, stepping forward, crying and hugging him.

"It was the only way," he said as he held her tight. They parted and he eyed her from top to bottom. "You haven't changed a bit," the silver-haired man said.

She wiped a tear from her cheek. "For three years they kept me in a camp. They have my daughters somewhere. My husband…" she choked on the rest of her sentence with sobs.

The VP put his hand on her shoulder and Andy himself felt like crying as she struggled with her emotions. "You're here now, safe; that's what matters."

Jack stood at the doorway. "They had an SE team surveilling her residence. Suffice it to say, if they don't know she's missing by now, they will shortly." Andy read between the lines and understood completely—the SE team was dead.

The President's daughter regained her composure for a moment, looking around the room and her eyes locked onto Charli. "Is she the one?" she asked, looking back at Jack.

"Lieutenant Charli Kazinski," he said as a form of short introduction.

The slender woman stepped in front of Charli and extended her hand. "He told me what happened. Thank you. I'm glad you were with him when the time came."

Charli fought back her tears, with little success from what Andy could see. "I'm sorry… I failed. Your father fought on until the very end."

The daughter of the former President leaned in and hugged Charli. "It wasn't your fault. It wasn't anyone's fault," she said parting with

Charli and sweeping the room. "We underestimated them. They had help from our enemies aboard. The liberals backed them like a secret army and turned them loose on us."

Jack stepped forward. "This is Andy Forrest," he said introducing the two of them. She held out her hand and Andy shook it nervously. "His father and other loyalists managed to save the Declaration of Independence and the Constitution. He and Charli managed to recover them, and a fairly significant American flag."

She gripped his hand with both of hers. "Thank you," she said.

Andy was unsure what to say for a moment and settled on. "There's no need to thank me." She didn't respond, which was the greatest compliment that he could have received. *I wish you were here, Dad. I'm with the Vice President and the daughter of the President on the cusp of starting to reclaim the country.*

Jack stood in the center room holding his arms out wide. "Tomorrow, the Ruling Council is planning to celebrate what they did to all of us, to the entire nation. They are going to give themselves a party. If the rumors are true, they are going to throw out the laws of the country and write a new Constitution. It is their attempt to validate and solidify what they did. They have swept their crimes under the rug, buried them or killed those that knew about them.

"They were not counting on us," he said, sweeping the room with his eyes. "That was their mistake. We will crash their party tomorrow and the whole world will know that America is not dead. People that have been under the boots of the Newmerica government will be given something new—hope—a reason to fight. For the first time in a half decade, they will experience what we have come to live with… fear.

"We all have a role in this. I won't lie to you; this is going to be tricky to pull off.

Andy watched him and realized that he was living in a moment in history. It was not some page in a book or some bullet point on a PowerPoint slide, it was *actual* history. If they succeeded, this would be the time and place people wrote about. *I'm just one of the people in the background of this painting, but I can't imagine being anywhere else.*

Charli moved over next to him as Jack went to his satchel and started to boot up his laptop to go over the plans. She handed him a Glock, one of those they had taken from Caylee. "You know how to use this?" she asked.

Andy shook his head. "Not this one. I've been shooting once or twice. They confiscated Dad's guns when he was arrested. I always figured I'd have time to learn, but they took all of the guns and it was too damned expensive for a permit to buy one of my own."

"Given your dad's affiliation with the SOL, you wouldn't have gotten one anyway," she said. Stepping next to him, she held the gun up for him to see, turning it over. "This is a G17. The mag goes in like this," she demonstrated inserting it. "You have seventeen shots. Here's how you chamber a round," Charli slid the slide back and forth. She then demonstrated unloading it for him. She showed him the magazine release and the safety. "Keep the safety on until you see things heading south. Don't fire panicked. Rookies always do that. Take your time and aim, gently squeeze the trigger. Jerking the trigger will screw with your aim." Charli handed him the gun and three magazines. They felt awkward in his hands and he set them on the table.

"Are you up for this?" she asked.

He nervously nodded. "Are you?"

"I'm getting tired of the cloak and dagger shit and constantly looking over my shoulder."

"It must have been hard."

Charli nodded once. "Tomorrow changes everything."

"My dad used to say, 'No plan survives contact with the enemy.'"

Charli grinned in response. "Your dad never knew me."

CHAPTER 25

"Social Justice Is Criminal Justice."

Manhattan, New York

Valerie Turner entered the long broadcast satellite control room of CBS casually, so as to not immediately arouse attention. She wore a black mask, a leftover from the virus months, black and perfect at obscuring her face. A lot of people still wore them, either out of lingering fear or force of habit.

The security guard outside the door had already been incapacitated, a chop to his windpipe had left him gagging long enough to take an AR-15 stock blow to his head. The lobby security staff had at least tried to put up a fight. Someone would likely find their bodies in the closet before the night was through, hopefully after she and her people were long gone. *I told Jack there would be breakage...*

One of the technical staff raised his eyes to look at her, but everyone else was focused on their tasks. The curious tech returned to his monitor in the dimly lit room, choosing to ignore her and her colleagues. Valerie allowed herself a moment of gloating. This was the start of the operation, but thus far it was going much better than she and Jack had anticipated.

Surveying the long, dark room filled with tightly-packed computer workstations with screens that flanked each operator, she knew she had to get their attention, and then force their compliance. Pulling out her pistol, she pointed it at the ceiling and fired. Dust from a pulverized ceiling tile fell over her Mets hat as she swept the gun through the room. "May I have your attention please?" Heads rose in panic and fear, several losing their headsets in the process. One of her people, Derek, a former Lieutenant in the NYPD, moved down the narrow aisle of the room, making sure there were no surprises. Eyes shifted from her to him and his AR-15.

"Nobody here has to die," she said. "Do as you're told and no one will." Two more of her people entered the room, weapons at the ready. One of the techs began crying—another person started to sob uncontrollably.

"Where's your production supervisor?" Valerie demanded.

A wobbly hand rose from a pale young man with a goatee. "I—I am."

"You have a name?"

"Walter?" he nervously said.

"Is that your name or a question?" she snapped. *Get your shit together!*

"My name," he said meekly.

"Well then Walter, you work for me, at least for the time being." He nodded apprehensively and the color drained from his already pale face. *Poor kid will probably throw up before this is over.*

"Wha—what do you want?" Walter asked.

"You are going to bring Studio A up on-line. You will continue to pipe in the feed from the District and the ceremony, but when I give you the word, you are going to cut to the studio. Got it?"

He nodded and took his seat. "I don't want any trouble," he said. The eyes of the others followed both him and her as she moved behind him.

"Some of my people are trained on this stuff," Valerie said. "Any of you decide to go off-script and try anything funny, we will know. If you do, Walter here will get a bullet in the back of his head, followed by each one of you."

"I—I don't understand, "Walter stammered. "The—the feed from the District... they'll know when we cut them off."

"Don't you worry about that Walter," Valerie said. "We have that covered. New Jersey's relay center is under our control already. Our broadcast *will* go out. You do what I say and nobody has to get their brains splattered all over their coworkers." One young woman's sobs turned to all out weeping and Valerie rolled her eyes at the sound. Derek moved behind one lanky Asian youth and shook his head. "Shit, this kid just pissed himself."

The tech turned to Derek. "You have guns—you're terrorists."

"Guns don't kill," Derek said flatly. "*I* kill. And we ain't terrorists."

"What are you then?"

Valerie opted to answer. "We're the good guys. You work for the terrorists."

Walter began to stab away at his keyboard as she hovered behind him. Two more of her team moved into the control room and made sure no one was doing anything they shouldn't. Satisfied, for the moment, Valerie pulled out her walkie-talkie. "Rabbit—this is the Fox. The studio is yours."

Jack's voice came back. "Good work, Fox. We are moving into position now."

Menlo Park, California

Former Navy SEAL Travis Cullen looked out at Facebook's five-building campus in the distance with a bit of grim satisfaction. An explosives expert, he considered his work in Silicon Valley to be one of his masterpieces. Five different complexes, each with a number of surprises planted and awaiting his signal. He had chosen to watch Facebook because their campus had the widest open views from a distance.

Travis had been a SEAL Lieutenant at the time of the Fall. He and his team had been forward-deployed to the Pentagon when the rioting had started to get out of hand. He had been expecting it. The BLM protests had been hijacked by ANTIFA and other militant groups for months—things were bound to get out of hand. Travis felt someone was clearly pulling the strings, but identifying *who* was a matter beyond his pay grade.

Loaded on two choppers, they were prepared to execute the Bifrost protocols when the White House was attacked; chopper in low and do a fast drop on the White House grounds to secure the building and the President if necessary. When the order came to stand down, Travis had ordered the pilot to take off anyway, to no avail. Orders were orders. He knew what was happening a short distance away. *I swore to protect my country, and in its time of greatest need, my superiors stabbed their Commander and Chief in the back.*

When he protested, they revoked his commission and took him away from his life. Jack Desmond had found him in a bar in South Carolina and told him there was a chance to set things right. Since that time, he had been Jack's demolitions expert. The bomb that took down the NSF building in Virginia? That was his, one of his best until now. The attack on Bumblehive... that had been him too. Jack had used his devices in Palo Alto weeks earlier to kill their bomb squad as well. Those had all been good in their own ways. This, however, was going to be his masterpiece.

Big Tech had always been part of the Fall. They had censored conservative voices for years. They twisted social media data to manipulate people. When news stories came up that were contrary to 'progressive thinking' they simply made them inaccessible, censored, or outright deleted. If you couldn't find or share the information, it was the same as not existing. Travis, like so many people prior to the Fall, had seen this, complained about it, but never thought it would be weaponized against America. When the White House and the Capitol fell to the anarchists, Big Tech enabled them to track down conservatives. Social Enforcement rounded them up swiftly, enabled by the technology companies being able to track their every move. The team that came for Travis, well, their bodies still had never been found. They did get his father, a twenty-year Navy veteran. He spent a year in one of their camps before allegedly coming down with pneumonia and dying. Travis had learned not to trust anything he was told by the Newmerica government—even about his father's death.

He sat in his truck on the service round outside the campus and watched the buildings and his chronometer. Jack was planning to release some information on the internet, things the government would not want out there. Newmerica's leaders relied on Big Tech to block such things and they were removed from the web with stunning efficiency. You couldn't find an image of the old American flag or the text of the Constitution out there—they simply made it impossible to find. They censored the internet behind the scenes and most of the country simply took it for granted.

Not today…

The blueprints for the buildings were on file with their respective counties, making it easy for him to identify weak points and places to plant his little surprises. Penetrating the building security had been relatively easy, especially Facebook. At Google, he had almost been discovered by the rentacop security team, but had talked his way out of the situation. Twitter's HQ in San Francisco had been easy to get into with Travis posing as a building maintenance tech. The bombs had been placed everywhere, especially near water pipes since he knew that water and electronics were an entertaining combination. The explosive devices he planted at their data farms outside of the urban sprawl were designed to cause massive damage as well.

Jack had used one of his devices to kill the Bomb Squad weeks earlier. Once the bombs started going off, the NSF would be crippled and unable to respond. They would have to assume that there were more devices that hadn't gone off. The buildings would be evacuated for days, if not longer, while non-experts conducted searches.

While the employees of the company could work from their homes, and many did during the COVID crisis, they relied on their secured links to the office—links that Jack ensured would be taken out. *These people have been beyond the reach of the people they have harmed. Snot-nosed college pukes that thought it was funny to push their little political agendas with mass censorship and list-making for Newmerica. They thought it was funny. They painted themselves as the rebels in their own version of Star Wars, but in reality, they had become the Empire. In a few minutes, they will learn that there is a price to be paid for their 'contributions.'*

At Facebook and Twitter, he had planned something special, something extra.

He checked his watch and used his burner phone to place the call. "Rabbit, this is David. I'm ready to take down Goliath."

"This is Rabbit," came Jack's cool voice. "Execute."

Travis shut off the phone and tucked it away. On the seat next to him was the transmitter and he opened the toggle covers on the switches for the companies he targeted. Twitter got theirs first. He could not hear the rumble across the bay, but knew that the half dozen bombs were going off on the second floor of their headquarters. It would take a few minutes for the effects of the blast to fully compromise the structure and bring it all down.

Google went up next, starting with their primary data farm, then their headquarters. Travis knew there would be panic and chaos. He hit the other switches, saving Facebook for last. When he hit the first two toggles for them, they saw the buildings of the campus erupt with deep resounding whomp sounds, followed by explosions of glass raining on the parking lot. Smoke rolled from where windows had been and fire alarms went off.

People poured out of the building a few moments later, running into the parking lot in sheer terror. Travis was amused by their panic; it was totally predictable. His time in Iraq had taught him a lot about how people react to explosions. They would get some distance, then stop, turn around to see the carnage rather than keep running. One building on the campus collapsed, falling inward, sending billows of gray concrete dust roaring through the air. A part of him hoped Zuckerberg was in there, trapped, not fully understanding what was happening. A few screams came from the group in the parking lot as they watched in horror.

One switch was left open on his control board and he stared at it for a long moment. Travis thought about his father and how he had not even been allowed to be with his father when he died. *He gave everything to this country, and in the end, it was his country that killed him. Those people out there aided the fucknuts that took my nation down. They have been manipulating the public for years, twisting what they saw and how they saw it. Now, today, for at least a while, that comes to an end.*

He hit the last switch without a bit of hesitation. The explosives in the parking lot of the Facebook campus went off, all four of them. Pillars of black smoke rolled skyward as screams filled the air. In San Francisco, the two fake post office boxes he had placed on Market and 10th Streets exploded as well—hundreds of pounds of high-grade explosives packed with nails, ball bearings, bolts—anything that could be used as shrapnel. The staff that had fled from the explosions was now caught in the secondary blasts. He was far enough away to hear the screams but not see the dead bodies. Travis didn't need to. *I've seen enough dead bodies for any person in their lifetime.*

He watched the carnage he had released with grim satisfaction. It wouldn't bring his father back, but it would do something that had never been done—it would frighten the Big Tech companies. Their employees would be afraid. *They* were now the targets rather than the citizens of the country. The bombs going off would make them wet themselves. *Now they can constantly look over their shoulders in fear.*

The first responders would be slow to react because they would fear more explosions. The fires and crippling effects of the blasts would consume each of the targets. *There aren't enough counselors in the state to take care of the fear I have created with these people today.*

Travis started the battered old Ford F-Series truck and drove away calmly as the rising pyre of smoke rolled like a mushroom cloud over Silicon Valley.

Valley Forge, Pennsylvania

Raul huddled behind the trunk of a pine tree, his shirt sticking to the sap every time he shifted. He was poised to rush the front gate once the vehicles hit the rear fence of the camp. He had two pistols, a battered green Glock and a SIG P365. The Glock was his backup weapon, stuffed into the oversized pockets of his green fatigue pants. Raul liked the SIG best, a little surprised that he had a preference in firearms to begin with. Firing the weapon on the makeshift range had chipped away at his bad memories of killing the man in Detroit. Now, though, he was going to be pressed again into using a weapon. While he disliked the thought of killing another, he knew that if he did, it was to save lives. *Father Ryan would approve… I know he would. I'm here to save people.*

Everyone was nervous. He could tell because no one had talked much on the ride in. Their faces were covered with smears of charcoal and they wore dark or green clothing. Jayden could sense it too. "If we save even a handful of these prisoners, it's worth it to their families," he said earlier as he drove the truck into the woods. He'd parked it for use later. The big truck was military surplus, something called a "Deuce-and-a-Half" that Jayden said he had found in a scrap yard and got running. The other two pickups were old rust buckets that never would have passed Newmerica's "Go Green!" emission standards. One burned so much oil it left a bluish cloud behind it and the engine seemed to knock hard. Jayden had told them that didn't matter; they were only needed for distraction.

While they rested near the vehicle, making sure they were prepared if they somehow were spotted, Jayden went off into the darkness, presumably to get the other vehicles ready. He was gone nearly half an hour before returning, with Sasha almost firing on him when he emerged from the brush. He checked his watch. "Five minutes," Jayden said, opening the door to the big vehicle and climbing in. Raul and the others silently followed, climbing in the back of the big truck. The old dump truck they were going to use was further down the trail.

"You afraid Raul?" Sasha asked.

He wanted to say *no* but couldn't. "*Si.* I have never done anything like this before."

"None of us have," she said. She leaned forward and kissed his cheek.

"What was that for?" he asked meekly.

"In case I don't get a chance later."

Five minutes seemed like an hour. Suddenly, from the other side of the camp, the night air was filled with the roar of two truck engines and the tires grinding into the dirt. Lights went on in the camp, as if the buildings themselves were awakened by the sound. Then the fireworks started, Roman candles, Phantom Fireworks mortars, and big bottle rockets lit up the tree line in the distance, beyond the camp. Raul peered over the edge of the vehicle and could see figures starting to move off to the other side, as Jayden had hoped.

The crashing sound of one truck hitting the fence filled the air, followed by a crunching bang as it slammed into a building, out of his field of view. Headlights flickered from another truck that hit the fence, tearing out barbed wire and chain link fencing as it sputtered and lost momentum, all amid the fireworks raining on the camp. Gunfire started as well, guards firing out of the camp either at the vehicles or at the source of the fireworks.

The Deuce-and-a-Half roared to life as did the dump truck behind it. Raul was jerked so hard he almost fell from his seat as the vehicle lunged out of the side road and headed for the main gate. The plan had been for the guards to be drawn off by the crashing vehicle to their rear, but suddenly there was a burst of gunfire from the left guard tower. The pinging of bullets hitting the vehicle filled his ears and terror gripped him. *This wasn't supposed to happen!*

Sasha raised up and fired at the tower that was closing quickly, so did three other members of the Order. Raul grabbed the side rail and stood long enough to fire at the tower too, not seeing the shooter but the small tower he was in. Bullets tore into the wood structure and the gunfire from there suddenly stopped, at least for the moment. The truck lurched hard when it hit the gate and Raul could hear the grinding of metal along the front and sides of his truck. Suddenly it stopped and everyone started scrambling out the sides.

He landed, gun at the ready. There were the cracking-pops of gunfire in the distance, now drowned out by the fire from his comrades. A bullet hit the ground off to his left, kicking up dirt. Jayden and a small group sprinted to the side of a building, using it for cover. He started to run to another barracks on the other side of the vehicle, hoping to get cover. Sasha sprinted beside him as they ran. Raul slammed hard into the side of the building, his ears roaring with adrenaline and gun shots. Across the narrow roadway at the entrance to the camp, just beyond the big truck, he saw Jayden and the others sweep from behind their building and unleash a torrent of bullets at the guards who were near the center of the camp hunkered down behind two buildings for cover.

His breath was heavy as he edged to the corner of the building to duplicate Jayden's move. Raul darted out a yard or so, looking for a target. He saw one figure, silhouetted by the lights, moving with a lumber—Lumpy. The figure held a large assault weapon and was firing at Jayden's position. Raul took aim slowly and fired. Lumpy's arm lurched back as Raul's bullet hit its mark and the guard cried out and dove for the ground. Raul drifted back so that he was partially covered by the barracks.

The wood on the corner of the building suddenly erupted next to Raul's shoulder, and he felt his body jerk to the side that was behind it. At first it felt like a bee sting in his upper right arm. Ignoring it proved impossible. As he tried to lift the pistol, a wave of agony washed over his arm and shoulder—it felt as if he were on fire.

Glancing at his arm, he saw a small chunk of flesh missing near his bicep and he saw blood, wet and reflective in the darkness. *I've been shot!* Staggering, he moved behind the building for full cover as the gunfire continued.

Sasha bent down next to him, trying to see the wound in the dimly lit darkness in the shadow of the building. Pulling out a penlight she shined it and Raul saw jagged splinters of wood stuck in his arm and a furrow where the bullet had wounded him in the upper arm. Seeing the blood made the pain surge even more. His entire arm throbbed.

"You're going to be okay Raul," she assured him. "I've got to pull out these pieces of wood so I can bind it." He looked up at her and nodded. Each one she removed hurt like a hot poker being pulled through his flesh. He wanted to put on a brave face for Sasha, but it was hard.

She took off her bandana and wrapped it around his wound. When she tied the knot, the pain was so bad he felt dizzy. The staccato of gunshots was still going on as she finished. "Can you stand?" she asked.

Raul switched the gun from his wounded right arm to his left hand and nodded. She helped him to his feet. Sweat stung at the corners of his eyes and he winced in pain. "I'm fine," he lied to her. Sasha flashed him a grin, then took his spot at the corner of the building, emptying her clip in a matter of seconds, before diving back for cover.

Then came the call from across the roadway. "Jayden's hit!" cried Darius.

Raul felt gut-punched. *This was not how it was supposed to go… not at all.* He turned to Sasha. "Get Maria. We'll move around the building, get on their side."

Sasha nodded and Raul moved the gun to the hand on his crippled arm. It hurt to use his hand to eject the clip and reload, but he didn't want to go into a fight without bullets. Gunfire still rang off, as did the occasional explosion of overhead fireworks from the distraction teams. Sasha and Maria came up next to him. "We're ready."

He was wet from sweat and the pain was excruciating, but he knew if he didn't take action, the shooting would not stop until they were all dead. "Follow me," he said through gritted teeth, rounding the corner of the barracks and into the darkness on the other side.

The District

The NSF Secretary sat behind a huge desk in the studio with other members of the Ruling Council. She had insisted on sitting next to the Chairman, and no one dared challenge her. "You need a female there, and a person of color, so that the entire country knows we stand by our principles." Her justification was for looks, which played well with the Chairman. Of course, there was more to it than mere appearance. It was a deliberate act on her part. Every time the camera would come to him, it would have her on screen as well. *I want the people to see me there... I want them to associate me with the Chairmanship.*

The Truth Reconciliation Committee had issued a press release about the death of her mother and brother. She did not allow herself to be seen as anything but strong and sorrowful, an expression she had practiced for several minutes in the private bathroom off of her office. The commentators would mention it as well during the celebration; she had seen to that personally. Even her harshest critics would have sympathy for her.

Manipulating the media had always been easy for her. She had taken a page from the Traitor-President and used her early years being a troll, often offering outlandish comments on current affairs. It drew her critics into the open so she knew whom to target. It made her a news topic almost on a weekly basis. *That was the one thing that the traitor was good at; he got his name out there—good or bad.*

The Chairman leaned over to her as the makeup people finished their work. "I met with Becky from the TRC and we think it best to introduce the new Constitutional Convention in my opening remarks, rather than at the end of the parade," he said in a low whisper.

"I approve of that," she said. "Best to get it out there and then move on. The less attention we draw to it, the better."

"I'm sorry for your loss," he offered. She wondered if his condolences were sincere given that she had already blackmailed him. *It doesn't matter if they are genuine or not. What matters is he's acknowledging me.*

"Thank you," she said.

"You should take some time off," he suggested. "A double-funeral... well, that can be a lot emotionally."

"I'll be fine."

"If there's anything I can do..."

"I may have them interred at Arlington. They weren't veterans but they are *my* relatives."

"Of course," he whispered back. "I'll call over to the Pentagon. I can't believe they'd refuse you."

"We are on in twenty," came the Director's voice. The makeup people scurried away and the Secretary turned her gaze to the camera, summoning her mournful expression to its fullest.

The Chairman spoke, firmly reading the words on the teleprompter as soon as the green light went on. "Good evening people of Newmerica. This is an important night for all of us. Five years ago tonight, the citizens of an oppressed and racist nation rose up and took back their freedoms. Five years ago, amidst the chaos that the traitors to our ideals caused, we stood up and reclaimed what was rightfully ours. We cast off the twisted and racist history of our past and embraced a new future, a diverse future, an inclusive future, a bright and shining tomorrow for everyone." Even she had to admit, he was a gifted orator, though most of the credit went to the Truth Reconciliation Committee team that that written the speech.

"I sit with you tonight along with the member of your Ruling Council. On this anniversary of that historic night, the time has come for us to pave the roads that will take us to even more greatness as a people. We will—"

Suddenly the producer's voice called out. "We've lost the signal," he said. "Standby."

Someone will lose their job, or worse for this. The Secretary had never liked the Director of the TRC. *Perhaps now is a good time to consider replacing her.* Hours of rehearsal suddenly seemed crippled by a technical flaw. *One can never pass up a catastrophe.*

"Are we on?" the Chairman demanded.

"No sir, we are not."

"What in the hell is happening?" he spat.

"I don't know. I'm pulling up the feed from New York right now," he said, activating an off-camera television monitor. The Secretary saw the image of a man she knew to be dead, aged, but his pristine silver hair and dark blue suit and red tie looking right at her through the monitor, like a ghost back to haunt her. *It can't be… he's dead. My people proved that.* Behind him was a flag, an older one, stained, torn in several places, but there—defiant.

"Good evening people of America," the Vice President said. "I'm interrupting the Ruling Council's little lovefest with a special broadcast of my own…"

CHAPTER 26

"The Good of All is the Good of One."

Valley Forge, Pennsylvania

The adrenaline pumping through his veins suppressed the pain in his right arm as Sasha, Maria, and Raul moved around the barracks, sprinting to the next building. The fireworks had stopped, but the gunfire had not. The popping of gunfire was not steady, but each crack made him flinch a little. The rest of the Order of the Bell were pinned behind the barracks and trucks by unseen shooters. His breath was ragged as they came to the edge of the barracks two up from where he had been shot. From the sound of the gunfire, the guards were around the corner.

Drawing a long, deep gulp of air, he let it out slowly, corralling his composure. "Alright," he whispered to Sasha and Maria. "We move as one. I will kneel, and come in low. Maria, you step out and fire—Sasha, you stand over me." They nodded silently in the shadow of the building.

"Now," he said firmly, under his breath.

He came down on a stone that dug into his kneecap hard, adding to his pain. Jostling his injured arm didn't help either. As he angled out on one knee, he saw the guards—the ones he had nicknamed Witch Hazel and Redneck. They were lying flat, facing away from Raul and his accomplices, some fifty feet away, firing off single rounds at the rest of the Order's party.

Using his left hand, Raul raised the pistol and fired. Sasha let loose with her rifle as well. Maria, stepping out, advanced two steps, raised her double-barrel shotgun and fired one shot after another. Everything happened at once and the ground around the two guards was churned up as bullets rained on them. Both tried to roll over to face the new threat, but the blasts from Maria's shotgun hit Witch Hazel in her side and turned Redneck's legs into a pulpy red mess that looked more like ground hamburger than human flesh. Redneck cried out, but one of the bullets hit him in the throat, ending his wail into the night sky.

A thin gray haze of smoke filled the air. The sounds of gunfire seemed to stop. Maria reloaded both barrels and walked over to the dead guards, unleashing overkill shots into both. "That's for my father," she said.

"All clear," Sasha called as Raul used the side of the building to stand.

The members of the Order emerged from cover and began to turn their attention to the barracks. Doors were flung open and they barged in, guns ready in case some guard was hiding. Raul made his way to the main street between the barracks and saw the prisoners brought out into the white/blue LED lights of the camp. Most wore faded tan clothing, some patched, others with holes in them. They were afraid. Raul could see it in their eyes and faces. More than one refused to come out of the barracks and had to be pulled out by his fellow prisoners or the members of the Order. *They are afraid this is all a trick.*

One woman with wild stringy hair, easily in her late 40s came up to him and hugged him, making his wound throb. "Thank you," she sobbed. She repeated it over and over. Raul ignored the smell of her, a nearly overpowering stench, and hugged her back. "You need to get in the truck so we can get out of here," he managed. As she broke her clutch with him, he saw her skinny arms and wrists jut out from her ragged sleeves. *Holy Father... they were starving these people!* He had suspected it during his surveillance of the camp, but now that he was here with the prisoners, he saw how bad it was.

Jayden appeared, limping badly, his head wrapped with a blood-soaked piece of cloth. Raul was happy to see him alive and could not help but smile. "It looks worse than it is," Jayden said, his eyes drifting to Raul's wound.

"Same here."

"We need to get these people out of here," Jayden said. "Then I want this place set on fire. They are never again going to put our people in places like this."

Manhattan, New York

Charli's eyes moved around the studio, from door to door, to the camera booth where the operator was being held at gunpoint. She was back on duty, protecting the legitimate leadership of the United States once more, and it felt like putting on a well-worn glove, strangely comfortable. She knew that the studio wasn't likely going to pose a threat; it was getting the Vice President out of New York—a hotbed of progressive fanatics, which would be a problem.

As he sat in front of the flag at the desk, she felt a surge of familiarity that she had not experienced in the last five years. The overthrow of the government—the execution and deaths of so many elected officials—there was nothing that looked or felt presidential. She knew that the Ruling Council had done that deliberately. They wanted no trappings of our past. Now, as her eyes darted to the VP, she felt a return to some degree of normalcy and wondered if the people watching would feel the same thing.

His words came flawlessly as he spoke. "This mob that overthrew your United States of America has lied to you from the beginning. They promised freedom, but have proven themselves to be more oppressive than any government in this hemisphere. They told you that I was dead. They told you that the President died in jail of a heart attack; that was a lie too. He died in West Virginia and is buried there in an unmarked grave. They promised that they would eradicate racism, but nothing has changed in our society… all they have done is pay Americans to turn in their fellow citizens, as if we were East Germany during the Cold War. They took away your guns so you didn't even have the right to defend yourself, making you dependent on them." As he paused his words hit Charli hard. They *did* lie about the President; they faked his arrest and his death. *I was there. Now the whole world finally knows the truth.* There was a feeling of great satisfaction at hearing him say that one line. Her burden that she had carried for so long was lifted.

"This lie called Newmerica is said to be progressive, but in reality, it is oppressive. Most of you have long suspected that they rounded up those with conservative views and took them away for so-called 'social quarantine.' These were concentration camps—plain and simple. Those they could not beat into submission were often starved or savaged in other ways. You may say I'm not telling the truth, but tonight, the Sons of Liberty have struck at five of these camps and have freed the prisoners there. In the coming weeks, you will hear their stories of the hardships that the Ruling Council inflicted on them.

"In alliance with the mainstream media and Big Tech, these anarchists, supported by the progressive wing of the Democratic Party, have twisted what you thought. They have played you. They have told you that we are experiencing prosperity, but you have stood in lines because your jobs disappeared or were sent overseas. Your roads are filled with potholes, your bridges rusted away, the streets littered with garbage, and drug users shoot up in front of your children. When you call for police, you get counselors or mediators. You have suffered shortages of food and other supplies and been told it was the fault of a man they labeled traitor. It is *they* who are the traitors! Lies are what they peddle. Tonight, they were going to celebrate their overthrow of a government and the deaths of thousands of innocent people. I say *they* are the ones that illegally control our nation. We are not Newmerica, we are *America*!

"They told you that the Constitution and the Declaration of Independence were dead documents and had been destroyed. That was another lie. Thanks to the dedication of true American patriots, they were saved." He gingerly held up the Declaration of Independence for the camera. Charli shot a glance to Andy who gave her a broad smile in response from his off-camera position. His face reddened and, in that moment, Charli had complete understanding of what he was feeling. *He has completed the journey his father began.*

"Pursuant to our laws of the land, I am ready to fulfill my duty." He rose to his feet and the former-President's daughter stepped forward, holding a battered black Bible in her hands. "Raise your right hand and place your other hand on this, and repeat after me," she said in a crisp voice. "I do solemnly swear that I will support and defend the Constitution of the United States against all enemies, foreign and domestic," she paused and allowed him to repeat the words. "That I will bear true faith and allegiance to the same; that I take this obligation freely, without any mental reservation or purpose of evasion," she said, a waver rising in her voice as she spoke. No doubt she was thinking about her father. The Vice President repeated her words, offering her an almost grandfatherly smile that seemed to give her strength. "And that I will well and faithfully discharge the duties of the office on which I am about to enter: So help me God." He finished the oath flawlessly, then turned to the camera.

"As the President of the United States of America, I declare the officials of the Newmerica movement to be enemies of the state. They are rebels and domestic terrorists. I assume full control of the Federal government and will immediately seek to restore our nation to its former glory and honor. As the legal Commander in Chief, I hereby order the military forces of the United States to acknowledge my authority under the Constitution and go on immediate alert. No order is to be followed from the Newmerican government or their so-called leaders. Any officer that refuses my order will be relieved of command. Orders for martial law in several cities will be released shortly.

"Countrymen; tough times will follow. These tyrants will not easily surrender what they have stolen. They will fight to remain in power. We will have to fight to take back what is rightfully ours. I know many of you, like me, were caught off guard by the mobs seizing control. Now is the time for you to take a stand. Join me. Follow me. We will restore our nation—*so help me God.*"

With that the camera went dark and the light above it flickered to red.

Jack gave no time for congratulations. "Sir, we need to get you on the move." Andy stepped in and rolled up the documents and folded the flag and quickly stored them.

"Did it go out on all of the networks?"

"It did—and on the net," Jack said with a grin that Charli had come to miss. "We caught them with their pants down. But we can't press our luck. We need to get out of the city." Jack turned to Charli. "Alright Slingshot, the Silver Eagle is all yours."

Charli Kazinski heard her old callsign and beamed. The last five years seemed to evaporate. Redemption came from strange places, and for Charli it was in fulfilling her duties. *I'm back!* "Very well. Mister President, I need you to follow me…"

EPILOGUE

"Lowering the Bar Ensures Equality."

Hackettstown, New Jersey

Caylee Leatrom sat alone in a booth at Marley's Gotham Grill taking a sip of her Long Island iced tea. It was a hole-in-the-wall restaurant and bar, one that only the locals likely knew. Most of the big chain restaurants had either gone belly up during the aftermath of the virus, or the economic downturn that had come after the Fall. Caylee preferred such places to the chains, not because of the food, but for the privacy they offered.

The TV over the bar had gone blank after the swearing in of the new President. When it flickered back on, a message of 'Technical Difficulties—Please Stand By,' was plastered on the screen. She admired Jack Desmond's style. "Go big or go home," she muttered to herself, allowing a rare chuckle out loud. There was a strange sense of pride in her newfound colleagues.

Several patrons of the small town bar pointed at the screen and their voices escalated. One was saying that it was some sort of stunt. "It has to be fake. Everyone knows he's dead." Two others were arguing right back. "You better hit the road Paulie. It looks like there's a new sheriff in town," one boasted jokingly. The first man stormed out. Caylee took it all in. *This is just the start.* No doubt all across the country fights were starting, some neighbor vs. neighbor, others within families themselves. *Things are going to get messy now, but that's how it should have been all along. At least now the playing field is fair.*

Caylee had been a tool of the Newmerica government—a pawn. It was a role she understood. She had a unique set of skills, mental and physical. They needed and used those skills. Only in her darkest moments had she ever considered the morality of what she did. Morality was a weakness for an operative. *It was easier to follow orders than to question why those orders came down in the first place.*

They used her. After she had done their dirty work, they made her a target. It was a massive mistake on their part. She had struck back, going right to the heart of it all—the Secretary of the National Security Force. Taking out her mother had been relatively easy, a simple pinprick of curare when greeted at the door had done the trick. She had a vial of it left over from her time as an operative. She had used a high dose, hitting her where her shirt rubbed at her collar so that the wound would be difficult to detect. She struggled to breathe as her diaphragm became paralyzed. Caylee remembered watching her on the floor of her hallway, struggling, then slipping off to sleep. The older woman's face was eerily like that of her daughter, which gave Caylee some strange sense of joy.

Now the time had come to inflict the fear she had so desired. Caylee opened the burner phone and dialed the number she had memorized. The Secretary's voice came on, hot and furious, more than she had ever heard before. "Who is this?"

"Your worst nightmare." Caylee paused, letting it sink in.

"*You.*" Pure venom came with that one word.

"How's your Mom and Bro doing?" she asked sarcastically. *I want her to know. I want her fear to be real.*

"You—you did that?"

"I have no idea what you are referring to," she replied coyly, taking another sip of her drink. "Can't a girl simply ask a friendly question of an old work buddy?"

"I will hunt you down. There is no safe place where you can hide. You will pay for that."

"Give it your best shot," she replied. "In the meantime, you might want to check the web. I think you're trending." She shut off the phone and smiled proudly to herself.

Her files, all her nasty covert missions, had been dumped onto the internet a few minutes earlier. Jack had assured her that the Silicon

Valley folks would not be taking it down for several days, and judging by the news broadcast she had seen of the bombings in California, she agreed. For the first time since the Liberat—no, the *Fall*, Silicon Valley had a reason to experience fear.

The truth was out there for the first time in years, unfiltered and unstoppable. With their iron grip on the nation suddenly challenged, they would be hard pressed to protect the Secretary. The whole world would know what kind of monster she was, what she had ordered Caylee to do. Her actions, releasing the information, would take her down too. The data was a double-edged sword. The people would know the amount of blood on her hands. It was a small price to pay for vengeance.

Besides, this fight wasn't over—it was just starting. *I'm not operating alone… I have new friends and allies. If I was dangerous before, I'm unstoppable now.*

Philadelphia, Pennsylvania

Raul looked at the crude crisscross stitches on his arm and winced again in pain. Delores, an ER nurse and friend of Jayden had come to the warehouse to tend their wounds and help with the former prisoners. Some could barely talk. When they tried, only hoarse empty sobs came out. Some looked afraid, as if their rescue had been some sort of trick and they were waiting for something bad to happen to them. Raul watched as they were given hot food and blankets and wondered what had gone on inside of the camp.

Sasha came over with a warm cup of coffee and sat on the tire that he was using as a chair. "How is Jayden?" he asked before taking a sip.

"One shot glanced off of his skull. More blood than damage, though his hairline is going to be messed up. He caught a ricocheted bullet in his shin. They had to dig it out. He's fine now, though he's going to have a hell of a headache for a while."

That gave him some relief. Jayden had been a mentor of sorts for him since he had arrived. "How are our guests?"

"Shaken up," Sasha replied. "Most are not well enough to travel yet. Even if they are, we can't just ship them back to their families. The NSF will be watching for them."

There was a distant cracking sound in the air. Raul sat his coffee down and rose. "What's that?"

"Fireworks," Sasha said. "They are going off all over the city. Apparently while we were freeing the prisoners, the Vice President came out of hiding and took the oath of office. He's our new President. Some serious shit is going down."

"Get out," Raul said, walking to the big door of the warehouse. In the night sky he saw the occasional burst of fireworks in the distance over the city of Philadelphia. Sasha stood at his side and pulled him close. "Jayden said we were just one of the teams that hit camps tonight. The whole thing was coordinated. The President has called on the military. It sounds like he's going to try to take the country back."

"Amazing," Raul said. "I had no idea." It struck him as strange and oddly comforting that he had been part of something else, something bigger. It was a feeling he had struggled with since the destruction of his Youth Corp troop.

"So what happens next?" he asked.

Sasha pulled him a little closer. "I don't know. We hurt them and they are not used to that. When people get hurt, they try to hurt back. That's for tomorrow. Tonight, we get to help the prisoners we got out of that place."

Raul looked off into the night as a red mortar round, an old Fourth of July firework, exploded in the distance. A few moments later he heard the retort. "Come on," Sasha said. "Let's go inside."

He didn't move. Instead he stared out into the night sky. "You go ahead. I want to enjoy this a little longer."

Bass River Toll Plaza, New Jersey

Andy sat next to Jack Desmond in the front seat of the unmarked box truck they had used to enter and leave the city. The President was in the back, along with Charli and the four additional protectors that Jack had brought with them. Getting out of the CBS building known as Black Rock had been relatively easy. The sirens of the New York NSF wailed in the air, echoing off of the buildings, seeming to get closer, but Jack's friend, Valerie, assured him that they would be handled.

As they approached the toll plaza, Andy saw the police cars parked nearby, their red and blue lights flashing. There was a line at each gate, and at each booth, there was an NSF officer. Jack took a newspaper and set it on top of his weapon on the seat between them. At Andy's side was the nation's most precious documents and the flag. Jack didn't verbally say anything to Andy, but his eyes darted from Andy's face to the gun. *I hope he doesn't expect me to shoot this guy!* Slowly he realized that might be what Jack wanted.

As they pulled up to the small toll plaza, the officer indicated that Jack should roll down his window. "What's up, Officer?"

"We're checking out of state vehicles," he said flatly. "Your plates are from Arkansas."

"Just dropped off a load of food up-state," Jack said. Andy looked around slowly, and saw that there were four officers total at the toll plaza. All seemed to eye the truck with suspicion.

"Sir, I'm going to have you pull over," he said firmly, gesturing to the area past the toll gate where their cars were parked.

"I have all my paperwork," Jack said, reaching across the seats as if he were going for the glove box. Andy wondered if he was going to make a grab for the gun instead, but his hand hovered just short of it.

"Sir, pull over."

"Of course," he said, grinding the gears slightly as he got it going, turning slowly over to a spot behind the two cars. The officer directed him to re-park, angling the rear of the vehicle away from the other officers at the toll plaza.

"I need you and your passenger to provide me your ID," he said.

Fuck... fuck... fuck. Andy started to fidget around for his identification. Jack produced a federal ID and Andy handed his ID over as well.

"Sir, I want you to step out and open the back of your vehicle," he said after reviewing the ID.

Andy marveled at how composed Jack was. "Happy to oblige," he said, casting a glance over at Andy and at the gun one more time. *This is not the time for heroics.* Andy opened his door slowly and dropped to the ground. "What's going on?" Jack asked the officer.

"You didn't hear? It was on the radio, TV, everywhere," the NSF officer said, walking to the back of the vehicle. "The Vice President of the United States hijacked the anniversary ceremony out of the District... got sworn in and everything, live, on the air."

"No kidding," Jack said as Andy came to the back of the vehicle. "Wow, we missed it."

"Yeah," the slightly portly officer said, taking off his hat and slicking back his red hair, then putting the hat back on. "They have us checking every out-of-state vehicle," he said.

"That's really something," Andy said.

"Alright," the officer said, "Let's take a look."

"Okay," Jack said. "Though I think you're wasting your time." Andy cringed and stepped back away from the door.

Jack fumbled with the keys, mostly to warn Charli and the others. He removed the lock and tugged it open a few inches, stopping there. The officer reached and jerked the door upward. It rolled and rumbled up. Standing before him were five people, guns drawn and leveled at him. Behind Charli was the President.

There was a moment where time seemed to stand still. Andy was expecting the roar of gunfire. For the longest few seconds, no one spoke, no one moved. The officer said nothing. He simply looked at the occupants with the guns trained on him. Casually, he climbed up, grabbed the nylon strap at the bottom of the door, and pulled it down slowly and carefully. He then took the lock and put it on the door hook.

Andy was dumbfounded. His mouth slowly dropped open. *What in the hell just happened? He had to have seen them.* The officer looked to make sure his colleagues hadn't seen anything, then turned to Jack. "Everything seems to be in order here," he said loudly enough for his fellow officers to hear. None even bothered to come over and look. Reaching into his uniform pocket, he retrieved a card and held it out for Jack. "You keep this. It says we inspected you and your cargo has been cleared. If you head west, instead of south, you will find less interference from checkpoints."

"Thank you, officer," Jack said slowly, almost in disbelief himself.

"No problem," he said, then leaned in so that only Jack and Andy could hear him. "God bless America," he said barely over a whisper. The officer gave him a wink. Even the tough Jack Desmond said nothing. His mouth hung agape.

It has begun...

And in that moment, when he heard those words, Andy realized that his father's suffering had not been in vain. *The country he believed in is still out here. It's not a place, it's a people. More importantly, now we have a fighting chance.*

AUTHOR'S NOTES

In 1775 Thomas Paine wrote *Common Sense* as a book designed to articulate and frame the moral and political arguments why America needed to exist on its own. In writing this book I wanted to explain the dangers of the far left, the progressives, but realized that a *Common Sense* approach would merely be ignored. People want stories, they want characters, they desire to be entertained more than lectured to. We live in a world where facts are challenged and counter-facts abound. A story… that is something that transcends data.

I harbor no illusions of this novel being on-par with *Common Sense*, but I wanted to provide conservatives with a perspective of the threats facing them. It began with a simple notion. What if the progressives got everything they wanted? What if the events of the later part of 2020 had taken that nudge down a darker path? What would the nation look like five years down the road? I have crafted a world that the extremist left-wingers crave, and the conservatives dread and fear.

While you may attempt to discredit the concepts of this novel, you will find that all of these concepts are based in reality. President Obama at one point suggested a nationalization of the police forces. Cries for reparations are all too real and the model I have presented, with them being another form of welfare, is a very real possibility. Gun confiscation and Green New Deals are not conspiracy theories, they are ideals embraced by many. Defunding the police is happening in some communities. Representative Alexandria Ocasio-Cortez claimed they had a list of Trump supporters, archives of their social media, purely for purposes of retribution. Media suppression of stories happens. A form of the Truth Reconciliation Committee has been proffered by members of Congress. Statues are being torn down or destroyed. Socialized medicine has long been a Democratic rallying point for their supporters. Social justice warriors, as idiotic as they appear, are a real thing, as is cancel culture. Imagine if these people were to get in power, real power. Social Enforcement is merely the next step in their evolution, if not checked.

In every election in recent years progressives cried for throwing out the Electoral College, but no one proposes to amend the Constitution to do so. That means that the only way to do it is to violently throw out our rule of laws and create new ones to their liking. ANTIFA wants to bring the entire system down, including capitalism. Insurrection is seen by many on the left as the means to an end if they cannot get their desires. The idea of a new Constitutional Convention, while it seems far-fetched, is actually a possibility. The left pushes 'rights' that do not exist in law, but only in their fertile imaginations. It is not hard to believe that if they were in power, they would cement those beliefs.

Conservatives like to believe that we would rise up if an attempt were made to overthrow the government. In reality, if it happened fast enough, there would be little that we could do. There would be little time to organize and the forces working against us are already organized. That is the scenario presented in this book.

All that I have done with this book is transform these concepts into a story so that it is digestible by the general public. Personally, I think it would make a great mini-series.

This book is designed to make you think. It is written to spark debate and discussion. It is intended to pull at your patriotic heartstrings. People who feel threatened by such a book are bound to label me a right-wing nut job, an extremist, or worse. I have always believed that the best heroes are defined by those that consider them their enemies. Labeling is what the left does best. I do not fear them. I have exposed them for what they really are. I have given you a glimpse of what they consider their utopia.

To anyone offended by this book—I offer zero apologies on behalf of millions of us who both loathe and fear what you so longingly desire. You may claim I have misrepresented aspects, but that is merely your opinion... mine differs.

I hope you have enjoyed the book and will encourage others to read it.

Made in United States
Orlando, FL
19 March 2024